The
Road
to
Zoe

ALSO BY NICK ALEXANDER

The Bottle of Tears
You Then, Me Now
Things We Never Said
The Other Son
The Photographer's Wife

The Hannah Novels

The Half-Life of Hannah
Other Halves

The CC Novels

The Case of the Missing Boyfriend
The French House

The Fifty Reasons Series

50 Reasons to Say Goodbye
Sottopassaggio
Good Thing, Bad Thing
Better Than Easy
Sleight of Hand
13:55 Eastern Standard Time

The Road to Zoe

nick alexander

LAKE UNION
PUBLISHING

Text copyright © 2020 by BIGfib Books
All rights reserved.

Published by Lake Union Publishing, Seattle

www.apub.com

Amazon, the Amazon logo, and Lake Union Publishing are trademarks of Amazon.com, Inc., or its affiliates.

ISBN-13: 9781542014120
ISBN-10: 1542014123

Cover design by @blacksheep-uk.com

Cover illustration by Jelly London

Printed in the United States of America

For Lolo

PROLOGUE

She stands in the middle of the kitchen, her hands on her hips as she surveys the devastation. Around her, what was once a clean, orderly family home has become a grubby mess – a zone of utter chaos. There are muddy footprints across the lino. Bits of paper and random items lie on every surface.

In many ways the mess strikes her as more appropriate. It seems to fit the circumstances of her life rather better than the superficial neatness of just a few days ago.

She continues to pull things, any things, all things, from the places they belong, the places they have occupied, often untouched for years, adding them to the contents of an open box on the kitchen table.

She'd tried to be logical at first, indeed had even managed to maintain order for a while. Thus, those early boxes, now at the bottom of a veritable wall of boxes in the hallway, truly do contain what it says on the packet, whether it be 'Recipe books' or 'Kitchen implements' or 'DVD's'. (Yes, she has erroneously added an apostrophe at the end of 'DVD', and it irritates her every time she sees it.) But she's beyond being logical now, beyond being able to decide into what kind of category a half-empty pack of AA batteries should go, and beyond caring, too. As a result, the last seven boxes have all been labelled 'Misc.'.

She takes the wooden bowl from the kitchen table and tips the contents into the current box (she sees a lightbulb flash by, then a key, an unrecognised USB cable and a box of Tic Tacs). She folds over the flaps and tapes the lid shut. With a chunky marker she writes 'Misc. #8' on the side. This one might actually be Misc. #9, she thinks; not that it matters.

She carries it to the hallway and deposits it on top of Misc. #7, then, taking a deep breath, she turns, walks the length of the short hallway and steels herself before yanking open the door to the cupboard under the stairs.

She drags Henry the Hoover towards the front door but then changes her mind and moves him into the lounge instead. The vacuum cleaner is going to have to be one of the last things to go, after all. Returning to the stair cupboard, she reaches into the semi-darkness and retrieves an orange extension lead, the mop and bucket, the ironing board and the iron. The iron should probably have gone in 'Electrical things' or 'Laundry stuff' but it's too late now.

She unhooks, from a nail, three school bags (an image of Jude at the school gates flashes in her mind's eye, and her heart twinges with love and loss), along with two old handbags that she should have thrown away years ago. These she dumps next to the sealed bin bags at the back door before hesitating, kneeling and checking the insides, one by one. They are all entirely empty except for the green canvas handbag, in which she finds an ancient restaurant receipt. Someone, somewhere, once ate spaghetti vongole in a restaurant called Paradisio but the date is faded and unreadable. While gently pushing one fingernail through a hole in the corner of the handbag, she tries to remember, but she can't even recall to which era the bag belongs.

Back at the cupboard, she drags some old coats from the depths, revealing two wooden shelves, one of which is packed with pots of home-made jam. They're so old that they're almost certainly inedible. From the lower shelf she pulls a dusty cardboard box.

She bites her lip as she carries it to the kitchen table. She sits and stares past it, out through the rain-speckled windows at the waterlogged green lawn beyond. She should probably tape the box up and look at it later, or not at all. That would almost certainly be the best thing to do.

But then the idiot DJ on Groove FM finally stops talking and plays a song instead, and it's one of Zoe's favourites. Mandy never much liked it herself, but Zoe had played it constantly, in . . . when was that? 2008? 2009? And how can 2009 be ten years ago? she wonders. Two thousand and nine sounds like last week. Lily Allen, she thinks now, as she listens to the song. When it reaches the chorus, she even remembers the title: 'The Fear'. An image of her daughter telling her that the lyrics are amazing pops into her head as clearly as if it happened yesterday.

For a moment, she stares out at the greenness of the wet garden again, and then, after glancing almost guiltily around the room, she runs her finger diagonally through the dust on the lid of the box and then removes it.

And here they all are, the actors of her life, smiling up at her. *All gone now*, she thinks, as she lifts a picture of Ian, suited, drunk and grinning, from the pile. Thirteen years they were married. Thirteen years! And here's Jude. Not entirely gone, that one, she thinks, but mostly absent all the same. She runs a finger gently across his cheek and lets out a deep bitter-sweet sigh. So much love, she thinks. Kids, they absorb so much time and effort and money. But the main thing is the love. And no one teaches you what to do with all that love once they leave. No one explains how you're supposed to cope when their fifteen-hour-a-day presence dwindles to a ten-minute call on Sundays (if you're lucky) and a two-day visit at Christmas.

3

She caresses the photo again and slides it to the edge of the box, revealing Scott's business card. Chunky, sexy Scott, who, despite everything else that was going on, gave her the best two years of her life. She'd bought her first digital camera just before they met and she's pretty sure she's never had a proper physical photo of him. Maybe even the digital photos have been lost by now and perhaps that would be just as well. Damn, Scott was sexy.

She delves further into the box and finds her official, mounted wedding photo. It's hard to decide which of the two of them looks the most uncomfortable in it. Ian, probably, she decides. Ian always looked a bit uncomfortable – a bit as if he wanted to be somewhere else. As it turned out, of course, there was a reason for that.

And then here she is, her first-born, and it's only when she finds the photo that she realises that it's what she's been looking for – that it's what she's been dreading. The photo, the Lily Allen song . . . Her heart lurches.

The idea that any of the main players might just step out of your life is hard to get your head around. Our brains are wired for permanence, really. Our parents will (we believe) always be on the end of that phone line. The husband will always be there for break-fast. But at least the concepts associated with losing these people are all around us. Our friends' parents die, and so we are forewarned. Other friends go from coupled to single. Shit happens. Separation, divorce: we have proper, useful words to describe these events. But a child? Well, you just don't get over that one, do you? There's not even a word for it.

'Oh, Zoe,' she murmurs. Lovely lost Zoe. Her vision is blur-ring, so she swipes at the corner of her eye and takes a deep, jagged breath. It's just too upsetting, and she can't do with being upset right now. She needs to be cool and efficient, like some suited female lawyer in a Netflix series. And so she slides Zoe beneath a

4

photo of Jude's first car, and then reseals the box, taping across the top.

She has just added the box of photos to the teetering pile in the hall when her mobile buzzes in her pocket. Talk of the devil, she thinks, but with a warm feeling and a hint of a smile.

'Mum?' It's Jude's voice.

'If that's who you called,' she says, 'then that's probably who it is. How was your holiday? Are you back yet?'

'Um, great,' Jude says. 'Yes, we just got back. Look, I need to see you. Can I come up?'

She grimaces. 'You need to see me?' she repeats, mentally listing the various reasons her son might want to see her. If he wants money, she's all out. If he's split up with Jessica and needs emotional support, her stock of that is pretty low, too.

'Yeah, it's kind of urgent,' Jude says. 'So is it OK? If we come up?'

'What? Now?' she asks. 'I'm right in the middle of packing. Everything's all over the place, sweetheart. The moving guys are coming tomorrow and I'm way behind schedule.'

'Then we can help you,' Jude says. 'We can stay the night and help you all day tomorrow.'

'But the bedrooms,' she says. 'I've packed all the bedding away. I wouldn't even know which box it's in.'

'We'll bring sleeping bags. It'll be fine.'

'But . . .' she sighs. 'This really isn't the best timing, Jude. I'd have to start unpacking stuff and tidying and this isn't the right moment for that. Are you sure it can't wait till next weekend?'

'Um. Well, no. No, it can't really,' Jude says. 'And don't tidy. We don't care how the place looks.'

'Tell me now, then,' she says. 'Tell me on the phone. You don't have to drive all the way here, do you?'

'I'd rather come,' Jude replies. 'We can be there in . . . How long?' he asks, and it's not until Jessica, in the background, shouts out, 'Four, four and a half hours,' that she realises the question wasn't directed at her. 'So, about sevenish?' Jude says.

'But the kitchen . . .' she says. 'Even the kitchen stuff . . . It's all packed away.'

'Then we'll bring pizza,' Jude says.

'Pizza,' she repeats.

'We can eat it out of the boxes.'

'Bring Chinese, then,' she tells him. 'If you must come, bring Chinese, from Ip's. I've still got plates somewhere.'

'Chinese it is, then,' Jude says. 'See you about seven-thirty.'

'And go to Ip's,' she says again. 'Opposite the Bull's Head. They were really rude the last time I went to the other one, so go to Ip's.'

'Yes, Mum,' Jude says. 'Don't worry. We'll go to Ip's. See you in a bit.'

'Just one thing,' she asks. 'Is it good news or bad?'

'Um, I'm not sure, really,' Jude says. 'It's certainly news, anyway.'

One

Mandy

My marriage ended on the 3rd of March 2007 at about 2.25 p.m.

There had been no warning signs; I had no suspicions. If anything, I felt blessed that we were one of those lucky couples who were destined to coast through life side by side. I didn't like to think about the end much, didn't want to consider which of us might go first, but that was about the only terror I could envisage on our joint horizon.

Other than that, I felt quite comfortable with the idea of getting older. What could be nicer, I thought, than lazy days in front of the (gas-powered) log fire, pausing occasionally to make a cup of tea for the person I'd spent my life with, someone so familiar to me that I hadn't needed to ask what he was thinking about for years. That's how well I thought I knew my husband.

Retirement, of course, was still a long way off, so I'm only telling you this to give you an idea of just how shocking that afternoon's revelations were to me.

I'd had one of my rare optical migraines at work that lunchtime, and after the obligatory lie-down on the office couch until I could see well enough to drive again, I'd rushed home, hoping to get to bed before the pulsing, throbbing headache that invariably followed the blindness got started.

Other than the hum of the refrigerator and the *pfff!* of the boiler starting up, the house was exactly as quiet as I expected it to be. Ian was out at work; the kids were at school. I'd take my Migrex and lie down in the darkened bedroom and, if I was lucky, it would pass by the time everyone got home.

As I entered the bathroom, I glanced towards our bedroom and saw, through the half-open door, a heeled leather shoe at the end of the bed. I noticed it without noticing it, if you know what I mean. I saw it as I saw the rumpled sheets and the wintry sunlight cutting through a gap in the curtains, but with the shimmering still present around the edges of my vision it didn't register, really. I certainly didn't consider, as I sat down to wee, that the shoe might not be mine.

What I did notice, when I stepped back out of the bathroom, the shimmering almost gone now and the lobe above my left eye beginning to throb, was that the shoe was no longer there.

Feeling more confused than suspicious, I headed towards the bedroom. The sheets, I noticed, were now smooth. The shoe I thought I'd seen had vanished. Had I imagined it? Was I having visions, now? Or had it just been a memory from a different day?

I sniffed at the air and thought I detected an unusual odour, a synthetic fruity perfume like fabric softener or perhaps cheap own-brand washing powder. But strange odours were a regular feature of my migraines, too, and so I ignored it and thought instead, as I kicked my own shoes off, about the shoe I thought I'd seen.

I crossed to the window and, even though this was physically painful, peered out at the street before pulling the curtains shut. The street outside was quiet. Everything seemed as it should be.

It was then that I heard a noise, or at least, I thought I heard a noise. Above the whistle of the WC tank filling it was hard to be

8

sure, but it had sounded like our conservatory door closing. The imaginary shoe, the fruity smell, the sheets, the noise . . . Something seemed out of kilter.

Not knowing quite why, I strode down the landing to Jude's bedroom and peered out between his Spider-Man curtains at the back garden, just in time to see Ian, my husband of thirteen years, surreptitiously pulling the back gate closed behind him. Then for a fraction of a second, no more, I saw the backs of two heads: Ian's, and a blonde woman's, before they vanished behind the neighbour's hedge.

I just about managed to change the sheets, but I was in too much pain to do anything more. But even with the sheets changed, I couldn't bear to lie down in that bed. I wondered if I ever would again.

After glancing around the room one last time and noting that Ian's tie was draped over the back of a chair, I crossed the landing to Zoe's messy bedroom, where I threw myself down and closed my eyes. The tie, I realised, was the same one Ian had worn to work that morning, the pink and blue striped one I had bought him (on Jude's behalf) the previous Christmas. Between spasms of physical pain, I thought about what I'd just discovered, and wept.

The pain had faded to a dull ache by the time the kids got home. I set them up with a film and some crisps and waited for Ian in the kitchen. They didn't seem to notice that anything was wrong. Kids are incredibly self-absorbed at that age.

Ian arrived just after six. He was whistling. I kid you not.

'Hi,' he said, bending down to peck me on the cheek. 'How was your day?'

'Not good,' I said. 'I got a migraine and had to come home, but then you know that, don't you?'

'Um,' he said, as if he hadn't even heard this remark. 'That's not good.'

'How was your day?' I asked, with meaning.

'Fine,' he replied. 'Uneventful.'

'Ian,' I said, in an attempt at getting him to stop what he was doing and look at me. But he continued to fiddle in his briefcase, retrieving first his phone and then the charger and then plugging them in.

'Ian!' I said again, and when this time he looked at me, I added, 'I know.'

He froze for quite a long time. I could see him reviewing the possible options. Denial. Incomprehension. Maybe a calculated argument about something else that would give him time to think. He opened his mouth to speak a few times, but then closed it. He pushed his tongue into one cheek.

And then I suddenly no longer wanted to hear what he had to say. I didn't want to discover which of the possible untruths he would choose. I didn't want to hold back what I knew or stoop as low as attempting to catch him out. It seemed too grubby, some-how. It didn't seem worthy of our thirteen-year marriage, or of our two beautiful children watching *Star Trek* in the next room.

'I saw you leave from Jude's window,' I said. 'I saw her shoes on the floor, Ian. You forgot your tie on the back of the chair, as well. I know, Ian.'

He nodded slowly. 'Oh,' he said.

I've seen too many films, perhaps, but I expected him to say, 'It was nothing.' I expected him to say, 'It was just sex.' And I'd been totally unable to decide how I'd respond when he did say those things.

Instead, he simply unplugged his phone and put the charger back in his briefcase. He slipped the phone into his lapel pocket and then gently lifted his keys from the kitchen counter.

'You're going?' I asked, flabbergasted.

'Uh-huh.'

'OK . . . Um, where are you going?' I asked.

'Linda's place, I guess,' he said, flatly, sadly. 'That's her name, by the way. Linda.'

'And what? You're just . . . going to . . . to leave? You're going to go there right now?'

Ian shrugged. 'Well, the cat's pretty much out of the bag now, isn't it?' he said.

'And you're going to . . . just walk out?' I asked again, through a mixture of sour laughter and rising tears. 'You don't have anything you want to say to me about any of this before you go?'

'Nothing that can't wait.' And then he swivelled on the smooth soles of his polished brogues and was gone.

That, then, is how my marriage ended. I didn't get to scream or shout or plead. My husband gave me no explanations or excuses. He simply turned and walked out of our (now my) front door.

I phoned him a few times over the next few days in varying states of mind – sometimes calm, reasonable, placatory even; on other occasions hysterical or raging. But Ian simply never picked up.

I had no answers to any of my questions. (How long had this been going on? Was he ever coming back? Did he want an actual divorce? And who would get the house we lived in if he did?) And I had no real answers for the kids either.

I'd told them that first evening their father had gone away for a while, and because they're clever kids, they'd pretty much worked out the rest themselves.

This was cruel to them and I think it was cruel towards me, too. But in retrospect, I don't suppose it was any worse than the traditional months of screaming and shouting at each other with which most marriages end.

Ten days after he'd left, Ian phoned and asked me to meet him for a 'walk and a talk' up at Solomon's Temple, the Victorian folly on the ridge above Buxton. It was about twenty minutes from the house and, other than a few dog-walkers, was likely to be quiet enough for me to scream without being overheard, so I agreed.

It was a cold spring day with a cutting icy wind, but it was sunny and dry, at least.

Ian was dressed in all-new clothes – that was the first thing I noticed. He had new jeans, new trainers, a new jumper and coat. A new partner, too. I remember wondering if he was in any way still the man I'd married.

We said hello timidly.

'I thought you'd want some answers,' Ian said, as we started to walk.

'I suppose I do,' I agreed.

'What do you want to know?' he asked.

And because I was unsure about quite how much I needed, or indeed wanted, to know I said, 'What do you think I want to know?'

'If I'm coming back?' Ian offered.

I laughed out loud at this. It was spontaneous and genuine if rather bitter laughter. Because if there was one thing I had decided, it was that he wasn't coming back. 'No,' I said. 'No, I think I already know the answer to that one, Ian. You're not.'

'That's right,' Ian said. 'Because I love her.'

I gasped at this and turned to look away at the horizon.

'I'm sorry,' Ian said, 'but it's true.'

'Right.'

'I don't suppose that's unexpected,' he continued. 'I mean, you and me . . . Well, it hasn't been right for years, has it?'

Even though I had known no such thing until that moment, I said, 'No, no, of course it hasn't.' Because if he'd said it, it had to be true, didn't it? Shame on me, I thought, for not noticing.

'I don't need my share of the house for the moment,' Ian said. 'So you can just carry on living there for a while. I guess that's probably better for the kids.'

'Yes,' I said. 'Yes, I suppose it is.'

'But I'd like to come and get some stuff,' Ian said, gesturing at his attire. 'While you're out at work, maybe? If that's OK?'

I nodded. 'Monday's fine,' I said. 'I'm out all day.'

'Monday, then,' Ian said.

'We need to tell them something. They need to know what's happening.'

'Of course,' Ian said. 'Do you want to . . . ? Or shall I?'

'No,' I said. 'No, you can have that honour.'

'Right,' Ian said. 'On Monday, then, I guess. When they get home from school.'

'I'll stay out till seven,' I said. 'So you'll have time.'

'Oh! You don't want to be there?'

'No,' I told him. 'I really don't.'

'Right, then . . .' Ian said, with a shrug. 'OK.'

'I think I'm going to go now,' I announced, stopping walking and glancing over my shoulder, homeward. A rage was building within me. A storm was brewing and I needed to get away from him before it broke.

'OK, then,' Ian said. 'I am sorry, you know.'

I stared at the ground and nodded. It was the best that I could manage.

'But we deserve to be happy,' Ian continued. 'We both do.'

I was happy, I remember thinking. But, 'Right,' was what I said. 'Of course.'

And then, just before the tears started to trickle down my cheeks, I turned and walked away.

◆ ◆ ◆

I kept all the drama out of sight, and of that, at least, I'm quite proud.

When the kids were out, I'd sit in my bedroom and run the phrase *I'm only thirty-three and I'm separated* through my mind over and over to make myself cry. For some reason, the fact that my marriage hadn't lasted until I was thirty-five seemed particularly unfair to me at the time. And once I was crying, I'd work myself into a frenzy and punch pillows and scream. But only ever when I was certain that no one could possibly hear me.

I never insulted or denigrated Ian in front of the kids. I never tried to get them to hate their father, even though that would, I think, have been a fairly easy thing to do.

◆ ◆ ◆

On the Monday evening when I got home, they were sitting in front of the TV. Onscreen, Homer Simpson was running away from a power station. The sound, unusually, was muted.

'Dad came and took all his stuff,' Jude said.

I nodded slowly and ruffled his hair. 'Yes, I know.'

'He said you both agree,' Jude said. 'He said you're not angry or nothing.'

'Not angry or anything,' I corrected him gently, thinking, *So, that's what we're telling them, is it?* And then, *Sure, I can run with that.*

'That's right,' I managed to croak. 'We both agree that it's for the best, really.'

'Not for us,' Jude said. 'It's not best for us, is it?' He glanced at Zoe, who shrugged sullenly in reply. 'It's rubbish is what it is,' Jude added, sounding momentarily close to tears.

'It is,' I agreed. 'It's rubbish. That's the perfect word for it.'

Jude sighed and then, spotting an opportunity, asked, 'Can we have pizza tonight? I mean, proper pizza, from Domino's?'

'We can,' I said. 'You can phone them and order if you want.'

'Great,' he said, jumping up and crossing to the bookshelf, where the pizza menu was stashed. 'Margherita?' he asked Zoe.

Zoe shook her head.

'What, then?' Jude asked, crossing the room and thrusting the flyer in her face.

'I'm not hungry,' Zoe said.

'What about you, Mum?' Jude asked, turning to me.

'I'm not hungry either, sweetheart,' I said.

'You have to eat something,' he said, looking between Zoe and myself, and for a moment I believed he was concerned for us, and my heart did a little somersault at the thought that my ten-year-old was trying to look after me. 'Otherwise we have to pay delivery,' he continued. 'Delivery costs almost the same as a pizza, so . . .'

'Margherita, then,' I said. 'A Margherita is fine. Zoe and I can share it.'

'I'm not hungry,' Zoe said again.

I went upstairs to see just how much of his stuff Ian had taken. The fact that his side of the wardrobe was entirely empty, the fact that not a single suit, shirt, tie or cufflink remained, made me gasp in shock.

In a way, clues to most of what was to come were present in those first few exchanges.

Jude would bounce through most of it with almost shocking resilience while Zoe would alternate between anger, sullenness and sadness. And Zoe, my lovely Zoe, would almost never be hungry again.

◆　◆　◆

Looking back, Zoe had always been difficult about food so, in a way, the fact that food should become the primary focus for her discomfort was predictable. But until Ian left, she hadn't seemed that much worse than most of her peers. Food phobias are a very adolescent-girl kind of thing and to start with, at least, though she'd suddenly decide she hated tomatoes or cheese or mushrooms, within a week she'd almost always forgotten which thing it was she was pretending not to like. So we'd got into the habit of saying nothing and simply waiting for each new phobia to pass.

We'd had the inevitable vegetarian thing, which, given I'm a keen cook, hadn't fazed me at all. Meat – or more specifically meat rearing – was apparently terrible for the planet anyway. So it was good for all of us, I told myself, if I cooked – and we ate – a little more variedly.

There had been a moment, a few weeks before Ian left, when the vegetarian phase had coincided with a hatred of all things tomato, and that, I admit, had been a challenge. But then Jude had spotted Zoe in McDonald's eating a Big Mac, which had calmed things down for quite a while.

With Ian gone, twelve-year-old Zoe's food phobias went into overdrive. As she wouldn't admit to being upset or sad, or to having any emotional reaction of any kind to Ian's departure, I suppose food was just how she expressed her angst. But Zoe's diet had been a feature of our family landscape for so long, it took me longer than it should have done to react.

I was perhaps, if I'm honest, too busy licking my own wounds to notice. I was worrying about my own weight, as well. It had a tendency to fluctuate in the exact opposite direction to Zoe's in times of stress, so eating tiny portions of whatever was on this week's restricted food list suited me, in a way. Or at least, I was able to convince myself that it suited.

Jude, as ever, was happiest when eating pizza, so as often as not, I caved in to the easy solution for making at least one member of the family happy by letting him do exactly that.

The watershed moment when I realised things had got out of hand happened about six months after Ian left.

I was in Morrisons one Friday evening doing the weekly shop, and I walked along the vegetable aisle picking things up and then putting them back in accordance with Zoe's current list of prohibited foods, which I carried around in my head. When I reached the end of the aisle, I looked down at my trolley and saw I had only two packages: potatoes and beansprouts. I froze and looked back down the aisle. Something had changed, I realised, and that something was that Zoe's phobias no longer replaced each other. They had become cumulative. And without being able to use fish or meat or beans or tomatoes; without dairy, onions or mushrooms, without rice or gluten, I couldn't think of a single thing I could cook for her.

I marched back down the aisle, slinging colourful vitamin-filled ingredients into my trolley. She would eat, I had decided, whatever it was that I cooked. I would starve her into submission and we'd become a healthy happy family again.

My battle plan lasted for just over two weeks. For two whole weeks, I cooked delicious nutritionally balanced meals and watched my daughter pushing food around the plate. For two weeks, I scraped whatever I had served her into the dustbin. And then, after a few phone calls, I booked us an appointment with Dr Belcore.

I picked Zoe up from school one day and drove us to the town centre. She asked me where we were going a few times, and I pretended it was a mysterious surprise. 'You'll see,' I said with a wink.

Dr Belcore was in a shared practice on Broad Walk. It was in one of those big stone houses overlooking the park and it had a plaque on the door that read Broad Walk Therapy.

'I don't know what this is,' Zoe said, the second she saw the plaque. 'But I'm not going.'

'He's really nice, apparently,' I said, gently taking Zoe's arm and steering her towards the door. 'And I just want us to have a chat.'

'A chat? About what?' Zoe asked, her body rigid as the door buzzed open.

'About how things have been since your father left.'

I got her as far as the reception desk, but when I gave our names to the receptionist, she asked, 'And Zoe, your daughter. Is she with you?' And I realised that she no longer was.

I stayed for the appointment anyway.

I was hoping for some pointers for how to deal with Zoe, but other than advising me to de-dramatise the food situation (by basically letting Zoe eat whatever she wanted) and asking whether perhaps I didn't need to be in therapy myself, he didn't tell me much that I didn't already know. He suggested I get Ian to make Zoe eat as a condition of seeing him while I myself stopped mentioning it at all. He thought this kind of role reversal might be helpful. And as I was leaving, he told me that if I wanted Zoe to come and see him I'd be well advised to negotiate that with her, rather than trying to trick her into coming, which was as obvious as it was impossible.

I only spoke to Jude about Zoe's food issues once, and it was his considered opinion that she was doing it for effect. 'She eats at night,' he told me. 'You do know that, right?'

'She eats what at night?' I asked him.

'Cornflakes, mostly,' he said. 'Bowls and bowls of the stuff.' And the second he said this I knew it was true. We were getting through three boxes a week at that time. 'Sometimes she puts a banana on top, too,' he said. 'But don't say you know about it or she'll stop. Honest, Mum, if you stop caring, she'll start eating. It's just to wind you up. It's just, you know, Zoe being Zoe.'

So for a while, that became my new strategy. I followed my now-eleven-year-old son's advice, which was surprisingly similar to what the shrink had suggested. I stocked up on fortified high-vitamin cornflakes and extra-protein soy milk (now with vitamin D and calcium!). I did my best not to show that I cared about, or even noticed, what Zoe ate.

And it seemed, for a bit, that this was a winning strategy. Zoe put on some weight. She even deigned to eat a jacket potato with beans from time to time, as long as she could do it alone, in her room, without anyone watching to see how much she ate.

Things with Ian got messy for a few months. He started to intimate that he might need his share of whatever the house was worth. But then suddenly they eased up again, for the saddest of reasons.

His mother, who I had always rather liked, had died unexpectedly. This meant that not only was he no longer strapped for cash, but he was far too busy clearing and selling his mother's house to care about ours. So the pressure that had been building around my own living arrangements simply fell away. We found ourselves getting on quite reasonably, which, considering the circumstances, was a surprise.

Zoe's mood, always somehow linked to how well I was getting on with her father, seemed to perform a brief upswing around then, too. It wasn't going to last long, because something was going to happen that would truly upset the balance. But around then, I was feeling quite proud of myself and how I was coping with it all. And I had no idea whatsoever just how bad things were going to get.

Two

Jude

My iPhone starts warbling at six in the morning, and for the first few seconds I can't remember why. But then it comes to me, and my first coherent thought of the day is, *This is a mistake*.

I throw back the quilt and all the hairs on my chest stand up on end. The room is freezing. I stand and head through to the bathroom to pee. The floor tiles are icy cold, and around me, the flat is silent. None of my flatmates ever get up before eight.

'Stupid, stupid idea,' I mutter, as I head through to the kitchen, pausing to peer out at the garden as I pass the hall window. But I can't even see if that's snow out there or just frost. The window is misty and beyond it everything's still pitch black.

By seven, I'm at East Croydon station, my backpack wedged between my trembling legs. I'm wearing my thickest suit and my longest overcoat. I have a woolly hat and a scarf on. But all of that's still not enough for this sub-zero January morning.

The platform opposite, the one I usually stand on for the 8.35, is already packed solid with commuters heading into London. But then a train slides into the station, hesitates for a moment, and then slides on out again, taking the entire contents of the platform with it. It crosses my mind that it looks like a magic trick. Now you see them, now you don't.

And here it is, the 7.03 to Gatwick. I scan the windows until I see Jessica jumping up and down, gesticulating madly.

'I'm so excited!' she says, the second the door slides open. Then, 'Hello!'

Jessica is always excited. It's pretty much her default state, whereas I tend to cultivate an attitude of restrained, defiant cynicism.

'I'm so cold!' I say, aping her tone of voice, as I follow her through the carriage to two seats she has spotted.

'I could hardly sleep last night,' she says, once we're seated.

'It's Bristol, Jess,' I say. 'It's just Bristol.'

'And then Cornwall!' she says. 'And I've never been to either. Can you believe it?'

'Well, let's hope they live up to your expectations,' I say. 'And I hope you have some warmer clothes with you.' Jess is wearing an incredibly cute woollen pink coat and a pink bobble hat, but down below she's in a polka-dot skirt, stripy bumblebee leggings and yellow Dr. Martens boots.

'I'll be fine,' she says. 'And you . . . What's with the suit? You look like you're going to work.'

I shrug. The truth is that I like wearing a suit. It makes me feel sharper, more adult. I can't really explain it, but I feel more myself, I suppose you could say, dressed this way than in just about anything else. Jess, like everyone else, assumes that I have to wear suits for work, and I'm happy to let them all think that's the reason. In fact, everyone at work took the piss out of me to begin with. Most of my colleagues at AMP wear jeans and three-day-dirty polos. It's one rare occasion where I'm totally happy to stand out.

At Gatwick, we find the car-hire place quite quickly. It's still not 8 a.m., and there are only two people in front of us.

21

I fill in all the paperwork and the guy – pleasant, polite and with an accent that makes him sound like a super-cute meerkat in an insurance advert – checks his computer screen and announces enthusiastically that he has good news. 'I have upgrade for you!'

'What upgrade?' I ask. My generation grew up on messages of the 'Good news! You have been selected for a free iPhone' variety. We're vaccinated against good news.

'I have no Vauxhall Corsa,' he says, 'so I give you Peugeot convertible. This is good, huh?'

'A convertible?!' Jess asks. 'What, with the top that folds down and everything?'

'Yes,' the guy tells us.

'And how much extra is this going to cost?' I ask, waiting for the punchline.

'None for the car,' Mr Meerkat says. 'Just little extra for insurance.'

'We don't want it,' I say. 'Just give us what we booked.'

'Hang on,' Jessica says. 'How much extra is it?'

'Only five pounds a day. It's excellent deal.'

'I'll pay it,' Jess says. 'It can be my treat.'

'But the original booking's only six quid a day,' I point out. 'This doubles it.'

'I don't care!' Jess says, her eyes glinting like a toddler's at Christmas. 'It's a convertible! Imagine how cool it will be.'

'It's January, Jess,' I say. 'It's minus five out. It'll be cold, not cool.' But I've already taken on board the fact that I've lost this battle.

'I want it,' Jess says.

'You know what?' I laugh. 'I spotted that!'

◆ ◆ ◆

'Gosh, it's brand new!' Jess comments. We're out on the car park loading our bags into the boot of the Peugeot. 'It even has that new-car smell.'

'It really is,' I say, as I slide into the driver's seat and turn on the ignition. 'It's brand new. Seven hundred miles on the clock.'

'You make that sound like a bad thing,' Jess says, pulling her seatbelt on.

'Well, yeah,' I explain as I adjust my seat and fiddle with the mirror. 'One tiny scratch anywhere on it and I'll lose my deposit. I prefer it when they give me a wreck, to be honest. I like my rental cars to be so fucked-up that no one can tell if these are new dents or old ones.'

We navigate our way out of the airport and merge on to the M23. 'This is back towards home, isn't it?' Jess asks.

'Just for a bit,' I tell her. 'And then we head off west, round the M25. It was cheaper to rent from Gatwick, that's all. Well, it was until you shelled out for a convertible.'

'It was a fiver a day,' Jess says. 'Let it go.'

'You're right,' I say. 'And I have, officially, now let it go.'

'Did you bring the printout?' Jess asks.

'Of course,' I tell her, patting my breast pocket.

'God!' Jess says. 'How exciting! Are you excited?'

'I'm nervous,' I reply. 'Does that count?'

◆　◆　◆

I wonder, as I drive, if I'm going to be able to stand Jess's enthusiasm and I have to stifle a sigh – Jess is very good at picking up on sighs. I wonder if this trip together isn't going to turn out to be a huge mistake.

Our relationship, since we met six months ago, has been very on and off. Very up and down, too.

23

Most of this is my fault, of course. I'm the one 'with issues', as they say. I'm the one who wakes up at 3 a.m. unable to breathe just because Jess is there beside me. I'm the one who feels trapped as soon as we spend an entire weekend together.

So this trip is something of a test, really. And I feel more scared than excited.

◆ ◆ ◆

I met the lovely Jessica through work, during one of my first-ever assignments.

I'd finished uni in 2018. Some of my friends were taking a year out to travel, and I'd hoped momentarily that Dad would sub me so that I could do so, too. But in the end, after pretending to consider it, he'd said, 'No.' He and his new wife were buying a house, and he simply didn't have any spare cash, he said. Mum had never had any spare cash, so I didn't even bother asking her. Instead, I grieved a bit for my lost gap year and then started applying for jobs.

The first month at AMP had been training. It had taken place in an overheated windowless office where I struggled to even stay awake, let alone learn anything. There had been a dead spider plant in one corner and even the trainer looked at death's door. He had grey hair and grey skin to match his grey suit, shirt and tie. He rarely modulated his tone of voice in any way.

But I had somehow survived it, and then was out on my own, travelling around London and going to fix software programs on clients' computers. I bought a couple of off-the-rack suits and some flashy ties and considered myself quite the man. Now I was working, I wanted to look a bit more like Dad, maybe. Dad's always been a bit of a dandy, so perhaps it's a way of feeling like we have at least that in common.

Just a week after the training ended, they sent me to Haringey social services. I was to move ten people's software from their ancient PCs on to new laptops. More and more of their staff were working from home, apparently. The third install was on Jessica's computer, and as soon as I walked into her office, I thought, *Wow*.

I'd had a few girlfriends at college but none of my relationships had been that successful. Perhaps, deep down, the whole Zoe business had affected me more than I cared to admit. Mum had gone a bit crazy for a while, and maybe that, plus my sister's unpredictability, had created some core beliefs about women. They're perhaps what made me run away whenever my own relationships with girls started to get serious. Women weren't to be trusted, I suspected, and I'm sure a shrink would link that somehow to my sister disappearing or my mum's dodgy relationships, or both.

Anyway, Jessica struck me immediately as gorgeous. She's from a multi-ethnic family, with deep olive skin, nice legs and a great figure. She's got huge brown eyes peeping out from beneath a *Pulp Fiction* fringe (she actually irons her hair, if you can believe that), and the result is that she looks a little dangerous and more than a little cool, sort of Alesha Dixon, only with a secret-agent Villanelle edge to her. She has a unique style of her own, largely because she makes a lot of her own clothes, mixing and matching style #1, which is kind of punky, and style #2 which has a sort of K-pop vibe – candy colours and stripes galore. Anyway, she was working when I arrived, and said she had to finish what she was doing. So I sat and watched her work.

'You're not allowed to see any of this,' she explained, pointing a fluorescent green fingernail at the screen. 'So you'd probably better look away.'

I asked what the data onscreen that I wasn't allowed to look at represented, and she explained how the software she was using worked, and even pulled up some very detailed information on what she called the 'chaotic trajectory' of one of the women she was helping. I thought of my sister immediately.

So even though I'd only known her for three minutes, I told Jessica a few details about Zoe and asked if her story might be in the computer, too. But Jessica, who it seemed took client confidentiality seriously, told me she couldn't look and wouldn't look and quickly shut down the program when I tried again to persuade her.

At the end of the week I asked her out. I'd had lunch with her and her colleagues a couple of times, accidentally on purpose (I suppose you could say that I stalked her) and it had been fun. I was pretty sure she was into me – she'd complimented me on my clothes a couple of times, after all.

Day after day I'd failed to ask her out, but by Friday I knew I needed to make a move because otherwise the probability was that I'd never see her again.

'I don't suppose you fancy getting a drink after work, do you?' I finally spat out, at 5.25 p.m. I was in the process of packing up my laptop.

'No,' Jessica said. 'Sorry, I don't think so.'

'Right,' I muttered, throwing a bit of fake laughter into the mix. I zipped up my laptop case and swung it over my shoulder. 'Well, at least that's clear. You, um, have a good one.'

But I couldn't bring myself to walk away. Instead I stood there, smiling like an idiot, and glancing back and forth between the doorway and Jessica.

Eventually, she glanced up at me. She frowned and then chewed the inside of her cheek. 'Look,' she said, 'I actually can't tonight, anyway. But if I give you my number, I suppose you could try hassling me repeatedly over the weekend. To see if I give in.'

I pulled a face. 'You want me to hassle you?' I asked.

She shrugged. 'Yeah, I suppose I do, a bit.'

'Oh, um, OK,' I said.

'It's just that . . .' she said, chewing a fingernail, 'we can't have you thinking I'm too keen, can we?'

'No,' I laughed. 'No, we can't have that at all.'

◆ ◆ ◆

We dated on and off. Actually, for Jessica it was mostly on, but I'd get my weird suffocating feeling and suddenly cancel on her, or lie and tell her I was busy. And unlike most of the girls I'd dated, she took this in her stride.

I asked her a few times if she'd reconsider looking in her computer for my sister, but she was quite adamant that it wasn't going to happen. And then on New Year's Eve, in a bar in Hoxton, she announced that she had some annual leave to take, and that she might as well take it at the same time as mine, in January.

Because one of her friends had told me that, 'The person you spend New Year's Eve with is the person you stay the year with,' I was already feeling a bit queasy, to be honest. The idea of spending my two-week holiday with her as well pushed me to the edge of a panic attack.

But then, just after midnight, she pulled a folded sheet of paper from her pocket and handed it to me. 'I thought we could maybe rent a car and go to Cornwall for a few days,' she shouted over the top of the music. 'For our holidays, I mean. My uncle's got a caravan we could use for free. And on the way, I thought we could maybe go here.'

I unfolded the page and looked at it. It had two addresses in Bristol.

'Bristol?' I asked.

Jessica shrugged cutely. 'Bristol!' she said, emphatically.

'Why Bristol?' I asked.

'Those are your sister's last known addresses,' she explained. 'Before she vanished from the social services radar, she was in Bristol.'

'Really?' I said. Unexpected tears were welling up and I was too drunk to even begin to think about why. 'But you said you couldn't. You said you'd get into trouble.'

'I guess I like you enough to take that risk.'

'God,' I said, looking at the sheet of paper again. 'Really?'

Jess grabbed my tie and used it to winch me in. 'Really!' she said, between kisses. 'Happy New Year, you lovely man.'

'Can we stop at the services?' Jessica asks, dragging me from my thoughts.

We've only been driving for about twenty-five minutes, so I'm reluctant.

'I need chocolate,' she says, and when she sees that I'm unconvinced, she runs her fingers through her hair, looks out of the side window and adds, 'And the loo.'

Once we've stocked up on chocolate bars and once Jess has roasted the poor cashier over the fact that there aren't any vegan chocolate options, we return to the car.

It's drizzling now, and I almost say something sarcastic about how lucky we are to have a convertible, but I manage to restrain myself.

'So how was Christmas?' I ask instead, as I merge back on to the motorway. 'You still haven't told me about it.'

'Uh!' Jess exclaims, pulling her stripy knees up and folding her arms around them. She starts to unwrap a dark chocolate Bounty. 'You really don't want to know.'

I shrug, check the mirrors, then move out to the centre lane.

'Do you?' Jess asks.

'Do I what?' I ask distractedly, thinking more about the traffic and the weather than the conversation at hand.

'Do you really want to know about my horrific Christmas?'

I shrug again. 'I'm just struggling to understand how Christmas can be that bad, I suppose.'

'I'll invite you next year,' Jess says. 'You can witness it first-hand. You'll love it.'

'You're not really selling it to me.'

'No,' Jess says. 'And at your place everyone is just, what, happy? It's all just peace and love?'

I laugh. 'Well, there was only me and Mum this year, but yeah, it was fine. It's not like it was when I was little, when there were three or four of us. Sometimes we had friends round too, so there were five or six of us. There's no piles of presents any more either. But it's fine. We give each other a gift; we eat Christmas dinner; we go for a walk. Some years Dad's there, too. What's not to like?'

'Right,' Jess says. 'Well, to start with, we don't do gifts.'

'You don't?'

'Uh-uh.'

'Why not?'

'I'm not sure,' Jess says, offering me a bite of Bounty, and then feeding it into her own mouth when I decline. 'We used to, till I was about ten. Actually, that's when Dad left – on Christmas Day when I was ten. So I suppose that's why Mum just sort of cancelled Christmas after that. I don't think we were very well off, but I mean, you can always find something to wrap up if you want to. She just got a downer on the whole thing, and from that point on Christmas never really happened again. Or not in any recognisable form, anyway.'

'That's harsh,' I say. I think about Jessica's dad leaving when she was ten. I knew he'd gone back to Jamaica, but until now I hadn't known when. It feels like a little something we have in common. 'Particularly tough when you're only ten.'

'I know,' Jess says. 'It wasn't good. Anyway, we just eat a normal meal nowadays, really. I had a fake turkey thing and Mum and Winston had chicken. I usually argue with Mum about something. This year it was the fact that she cooked the potatoes with the meat.'

'Meaty juices not being veggie.'

'Exactly. And then Mum argued with Winston.'

'About?'

'His job, mainly,' Jess says. 'Mum thinks he should aim higher than Pret. But, I mean, at least he has a job now, right? And then I argued with Winston as well. I was actually trying to defend him, but he took it all the wrong way. Which was probably at least partly my fault. I tend to suffer from foot-in-mouth disease where my brother's concerned.'

'What did you say?'

'Do I really have to tell you?' Jess asks.

'Not if you don't want to,' I say. But I know that of course, she will.

'I just said that not everyone can be a bloody astronaut,' Jess says. 'Like I say, I was trying to defend him. To Mum.'

'And that didn't go down well?'

'No. Winston was all, like, "Oh, and of course you are an astronaut, aren't you? Because social services is soooo important." And I said that no, I wasn't, and nor did I feel I needed to be an astronaut because I have a perfectly good job, and I was actually helping people and I like that and I was just saying that Mum should respect our choices and blah blah, and so Winston got all uppity and said he had a perfectly good job at Pret as well, and that he was helping people too, even if he was only helping them to eat shitty sandwiches, and even if it was just a zero-hours contract, he's happy, and that the zero-hours thing was hardly his fault, was it? It was Mum's fault for voting Conservative, and so Mum got all spiky about that and everyone ended up sulking. Honestly, we could argue about the weather in our family. Actually, we quite often do.'

'Sounds great,' I say. 'Full of Christmas cheer.'

'Exactly,' Jess replies.

'And your mum's a Conservative voter? That can't be easy for you.' Jess is one of the most political people I know. And Conservative, she is not.

'Yeah,' Jess says. 'Mum thinks that voting the same way as rich people somehow makes her one of them. Something like that, anyway.'

'Right,' I say.

'God, I love Bounties,' Jess says. 'I wish they'd make them vegan, though, because they do make me feel guilty.'

'So what about if you took loads of gifts for everyone?' I say. 'If you tried to force them to have a proper Christmas? What would happen?'

'They'd just turn their noses up at whatever I brought,' Jessica says. 'Honestly, it's a no-hoper. It can't be fixed. I've tried.'

By the time we arrive in Bristol, it's bucketing down. The windscreen wipers are sloshing the rain back and forth, and occasionally lorries coming the other way chuck whole buckets of water in our direction making navigating the city streets, where major roadworks are in progress, anything but easy. Still, at least it isn't snowing, I suppose. The Peugeot's thermometer is only reading two degrees, so things could get worse at any minute.

Google Maps, into which Jess has fed the address of our Airbnb, leads us around the edges of the city, and then on south into what appears to be a massive, endless council estate.

Jess, who has taken control of the music, is playing The Cat Empire, her absolute favourite band of the moment. They're really not my favourite band at all, but due to forced and repeated exposure I'm starting to at least get used to some of the songs. Today, as the grey rainy streets slide past, the contrast between the upbeat 'Steal The Light' and everything beyond the windscreen makes it seem like a kind of depressing, post-apocalyptic music video. The kind of thing Ken Loach would produce. If he did music videos, obviously . . .

I glance at Jess's phone and note that we're a mere minute away from our destination. 'Are you sure this is the right address?' I ask. 'It's pretty grim out there.'

'Yep, definitely!' Jess says, brightly, and I wonder if we're even seeing the same thing.

'I thought Bristol was supposed to be all hipstery and cool,' I comment, as Mister Google directs me to turn on to Filwood Broadway.

'I'm guessing that not all of Bristol is,' Jessica says.

'And you chose this particular area because . . . ?'

'Because Zoe chose this particular area,' Jess says. 'Plus, the Airbnb is supposed to be really cool.'

'Right,' I say, doubtfully.

'There!' Jess shrieks, pointing. 'That's it.'

I pull over to the side of the road and open Jess's side window so that we can peer out through the rain. Beyond a high grey spiked fence – the kind they put along railway lines – sits a hefty and quite funky-looking pine-clad Portakabin. It's bang in the middle of a tatty car park, which itself is behind a run-down-looking community centre. The cabin looks as if it has been beamed down by eco-aliens or something. And it looks like they got their GPS coordinates mixed up and delivered it to completely the wrong place.

'We can't stay here,' I mutter, frowning at Jess.

'Of course we can,' she says, and just to prove it, she pushes the door of the car open and steps out into the rain.

After a few minutes fiddling with various combination locks, we have managed to get through the steel gates and into the eco-lodge. It's basically an ultra-modern, super-insulated one-bed unit, built from wood and straw bales, and triple glazed.

The interior is warm and modern, very Scandinavian-looking, and it's well furnished and fully equipped with expensive modern appliances. It's smart and well heated; it feels cosy and chic. The only real mystery is how it ended up in the Filwood Community Hall car park in the first place.

'It's lovely,' Jess says, running one hand across the countertops and then swinging on the door jamb as she makes her way through to the bedroom. 'Isn't it lovely?' she calls from the next room. 'I'd love to live in one of these.'

'Yeah, just not here,' I say. I'm peering out through the venetian blinds at a woman with a pushchair who is passing. She looks about eighteen, is soaked to the skin and is vaping aggressively, if such a thing is possible. She seems to detect my presence as she passes and turns to stare straight at me, causing me to duck back behind the blinds, but not before I see her raise her middle finger at me.

I follow Jess through to the bedroom, where she's bouncing on the edge of the bed contentedly. 'It's nice, isn't it?' she says again. 'A bargain!'

'It is,' I agree. 'Weird place to have it, though.'

'I know,' she says. 'But that's half the fun, right?'

◆ ◆ ◆

We drag our suitcases in from the car and head out in search of food. As we lock the gates behind us, the rain has almost stopped. I worry that someone is going to key the side of the car. All the other cars in the street are old bangers and our brand-new, bright green Peugeot looks dangerously conspicuous.

We head on foot towards some shops Jess spotted as we drove in, but when we get there we realise that everything is closed. There's a boarded-up graffitied cinema, a butcher's, a pharmacy and a Salvation Army shop, all shuttered, apparently permanently.

'Jesus, what happened here?' I ask. 'A nuclear war?'

'Bad governance,' Jess says. 'Unbridled capitalism. The Tories. Take your pick.'

'Could you have chosen a nicer spot?' I ask.

'Hey, half of Britain looks like this these days,' Jess says.

'Just not the half I hang out in.'

'Well, no,' Jess says. 'Quite.'

'Do you think it was ever better?' I ask. 'I mean, when Blair was in power, did it actually make any difference?'

'A bit. But not much, I don't think,' Jess says. 'Perhaps there was a bit more hope back then. People at least had the hope that things might change. But change takes a long time. A long time and a lot of money.'

At the end of the row, we come to the sole surviving shop: a combined newsagent, tobacconist and corner shop. 'Yay!' Jess says. 'I knew there'd be something.'

We say hello to the friendly Asian owner and then scour the shop for vegan food options. There are no fresh vegetables or fruit on sale, just chocolate, white bread and ready meals, so we finally leave with beef-flavoured Pot Noodles, which amazingly Jess says are vegan, plus packets of crisps.

'So Zoe lived near here?' I ask, as we walk back towards the community centre. 'You looked up the address?'

'Yeah, it's just up there,' Jess says, pointing towards the derelict cinema. 'Or maybe there,' she says, pointing behind us. 'I'm a bit confused now.'

'Classy, my sister,' I say.

'I expect she had her reasons,' Jessica says. 'Do you know anything about how she ended up in Bristol?'

'Nothing,' I reply. 'I didn't even know she was in Bristol until you gave me that printout.'

'So shall we get these inside us and go Zoe-hunting?'

'I suppose,' I say. 'Are we just going to go and knock on the door?'

'Sure. Why not?' Jess says.

'Aren't you scared?' I ask. I nod at the junk-filled garden we're passing. It contains the remains of a broken burnt-out scooter, two mattresses and no fewer than three rusting supermarket caddies. 'Aren't you nervous about knocking on doors around here?'

Jess laughs. 'I'm a social worker,' she says. 'Knocking on doors like these is what I do all day, every day.'

'I suppose,' I say, suddenly grateful that she's there with me to do this.

'And you, are you scared?' Jess asks.

'A bit,' I admit.

'Scared you'll find her, or scared that you won't?'

'Oh,' I say. 'Oh, I thought you meant . . . Um, scared of both of those equally, I think.'

'Right,' Jess says.

But what I'm most scared of is that she'll be dead, if I'm honest.

'I'm sorry?' Jess says, and I wonder for a minute if I've said that out loud.

'Nothing,' I say. 'Just, you know . . . Yeah. A bit nervous.'

Three
Mandy

About a year after Ian's mother died and about two after I'd spotted that shoe on the floor, I, too, met someone new.

Nothing could have been further from my mind than a relationship. Oh, the idea that one day, just perhaps, there would be someone else had crossed my mind a few times, but when I tried to actually visualise such a thing, it was impossible. I struggled to imagine how I could find someone new attractive. When you've spent thirteen years with the same person you can come to think that it's the familiarity you're in love with, rather than something specific about them. And if I struggled to imagine being attracted to someone who was essentially a stranger, I struggled even harder to imagine them fancying me.

I'd put on a few kilos since Ian had left and hadn't, I don't think, bought a single item of clothing. The phrase 'letting myself go' describes it quite well.

Anyway, I was walking back from town with a bag of shopping when a voice from above shouted, 'Look out below!' I glanced up just in time to see a branch on the end of a rope swing my way. It missed my left ear by about a foot.

I jumped sideways to avoid the return of the pendulum and peered up into the tree, shielding my eyes against the sunlight with my free hand. 'Oi!' I shouted, my shock turning to anger. 'You nearly killed me!'

'I know, I know, I'm so sorry!' came a reply, and a man came into view, hopping with agility from branch to branch and then quickly climbing down the ladder to street level.

'Jesus!' I said as he fiddled to unclip his harness from a rope. 'You really could have killed me there.'

The man turned to face me. He was young, tall and fit with a fuzzy beard and big, brown, touchingly concerned-looking eyes.

'You are OK, aren't you?' he asked, stepping towards me and reaching out to touch my shoulder. 'I'm so, so sorry.'

I licked my lips and nodded. 'My life flashed before my eyes, but I seem to be fine,' I said. 'Whatever happened to health and safety?'

'I'm so sorry,' he said again, grabbing and steadying the still-swinging branch. 'My mate'll be along in a minute to put barriers up. I was just getting everything ready, but it snapped. I didn't cut it or anything. The branch just snapped. It's a good job I had it tied off.'

'It's a good job I wasn't a foot to the left,' I said.

'I know, I know! Come and, um, have some coffee. I've got some in the van. You look a bit pale.' He would later admit that this was a lie – that I hadn't looked pale at all.

'I do feel a bit funny,' I said, a fib of my own. 'So I might just take you up on that.'

◆ ◆ ◆

I found Scott instantly attractive. He was, as I say, tall and rugged-looking. His work gear, the green overalls, the safety hat, his climbing harness . . . well, it all somehow added to that. But it was his eyes that really got to me. It was his big brown eyes and, if I'm being brutally honest, that muscular arse of his, too.

We sat on the back step of his van and drank surprisingly good coffee from a flask.

'You live around here?' he asked.

'Just up there,' I said, pointing.

'It's funny we've never met, then,' he said. 'We've been doing the trees around here for weeks.'

'Well, I spend most of my time at street level,' I said, with a wink. 'Perhaps I need to look skywards more often.' Was I already flirting? Perhaps, unconsciously, I was.

I was definitely enjoying the company of this fit, smiley young man. I was perhaps even milking the situation a little in order to prolong the moment. But I honestly hadn't imagined for one second that the feeling might be mutual.

Scott was astoundingly straightforward. That was the first non-physical thing I noticed about him. With Ian, there had always been a subtext. You always had to read between the lines to work out what he was really trying to say. But with Scott, things were much more direct. Even the way he asked me out that first day was typically literal, which was just as well, as I'm pretty sure that if he'd been subtle in any way I would have assumed that he was just being polite.

'Um, you know what? I really like you,' he said, as I handed back the plastic cup and stood regretfully to get on with my day. 'I don't suppose I could take you out to dinner one night or something, could I?'

I frowned and turned back to look at him.

'Oh, I bet you're already taken, aren't you?' he said. 'Are you married or something?'

I laughed at this and, I think, blushed.

'No,' I said. 'No, I'm not taken at all.'

'Wow,' Scott said. 'Well, there's a stroke of luck!'

◆ ◆ ◆

It was a week before I saw him again. I needed a week to get my legs waxed, my hair cut and my nails done. I bought some new underwear, too.

We met in the Cheshire Cheese, which was a mistake. It was quiz night and we could hardly hear ourselves think, so Scott downed the remains of his pint and we moved down the road to a tapas place. Wearing cargo trousers, trainers and a sweatshirt, he looked even younger than I remembered.

'So, how old are you, Scott?' I asked as soon as the waitress had brought us our drinks. I wanted to get the age thing out of the way.

'Twenty-six,' he said. 'And you?'

'Thirty-five,' I told him, pulling a face.

'Right,' Scott said. 'Is that going to be a problem, then?'

'I don't know,' I said. 'Is it?'

Scott laughed at this. 'Not for me, it isn't. That's for sure. Thirty-five is nothing.'

'Really?' I asked, wondering if it was going to be a problem for me while blushing at the flattery. Despite how much life I seemed to have lived through and how old all that experience seemed to make me feel, perhaps I wasn't too old for romance after all. 'Nine years is quite a gap,' I said, protesting weakly.

'Not for me,' he said again, sipping his beer. 'I've always dated, you know, older girls. People my age don't really interest me. I'm a bit weird that way, I suppose.'

'Gosh,' I said. 'OK.'

'OK?' Scott repeated. 'That was quick. I thought I was going to at least have to get you drunk.'

'That wasn't *OK*,' I said. 'It was just . . . OK!'

'So what you're telling me is that I do have to get you drunk?' Scott asked, grinning.

'Let's say that getting me drunk is probably a good place to start,' I said.

◆ ◆ ◆

We dated for three months before I introduced him to the kids. I suppose even three months will sound a bit short, but I'd fallen in love with Scott almost immediately.

I had tried quite hard not to do that. Falling in love at my age, falling in love with someone his age – falling in love when I was still waiting for my divorce to come through – well, it all seemed ridiculous. Actually, it felt worse than ridiculous. It felt somehow sinful.

But Scott was funny, easy-going and sure of himself, and in many ways more adult than most of my peers. He laughed at all my jokes too, which after Ian's almost constant incomprehension was a huge and much-needed ego boost. The sex was quite something as well, and being twenty-six, Scott was up for it all the time.

I was happy, really happy, for the first time in years. I'd forgotten just how all-absorbing it was to be in love. I'd forgotten how obsessive it could feel, how many hours you could spend daydreaming about someone, how magnetic the attraction between two bodies could feel. Because when we were together in a public place, I was only ever thinking about how much I could get away with touching him without people noticing, and when we would next be alone together. It was all absurd and naughty and totally unreasonable. But it felt totally magical, too.

◆ ◆ ◆

Because I was scared of how Zoe would react, I introduced Scott to Jude first.

Zoe had been a little easier to live with over the previous year, so there was some cause for hope that it might go better than expected. If it didn't, I was terrified that Scott's appearance would simply upset the apple cart all over again. I hadn't begun to imagine just how upset an apple cart could get.

Scott and Jude hit it off almost immediately. They had similar interests: the outdoors, computers, sports . . . They were Apple fans and Manchester United supporters, both of which were like religions to twelve-year-old Jude. But there was more to it than shared spheres of interest. They had similar ways of communicating, too.

Zoe had always been a bit more like Ian, really. You always had to work out what she meant, whereas Jude was forthright, like Scott.

I'd engineered the meeting bang in the middle of Jude's comfort zone, namely Pizza Express, one night when Zoe was staying at a friend's house.

Scott, who seemed quite good at the whole bonding business, asked Jude's advice about the menu and ordered the exact same things as my son.

'So are you Mum's new boyfriend?' Jude asked, once our drinks had arrived.

'I think so,' Scott replied, glancing at me for confirmation. I nodded vaguely. 'Would you mind if I was?' he added, turning back to Jude.

'Not really,' Jude said, matter-of-factly. 'But thank you for asking. That's very considerate of you.'

For the most part, they talked about football. Manchester United were riding high in the Premier League, and there was lots of talk about Rooney and Ronaldo, as I recall. But to be honest, it went over my head. I was too busy watching Scott's lips move, too busy thinking about kissing them to feign that much interest in football. Watching him getting on so well with my son had sent my feelings towards him into overdrive.

As we were leaving the restaurant, Jude asked Scott if he was going to move in. He actually sounded quite upbeat about the possibility, so I expect the idea of another male in the house, and above all, someone to talk about football with, seemed quite appealing.

'I don't think so, mate,' Scott replied. 'I've got my own little place out in Bakewell. And I quite like living on my own, to be honest.'

'OK,' Jude said, thoughtfully. 'Can we come and see it? Your house, I mean?'

'Of course you can,' Scott said.

'Has it got a big garden?'

'It has,' Scott told him.

'Big enough to play football in?'

'Well, not really. Because I grow lots of vegetables in it.'

'Oh, OK . . .' Jude said. 'But we can definitely come and visit?'

'Definitely,' Scott confirmed. 'You can come anytime you want.'

◆ ◆ ◆

For thirteen-year-old Zoe, a few days later, I booked a table at Simply Thai. Incredibly, their tofu curry had been an almost constant throughout the many phases of her eating disorder, but that evening she wouldn't even touch that. Instead, she glowered at some point in the distance beyond the window, occasionally deigning to lift a prawn cracker to her lips.

Scott did his very best to charm her, but it was never going to happen, really. It was actually quite painful to watch.

'Is there something exciting going on out there?' I eventually asked, an attempt at making her at least look at us.

She turned to me and rolled her eyes.

'Oh, come on, Zoe,' I said. 'It's really nice of Scott to bring us to your favourite restaurant, don't you think? You could at least talk to him a bit.'

Zoe sighed and swivelled robotically to face Scott. 'So are you shagging my mother?' she asked him. 'I mean, I assume that's why we're here.'

'Zoe!' I gasped, glancing round the restaurant to see if anyone had overheard. 'How dare you!' I actually sat on my hand to avoid slapping her in public.

She shrugged. 'You asked me to talk to him,' she said. And then she pushed her chair backwards and stormed from the restaurant.

'Just let her go,' I told Scott, when he, too, started to stand. 'She knows her way home.'

◆ ◆ ◆

Zoe's was such clichéd angst, it was almost as if she'd looked up how to behave in a psychology textbook. She would position herself in constant opposition to Scott, seemingly with the sole aim of reminding him that he wasn't her father, should he finally attempt to overrule her.

Scott, bless him, had the patience of a saint, and would explain every time that he wasn't trying to be her father, but that he was there for her if ever she needed him.

Like with the food issues, I tried pleading with and/or bribing her. I tried threatening and punishing her, too. But as ever, nothing worked. Zoe never treated poor Scott with anything other than disdain.

A couple of months after they'd met, by which time Scott was staying over a couple of nights a week, I heard him lose his cool for the first time. It was a miracle, really, that it hadn't happened before.

I was in the kitchen checking my Visa statement on the laptop and, because Scott wanted to watch the match, he'd headed through to the lounge, only to find Zoe had left her almost untouched sandwich on a plate bang in the middle of the sofa.

'Are you eating this?' I heard him ask.

I paused what I was doing and listened more intently.

'Does it look like I'm eating it?' she replied.

'OK. Let me rephrase that,' Scott said. 'If you're not eating that, how about you carry it through to the kitchen, put it in the bin and put your dirty plate in the dishwasher?'

'Why should I?' Zoe asked in her most belligerent tone of voice.

'Because leaving our dinner plates in the middle of the sofa isn't sustainable behaviour,' Scott explained, reasonably.

'You what?' Zoe said. To my despair, she was starting to sound a lot like Vicky Pollard from *Little Britain*.

'Sustainable behaviour is something that everyone can do without it being a problem. Unsustainable is something that everyone can't do,' Scott explained. 'So, for instance, if we all left our dinner plates on the sofa, then none of us would be able to sit down, would we? So we can't all do that. It's unsustainable.'

'Whatever,' Zoe said.

I blew through my lips and closed the lid of the laptop. I was loth to stop what I was doing, but my daughter's rudeness was becoming intolerable. But as I started to stand, for the first time ever Scott spoke up.

'Just do it, Zoe!' he shouted. 'Take your bloody plate through to the kitchen before I ram it down your throat.' I shuddered to hear him talking to her this way, but she'd been so consistently foul to him I had kind of been waiting for it to happen. As I hesitated over whether to intervene, Zoe said, predictably, 'You're not my father. You don't get to tell me what to do.'

'You're right,' Scott said. 'And thank God I'm not. Because being the father of such a rude, gutter-mouthed, sulky, ungrateful daughter would be a real f— a real effing downer, wouldn't it?'

'And so would having a dad like you,' Zoe replied childishly, but with a quiver in her voice I hadn't heard for a while.

I was unconvinced that this was a constructive way for Scott to build a relationship with my daughter but, after all, everything else had failed. He'd been as nice as pie to her for months and it had got him precisely nowhere. So as she entered the kitchen and dumped her plate in the sink, sandwich and all, I said nothing. I just watched and waited to see if things might now improve.

A few days later I got my friend Ellie to phone her psychologist brother for advice. He said that Zoe's reactions were all pretty normal and that I should just keep things as calm as possible. I should ensure Zoe felt loved and safe, he said, and wait for her to get over it. So even though I was finding the love bit increasingly challenging, that's what I tried to do.

◆ ◆ ◆

In the beginning, Scott and I just seemed to get on better and better. I could barely believe my luck.

The main reason for this was his honesty, I think. He was so truthful about everything that I never really doubted his word. So if Scott said, 'I'm going to go home for a bit. I need a bit of quiet time. It's just the way I'm built,' I'd know that it was exactly as he'd said. It didn't mean, 'You've annoyed me,' or 'I'm going off you,' or even 'Your daughter is driving me insane,' though he often enough said that last one, too.

I found I was happier, that I was more satisfied sexually as well, than I had ever been before. It will sound clichéd, but I really did find myself singing in the shower of a morning, and it seemed to me that perhaps I'd been in the wrong relationship all along. I even occasionally felt grateful towards Ian for having prompted the break-up. And that took all the anger out of our separation.

He started stopping by for a cuppa about then. He'd bring the kids home and then stay for a cup of tea or, depending on the time of day, even a bite to eat. He'd split up with Linda so he had time on his hands, I suppose. I have to admit to feeling a bit smug about the fact that their relationship hadn't worked out.

The mealtimes when Ian ate with us were the only times Zoe was bearable. She was never happier than when Ian and I were being civil to each other.

But there was someone who didn't have such a positive view, and that person was Scott. Finally, the man with no faults revealed that he wasn't so perfect after all. He suffered from jealousy, and it was all directed at my ex.

Of itself, we could probably have worked around it. After all, I was as in love with Scott as I was comfortable with the fact that I was no longer with Ian. So all I had to do was avoid mentioning the one to the other and everything would be fine.

But Zoe soon discovered she could wind Scott up about it. She'd compare them constantly, and within earshot, always painting Ian as Scott's far superior rival. She'd tell Scott what a great father Ian was, how he earned so much money, or how much his new suit or car had cost. If Scott gave me a gift, usually something cute and home-made, or tasty and home-grown, she'd mention some previous expensive gift I'd had from Ian, exaggerating freely. She was turning into a sort of Glenn Close of daughters and if Scott had owned a pet rabbit, I'm pretty sure she would have boiled it.

Once she'd twigged that I was avoiding mentioning Ian, things really got difficult to manage. Zoe started to note when Ian lingered for a drink and then make me look like a liar by mentioning it.

'You didn't tell me Ian stayed for dinner,' Scott said accusingly one night, and I knew instantly that Zoe was behind it.

'He brought the kids home,' I said. 'That's all. He is their father, Scott.'

'But you invited him to dinner.'

'I was serving up, Scott. I could hardly not invite him, could I? He stayed just long enough to wolf down a jacket potato and then he left.'

'That's not what Zoe said.'

'Well, no. Of course it isn't. But I can assure you, he ate a potato and left.'

'He didn't have dessert?'

'Yes, he ate a yoghurt, if you must know.'

'And wine.'

'And he drank a glass of wine.'

'But you decided to keep that a secret?'

'I didn't keep it a secret, Scott. I just didn't think it worth mentioning.'

'You didn't think it was worth mentioning,' Scott repeated. 'Funny, that. We spoke for half an hour last night and you didn't think to tell me.'

'OK, if you must know, this is exactly why I didn't mention it. Because it makes you get like this.'

'Like what?'

'Jealous. Absurdly jealous.'

'Right,' Scott said, pulling his still-warm jacket back on. 'Whereas knowing you've been seeing your ex-husband behind my back doesn't make me feel jealous at all.'

No sooner had the front door slammed than Zoe appeared, looking smug. 'Scott didn't stay for long,' she said glibly.

'You're right,' I replied, as neutrally as I could manage. 'He didn't.'

Four

Jude

It takes us less than ten minutes to walk to the house on Bantry Road.

Our lunch of Pot Noodles and crisps hasn't really hit the spot for me, and my stomach is grumbling as we walk. But when I mention this to Jess, she suggests it's probably just nerves, so I wonder briefly if she might be right before deciding that, no, I simply haven't eaten enough. Jess always likes to find a psychological explanation for everything, and sometimes, for instance when you're just hungry, that can be quite annoying.

The rain has completely stopped now, and there are even occasional glimpses of sunshine bouncing light off the glistening pavements, making the whole place look just a touch less sinister.

'So, what would you say to her?' Jessica asks as we walk. 'I mean, she's obviously not going to, but just suppose Zoe opened the front door. What would you say?'

I think about this for a moment, and then tell Jess the truth: that I haven't the faintest idea. As we continue to walk, I try out various ideas in my mind, but none of them quite seems to work.

When we get to number forty, it's a council house surrounded by other identical council houses in a street surrounded by other identical streets. It has a small, rather absurd iron gate across the narrow concrete path that leads through the overgrown front yard to the door – absurd because there is no fence on either side of it, so we could just step around it if we wanted to. I open the gate and theatrically bow and beckon to Jess to enter.

The paintwork on the front door is peeling, one of the panes of glass has been replaced with cardboard and to the left of the door, pushed up beneath the lounge window, is an old rain-soaked fake-leather sofa. 'This is nice,' I murmur.

'Just stop it,' Jessica mutters, knocking boldly on the front door. I think I see the net curtains in the upstairs window twitch, but I'm not sure. After a moment, Jess raps on the door again before bending down to peer through the flap of the letterbox. 'Hello?' she shouts out. 'Anyone home?'

She straightens and pulls a face. 'The problem is that you look like trouble,' she says.

'What do you mean, I look like trouble?'

'Men in suits,' Jess says. 'They rarely bring good news to ordinary people. They're usually here to seize the telly or serve a writ or something. You look like a lawyer or a judge. You look like trouble.'

I fiddle with my tie as I consider this. 'OK . . .' I say doubtfully.

'I nearly said something when we left the unit,' Jess says. 'I nearly asked you to change. I wish I had now.'

I give her an exaggerated once-over of my own, taking in her candy-pink coat, the leggings, the yellow Dr. Martens.

'What?' she says. 'I'm not saying you have to look like everyone else. I'm just saying that looking like a plainclothes cop isn't perhaps ideal.'

'I think I preferred it when you said I look like a judge.' I laugh.

'Whatever,' Jess says, waving one hand at me dismissively. 'You know what I mean.'

We step back from the front door and look up at the bedroom window. I still think I can sense someone there, peering out at us. 'This isn't going to work, is it?' I say miserably.

'What d'you mean?'

'Well, I'm just realising. It's like, I thought we'd find her, or, you know, not be able to find her. Definitively. But the probability is actually just this, isn't it? It's just no answer.'

At that moment, a yellow DHL van comes hammering up the street, then scrunches to a stop in front of where we're standing. A young guy with a blond ponytail climbs down, retrieves a package from the rear of the van and then, ignoring the ironic gate, jogs across the patch of grass to join us. 'All right?' he says. 'Anyone in?'

'We're not sure,' Jessica tells him, standing back. 'You try.'

He knocks loudly on the door and raps his knuckles on the window. 'DHL!' he shouts. 'Delivery for you!'

Surprisingly, the front door opens immediately, revealing a middle-aged woman in a velour dressing gown. 'Oh, is that my Amazon stuff?' she asks, reaching out to take the package from the DHL chap's outstretched hand.

'Just sign here,' he says, stuffing a touchscreen device in her face. The package signed for, he jogs back across the garden and climbs into his van.

The woman starts to close the front door again, but then hesitates briefly. 'If you're Jehovah's or whatever, I'm not interested,' she says.

Both Jess and I grin at this.

'We're not,' Jess says.

'No, we're really not,' I add.

'And if you're selling something . . .' the woman begins.

'We're actually just looking for his sister?' Jess interrupts. 'Zoe Fuller. Do you know her?'

The woman freezes. It only lasts a split second, but I can see the name means something to her.

'You know her?' I ask.

The woman shrugs. 'I might do. She in trouble?'

'Not at all,' Jessica says.

'I'm her brother. Like I said, I'm just trying to track her down.'

'You don't look like her brother.'

'Well, no,' I say, unsure how to respond to that. 'Apparently I look like a Jehovah's Witness. But I'm not. I'm Zoe's brother.'

'She was here, then?' Jess asks. 'At this address?'

'Ages ago, she was. She was 'ere with Dwayne.'

'Dwayne?'

'My son. But they only lasted a couple of months. His relationships never last. Too selfish. And then they both fucked off. Separately, mind.'

'Do you know where to?' Jess asks.

The woman shakes her head. She pulls back the flap of her Amazon package and peers inside. I can see that she's already losing interest in us. 'Nah,' she says. 'Dwayne went back to his dad's, I expect. As for Zo, I really couldn't say. Nice girl, though. I liked her. It was just a shame she got into smoking that rubbish.'

I open my mouth to ask her what rubbish, but Jess is already saying, 'Do you have an address for Dwayne, maybe? Or a number?'

'Of course I do,' the woman tells us. 'He's my son. But I ain't giving it to you. I'm sorry, love, but I don't know you from Adam.'

She starts to push the door closed, but Jess positions one foot in the gap. 'Just one quick question,' she says brightly. 'We have this other address for Zoe. Do you know it, by any chance?'

The woman reopens the door a little and shoots Jess a glare designed to kill. 'Take your foot out of my door, and maybe I'll answer that,' she says.

'Yes, sorry,' Jess says, withdrawing her boot from the opening. 'Here,' she says, plucking the sheet of paper from my grasp and handing it over.

The woman studies it. 'Sure,' she says. 'That's over in Lawrence Hill, that is.'

'Is that a walk, or, like, a drive away?' Jess asks.

'It's a long old walk. Or you could get a bus. The number . . .'

'We have a car,' I interrupt. 'So we'll probably drive.'

'Right,' the woman says. 'Well, watch your backs. It's rough up there.' And then the door clicks shut, and it's over.

As we walk back towards the car, I repeat the woman's warning. '*Watch your backs*,' I say. '*It's rough up there.*'

'I know,' Jess says. 'The mind boggles.'

'And what do you think Zoe was smoking?' I ask.

'Let's just hope she only meant weed,' Jess says.

'Yes,' I say. 'But it didn't sound like she meant a bit of weed, really, did it?'

'Not everyone knows to differentiate,' Jess says. 'Plenty of people think that all drugs are basically heroin.'

'And what do you think she had in the package?' I ask.

'A vibrator, I reckon,' Jess says.

I snigger. 'Yeah, she was kind of in a hurry, wasn't she?'

'Definitely,' Jess says. 'A rabbit, probably. I hope she remembered to order batteries, too. Otherwise there's going to be a frantic nip down to the shops.'

It takes us fifteen minutes to drive to Lawrence Hill and another five to park up and walk back to Queen Ann Road. Most of the area looks as if it was redeveloped in the sixties or seventies: low-rise tower blocks vie for space with ugly industrial units.

Number 127, when we reach it, is the address of a long-out-of-business garage in the middle of yet another row of boarded-up shop fronts.

To the right of the defunct garage is a grubby off-white door with a carefully stencilled plaque that reads, 'Flat 1. 127 Queen Ann Road'. Above this is a dilapidated sign, the remaining letters of which read, 'TY E & E HAUST CHANGE • BO YWO K • VAL TI G • MOT'.

'Queen Ann Road is pretty majestic,' I comment as we stand in front of the doorway, peering up at the yellowed net curtains in the first-floor windows. 'Zoe's tour of the world's most glamorous hotspots.'

'I know,' Jessica says, as she knocks on the door. 'She's not been moving up in the world, has she?'

The door is opened almost immediately by a young man in a dirty Nike tracksuit. 'Yeah?' he asks. He smiles at Jessica and then turns to look at me, actually scratching his balls as he does so.

'We're looking for Zoe Fuller,' Jess tells him. 'Do you know her?'

The guy shakes his head. 'Should I?' he says.

'She used to live here,' Jess tells him. 'Or at least she told us she did. This is her brother. We're trying to track her down.'

'Our mum's ill,' I tell him, deciding to create a heart-rending narrative to get a maximum of information out of him, but then almost immediately feeling guilty for having invented an illness for my mother. I worry that I have somehow tempted fate. 'I thought Zoe needed to know.'

'Shit,' the man says. 'Sorry, but I've only been here a couple of months.'

'Have you seen any post for her?'

The guy half-glances at a shelf behind him, which is piled up with junk mail. 'Never,' he says.

'And does anyone else live here?' Jessica asks. 'Is there anyone else who might know something?'

'You could ask Kira, I s'pose,' he says. 'Kira's been here years. She knows everyone, Kira does.'

'That would be great,' I say. 'Is Kira here now?'

The man sniffs noisily, snottily. 'Not till seven,' he says. 'Maybe eight.'

'This evening?'

'Yeah. I'll, um, leave her a note or something. Otherwise she probably won't open the door. She gets nervous, Kira does.'

◆ ◆ ◆

'He was pretty helpful,' I say as we walk back up the hill to the car.

'He was,' Jess agrees. 'Actually, so was the woman in the other place, really. Once she got over finding a couple of Mormons on the doorstep.'

'Jehovah's Witnesses, actually,' I correct her.

'Yeah, but you look more like a Mormon. Always nicely dressed, those Mormon boys.'

'Are you taking the piss out of my clothes again?' I ask.

'Maybe just a bit,' Jess grins.

'I thought you liked the way I dress. You told me it was sexy.'

'It is, actually,' she says. 'But I'm thinking you might need to broaden your wardrobe. One suit does not fit all circumstances, you know?'

'I could always get some Nikies,' I suggest, jokingly.

'I think you'd look pretty hot in activewear,' Jess laughs. 'There's more than one way to look sexy, you know.'

◆ ◆ ◆

From Lawrence Hill, we drive out to Clifton, where they don't appear to have any council houses. Instead, the streets are lined with grand Georgian townhouses. It reminds me a bit of Chelsea.

We wander past leafy padlocked parks and peer at the menus of organic vegan restaurants – the contrast with Filwood is quite shocking, really. The final clouds have vanished, too, so it feels as if even the weather might be better in this part of town.

We duck into a coffee shop called Himalaya. It has stripped floorboards and mismatched funky furniture. Jazz is playing through Bose speakers. The facade has curved-glass bay windows through which the sun is streaming. We order soya cappuccinos and a slice of vegan carrot cake to share.

'It's a whole different world here,' I say, glancing out at the street to where a bearded man is cycling past, his daughter in the child-seat on the back.

'Different to where?' a voice asks, and we look up to see the owner standing over us with our drinks.

'Oh, we're staying on the other side of town,' I explain. 'It's not quite the same.'

'We're in Filwood,' Jess explains.

'Now why would anyone want to stay in Filwood?' the guy laughs as he puts our drinks down, and though we both know what he means, and though his laughter is genuine enough, something about the comment troubles me.

It's not until we're back outside that Jess puts words to my unease. 'That was really quite revealing,' she says. 'About the state of Britain today, I mean.'

'How so?' I ask.

'Well, there wasn't any compassion there, was there? No sadness over the state of the other side of town. No outrage that there's masses of money here for vegan cappuccinos but not enough five miles away to even keep a Salvation Army shop open. Just that sneering British determination to avoid ever having to be confronted with the riff-raff.'

'He wasn't exactly sneering,' I say.

'No,' Jessica agrees. 'But I honestly don't think he gives a shit about the state of Filwood, do you?'

'No,' I say. 'Perhaps not.'

After consulting some online guide on her phone for a bit, Jess leads us to the Lido. 'It's supposed to be beautiful,' she tells me. And with its vast blue-tiled, heated outdoor pool and gourmet restaurant down one side, beautiful is what it is.

As an excuse to visit, we take seats in the café and order over-priced cups of tea.

Occasionally people appear from the far end of the pool before disappearing into the individual changing booths along the far side. They then reappear in their bathing costumes before plunging into the glowing pool. It looks a bit like one of David Hockney's California paintings.

'So, guess how much it costs to swim in here,' Jessica says, after a fresh bout of googling.

'Um, too much for the folks who live in Filwood?' I ask, trying to head off her next rant before it gets started.

'Yeah,' Jessica says. 'I would say so. It's twenty quid a pop.'

'Twenty quid?! Just to swim?'

'Well, you get access to the sauna, too. Lovely, though. I mean, I would, if I was loaded. If money was no limit, I'd be here every day, wouldn't you?'

'Yes,' I admit. 'Yes, I think I probably would.'

'We all would. That's the trouble. There was a public pool in Filwood until 2006, you know,' Jess informs me while scrolling down her screen. 'But they closed it due to government cutbacks.'

'Nice,' I say, sipping my tea and discreetly watching a very fit woman behind Jessica's head as she dives perfectly into the far end of the pool. 'Why would poor people possibly need access to a pool?'

'They're even closing that community centre behind where we're staying,' Jessica says, waving her phone at me. 'There's a whole article here on the fight to keep it open.'

'God, that's not right, is it?' I say. 'I mean, it's the only thing left. There's nothing else there at all, is there?'

'No,' Jess says. 'No, there isn't.'

◆ ◆ ◆

From the Lido, we walk out to the famous suspension bridge. It's really just something to do, a destination to head for, but when we get there, the bridge is pretty impressive.

A plaque tells us that it was built in 1864, and after a brief discussion about quite how, in 1864, they managed to drag the massive cables that hold the bridge up across the River Avon, we decide to cross to the far side where there is apparently a visitors' centre.

'Loads of people throw themselves off here,' Jessica informs me, as we pass by an advertisement for the Samaritans.

'That's a cheery thought,' I comment. 'I love travelling with you.'

'You know, my mum tried to kill herself when Dad left,' Jessica continues, making me feel bad about my flippant comment. 'I mean, only in a half-hearted sort of way. I don't think she ever thought she'd actually die. But it was tough, as a kid. It was hard to convince ourselves that we really mattered that much to her after that. I can't say it left me feeling particularly important. Or especially loved.'

'No,' I say, taking her hand. 'No, that's awful.'

'Was your mum OK?' Jess asks. 'I mean, when your dad left? I'm assuming he left her, did he? It's generally the dads who go.'

'Yeah, she was OK,' I say. 'She's quite tough, my mum. And I'm not sure who left who, really. I mean, Dad moved out, but I'm not sure whose decision that was. We never really talk about it. I think they both agreed.'

'But he remarried, right?'

'Not for years. But yeah, he did eventually.'

'That's weird,' Jessica says.

'What is?'

'Not knowing whose fault it was.'

'It's always everyone's fault in a way, isn't it?' I say. 'Sort of everyone's fault and no one's fault at the same time.'

'I suppose,' Jessica says, frowning in a complex manner, as if she's trying the thought on for size. 'Perhaps.'

◆ ◆ ◆

Mainly because it's so warm inside, and so very, very cold outside, we spend quite a while in the visitors' centre. Looking at images of the bridge being built is surprisingly interesting, even if the presentations are rather sketchy about quite how they got those impossible cables across the river.

By the time we get back outside, it's pitch black. I check my phone and announce that it's five-thirty. 'So what do you want to do now?' I ask.

'Shall we go somewhere nice and eat a bit early?' Jess suggests. 'I'm a bit tired and hungry, to be honest. Then we can check Zoe's place on the way back and get an early night – maybe pick up a bottle of wine or something?'

She winks at me as she says this, and I think about the implications of an early night with a bottle of wine and have to struggle not to think about it any further. I find Jessica incredibly fit, and it doesn't take much to get myself all worked up. 'That guy said she won't be there until eight,' I remind her, 'so we can't go back too early.'

'Sure, but by the time we've found somewhere and eaten, that'll be fine, won't it?' Jess says. 'Come on, I saw some vegan places on TripAdvisor. They're in, like, shipping containers or something, down on the riverfront. Wapping Wharf, I think it's called. Let's try there.'

◆ ◆ ◆

We park in a scrappy car park behind the wharf and walk down to the dockside. The streetlamps are reflecting prettily in the rippling water, but an icy wind makes it all but impossible to stay outdoors, so we duck into the first bar we come across.

'It's cold out there, huh?' The smiling, hipster barman laughs as we unbutton our coats.

'It is,' I agree, even though the truth is that it isn't much warmer in here. I scan the empty bar and see that there are four cheap blow heaters in the corners of the room. The architects don't seem to have given much thought to how to heat this particular shipping container in winter.

We order two craft beers from the massive list and then move to the two seats closest to a blow heater.

'Everywhere's so quiet,' Jess says.

'Monday night in January,' I say. 'I bet it has a different feel to it in summer.'

Jess nods and sips at her beer. 'Well, everywhere's nicer in summer, isn't it? I often think that all these trendy redevelopments are basically attempts to be more European. We all want to be Spanish, really, don't we? It's just that we don't have the weather for it, so it's all a bit hopeless.'

I nod and lick my lips. I've been thinking, most of the afternoon, about what Jess told me about her mother and how I didn't really respond. I feel like I should have said something caring or profound, perhaps. But the truth is that it took me a bit by surprise. I'm worried I appeared indifferent.

'You OK?' Jess asks. She's clearly picked something up in my expression.

'I was thinking about what you told me,' I admit. 'About your mum. I'm sorry. I didn't know what to say when you told me that.'

Jessica shrugs and reaches for my wrist. 'Hey,' she says, 'don't worry. There's nothing to say. I only mentioned it because of that Samaritans sign on the bridge.'

'All the same,' I say. 'I sounded like I was making light of it, but I really wasn't.'

'Don't worry. Winston and I joke about it all the time. We call it Mum's fake suicide. I mean, she survived, after all.'

'I just hadn't realised what a hard time you had,' I say, flipping my hand over to take Jess's within my own.

'You know,' Jessica says, 'when you're a social worker, you realise that most people have had a hard time. And a lot of them have had a much harder time than yourself. When you're dealing with kids whose parents are in prison and who are constantly shuffled from one foster family to another, it tends to put your own shit into perspective.'

'I suppose it must,' I say. My phone buzzes at that moment, so I slide it from my inside coat pocket and check the screen.

'Take it if you want,' Jess says.

I shake my head. 'It's just Scott,' I explain. 'I'll phone him back another time.'

'How long were they together?' Jess asks, once I've put my phone away. 'Scott and your mum, I mean. Two years or something, wasn't it?'

'Yeah, something like that. A bit more, maybe.'

'And does she mind that you've stayed in touch?'

I laugh. 'No,' I say. 'Because she doesn't know.'

'So, she would mind?'

'I don't think she'd be particularly comfortable with it. I mean, they're not on speaking terms or anything.'

'But you decided to keep in touch all the same?'

'I didn't really decide,' I tell her. 'It more just sort of happened. Because we get on really well.'

'So you weren't jealous when he turned up?'

'Jealous?' I ask. 'Of what?'

Jessica shrugs. 'Kids often are,' she says. 'They generally resent their parents' new partners. The only time my mum ever dated anyone, I hated him. I mean, he was an absolute tosser, so that wasn't entirely my fault. But even if he'd been nice, I doubt we could have been mates. I was way too angry about Dad leaving to be nice to Mum's new boyfriend.'

I nod. 'That's what Zoe was like,' I say. 'She hated Scott's guts. But not me. I really liked him.'

◆ ◆ ◆

I loved my dad, but unlike Zoe, I didn't feel I'd lost him. He was still there, if anything more present than when he'd been living at home. He was forever bringing us presents and taking us places at the weekend. And in addition to this, we suddenly had Scott.

Where Dad was a clever but, I suppose, quite a rigid sort of a bloke, Scott was fun and sporty. You could wrestle with Scott, if you know what I mean. Perhaps it's because he was younger than Dad, or maybe it's just because he wasn't my dad, but he really felt more like a mate.

I'd never tell Dad this, of course, but in a way Scott suited me better. Though Dad had always made a champion effort to seem interested in football or iPhone apps or space rockets or whatever I was currently into, he was never really that convincing. He always seemed like an adult who was humouring me just a bit, whereas Scott was genuinely interested in these things. Sometimes Mum had to interrupt us when we got yakking. 'Can we talk about something other than the moon landing?' she'd ask. 'Because I'm feeling a bit left out here.'

Scott was cool to hang out with, too. Where Dad warned me not to climb trees, Scott taught me how to do it better – how to get right to the top and how to use a harness so that when I fell, all I did was swing around. Scott had no objection to spending two hours up on the field in drizzle so I could improve my goal-keeping skills either. And unlike Dad, Scott was actually a decent striker. So I suppose that, if I had to sum it up, I felt like I'd gained an extra dad. Or at the very least, a new best friend.

Zoe didn't see things like that at all, of course. She'd been up and down and all over the place ever since Dad had left, but when Scott appeared on the scene she lost the plot completely.

She seethed with resentment at the fact that Scott was supposedly trying to replace our father. She'd get angry if she got home and Scott was there, but even angrier if Mum went over to Scott's place instead. If I told her to lay off, or that I liked him, it made her furious. Zoe's reasons to dislike Scott seemed endless, really.

He tried being nice to her, to begin with. He offered to drive her places, or help her with her homework. He cracked jokes and even bought her stuff. But nothing worked. She'd 'set against him', as Mum would say, from the very first moment they'd met. And there was nothing he could do that would ever change her mind.

The funniest thing was what happened if he touched her, because Scott was a very tactile person, forever touching your arm when he spoke to you, or stroking your head when he walked by. But when Scott touched Zoe, who really wasn't tactile, she shrieked. It was quite weird, actually, almost as if he'd given her an electric shock or something. If she was standing when he touched her, she'd literally jump back a few feet. Scott and I used to joke about that. He'd reach out with one finger to touch me and I'd throw myself back against the wall as if he'd been holding a phaser gun and then die, loudly, on the lounge carpet. 'You have been Zoe'd!' he'd say.

Sometimes I wondered if the problem wasn't actually that Zoe fancied Scott and was embarrassed about it. He was certainly a good-looking guy, and his age difference with Zoe wasn't that much bigger than the difference between him and Mum, after all.

Anyway, I was happy, Mum was happy; Scott was happy. It was just Zoe who was out of control.

It wouldn't have been too much of a problem; I mean, we'd all got used to working around Zoe's moods. She'd been difficult for as long as I could remember. But then she wilfully began to wind Scott up. And as time went by, she discovered that she was really, really good at that. In a way, winding Scott up was Zoe's super-power. And once she'd discovered it, there was no real way that the relationship could last.

◆ ◆ ◆

Once we've finished our drinks, we button our coats back up and head out into the icy evening. We check out the various restaurants on Wapping Wharf, but the vegan place that Jess had hoped to eat in is closed on Mondays, and the others are either totally empty, which is somehow intimidating, or full, or outrageously expensive.

We almost eat in a little Indian place, but then the owner comes running outside to urge us indoors, and for some reason, because her desperation somehow embarrasses us, we stare at our feet and shuffle away. 'I feel like we should eat there,' Jess says, once we're out of earshot. 'But she was just that bit too intense.'

We end up in a place called Root, which at first glance seems to combine both affordable food and some vegan options for Jess.

Once we're seated, however, once our drinks have been served and it's too late to leave, the waitress asks, 'So, have you eaten with us before? Do you know how it all works?'

There's something pretentious about her introduction, and Jess, who apparently had the same thought, makes me splutter into my beer when she replies, 'Well, I assume it's, like, a restaurant? So I'm guessing that we order food and then eat it?'

The girl, who I now realise is American, replies, 'You're so funny! This is a small-plate restaurant, yeah? So we generally advise that you order a few things to share. Say two or three each, tapas-style. I'll leave you to make your choices, yeah?'

'A small-plate restaurant,' I repeat, once she has left. 'Is that a thing?'

'Apparently so,' Jess says. 'Not the most reassuring way to describe your restaurant, though, is it?'

I order the grilled sardine and mushroom risotto, while Jess plumps for gnocchi with chestnuts and cauliflower pakora.

Ten minutes later, when our food arrives, Jess comments, 'It is a thing! Oh God. It's definitely a thing!'

'I'm sorry?' the waitress asks.

'Nothing, just an in-joke,' Jess tells her. 'I hope you're not hungry,' she adds, once we're alone again.

'Unfortunately, I am,' I say. 'I'm starving.' I reach for the menu. 'Oh,' I say, once I find what I'm looking for. 'Grilled sardine.'

'Singular?' Jess asks, grimacing at my tiny plate.

'Yeah, I should have spotted that missing "s".'

'I actually noticed,' Jess says. 'I'm sorry, I should have said something. I just didn't think anyone would dare serve a single sardine. Especially not for nine quid.'

'No,' I agree, stabbing at said sardine with my fork. 'Do you remember a few years back when the plates got bigger and the portions got smaller? They were huge, the plates, everywhere. You could barely fit two of them on the table.'

'Yeah, nouvelle cuisine, wasn't it?' Jess says, daintily forking one of her mini-gnocchi. 'With a swirl of ketchup or whatever, to make it look pretty.'

'That's right,' I say. 'Anyway, it looks like the plates got smaller again.'

'Yeah, I think they did,' Jess says. 'It reminds me of an episode of *Absolutely Fabulous* where she eats with dolly cutlery to convince her brain the portions are bigger. It's a way of dieting, apparently.'

'Let's hope it convinces my stomach,' I say.

The bill, including drinks, comes to almost fifty quid, but by the time we leave I'm genuinely no less hungry than I was on arrival. But in true British style, we tell the waitress that everything was fine. I even chicken out from removing the 'discretionary' service charge that the waitress has helpfully added to our bill.

'I'm still hungry,' Jess says, almost as soon as we step back outside. 'Can we stop at a chippy on the way home?'

It's exactly what I had been thinking.

We drive back to Queen Ann Road. I'm a bit nervous about returning there after nightfall, but as the streets are entirely deserted on this arctic January evening, it ultimately feels no less menacing than by day.

After a reminder from Jess, I remove my tie and stuff it into my coat pocket, and then I steel myself and knock on the door.

The same young guy as before opens up, only this time he invites us indoors. This is a surprise. 'Come up,' he says. 'You're in luck.'

At the top of the staircase, where the landing opens out into a lounge area, what greets us is almost surreal in nature.

Other than in a junk shop, I have never seen so much furniture in such a small place. There are three tatty sofas, one of which is stacked upside down on top of another. There are five or six armchairs, three tables, one of those old sewing machines built into a table, a pinball machine, and against every wall, stacks of records or pictures or mirrors. It's all astoundingly tatty, and so ugly that these can only really be items people have discarded.

'Come, come!' the guy is saying, as he weaves his way through the maze of furniture towards the far side, where a massive television is playing the intro to *EastEnders*. And so, after exchanging the briefest of knowing looks, Jess and I follow him.

Only when we reach the far side of the room do I realise that a woman is sitting in the wing-backed armchair. She's in her thirties, with patchy hair and heavily acned skin. She has a one-bar radiant electric fire pointed at her knees, but the rest of the room is icy.

'Kira!' our young friend says, and she half-heartedly glances in his direction without really turning her head enough to actually look at him, before returning her gaze to the television.

I become aware of a smell; a stench, really, and I'm forced to breathe through my mouth to avoid gagging.

'These are those people,' the young man says enthusiastically. And then, even though all of the chairs are piled high with junk, he gestures, I think, for us to sit. 'Please!' he says. And then, suddenly embarrassed, he adds, 'I'll, um, leave you to it,' and vanishes through a door in the far wall.

Kira glances at me very briefly and then returns her attention to *EastEnders*, the theme tune of which has just ended.

'Um, Kira?' I say, and she gestures vaguely with one hand, though I'm not sure quite what, if anything, the gesture is meant to imply.

'Kira?' I say again.

'S'me,' she replies.

I glance back at Jess, who is still standing behind Kira's armchair. 'Drunk?' she mouths. 'Stoned?'

I shrug by way of reply.

Jess grimaces, and then squeezes her way around the far side of Kira's chair until she, too, is facing her.

'Hello, Kira,' she says, crouching down and sounding for all the world like a social worker taking control of a difficult situation. 'I'm Jess and this is Jude. We'd like to chat to you about Zoe Fuller, if that's possible?'

I'm impressed. I've never heard her professional tone of voice before. She sounds like a different person. She sounds like someone I don't yet know.

'We're trying to track Zoe down,' she continues. 'Do you know her? Do you remember her living here?'

Kira nods vaguely. ''Course,' she says. ''Course I know 'er.' She reaches down the side of her seat cushion, and for an instant I think that she's going to produce some piece of evidence: a photo or a letter, or an address book. A mobile phone, perhaps, to call her. But when her hand comes back into view, what she's actually holding is a half-bottle of vodka. She takes a swig and then, bless her, offers the bottle to me.

'No, thanks,' I say. 'You're all right.'

'So how long ago was Zoe here?' Jessica asks. 'Do you remember when it was?'

'A while,' Kira says. 'Ages, prob'ly.'

'Do you know where she went afterwards?' I ask. 'Do you have, maybe, a forwarding address or something?'

'She owes me twenty quid,' Kira slurs. 'Thirty, actually. At least thirty. Never paid me for her skunk, did she?'

'Oh,' I say.

'You her mates?' Kira asks, glancing up at me, and then looking back at Jess. 'Is that it?'

'Her brother,' I say again. 'I'm her brother.'

'Got any cash on you?' Kira asks.

I part my lips to reply, but Jess wiggles one finger at me discreetly, indicating that whatever I'm about to say, she thinks I shouldn't say it. Which is amusing, really, as even I'm not sure what I was going to say.

'If we could track her down,' Jessica says, 'then maybe we could get your money back for you.'

Kira laughs at this. 'You won't get nothing out of 'er,' she says. 'Tight as a duck's arse, that one.'

'If we were sure we were going to find her, I might be able to help out,' I say, and despite Jessica's violent head-shake, I slide my wallet from my pocket and pull a crisp twenty-pound note out.

Suddenly, I have Kira's full attention. She makes a swipe for the banknote, but I raise it above my head, out of reach. 'An address?' I say. 'Or a phone number.'

Kira sighs deeply. She looks back and forth from the banknote to me, and her face crumples. I wonder for an instant if she's actually going to cry.

'I can tell you where she works,' she offers, brightening.

'Yeah?' I say. 'Yeah, that would do the trick.'

'Give me that first,' she says, nodding at the banknote. 'She owes me.'

'Tell me where she works first,' I retort.

'The Poseidon,' Kira says. 'Out in Knowle.'

'The Poseidon?' I repeat.

'What is that?' Jessica asks. 'A bar? Is the Poseidon a bar, Kira?'

Kira laughs at this as if it's the stupidest suggestion Jessica could have made. 'No!' she says. 'It's a takeaway, innit.' And then, in a shockingly fluid gesture that I would never have thought her capable of, she lurches from the chair, swipes the banknote from my hand and stuffs it down the front of her T-shirt.

'The Poseidon,' I say again. 'And that's where, did you say?'

'S'in Knowle,' she says.

'Is that in Bristol?' I ask.

'It's up by where we're staying,' Jessica replies. 'I saw it on the map.'

'And do you know what road it's on?'

But Jessica already has her phone out. 'Found it,' she says. 'You wanted chips? Well, it's a fish-and-chip shop.'

'Is that the one?' I ask. 'Is it a chippy?'

'Yeah,' Kira says, swigging again at her bottle. 'Yeah, she worked there. Maybe she still does.'

'Well, that was weird,' I say, once we're back at street level.

'Totally weird,' Jess says. 'And that smell! What was that?'

'I don't know. I was gagging. It was spaghetti Bolognese, I think. Mixed with . . . I don't know . . . cat's piss?'

'You know, I wondered if someone hadn't pissed in that chair she was in,' Jessica says. 'When I crouched down . . .' In lieu of ending her sentence, she pulls a face.

'Yeah,' I say. 'That crossed my mind, too. And skunk . . . that's . . .'

'Could be cannabis, could be heroin,' Jess says.

'Yes,' I say, swallowing with difficulty. 'Yes, that's what I thought.'

The Poseidon is an entirely traditional fish-and-chip shop: a high counter to lean on, a thousand watts of neon illuminating the place like a lighthouse, and pickled eggs next to the till.

It's empty when we get there, and the owners or employees, two women who are perhaps mother and daughter, are sitting at a plastic garden table at the rear, drinking mugs of tea. The younger of the women, who is in her forties, finishes at some length her inaudible conversation before finally coming to serve us.

'What do we want?' Jess asks, peering up at the overhead menu. 'Just chips?'

'I suppose so,' I say. 'Let's get a big portion and share.'

'Large chips, that's two pounds,' the woman says, ringing up our choice on the till.

'And curry sauce,' Jessica says. 'Can we have curry sauce?'

'Sure,' I say. 'Knock yourself out.'

We argue briefly about who should pay, and I cave in and let Jess do it.

'Does Zoe still work here?' she asks, as the woman hands back her change.

'Zoe?' she repeats, looking genuinely confused. 'Sorry, there's no Zoe here. It's just Mum and me.'

'Oh,' I say. 'That's weird. She definitely said she was working here. I'm her brother, by the way.'

She shrugs and then wanders back to where her mother is agitating the chip basket. They have a discreet conversation during which her mother glances up at us repeatedly over the tops of the deep-fat fryers.

Eventually, she returns to front of shop. 'Mum knows who you mean,' she informs us. 'She was only here for a while. It was years ago, though. She stood in when I was . . . indisposed.'

'Right,' I say, stifling a smirk at her surprising use of the word 'indisposed', which she has pronounced, for some reason, in the voice of Queen Elizabeth II. 'I don't suppose you have an address for her, do you?'

'Or a phone number?' Jess asks. 'Anything at all, really. We've been tramping all over, trying to find her.'

'I doubt it,' she says. 'But I'll ask Mum.'

She retreats once again behind the fryers and has another mumbled conversation with her mother, who finally tips her batch of chips out into a tray, salts them and packages up our massive portion and a pot of curry sauce before crossing the shop to address us. As she walks, I see she has massive wing-like flaps hanging from her biceps, and I remember from somewhere the terms that describe them: bingo wings. Or chip-shop arms.

'So what do you want with Zoe?' she asks, as she hands me the carrier bag.

'I'm her brother,' I explain again.

'Their mum's ill,' Jessica says, reusing the alibi that I'd promised myself never to use again. 'We've been trying to track Zoe down, so we can tell her.'

'Oh,' the woman says, looking concerned. 'Very ill, is she?'

'I'm afraid so,' Jessica says. 'I'm afraid she's not very well at all.'

'Well, I'm sorry to hear that,' she says, glancing back at her daughter, who is lingering beside the till. 'She's a nice kid, Zoe is.'

'Yes,' Jess says. 'Yes, she's lovely, isn't she?'

'Look, I might have something,' she says. 'I'd have to look. It was ages ago. But I think I sent her P45 on somewhere, so, maybe. It'd be at home, though, not here.'

'Could you look?' I ask. 'That would be amazing if you could look.'

'Of course, love,' she says. 'Come back later in the week, and if I've found anything . . .'

'We're checking out tomorrow,' Jessica reminds me.

'We live in London,' I explain.

'Oh,' the woman says. 'London, is it? Well, come back tomorrow then.'

'Tomorrow lunchtime?' I ask.

'No, tomorrow evening, love. We don't open till six.'

'But we have to check out by eleven,' Jess points out.

'Then could I phone you?' I ask. 'Could I maybe get your number and call you?'

'No,' the woman says. 'Give me yours and if I find anything, I'll call you.'

◆ ◆ ◆

Ten minutes later, we're back at our cabin with a bottle of South African Chardonnay from the corner shop and our sweaty packet of chips. When we unwrap these, they turn out to be almost inedible. The Poseidon have somehow managed to both undercook them and dry them out. We eat two or three each, and then dump the remains in the bin.

'I hate throwing food out,' Jess says.

'Yeah, well . . . define food,' I say, and she laughs.

'Yes, you're right there,' she says. 'Let's hope that wine's better.'

She unbuttons her coat and pulls off her boots before throwing herself, quite suggestively, across the sofa. 'Come here, little Mormon boy,' she says, 'and bring that bottle of wine with you.'

'I think you need to stop calling me that,' I say, as I unscrew and pour the wine. 'I don't think Mormon boys are allowed sex outside of marriage.'

'I know,' Jess says. 'But I'm quite into the idea of perverting you.'

'Now that,' I say, as I pull off my own coat and jacket, 'sounds more like it.'

In the morning, I wake up first. Jessica is gently curved against my back, and almost as soon as I understand that I'm awake, I also realise that I'm feeling panicky. Though we've been dating for almost six months, I can count the number of times we've woken up together on my fingers. Which, of course, is why this trip is so risky.

I wonder briefly if this panicky feeling, this inability to breathe, might be somehow linked to searching for Zoe. But though I'd love to be able to hang it on something else, the feeling is so familiar that I can't deny, even to myself, where it springs from. My 'issues' are back, and if I don't get my head sorted out before Jess wakes up, then this whole trip could go tits-up.

I try to concentrate on my breath, yogi-style. Breathe in. Breathe out. Breathe in. But my mind refuses to stay focused. I think about previous panic attacks and how I've dealt with them – essentially by walking away and hiding for a few days until it has passed. If that's not possible, I've often shamelessly engineered an argument so that it's Jess who walks away. That's clearly not an option today.

I try to analyse, for the umpteenth time, why going steady makes me feel so scared – where this sudden desire to break free comes from. Actually, the word 'desire' doesn't really cover it. I feel pushed – driven, even – to escape. It can feel sometimes as if my life depends on it.

These crises, which I'll happily admit are entirely unreasonable, have been the death knell of most of my previous relationships.

Jessica, unlike every other girl I've dated, seems able to cope. Perhaps it's because she wants to be a psychologist one day. Maybe it's because of all the shrinky-dinky books she reads. But whatever the reason, she somehow treats my weird moods as interesting case studies rather than considering them personal affronts.

'Oh, I see,' she'll say. 'It's "Let's argue with Jess" time, is it? You know, I think I'll skip the whole thing and just go home and read a book, if it's all the same to you.' Then she'll calmly pick up her stuff and leave. 'Text me when you're over it,' she'll say as she heads out the door. 'And if you never are over it, that's fine, too. No pressure. Love you!'

Most of the time I feel better, physically at least, almost imme-diately she has gone. Within two days I'm actively missing her, and on the third or fourth, I'll text her to say everything's OK again. I generally go for something like, 'Sorry about that. I'm a nob. I don't mean to be, but I am. But I'm a nob who misses you.' And she'll reply, 'Great! See you tomorrow.'

She snuggles a little closer to my back now, and I struggle not to jump out of the bed. I tell myself to be reasonable. 'Nothing's happening here,' I tell myself. 'There is no danger, there is no reason to feel stressed here.'

'Umh,' Jessica murmurs, followed by a huge yawn. She shuffles even closer to me and lays one hand across my stomach.

'You OK?' she asks after a minute or so. 'You're as rigid as a plank and your breath's all funny.'

I clear my throat. 'Um, weirdly stressed this morning. Panicky. Sorry.'

'Oh,' Jessica says, momentarily relaxing her grip on me. 'Poor you.'

She seems to consider her options for a moment before sliding her hand down my chest. She takes my limp dick in her hand. 'Does this help?' she asks, giving it a squeeze. 'Or does that make things worse?'

I'm not going to be able to, I think, even though with Jess that has never happened yet. For an instant my fear of being unable to perform does make things worse.

'I'm not sure,' I tell her, eventually. 'But I don't think that thing in your hand is in working order this morning.' And yet, less than a minute later, my body starts to react to her touch.

'Something seems to be happening,' Jessica sniggers in my ear.

'Yeah,' I say. 'Yeah, it does, doesn't it?'

'Good,' she says, and then a minute later, I'm hard and she's rolling me on to my back and climbing on top of me. 'Perhaps we've discovered the antidote.' She reaches down and pulls me inside her, and I gasp. I'm breathing freely again – breathing heavily, even.

'Yeah,' I say. 'Maybe we have.'

When I step out of the shower, Jess, who's sitting cross-legged on the sofa, ironing her hair while watching breakfast TV, calls out, 'Your phone rang when you were in the bathroom.'

'Yeah?' I say, tying the towel more tightly around my waist as I enter the living area. 'Did you see who it was?'

Jess vaguely shakes her head. She seems pretty engrossed in whatever's on the TV.

I pick up my phone and dial voicemail, then grab a prospectus for Bristol Zoo on which to note down the address, before listening to the message a second time.

'So, it seems that Zoe . . .' I start. But Jess raises a finger and shushes me. 'Hang on,' she says. 'This is interesting. Annoying, but interesting.'

Feeling vaguely peeved that she's more interested in Brexit than in my sister, I head through to the bedroom to dress. As a result of Jessica's remarks yesterday, I choose jeans and a jumper. I'll be warmer this way anyway, I reckon.

When I return to the lounge, the TV set is off. 'You didn't have to turn that off for me,' I tell her.

'Oh, it just makes me too angry,' Jess says. 'I can't stand it.'

'Brexit again?'

She nods. 'I mean, when you visit places like this, you can understand why people voted that way, but . . .'

'You can?' I interrupt. Jess has railed so many times about her inability to understand why anyone would have voted for Brexit that I'm surprised.

'Well, if you live in Filwood, you're going to vote for anything that's likely to shake the system up, aren't you? You're going to think that things can't possibly get any worse, no matter what changes. So you're going to vote for anything rather than what you've got now. I mean, I wouldn't mind so much if it was going to fix anything. But it's not like places like this are going to suddenly get an explosion of investment after Brexit, are they?'

I shrug. 'Maybe they will,' I say. 'Who knows?'

'But the whole country's going to be poorer,' Jess says. 'Just about every economist says so. So how does that help? My bet is that places like Filwood will get even worse.'

'Unless it takes people over the edge,' I suggest. 'Maybe the proletariat will finally get fed up enough to riot, or vote for comrade Corbyn. Maybe he'll tax the hell out of Google and Facebook and spend all the money in Filwood.'

Jess smiles at me lopsidedly. 'Actually, that's quite clever. Maybe that's what he's counting on. I always find it hard to imagine that he doesn't have some kind of strategy, so maybe that's it. An actual meltdown of society, caused by a Tory Brexit.'

'Who knows?' I tell her again. 'I'm just saying that no one knows exactly how things will pan out. The ricochets of events can be pretty complex. Sometimes the right decision leads to the wrong outcome. And vice versa.'

Jess nods thoughtfully. 'I love it when you're being clever,' she says.

I go to fiddle proudly with my tie, Stan Laurel-style, but then realise that, for once, I'm not wearing one. I make the gesture anyway. 'I'm always being clever, sweetheart.'

'So, who was on the phone?' Jess asks. 'Nice jumper, by the way.'

'Oh, the woman from the chippy!' I say. 'You know, I didn't even get her name. Anyway, she's given me an address for Zoe. Apparently, she sent the P45 here.' I hand the prospectus to Jess, who frowns and says, 'Why would she send it to Bristol Zoo?'

'No!' I laugh, taking the sheet from her grasp and flipping it over so she can see the address I've noted down.

'Morecambe,' Jess says. 'I don't even know where that is.'

'It's up north,' I explain. 'Above Liverpool. Near Blackpool and Lancaster, if that helps? It's weird she chose Morecambe, though.'

'Why?' Jessica asks.

I shrug. I don't feel like telling her that particular story right now. 'It's just a long way,' I say. 'She's been zipping up and down the country like crazy.'

'Sure, but Blackpool!' Jess says, flashing the whites of her eyes at me, clearly channelling her inner child. 'That's the seaside! Can we go? Can we?'

'Really?' I ask. 'What about Cornwall and your uncle's place and all that?'

'Oh, who cares!' Jess says, waving the prospectus at me. 'This is your sister's address, Jude.'

'Well, it was her address, two years ago. There's no guarantee that—'

'We still have to try, though, don't we?' Jess interrupts. 'Did she give you her phone number or anything?'

I shake my head. 'She said she tried the number she had for her, but it's been disconnected.'

'The pay-as-you-go generation,' Jess says. 'We come up against that at work all the time. No one ever keeps the same number any more.'

'Umh?' I say. I've been momentarily lost in my phone. 'Sorry, I was checking the phone book,' I explain. 'She hasn't got a landline number either.'

'Who has, these days?'

'I know,' I say, glumly.

'So we're going to Blackpool!' Jess says.

'Morecambe,' I correct her. 'But are you sure you wouldn't rather go to Cornwall? We don't have to do this right now.'

'No, I'm excited about going to Blackpool.'

'Morecambe!' I correct her, again.

'But you said it's nearby. We could still stay in Blackpool, right? We could go to the funfair and everything, couldn't we?'

'I doubt it,' I tell her. 'It'll be closed for the winter.'

Jess tuts. 'Oh, what a bummer,' she says. 'Funfairs are fab. But can we stay there? I love those seedy seaside towns. I bet they have amusement arcades and candyfloss and everything. I went to Margate last summer and I loved it. I can look now and find a place to stay, if you want.'

'I'd still rather stay in Morecambe,' I say, as I return to the kitchen area to finish making tea. 'I mean, that's where Zoe was last. Plus, I seem to remember Blackpool was pretty seedy. Morecambe's not exactly hipsterville either, but it's a bit less full-on than Blackpool. You're less likely to actually get mugged.'

'Lunch, then?' Jess says. 'Can we do lunch there? How long does it take to get there, anyway?'

'Sure, lunch works,' I say. 'Just about. It's on the way. If we leave by nine, we could be there about one, I suppose. But are you totally sure you wouldn't rather go to Cornwall?'

'I'm sure,' Jess says. 'You can buy me lunch.'

'Oh, I think I can run to fish and chips on Blackpool seafront,' I tell her.

'You can buy me a vegan lunch,' Jess says.

'Oh, I think I can run to a portion of chips on Blackpool seafront,' I say, sotto voce.

'And you're not feeling weird any more?' Jess asks, her concerned tone of voice returning.

I take a deep breath and take stock of my body. 'No,' I say. 'No, I appear to be fine. That particular crisis seems to have passed.'

'God, imagine if that was the answer,' Jess says.

'If what was the answer?'

'Sex!' she says. 'Imagine if we just had to shag, like, hourly, just to keep you from having panic attacks.'

'That would be truly awful,' I mug.

'I know,' she says. 'It would be horrific. I'd be exhausted. But in a good way.'

Five

Mandy

As summer arrived, Scott's jealousy, efficiently leveraged by Zoe, became more and more problematic.

Ian, who apparently had met someone else (I never even knew the name of this one), started coming around less and less, and that suited everyone except Zoe. Not only did it limit her ability to wind Scott up about it, but I think she genuinely missed us all spending time together.

She started starving herself about then – began, quite literally, to eat nothing at certain meals. Her weight fell from forty-two kilos to forty and then to thirty-eight. She was looking pretty gaunt, but when I took her to see our GP he prescribed counselling, which Zoe refused point-blank.

Her schoolwork began to suffer as well. I think she must have been too hungry half the time to concentrate. Where her averages had once been top-of-the-class, by that summer they were bad enough for the school to start calling me in for meetings.

Don't imagine for an instant that I just let all of this happen without intervening. I didn't. I tried forcing her to eat. I tried forcing her to work. I tried bribes and punishments; I tried pleading and crying. Nothing ever worked.

Eventually the school sent me an appointment for Zoe to see their in-house shrink, Dr Stevens. I felt grateful that someone external had decided to intervene. For a while, I thought everything might now get sorted out, and that was a huge relief.

It took three missed appointments before we got Zoe to attend, but when she finally did, she sat in glum silence throughout. She may have grunted and shrugged a couple of times, but that was as far as her involvement would go.

Afterwards, Dr Stevens said that as Zoe was fifteen, he'd like to carry on seeing her alone. But as this required her actually going to appointments, and because Zoe was the most determined, recalcitrant teenager ever, it was never really going to happen. The first time, she simply didn't turn up. I didn't even find out that she had lied to me about that until two days later, when the school phoned.

The second time, I took an afternoon off work to pick her up from her final class and chaperone her to the meeting. But she gave me the slip by climbing out of the window of the girls' toilets, leaving me standing, like an idiot, in the hall. I was so angry about it that when she did deign to come home that evening I, to my shame, slapped her cheek. It was only the second time I had ever slapped her, the first having been a quick slap to the legs when she was about five and had run out into the road. Unexpectedly, she seemed quite thrilled by this new development, almost as if it was what she'd wanted all along. She raised one hand to her cheek and looked me in the eye. 'Do you see what you're like?' she asked. 'And then you wonder why I hate you?'

I cried about that on Scott's shoulder, later that evening. Being told I was hated by my own flesh and blood had really cut me to the core.

We booked three more appointments and Zoe vanished every time, sometimes just before the appointment, on other occasions for days either side of it.

In the end, even Dr Stevens gave in. Until Zoe had reached rock bottom and actually wanted to talk, he wasn't going to be able to help her, he said. When I asked him what rock bottom implied, he shrugged, and when I asked him what my options were, he suggested, surprisingly casually, that I might want to consider sectioning her under the Mental Health Act.

I met up with Ian in Costa so that we could discuss this new, terrifying development.

'She hates Scott,' he told me. 'That's the problem.'

'She can't be not eating because she hates my boyfriend,' I said. 'It can't be that simple.'

'But what if it is that simple?' Ian asked.

'I'm not leaving my partner because my daughter doesn't like him,' I informed him.

'Well, no,' Ian agreed. 'I'm just saying . . . Actually, she wants to move out, you know? She wants to live with me.'

'Then let's try that,' I said, immediately.

That will sound terrible, I suppose. As a mother, you're supposed to love your children unconditionally. You're supposed to care about them through thick and thin.

And I did care, that's the thing. It was just that, despite all my caring, I was failing. I was failing as a mother. I was failing my daughter, and that was really starting to hurt. Zoe had got so skinny by then – you could actually see her ribs – that I'd begun to envisage her dying at some point in the future if something didn't change. Yet I imagined that if I sectioned her, she'd end up hating me for ever more. I felt it was the sort of thing that we'd simply never get over.

I'd spent a year by then trying to get her to psychologists, and almost two reading articles about anorexia. Zoe's illness had come to dominate almost every waking moment of my day. I'd even

begun to have nightmares about her, so I suppose she was imping-
ing on my sleeping hours as well. It was exhausting. I felt exhausted.

The only rare moments of harmony in the house were when
Zoe was elsewhere. Scott, Jude and I would spend a family evening
in front of the television and I would just about get to relax. And
then I'd suddenly remember that Zoe would be home soon, and
I'd tense up all over again.

So yes, if Zoe wanted to live with Ian, let her live with him,
I thought. Maybe she'd be happier there. Maybe she'd escape the
feeding tube. Maybe she'd avoid having to be sectioned.

Ian, rather creepily, took my hand then, and grimaced. 'I'm
sorry,' he said, 'but I can't have her.'

'Why the hell not?' I asked, pulling my hand away. 'She's your
daughter, too. I think it's your turn to see if you can help. Don't
you?'

'I'm moving,' he said. 'I'm sorry, but I'm moving in with Linda.'

'Linda?' I repeated, frowning. 'I thought there was a new one,
from Manchester or something.'

'No, we split up,' he said. 'I'm back with Linda now, and, well,
it's serious.'

'And this absolves you from responsibility for your daughter
how, precisely?' I asked.

'It's not that, love,' Ian said. 'It's just that Linda's already got
three kids. And they already share two bedrooms. We simply don't
have room for Zoe right now.'

'Then buy somewhere bigger,' I told him. 'You've just inherited
a shedload of money, haven't you? Move!'

'I suppose I could,' Ian said, thoughtfully, doubtfully. 'It's just
not what Linda and I have decided to do.'

'Have you told her?' I asked then. 'Have you actually told poor
Zoe that you don't want her?'

'It's not that I don't want her,' Ian said. 'It's that I can't. And no, I haven't told her yet. I thought you might want to.'

'Oh, no!' I said, angrily. 'No, no, no! You can own that one, Ian. And if she ends up in some psych ward, well, you can own that one as well.'

At this, Ian shook his head sadly and stood. 'You're quite revolting when you want to be,' he said, nastily. 'I'm not surprised she wants to move out.' And then he turned and walked out of the coffee shop.

◆ ◆ ◆

Ian did tell Zoe she couldn't live with him. I know this because about a week later she came home and, waiting until Scott was there for maximum destructive capability, she asked why I'd had a 'secret lunch with Dad'.

'It wasn't secret, and it wasn't lunch,' I said. 'I had to meet him to discuss what to do about you. Because we're worried. We're all worried. And the options are getting—'

'It wasn't secret? Well, you certainly didn't tell me. Did you tell the gardener?' she asked, nodding towards Scott. That was her latest thing, referring to him as the gardener.

'I forbid you to call Scott the gardener!' I told her.

'Forbid away!' Zoe said. 'It's the only thing you're any good at.' And then, before I could even get out of my chair, she was gone, slamming the front door behind her.

It took mere minutes for that to become a fresh argument between Scott and me. 'It wasn't lunch,' I told him. 'It was a cup of coffee in Costa. And I only met him there because it annoys you when he comes here. And if you must know, all we did was argue about Zoe.'

But Scott wasn't having any of it. It was his nature to be unreasonably jealous, but beyond that, I suspect he was getting sick of the stress levels in our household. He was starting, I think, to look for get-out clauses. And who could blame him for that?

He stayed away for two weeks that time, and I feared I had lost him definitively.

That two-week break made me notice just how in love with him I was. It made me realise how dependent I was on him for my own well-being, too. Because other than his weakness for being wound up by Zoe about Ian, Scott was perfect. He was generous and multitalented around the house. He was funny and sexy and cute and was amazing in bed.

Without him, the house felt no less stressful, because even then, Zoe didn't calm down. But it did feel incredibly lonely. It felt far sadder, too.

So, when Scott returned – oh miracle! – I told him I'd decided to stop seeing Ian completely. He'd proven himself to be utterly useless anyway, I said, and that was basically true.

Avoiding Ian turned out to be easier than I'd expected. He pretty much vanished from our lives about then. Though I'm sure he'd deny it, the truth was that he'd simply lost interest in us.

Zoe was at her worst, and frankly, nobody needs that kind of stress in their lives.

Jude, for his part, was so into Scott that I feared he might have a crush on him. They wrestled and climbed and ran around fields together. They were all-but-uninterruptible at the dinner table, too. So I honestly thought back then that Jude might turn out to be gay. Though that of itself wouldn't have posed the slightest problem for me, his having a crush on my boyfriend could have been extremely challenging to deal with. So it came as something of a relief when that turned out not to be the case.

As far as Ian was concerned, neither Zoe nor Jude were really massaging his ego back then. As that was always the one thing Ian needed from the people around him, he chose the easy path. He chose Linda's life instead.

She was a yoga teacher, rumour had it. And according to Jude, the whole family did yoga together on Sunday mornings in the garden. It was an easy enough choice to make, I suppose. If it had been possible, I probably would have moved in and done a spot of yoga myself.

The yoga-teacher thing got to me a little, I'll admit. I couldn't help but imagine her sylph-like figure. I couldn't help but think about the athletic positions she'd be getting into for Ian of an evening, too. I could picture with shocking ease how they'd be working their way through the entire *Kama Sutra*.

But then I'd roll over and look at the bearded beauty sleeping beside me, and convince myself that it didn't matter. Whatever she looked like, she'd ended up with Ian while I'd ended up with my toy boy. I knew who'd drawn the short straw there, and it certainly wasn't me!

A few months later I caught sight of them in town. I was coming out of Morrisons while they were heading in, Linda's little girls trailing sweetly behind them like a row of ducklings. I felt a spike of vicious, selfish joy at the sight of her. Because Linda, sweet Linda, was big. She was a seriously overweight yoga teacher! Who even knew such a thing existed?

Zoe discovered Quorn sausages around then and decided that she liked sausage sandwiches. She wasn't eating anything else, so it obviously wasn't ideal, but just the fact that she wanted to eat anything was such a relief I decided to go along with it.

Every evening, I'd cook a healthy meal for the three of us, and Zoe would make her sandwich: two slices of bread, two Quorn sausages, margarine (not butter!) and tomato ketchup. This she'd take up to her room, where she'd eat alone.

I tried, once or twice, to force the issue of us at least eating in the same room, but when I did she silently protested by eating nothing. Better that she eat alone in her room, we all agreed, than that she ruin everyone's mealtime by not eating anything at all.

So we settled into a kind of routine, for a while. Zoe wasn't actually with us, but at least I knew she was safe upstairs, doing whatever teenagers do on her iPad. It felt almost like normal family life.

It was on one of these evenings, the three of us eating pizza in front of *Doctor Who* while Zoe ate her hundredth Quorn sandwich in her room, that Jude suggested a trip to the seaside. It was the August bank holiday weekend, after all. It would be fun, he said.

'What about Zoe?' Scott asked.

'Oh, Zoe will be up for the beach,' Jude said.

I laughed. 'You can't really believe that,' I told him.

So Jude ran to the bottom of the stairs and shouted up to his sister, 'Zoe? Zo! Zoeeee! How do you fancy a trip to the beach?'

There was a pause during which I think we were all holding our breath. And then Zoe's bedroom door creaked open. This alone was unexpected.

'You what?' Zoe called down.

'Do you want to go to the beach?' Jude asked again. 'I'm trying to convince 'em to take us.'

'Trying to convince who to take us?' Zoe asked.

'Well, Mum and Scott, of course.'

'Humph,' Zoe said. Then, 'Which beach? Where?'

'I dunno,' Jude said, then, turning to face us, he asked, 'Where would we go?'

'Blackpool, maybe?' I suggested. From Buxton it was the obvious choice. But Scott was already pulling a face.

'There's, like, an amusement park in Blackpool, right?' Zoe said, deigning to descend three steps and actually peer over the banisters at us.

'You see!' Jude said, triumphantly. 'Zoe wants to go, too.'

'I haven't said yes yet,' Zoe informed him. But it was clear from the simple fact of her engagement in the conversation that he'd struck lucky.

Scott had – a detail I'd forgotten – briefly lived in Blackpool as a child. As he didn't seem to have particularly fond memories of the place, we booked a bed and breakfast in Morecambe Bay instead – promising to take the kids to Blackpool Pleasure Beach on the way up.

◆ ◆ ◆

We left about ten the next morning, all piling into Scott's old Toyota. Zoe ate breakfast for once – two sausages and a piece of toast, and packed her own bag without complaint.

At one point, as we were loading the bags into the car, Scott nudged me and nodded back towards the house. 'What's going on with that one?' he asked.

'I don't know,' I whispered. 'But I'm not complaining . . . We can go to the seaside every weekend if she's like this. Hell, we can move to the bloody seaside.'

The traffic was heavy, but not unbearable. Only the final section from the motorway to the seafront was horrific, taking forty minutes rather than the ten predicted by Scott's GPS. But it was a beautiful day with a wispy blue sky, so we rolled down the windows and stared at the other participants in the traffic jam, who'd clearly all had the same idea as us.

We finally found a parking space in a tatty little side road behind the Pleasure Beach. I'd wanted to get lunch first, but as the kids were gagging for the funfair, I simply made them promise to eat something once inside.

We queued for half an hour to pay and then we queued for another fifteen minutes to get in.

Once inside, Scott bought everyone bags of chips. Well, everyone except for Zoe, that is. But even Zoe accepted the idea of a veggie burger. She dumped the actual burger in a bin pretty quickly, but ate all of the bun. Such things were considered major victories at the time.

The queues for the rides were horrendous, so we quickly began to split up so we could avoid queueing for rides that didn't interest us personally.

Jude wanted to go on every single roller coaster, while Zoe seemed drawn by anything that would spin her around or drop her from a height.

Personally, anything circular makes me sick, but I'm also scared witless of roller coasters, so I tend more towards sticking whoever is in my charge on a ride and then waiting by the exit.

While Scott took Jude on the Big Dipper, I waited for Zoe to be dropped from a platform two hundred feet high. Then while Scott took Jude on the Big One, I photographed Zoe spinning crazily across the summer sky on a ride called Bling. Where most of her fellow riders stepped off Bling looking quite green, Zoe, most unusually, was grinning from ear to ear. I had rarely seen her so happy.

Once Jude had sampled the Big One he didn't want to go on anything else. But Scott, who'd jarred his neck on one of the bends, wasn't so keen to repeat the experience.

Jude begged and begged both Zoe and me to take him back on the ride, and in the end I gave in. By the time we reached the final zigzag of the queue, however, I'd broken out in a sweat. The carriages thundering overhead and the screams of the passengers had pushed me to the edge of a panic attack. And so, wimpy mother that I am, I got a woman who was queueing alone behind us to take my place.

'You will look after him?' I made her promise.

'Of course!' she said. 'It's going to be great, isn't it?'

Jude rolled his eyes at this. 'You're such a wuss, Mum,' he told me as I threaded my way back out of the queue.

As Scott and Zoe were on the Wild Mouse, an ancient wooden roller coaster that scared me because of how rickety it seemed more than anything else, I wandered through the crowds, letting my nerves settle back down and thinking about what an amazing success the day was turning out to be. After all, Zoe, recalcitrant, moody Zoe, was currently crushed into a Wild Mouse with Scott, my beloved. Perhaps, I dreamed, they'd even start getting on together.

I was standing at one end of the ride, peering up at the mice rolling overhead and trying to spot Zoe and Scott, when someone tapped me on the shoulder. I turned to see Ian grinning at me.

'Hello, stranger!' he said. 'This is a coincidence!'

'It is!' I laughed. I glanced up at the ride to check that neither Zoe nor Scott were watching, and then stepped a little further into the shade of the hot-dog stall before leaning forward to accept Ian's peck on the cheek.

I'd hardly seen anything of him for months, and, strange as it may seem, I'd been missing him. I suppose we'd lived together for thirteen years, after all. Plus, he'll always be the father of my children, no matter what happens.

'You're here with the kids, I take it?' he asked.

I nodded. 'Scott's here, too. We thought what with the bank holiday and everything . . .'

'Great minds think alike,' Ian said. 'How's Zoe doing?'

'Actually, today she's fine,' I said. 'It's most unusual, but today is a good day.'

'And they're where?' Ian asked, scanning our surroundings.

'Oh, Zoe's up there somewhere,' I said, pointing. 'And Jude's on the Big One for the second time. I think he's going to spend the whole day on it, to be honest. And your lot?'

Ian nodded vaguely into the distance. 'Queueing for the loo,' he said. 'My mission is to buy hot dogs.' I wrinkled my nose at this, prompting Ian to continue, 'I know, I know . . .' He was familiar with my distrust of the unidentifiable ingredients of hot dogs. 'But Linda's kids love 'em, so, what-ya-gonna-do?'

I shrugged. 'At least they eat, I suppose,' I said. 'Look, I'd better be getting back to Jude. He'll be finishing soon. Unless you wanted to see them?'

'Better not,' Ian said. 'It would only make everyone jealous of everyone else. I mean, if we bump into each other again, then, well, that's unavoidable. But I don't think I want to go out of my way to make it happen.'

'I agree, actually,' I said. I'd been imagining how Zoe and Jude would feel if they saw their father out with his new family.

'Well, that's a turn-up for the books,' Ian said. 'Us agreeing!'

'Like I said,' I told him, turning my face towards the sunshine. 'Today is a good day.'

'You look well,' Ian said, surprising me by taking hold of my hand and giving my fingers a gentle squeeze.

'Why, thank you,' I said. 'So do you.' And it was true. Ian was looking tanned and slim and well dressed. I could almost remember why I'd fallen for him all those years ago.

'I am sorry,' he said. 'About everything. I just wanted you to know that.'

'Yes,' I said. 'Yes, I knew that, deep down, I suppose.'

'And I'm sorry we fell out about Zoe,' he continued. 'We might actually be moving if we can just find a place that suits everyone. So maybe I could have her more often, after all. If you still want me to, that is.'

'If Zoe still wants it, more like.' I glanced at my wrist, even though I wasn't wearing a watch. 'I really do need to get back to the Big One,' I said.

'Sure,' Ian replied, releasing my hand and smiling sadly at me. He opened his arms, inviting an embrace and said, 'May I?'

I hesitated for a second, then, thinking, *Oh, why spoil the moment?*, I replied, 'Sure,' and let him crush me in his arms.

'You are great, you know,' Ian said, leaning back just far enough to look me in the eye. 'I don't think I ever told you that enough, but you are.'

'I don't think you ever told me that at all.' I started to lever myself from his hug. 'But thank you. Better late than never,' I added with a fake laugh designed to cover my embarrassment. I'd noticed his eyes were looking shiny and had decided our 'moment' had reached its sell-by date.

'Right then!' Ian said. And then he lurched at me and kissed me on the lips. I was so surprised I didn't respond at all. 'Right,' he said again. 'Better go!' And then he turned on one foot and strode away into the crowd.

'Well, that was intense,' I murmured to myself.

Fearing that Ian would remember his mission to buy hot dogs and return, I also strode away, but in the opposite direction.

By the time I reached the Big One, Jude had already rejoined the queue. 'Mum!' he called out, once he'd spotted me behind the barrier. 'I thought I'd lost you! I couldn't decide what to do, so I thought I'd just queue up again.'

'I'm sorry,' I called back, walking closer. 'I got held up.'

'Held up with what?' he asked, when I reached him.

'Um? Oh, the toilets,' I lied. 'There was a queue.'

'So is this OK?' Jude asked. 'Can I go again?'

'Of course,' I said. 'If you're sure you don't want to try something else?'

'I'm sure,' he said, grinning. 'It's awesome.'

'Then I'll meet you at the Wild Mouse after, OK? That's where Scott and Zoe are.'

'OK,' he said, happily. 'See you there.'

When I returned to the Wild Mouse, only Scott was waiting, looking anxious.

'Zoe's not with you?' he asked, immediately.

'No!' I said. 'I thought she was with you.'

'Well, she was,' Scott said. 'But when we got off the ride she stomped off. You know what she's like. I was hoping she'd come to find you.'

'I'll call her,' I said, pulling my phone from my handbag.

'I've tried,' Scott said. 'But her phone's switched off.'

Six

Jude

By ten past nine, we're out of our lodgings, keys dropped off, and we're heading towards the motorway. It's a sunny morning, but cold enough that I've had to scrape the frost off the windscreen before moving the car.

Jess fiddles with the radio as I drive, but as everyone's talking about Brexit, and because after weeks and weeks of no progress whatsoever that's not the most interesting thing to listen to, even for Jess, she eventually gives up and plugs her phone in. She chooses the new My Baby album, which I love, and I tap my fingers against the steering wheel as I drive and feel that all's right with the world.

'Maybe we can have the top down later,' Jess says. 'It's lovely and sunny today.'

I point at the dashboard, where the temperature reading is -4°.

'Have you ever noticed how -4° looks like a man having a poo?' Jess asks.

I shoot her a grin. 'Yeah, I saw that somewhere online,' I say. 'On Instagram, I think. Or Facebook.'

'Anyway, you've got a scarf, haven't you? I've got my bobble hat. It'll be fine.'

'We'll see,' I tell her. 'Maybe when we get to Blackpool.'

'Well, we have to open it at some point,' Jess says. 'I've always wanted to drive an open-top car.'

I wonder what kind of driver she is. She has never yet driven me anywhere.

We chat about Bristol for a while, laughing again at my nine-quid grilled sardine and Jessica's micro-gnocchi before settling into a comfortable silence.

I alternate between listening to the music, basically singing along (in my head – I have a terrible singling voice), and daydreaming, running the events of the last twenty-four hours across the cinema screen in my mind.

I think about the fact that, somewhat ironically, we've solved my most recent panic attack not by separating, but by moving as close as two human bodies can possibly get. I wonder if it's perhaps like homeopathy or something, where whatever makes you ill supposedly also makes you better. I wonder if it will work every time and how much sex that might involve and start to feel horny, and so try to think about other things instead.

Once the car has warmed up, Jess puts her feet up on the dashboard. She's wearing green plimsolls today, along with a black-and-white striped jersey dress featuring a red velvet bleeding heart that she has sewn on herself, and red-and-white polka-dot leggings. I wonder if Blackpool's ready for her. Personally, knowing what the town is like, I'm glad I chose to dress down again.

Jess catches me looking over at her and smiles briefly before turning her attention back to the side window, but not without resting one hand on my leg. It feels nice in this car, I think. What with the music and the heater and, yes, with Jess, it feels cosy and warm and somehow safe.

'What are you thinking about?' Jess asks, out of the blue. We've been driving for about forty minutes and the My Baby album has just ended.

I laugh. 'I was thinking about Worcestershire sauce,' I tell her honestly.

'Really?'

'Yeah, I was thinking about how you never see it any more. Lea & Perrins Worcestershire sauce.'

'Any particular reason?' Jess asks. 'I actually hate Worcestershire sauce.'

I point to a sign we're passing. It reads, 'Worcester 11. Birmingham 60. Manchester 120.'

'Ahh, right!' Jess says. 'Do you think they really make it there?'

'You know, I have no idea,' I say.

We drive for ten more minutes and then I ask Jess the same question.

'Um, if you really want to know, I was thinking about Zoe,' she replies.

'Any reason in particular?'

'I'm not sure if . . .' Jess starts, before pausing and starting again. 'Actually, I was wondering what went wrong with her. I mean, you're one of the most together people I know, so . . .'

'Me?' I say, pulling a face. I don't feel particularly together.

'Yeah, you. You're so together you're like, I don't know what.'

'Nice simile.'

'I know. I'm good at similes. But, I mean, you grew up together, so what was different for Zoe? Of course, if you don't want to talk about it, that's fine. I'm just thinking about the whole nature/nurture thing.'

'Right,' I say, thoughtfully. 'No, I don't think I mind.'

'So was it the fact that your parents divorced?' she asks. 'Did she just take that differently to you? Or was there something else?'

'Pretty much,' I say. 'I mean, the potential was already there, if you know what I mean. She was never easy, our Zoe. And she always had issues, like with her food and stuff.'

'Anorexia?'

I nod, check the mirror, and then indicate to change lanes. 'On and off, yeah. Mainly on, though, unfortunately.'

'That's a tough one,' Jess says. 'My best friend went down with it when we were fifteen. She ended up in hospital being force-fed and everything.'

'Zoe nearly did as well. But she tended to come back from the brink just in time to avoid it. It always seemed to me like she was more in control of it all than people thought.'

'And that all kicked off when your dad left?'

'No, like I say, it was already there, lurking. She was forever refusing to eat this or that. But I suppose it got worse once Dad left. Much worse.'

'And there was never a question of you living with him?' Jess asks. 'Was it just a given that you would both stay with your mum?'

'Pretty much,' I say.

'Me, too,' Jess says. 'But then Dad had buggered off to Jamaica, so it wasn't really an option.'

'Zoe actually wanted to live with Dad. But he said no.'

'Ouch,' Jess says. 'That must have hurt.'

'Yeah, I know. The real reason was that Linda – his new girl-friend, now his wife – had three young girls already. I think she was worried, quite rightly, that Zoe would screw them all up. And I mean, Zoe was really no fun to live with, so you can see her point of view. But because Dad was such a wuss, he never told Zoe why. He was still trying to be our best mate all the time. So I think he told her, or at the very least he let her believe, that it was Mum who'd vetoed the idea.'

'Eww,' Jess says. 'What a weasel! I mean, I'm sorry and I know he's your dad and everything, but that's just so unfair to your mum.'

'Well, Dad's a wimp,' I say, feeling slightly uncomfortable now that Jess has joined me in slagging him off. 'But he has qualities, too. He's not all bad.'

'And no one ever told Zoe the truth?' Jess asks.

'I tried,' I explain. 'I told her she'd got the wrong end of the stick, but she just looked at me in that big-sister way – like it was sad how stupid her little brother was. She told me I was naive or something, I think. Zoe always thought she knew better than everyone else. You could never really tell her anything.'

◆ ◆ ◆

As we drive on, passing Worcester, I try to work out why I haven't mentioned the Blackpool/Morecambe connection to Jess. Because though it's undoubtedly true that Dad leaving was the thing that lit Zoe's fuse, the main event had been Blackpool. That's when everything had actually exploded.

I'm not really sure why I don't want to tell her, which is worrying. It's never a nice feeling having to accept that you don't fully understand your own psyche, and today is no exception. I'm left feeling distinctly unsettled.

'Cat Empire?' Jessica asks. She's waving her phone at me.

'Oh, no, please . . . no,' I say. 'Can we have something else this time?'

Jessica sighs. 'I don't know why you don't like them,' she says.

'I do like some of them,' I tell her, even though 'like' might be overstating it. 'It's just those Latin beats they sometimes do. It's all a bit Manu Chao.'

'I like Manu Chao,' Jess says.

'Yeah, well, sorry . . . I don't. And I just fancy something a bit more . . . I dunno. Something funkier, maybe?'

'Jake Bugg?' Jess asks.

'I said funkier,' I laugh. 'I like Jake Bugg, but funky he is not.'

'God, being a DJ for you is like . . .' Jess says. 'Like . . . I don't know. Like a really bad simile, or something.'

'What about that French guy?' I suggest. 'The one who does the electro stuff.'

'David Guetta?' Jess asks, her nose wrinkled.

'David Guetta?' I repeat, astonished. 'Is he French? Is David Guetta French?'

'Yeah, I think so.'

'Wouldn't it be Davide Guetta if he was French?'

'I don't know. But I'm pretty sure he is.'

'And you have David Guetta on your phone?' I ask.

'Nope.'

'Well, thank God for that!' I laugh. 'No, I meant the young guy. With the cute accent.'

'I don't know who . . .'

'You played it at that party we went to.'

'Oh, I know who you mean!' Jess says theatrically. And after a few swipes on her phone, the music starts.

'That's it,' I say. 'I love this.'

'It's brilliant to dance to.'

'I remember,' I say. 'People went crazy. What's his name?'

'Kazy Lambist,' Jess says. 'Weird name, huh? But I suppose it must mean something in French.'

It is twenty past one by the time I park the car in Blackpool. The side street, just two back from the seafront, is in a terrible state. A number of the houses have been boarded up, and the paint is peeling off all of them. I glance up and down the street at the other cars parked there. There's a rusty Ford Cortina, one of those Simcas people always use for rally driving, and an ancient Rover P6 that looks almost new.

I nod at the street. 'It's like – what was that TV series where he found himself back in the seventies?'

'*Life on Mars?*' Jessica says. 'I was just thinking the same thing. It's freaky. Who knew that Peugeots could time-travel, eh?'

We walk to the seafront, passing a long-closed UFO Exhibition and a shuttered Chinese restaurant. Then we cross the road to the wide promenade and turn towards the tower.

'They have an Eiffel Tower and everything!' Jessica says.

'It was inspired by the Eiffel Tower, actually,' I say. 'Though I have no idea why I know that particular fact.'

Despite the sunshine, there's a chilling sea breeze, and as a result the seafront is all but deserted. We pass a beggar who, between swigs of Tennent's, asks us for change, and a couple our age who sound like they're speaking Russian.

'You see,' Jess says, once they're out of earshot. 'Blackpool is very cosmopolitan.'

'Yeah,' I say, through a grin. 'Yeah, of course it is.'

At the tower, we cross and head in towards the shops, looking for lunch. As we pass a packed fish-and-chip bar, I pause. 'Here?' I ask.

'Sure,' Jess says. 'It's busy, which has got to be a good sign. Plus, I'm bursting for the loo.'

I queue at the counter and when Jess returns we attempt to order one fish and chips and one veggie burger and chips. But the cashier informs us that they're out of veggie burgers.

'Oh, what the hell, I'll have cod,' Jessica announces.

This is a surprise to me, as I have never once seen her eat fish; so, once we're seated, I ask her about it.

'Oh, I'm quite flexitarian, really,' she says. 'I mean, I'd rather eat without anything having to die for me. And I'm never going to order some factory-farmed beefburger. But if I'm stuck, I'll eat fish. If I'm really stuck, like I was in Paris one time, I'll even eat chicken, as long as it's free range. Though I can't say that I'm particularly keen.'

'Gosh,' I say. 'I never knew you were so pragmatic.'

'There are so many parts of my amazingly complex personality that you know nothing about,' Jessica mugs. 'Maybe you'll have to hang around a bit longer to discover them all.'

'Maybe I will,' I say.

'Actually, don't ever tell anyone this,' she says, raising a forkful of cod to her lips, 'but I was secretly hoping they'd be out of veggie burgers. I love fish and chips.'

'Mm,' I say. 'Me too. And this is good.'

'It's really good,' Jess agrees.

Once we have eaten, and drunk our cups of tea, we return to the promenade.

'So is that the funfair, up there?' Jess asks, pointing into the distance.

'It is,' I tell her. 'You know it's going to be closed, right?'

'I don't care,' Jessica says. 'I just want to see it. Plus, it's a lovely day for a walk.'

And it is a lovely day. The bracing wind is whipping the white caps of the waves and creating a sea mist through which the low winter sun appears haloed.

'It's that smell, isn't it?' Jess says. 'That iodine smell. One day I'd love to live by the seaside.'

It takes us twenty minutes to walk to the Pleasure Beach, a walk during which I unexpectedly start to feel tense.

There are very few walkers out today – we must cross paths with only twenty or thirty people the whole time – but they are all, almost without exception, in trouble.

We see a bag lady with a supermarket caddie full of her stuff. We see three utterly inebriated men, staggering along clutching the railings, which at 2 p.m. on a January afternoon takes some doing. Two separate beggars ask us for money – I give the sober one with the cute dog a quid – and we see a young couple who appear to have mental health issues, muttering and swearing to themselves, or perhaps to each other; it's hard to tell.

'I can see why you didn't want to stay here,' Jess announces when we're three-quarters of the way to the funfair. 'Blackpool's a bit down on its uppers, isn't it?'

'It's always been rough, I think,' I tell her. 'Well, not in the fifties, of course. But ever since cheap flights to Spain were invented, it has. I think it's got worse recently, though.'

'It's like Bristol,' Jess says. 'I tell you, half of Britain is crumbling. But they just keep voting 'em back in.'

When we reach the Pleasure Beach, it is indeed closed, so we simply cross the road and peer through the railings.

'Are you OK?' Jess asks as we turn and walk back the other way. 'You've gone very quiet.'

'I'm fine,' I tell her – a lie. In truth I'm feeling a bit queasy. I'm not sure if it's Blackpool doing this to me or the fish and chips we ate.

'Is it good in there?' Jess asks. 'When it's open, I mean.'

'I went years and years and years ago,' I tell her. 'I was fourteen, I think. And all I really remember is the Big One. It's that roller coaster.' I pause to point back at the structure. 'I must have gone on it five or six times.'

'Obsessive compulsive disorder?' Jess says.

'Yeah, something like that,' I agree.

When I turn to face north, I see a rowdy group of adolescents heading our way. There are five girls, one of whom is pushing a pram, four guys and a child of about eight, and they are larking around together, very possibly drunk.

One of the girls – she's wearing bleacher jeans and has a Mod haircut – breaks free from the group and crosses the path to intercept us. 'You got any change?' she asks, cockily blocking our progress.

'Sorry,' I say. 'No.'

'What?' she asks, glancing back at her friends – her audience. 'What, nuffink at all?'

'Sorry,' I say, tugging on Jessica's hand, urging her to walk around this human obstacle.

'Where you from?' one of the lads asks, jogging across now to join his friend.

'Just don't engage,' I warn Jessica, but it's too late.

'We're from London,' she's replying. 'What about you? You live here?'

'London!' He laughs. 'She's from fucking London!'

I'm starting to sweat here. They may all be a few years younger than me, but there are ten of them. Actually, the five girls alone look pretty scary. I really don't want to get into a fight so I grab Jessica's hand even more tightly and increase my pace dramatically.

The kid now starts running around us while making monkey noises and scratching his armpits. 'Oi!' he says. 'D'you wanna banana? Do you? D'you wanna banana?'

This catapults me immediately back to some of the worst moments of my school days. It's then that a handful of gravel hits the back of my head, which reinforces the feeling even more. It stings, but doesn't, I don't think, actually injure me.

Jess hesitates and tries to turn around to confront them, but I tug on her hand the way you urge on a child. 'Just leave it,' I mutter. 'We're seriously outnumbered, Jess. And they're pissed.'

I spot a group of people waiting at a tram stop and tack diagonally towards them, and thankfully the pack of hyenas behind us begins to lose interest, following slowly, still shouting insults, then pausing, and then finally, in a foray of monkey noises, turning and continuing on their way.

'Now that's why I didn't want to stay in Blackpool,' I say.

'Yep,' Jessica says, icily. 'Yep, I got that, Jude, thank you.'

We return to the car immediately, without even having to discuss it. I type the address of our Airbnb into Waze, start the engine and pull away. It's not until we hit the M55 that my stress levels start to return to normal.

Jess remains silent. In fact, she hasn't said a word since the incident on the prom.

She has her legs crossed away from me and is looking out of her side window. Now that I think about it, she's sitting as far away from me as she can within the space provided by the small car. This cannot be a good sign.

I open my mouth to speak a few times, but then close it again, because I can't quite work out what to say first. In the end, choosing humour, I say, 'So, Blackpool was fun!'

'Yeah,' Jess says, flatly. 'Yeah, Blackpool was great.'

We continue in silence for a few more miles before I ask if something's wrong.

'Noooo,' she replies, mockingly. 'Why would anything be wrong?'

I drag my eyes from the busy motorway and turn briefly to check her expression, but get no clues. She's still resolutely facing the other way.

'Jess!' I say. 'Tell me.'

Only now does she turn her head towards me. She looks confused at first, but then her expression shifts to anger instead. 'Really?' she asks. 'You really don't know?'

'Uh-huh,' I say, shaking my head. 'I really don't know.'

'Huh!' Jess spits, turning away again.

'Jess,' I whine, reaching out to touch her leg. 'Don't do this. We never do this. Tell me. Or do I need to stop at the services or something?'

'Jesus,' Jess mutters. She glances at me, shakes her head in apparent dismay, and then looks back the other way as she says, 'Well, let's just say I didn't much enjoy being called a monkey.'

My initial reaction is to feign confusion. 'But that was me,' I tell her. 'I mean, he wasn't calling you a monkey. He was talking to me.'

Jess laughs sourly at this, and shifts her body to face me, finally engaging fully in the conversation, which I suspect is in danger of becoming an argument. 'Really?' she says again. 'You really think that was about you?'

'It's my arms,' I tell her. 'They're really long, like a gorilla's or something. Everyone used to call me Monkey Boy at school. I'm used to it.'

'Jude,' Jess says, and I know, because of her use of my name, that this is serious stuff. 'They were calling me a monkey. Because I'm black.'

'They weren't,' I protest, even though I suspect that she's right. 'Were they?'

When I glance at Jess, she's nodding pedantically. She reaches out and raps her knuckles on the side of my head. 'Anyone home?' she asks. 'Anyone at all?'

'But that would be horrifically—'

'Racist?' Jess says. 'Oh yeah!'

'Are you sure?' I ask. 'I do have really long arms.'

'I'm sure,' Jess says. 'Trust me. And when they said, "Fuck off back to where you came from", that was directed at me, too.'

'It crossed my mind,' I say. 'But I didn't want to admit it. And I didn't want you to think it either. So I told myself he meant London, because you'd said that's where we were from. I told myself they meant fuck off back to London.'

'Yeah, I get it, Jude. But no. They meant fuck off back to Ah-fric-ahhhh,' Jess says, in a fake mocking accent. 'Where da bananas grow.'

'That's horrendous.'

'Yep!' Jess says. 'Welcome to multiracial Britain. I wondered why you didn't react. I was actually quite angry about that. I still am, in a way.'

'There were ten of them, Jess,' I point out.

'I didn't expect you to fight them,' Jess says. 'I didn't think you were going to change into your Superman outfit in the phone box and fight them all off. I just thought you might . . . I don't know . . . react somehow. I thought you might try to console me . . . or apologise for your fellow countrymen or something.'

I nod thoughtfully as I think about this. 'I'm sorry,' I finally say. 'I just didn't want to admit that that's what was happening.'

'White privilege,' Jess says.

'I'm sorry?'

'It's called white privilege.'

'What is?'

'Being able to avoid thinking about that stuff. Not letting it cross your mind. It must be very relaxing for you. I'm jealous.'

'Right,' I say. 'Well, I'm sorry about my white privilege, too.'

'OK,' Jess says.

I drive on for another ten minutes before I dare speak again. 'I have a question, though,' I tell her. 'If I might?'

'You might,' Jess says, thankfully sounding more relaxed now.

'So, you said "my countrymen". You said I might have apologised for my countrymen.'

'Yeah?' Jess says. 'And?'

'Well, are they?' I ask. 'Are they my countrymen? I mean, are they more my countrymen than they're yours?'

'Um,' Jess says. 'OK, good point. You win that round.'

'I'm not trying to win anything, Jess,' I say. 'I'm just trying to understand. I mean, I'm sorry that happened to you. Really. You know me, so you know that's true, yeah? But is it something I should apologise for? Are they somehow my responsibility, because I'm white?'

'No,' Jess says. 'No, of course not. Sorry, I was being irrational. Because I was angry.'

'OK,' I say.

'Just, maybe next time you hear someone being called a monkey, or told to go home . . . maybe look around you carefully. Because I can assure you that it won't be aimed at you. Despite your very long arms.'

'No,' I say. 'No, I get that, now. Despite my very long arms. So does that kind of thing happen a lot? To you, I mean? In London?'

'A fair bit,' Jess says. 'Most of it's a bit more subtle than that, but yeah, there's some kind of event or remark, I'd say, almost daily.'

'More subtle, how?'

'Oh, like . . . I don't know.' Jess thinks for a moment before continuing. 'OK, so, before I started ironing my hair, when it was frizzy, yeah? Well, people were always touching it. As if it was funny, or intriguing, or exotic or something. As if white people had some God-given right to touch my hair, yeah?'

'And is that why you iron it?'

'No. I iron it because it looks like shit if I don't. Because I look like I'm wearing a Jackson Five wig. But it does have the advantage that strangers have stopped trying to touch my head all the time.'

'Yeah, I can see how that might be irritating.'

'Or people will ask where I'm from,' she says. 'Like he did, back there. If I'm at a party someone will always ask where I'm from, and then not be entirely satisfied with my answer.'

'Which is?'

'Well, Brixton, of course. I mean, I was born there. I grew up there. I went to school there. If you want to know where I'm from, then the only reasonable answer is Brixton. But people will say, "No, where are you really from?" I think I'm supposed to say Jamaica or Ah-fric-ahh or something. Something that might explain why my skin isn't milky white like whoever is asking the question. Because being English, being British, just doesn't make any sense to people if you look the way I do.'

'So when he asked us where we were from—'

'He didn't ask us, Jude. He asked me. And yes, it's annoying. And the hundredth time it happens, it's really fucking annoying.'

'Again, I'm sorry that happens to you.'

'Well, I thank you for your concern, kind sir.'

'I'm . . . well, I'm shocked.'

'You'll get over it,' Jess says. 'Though I probably won't. And did they really call you Monkey Boy at school?'

'Unfortunately so,' I tell her. 'But I do have long arms. I have to get shirts with extra-long sleeves. I have to get my jackets adjusted, too, because I'm too skinny for my sleeve length. So yes, everyone took the piss out of me at school.'

'Well, I love your long arms,' Jess says. 'And I love the way you swing them when you walk.'

'Really?' I ask, glancing across at Jess to see if she's taking the mickey.

She wrinkles her nose, cutely. 'Yeah,' she says. 'I think I love you, Monkey Boy.'

◆ ◆ ◆

It's almost 4 p.m. as I drive into Heysham, the tiny village just south of Morecambe where our holiday let is situated. The sun is already low, lighting up the horizon with a pretty swathe of orangey-yellow light.

We park up next to a brand-new Bentley and phone the number we were given when we booked this morning. A young guy appears from next door to let us in.

'Am I OK parked there?' I ask, indicating our car.

'Sure,' he says. 'As long as I can get the Bentley out, you can park anywhere.'

Once inside the apartment, it becomes clear that the cost of this rental – three times what we paid in Bristol – has far more to do with the owner's need to pay for his Bentley than anything to do with the accommodation itself.

Though the view through the small lounge window is admittedly stunning, everything else about the place is depressing. The armchairs, sofa and carpets are all decidedly old-fashioned, while the mattresses are simply old. It feels like we're visiting someone's grandma.

Once he's gone, Jess puts her hands on her hips and combines a grimace with a toothy smile. 'So, whaddaya think?' she asks. She crosses the room and gestures amusingly at a horrible 3D Alpine landscape above the fireplace.

'I know,' I say. 'Naff, huh?'

'It's OK,' she says. 'But I can't say I wasn't expecting more. For the price, I mean.'

'Nice setting, though,' I offer. It's my attempt at optimism. 'I suppose it's the view that we're paying for.'

'The view of the power station?' Jess asks, peering out of a side window.

'Yeah,' I say, joining her. But with the orange sun reflecting across the wet sands, even the power station looks pretty this evening.

'You're right,' Jess says. 'I'm just being . . . you know . . .' She shrugs. 'So can we walk to Morecambe from here?'

'Yep,' I say. 'It's a biggish walk, though.'

'Then let's go now,' Jess says. 'Before it gets too dark. I could do with the exercise.'

She pulls on her bobble hat and I tie my scarf tightly around my neck, and then we head out along the coastal path towards Morecambe.

The sun is skimming the horizon now, and the sand flats look beautiful in the evening light, so we stop repeatedly to take photos – first of the sunset, and then of the elegant grey railings set against the icy grey sands beyond. 'I like the minimalism of it all,' Jess says. 'I was expecting something more glitzy, but this is really pretty.'

It takes us an hour to reach Morecambe seafront proper, which is a little more glitzy, and by the time we get there night has fallen and with it the temperature. It's bitterly cold.

'Can we get a hot drink?' Jess asks, dragging me across the road towards a coffee shop. 'I'm freezing.'

'I'll bet you are,' I say. 'I'm frozen, and I'm in jeans. I can't imagine what it must be like in leggings.'

'Oh, it's not my legs,' Jess says. 'It's my ears.' She pulls her hat as low as it will go. 'I'm worried they're going to drop off.'

Once we're seated with our drinks, a hot chocolate for Jess and a tea for me, Jess says, 'So, I need to ask you something. Something important. Something serious.'

I finish unravelling my scarf and unbutton my coat to let the heat in. I glance around the coffee shop, but the only other clients are at the rear, out of earshot. 'Go on,' I say, not without apprehension.

'It's my ears,' Jess says.

'Your ears?'

'Yeah, will you still want to date me? If they fall off, I mean? Would you date a girl with no ears?'

I laugh in relief. 'Do you think they really might?' I ask, reaching across the table to cup her head in my hands. 'Wow, they are cold,' I say.

'So would you?' Jess says. 'I could wear a hat. I could even stitch some fake ears into the brim.'

'Lack of ears would change nothing,' I tell her. 'Ears, ultimately, are neither 'ere nor there.'

'Cold ears, warm heart,' Jess says. 'That's what they say, isn't it?'

'Something like that.'

She pulls her phone from her pocket. 'Can you give me that address?' she asks, her finger hovering above the screen. 'The one the chip-shop lady gave you.'

'I left it back there, in the car,' I say.

'Oh,' Jess says, putting her phone away again. 'Did you do that on purpose, or was that an accident?'

I shrug vaguely. 'Tomorrow,' I say, simply. 'I don't think I can face much more excitement today. Or disappointment, for that matter.'

'Fair enough,' Jess says. 'It's your mission, after all. So what do you want to do this evening?'

'I was thinking we could go back to the Midland Hotel,' I say.

'The posh place on the seafront? The one we walked past?'

I nod. 'For a drink, I was thinking. Or a meal. It's all been redeveloped by some big architect. I saw a thing about it on TV. It's supposed to be amazing.'

'It'll be like Root, though, won't it?' Jess says.

'Root?'

'Yeah, you know. A grilled sardine for twenty quid.'

'Yeah, I suppose it might.'

'I'd rather find a pub with something filling,' Jess says. 'I'm pretty hungry, despite eating a billion calories of fish and chips. I looked at a pub near where we're staying. In Hailsham.'

'Heysham,' I correct her. 'Hailsham's down south. Way down south, near Eastbourne.'

'Heysham, then,' Jess says.

'Cheap to run,' I comment approvingly, and when Jess unexpectedly frowns, I expound, 'You . . . you're cheap to run.'

'Oh,' Jess says. 'Hardly! Our two nights in the world's most expensive retirement home is my fault, remember.'

Our drinks finished, we head back into the icy evening. A breeze is rising, and it's even colder now. Overcoat-piercingly cold.

We walk the full length of the seafront, and then when the temperature gets too much for Jessica's poor ears again, we duck into an amusement arcade. It's quite surreal moving from the dark, silent evening outside to the mad, flashing noise of the interior.

We race each other on Sega motorbikes (I win) and then play a few rounds on a slot machine (we both lose) before heading back outside.

'Well, look on the bright side. At least we know we're not epileptic,' Jess comments, as the night once again envelops us.

'Yeah,' I say. 'That was pretty full-on, wasn't it?'

It's truly too cold and too dark to walk back along the ragged coastal path, so I attempt to book an Uber on my iPhone. On discovering that Morecambe is an entirely Uber-free zone, we wander around the deserted streets looking for a taxi for twenty minutes. When we don't manage to find one of those either, Jess checks Google for buses. 'There's one to Heysham every twenty minutes,' she informs me.

'A bus?' I repeat.

'Yeah, come on. It'll be worth it just to see your face. It'll be a whole new experience for you.'

I'm famous, apparently, for my aversion to buses.

We sit upstairs, which takes me back to my childhood. When Dad first left, I had to go to school by bus for a while. And I always chose to sit upstairs, and whenever possible in these same front seats.

We alight in Heysham, right next to the pub Jessica suggested, so feeling a bit like an old couple, we duck inside and, after a single drink each, we eat early, warmed by the crackling, spitting log fire.

'So what now?' Jessica asks, once we've let ourselves back into our granny flat. 'God, it's only eight,' she announces, pointing her phone at me as proof that this is so. 'It feels like midnight.'

'Um, we could see what's on TV,' I suggest. 'Or just, you know, go to bed?'

'I don't think I'm sleepy just yet,' Jess says, pulling off her pink woolly coat and slumping on to the horrific faux-leather DFS sofa. She reaches for the TV remote.

I clear my throat. 'I . . . didn't actually say anything about sleep,' I point out. 'I said bed.'

'Oh!' Jess says, sitting bolt upright and then putting the remote on the coffee table. 'Oh, OK then. Sure. Bed gets my vote. Definitely. Just don't touch my ears until they've thawed. I don't want you breaking them off.'

Seven

Mandy

For more than three hours, in the baking August sun, we hunted for Zoe.

To start with, I alternated between looking for her and greeting Jude after each ride on the roller coaster, but in the end, as my panic levels started to rise, I decided he was better off out of it. It made more sense to concentrate on finding my daughter, too. And so I told him to stay on the Big One – it was all he wanted to do anyway. I said that eventually we'd come and find him, but that he wasn't to move under any circumstances from that ride.

'Don't worry,' he told me. 'I don't want to.'

Scott and I searched together at first, exploring the funfair in ever-decreasing circles. But I was worried that we were somehow following Zoe around the park, even as she was hunting for us, so we split up and went in opposite directions.

At one point I thought I'd found her, and I sprinted across the tarmac, dodging through the crowds as fast as I've ever run, only to find that it was another teenager in an identical denim jacket.

Scott got a park employee to call out Zoe's name over the tannoy system, but if Zoe heard it, she certainly didn't reveal herself.

Just before five, as I was preparing what I was going to say to the police, who I'd finally decided we needed to call, she was there, as if she'd been teleported, standing right in front of me, nonchalantly nibbling at some candyfloss.

My mood switched from worry to steaming anger in milliseconds, and I shrieked her name so loudly that bystanders paused to stare.

I grabbed her arm and shook it violently, causing the candyfloss to fall to the ground. I told her we'd been looking for her for hours and asked where the hell she'd been, to which she replied with a shrug, no more. 'Where were you, Zoe?' I insisted.

'Around,' she said, pointing vaguely. 'Over there.'

'And your phone. Why aren't you answering your phone?' I asked, my voice trembling in fury.

'Battery's dead, innit,' she said. 'I told you I need a new one.' It was as much as I could do not to hit her.

I phoned Scott to give him the 'good' news, and dragged Zoe off to find Jude.

Once we were all together, I asked her to apologise, but she remained staunchly silent.

'You've ruined the whole day! Apologise!' I shouted, loud enough to draw attention to myself once again, and this time Zoe complied.

'Sorry, Mum,' she said, investing the phrase with as little energy as possible.

'And apologise to Scott,' I instructed her. 'He's spent the entire afternoon looking for you, too.'

Zoe pouted and shook her head silently.

'If you don't apologise immediately, I'll . . . I'll . . . drive us all straight home,' I told her.

But Zoe knew it was an empty threat. The bed & breakfast was booked and paid for. Jude was already protesting that he wanted to go to the beach the next day, that we'd promised and that it wasn't fair. And Scott, lovely Scott, was already saying that it didn't matter, and that he'd had a great day wandering around anyway.

'I hate you sometimes, Zoe,' I told her quietly, as we walked separately back to where the car was parked. 'I love you, too. I'll always love you because you're my daughter. But sometimes you make that really, really hard work.'

Once again, her reply was nothing more than a shrug.

◆ ◆ ◆

Our weekend in Morecambe was tense, to say the least.

Scott and Jude managed to have a reasonably good time, running around the beach flying a cheap kite they'd bought and hunting for crabs in rock pools.

But Zoe, my dear darling daughter, drove me to my wits' end. She sulked constantly, and nothing anyone did or said was sufficient to get her out of her dark mood.

She answered questions, when she answered at all, with a shrug. The rest of the time, she refused to even grace us with a shrug, feigning deafness to whatever was going on – ignorance of whatever choice needed to be made.

Our accommodation was an old-fashioned B&B, one of those places with a 'VACANCIES' card in the window and a list of rules pinned to a corkboard in the hallway.

Zoe and Jude shared a room on the fourth floor while Scott and I were on the third.

When we got to our room, we made love, albeit briefly, on the ancient squeaky bed, and this relaxed me just enough to carry on with my day. Because until that moment I'd been feeling as if I might just implode with the stress of it all.

Afterwards, I went upstairs to fetch the kids for dinner. I paused outside their door in surprise, because from the interior I could hear both their voices, and they were talking relatively happily about the funfair. For a moment I thought everything was going to be all right, but the second I opened the door and tried to join in, Zoe fell silent.

'Can you go downstairs and join Scott?' I instructed Jude. 'I need to have a chat with Zoe.'

'Good luck with that,' Jude said as he grabbed his Nintendo from the sideboard and skipped from the room.

Once the door closed, I sat on Jude's bed, opposite Zoe.

'So, what's going on with you?' I asked, softly.

A shrug.

'You seem upset. Is it because I was angry with you?'

Another shrug.

'I was worried. You really scared me back there. We looked for you for three hours, Zoe. Do you understand that? Do you get why I was angry?'

Zoe nodded. 'I said I'm sorry,' she reminded me.

'So what's happening?' I asked. 'Why are you so miserable?'

'I hate him,' she said, simply. 'You shouldn't have made me go with him on that ride.'

'Scott?' I said.

Zoe rolled her eyes at this, and it was true that it was obvious who she was talking about.

'You know, I didn't make you do anything.'

'No,' Zoe said. 'Right.'

'And you don't like Scott,' I said. 'I know that. You've made it quite obvious, but . . .'

'I don't not like him,' Zoe said. 'I hate him.'

'Right,' I said, doing my best to stifle a sigh. 'Then why don't you tell me why?'

Another shrug.

'Please, Zoe,' I said. 'Tell me why you hate Scott so much and then maybe we can move on.'

'I can't,' she said.

'You can't?'

Zoe shook her head.

'You mean, you won't?'

Zoe bowed her head and stared at her feet, which she started to kick together.

'Just give him a chance,' I said.

'A chance to do what?' Zoe spat.

'Just, give him a chance,' I said. 'Try to get on with him.'

Zoe laughed at this. She actually laughed. 'Yeah, right,' she said, sarcastically.

At that, my patience ran out all over again. 'I give up, Zoe,' I said, standing. 'You've worn me down, and I'm tired. So, I give up.'

'So, Scott goes?' Zoe asked, looking up at me with genuine optimism in her eyes. My heart fluttered a little then, because I remembered that she was a child – a child who could imagine that such an outcome was possible. And I actually considered it, for a moment. The thought lasted less than a second, but I imagined dumping Scott so that Zoe would be happy again. And if Scott had been anyone else, I seriously might have done so. But Scott was Scott. I was in love with him.

It was my turn to laugh then, but with sadness. 'No, Zoe,' I said, reaching out to ruffle her hair, but failing when she ducked away from my touch. 'No, Scott isn't going anywhere. But I give in trying to fix it. Get on with him or don't. I don't care any more.'

◆ ◆ ◆

She was awkward all weekend. She was silent and on hunger strike when we ate in a fish-and-chip restaurant on the seafront. She was solitary and miserable on the beach. She even ignored Scott's offer of money to play the slot machines. This was all pretty par for the course, and yet something was different. Something had changed, and it took me a surprisingly long time to work out exactly what that was.

It wasn't until we were almost home that I figured it out.

We were driving over the hilltop road everyone refers to as the Cat and Fiddle and Jude had been blathering on for what felt like hours about seawater aquariums and how cool it would be to have one, and how he could keep those crabs as pets if that were the case, and what he would feed them, and on and on and on.

Scott interrupted to ask if we wanted to stop off and get a takeaway on the way through town. It was my opinion that we'd spent quite enough money over the course of the weekend, and there was plenty of food at home I could cook.

But Jude wanted pizza, and Scott felt it would finish the weekend off nicely, so I caved in.

'What about you, Zoe?' Scott asked her. 'Will pizza work for you or do you want something else?'

Zoe didn't reply, and as it was rare for her to not have a negative opinion about a food option, I turned in my seat to look back at her. I was thinking that she might have fallen asleep.

But Zoe was awake, her features neutral. It was as if she hadn't heard Scott's question at all.

'Scott just asked if pizza works for you,' I said. 'Or would you rather we stopped somewhere else?'

'Oh, I don't mind, Mum,' Zoe said, sounding polite, sounding quite reasonable, in fact. 'I'll just make one of my sandwiches when we get home anyway, so get what you want.'

'Do we have enough sausages?' Scott asked her then. 'And what about bread? Do we need bread? I can always stop at the Sainsbury's Local if you want.'

Again, Zoe didn't reply. Again, she looked like she genuinely hadn't heard him. It was just that, within the confines of the car, not having heard was impossible.

'Zoe!' I said, trying to keep the exasperation from my voice. 'Do we need sausages or bread?'

'Oh, no,' she replied. 'There's two whole packs in the freezer. There's loads of bread left, too.'

It was then that I understood she was blanking Scott. I scanned through the last forty-eight hours in my mind and realised that she hadn't, as far as I could remember, spoken to him, or even acknowledged his presence in any way since Blackpool.

I didn't challenge her about it immediately. Instead, I waited to see if I was right, and once I'd confirmed that I was, I waited a little longer to see if it would pass.

I hadn't been joking earlier when I'd told her she'd exhausted me. The weekend had left me feeling reluctant to engage with her in any way. It's a terrible thing to say, but I felt bored with the subject of my daughter, the special kind of 'bored' that really means 'resentful as hell'. I did, however, ask Scott about it in bed that night.

He was dismissive. He said something like, 'Oh, you know what she's like.' He said she'd get over it, that it was just another phase.

'Get over what, though, Scott?' I asked. 'Did something happen when you were on that mouse ride? Did you argue?' It had been after the mouse ride that she'd run off, after all.

Scott just shook his head. 'Nope,' he said, visibly trawling through his memories. 'She was fine, actually. She was in quite a good mood. And then when we got off, she ran away.'

I wondered if it was maybe my fault. Perhaps saying that I didn't care if they got on had been a major strategic mistake.

But then Scott rolled on top of me, and for twenty glorious minutes, I didn't think about Zoe at all.

◆ ◆ ◆

The months that followed were excruciating.

If you'd asked me what Zoe could do to make my home life worse, I would have said that there was nothing. I would have told you that we'd already reached peak-Zoe-angst. But I would have been wrong, because Zoe's blanking of Scott would turn out to be exceptionally destructive of what remained of our home life.

She never stayed in a room where Scott was present, and when, just occasionally, circumstances forced them together – in the car, for instance – she quite literally never spoke to him, or reacted to anything he said, ever again.

If I sat her down to ask her what was wrong, and I did do that quite regularly, she'd say, 'I hate him,' or, 'I don't want to see him.' But that was all the information I could get.

Only once did I get anything more from her. In response to my quite specific question, 'Did something happen in Blackpool? Did something happen on that mouse ride?' she replied with something other than dumb silence. 'What do you think, Mother?' she asked me.

'I don't know, daughter,' I replied. 'That's why I'm asking you.'

'Well, of course it did,' she said. 'Of course something happened! Jesus!'

And then she ran through the house and vanished for the rest of the weekend.

I played the scenes of that day over and over in my mind. Here was Zoe agreeing, quite enthusiastically, to go on the ride with Scott. And here she was afterwards, sullen and silent and brooding.

I thought about it obsessively. And when we were all together I listened to the oppressive silence between them. Often the air in the house would feel so unbreathable that I'd have to go for a walk around the block just to find some oxygen to stop my head spinning.

I asked Scott endlessly what had happened that day. Because try as I might, I just couldn't convince myself that he had no idea whatsoever. In the end, the fact of my asking – my inability to believe his answer, as he saw it – became a problem for our relation-ship as well. Things became tense between us and I was at a loss to know why or how to fix it.

Scott didn't seem to care as much as I felt he should that Zoe no longer wanted to speak to him. Within a few weeks he had given up addressing her as well.

Questions of the 'will you ask your sister?' kind directed at Jude had stopped working by then, so Scott began to act like he couldn't tell if Zoe was in the room either. It was as if they were in parallel universes, gliding through the same space but never quite aware of the other's presence.

Only once did Scott lose his temper with her, grabbing her arm as she walked out of the room and saying, 'What is wrong with you?'

Zoe screamed, and I mean she really screamed, until Scott let go of her, before running upstairs and locking herself in her room. Scott stormed out, leaving Jude and I sitting in silence. I caught my son's eye, then, and he simply raised an eyebrow, in what struck me as a terrifyingly adult gesture.

Later in the evening, I asked him if he could try to find out what was wrong, but he told me he'd already tried. 'She doesn't like Scott,' he informed me, as if that explained what was happening. Perhaps to a fourteen-year-old it was reason enough. Maybe to Zoe it seemed that way, too.

But I felt there had to be more to it. Everything had a cause and everything had a solution. And so I started to drag her, some-times quite literally kicking and screaming, back to see the school psychologist.

Eight
Jude

I sleep badly that night, and I wake up extra early, too. Unable to get back to sleep, I slip from the bed, leaving Jess snoring gently, dress and head to the village for breakfast supplies.

When I get back forty minutes later, she's in the shower, and by the time she's finished messing with her hair I've given up waiting and eaten.

Later, I toast a couple of crumpets for her and make a fresh pot of tea. In keeping with the granny theme, there's a teapot with a knitted tea cosy, which, when I put it on like a hat, makes Jess giggle gorgeously. Still wearing my comedy hat, I sip my tea and watch her bite into the crumpet with gusto.

'Did you ever want to work in fashion?' I ask. She's wearing a tartan skirt and a grey jumper with mad zigzag stripes this morning.

'Do you want us to go into business together selling tea-cosy hats?' she asks. She looks down at her chest and adds, 'Or is that your way of telling me this is too much?'

'No! You look great,' I say. 'I was just wondering. I mean, you like clothes and you're really good at putting them together. Did you never want to be a designer or a model or anything?'

'Um, modelling was hardly an option,' Jess says, laughing.

'Why not?'

'Well, my boobs are too big and my hands are too ugly, to start with. Add to that my huge forehead and uncontrollable hair, and . . .'

'Wow! All that, huh?' I say. 'God, you girls are so hard on yourselves! I think you'd make a perfect model. And there's nothing wrong with your boobs, your hands or . . . what was the other one? See, I can't even remember.'

'My huge forehead.'

'Yeah, there's nothing wrong with that either.'

'Which shows just how much you know,' Jess says. 'You guys have no idea.'

'And designing stuff?' I ask. 'I mean, you're always changing everything, sewing bits on and pulling bits off.'

'I suppose I thought about it,' Jess says. 'When I was a kid, I did consider it. But the fashion world's just so vacuous, isn't it? I'd rather be actually helping people, I think.'

'That sounds fair,' I say.

'By the way,' Jess says, 'while we're on clothing, I hope I didn't upset you about your suits?' She nods at my clothes, jumper and jeans again, as if that is somehow proof of what she's saying.

'No,' I tell her. 'Not at all. I just thought because we're going Zoe-hunting, this is better. Don't want them thinking we're Jehovah's Witnesses again, do we?'

Jess chews and swallows before replying, 'I do think you look better in a suit. Just so you know. It's weird for a young guy – I mean, unusual, not weird. But it suits you. Especially that blue check one.'

'Well, thank you, ma'am,' I say.

'I kind of think we look cool together, too, don't we? I saw our reflection the other day in a shop, and your serious thing kind of offsets my mad thing, if you know what I mean.'

I laugh at this. 'If you say so,' I say. 'You're the expert.'

'Plus, it's sexy,' Jess says. 'Much sexier than the jeans and T-shirts the rest of the world is wearing.'

'You can stop now,' I tell her. 'But thank you.'

'Right,' Jess says. 'Well, at least I've said it. I was worried you were going to burn all your clothes and buy activewear.'

'No chance,' I say.

Jess pulls out her phone now, and starts to read the *Guardian*, her daily morning ritual, so I leave her to it and move to the lounge, where I can look out at the seascape.

I daydream about Zoe, then remember my childhood visit to Morecambe and kite-flying with Scott. I feel a sense of nostalgia, of loss, really; for even though, thanks to Zoe, the weekend had been pretty awful, it had been the last time I'd ever really had fun with Scott.

I think about the fact of Zoe coming back here and wonder why that might be, and then if maybe it somehow holds the key to understanding what went wrong.

Perhaps, I figure, she met someone that day at the funfair. Maybe she ran away later to join him.

I must be staring out to sea for some time, because the next thing I know it's ten o'clock and Jess is placing one hand on my shoulder. 'Are you OK?' she asks. 'You've been there for ages.'

'Sure,' I say. 'Just, you know, daydreaming.'

'About Zoe?' she asks.

'Yeah, mainly,' I admit.

'Do you think we'll find her?' Jess asks, and then when I shrug, she adds, 'In your guts, I mean. What's your gut feeling?'

I tell her honestly that I don't have a gut feeling, and that I'm wondering if that might mean she's dead. 'I used to think she had a death wish,' I tell her.

'A death wish?'

'Yeah, the not-eating thing. She scared me sometimes.'

'No,' Jess says, with surprising certainty. 'She's not dead.'

I sigh, unconvinced.

'Have you been here before?' Jess asks. 'I mean, you've been to Blackpool, haven't you? Have you been here as well?'

I smile and turn to face her. 'Now, why would you ask me that?' I say.

'Just a feeling,' she says. 'A woman's intuition, maybe?'

I decide to tell her the truth. I've been feeling uncomfortable about avoiding the subject anyway. Uncomfortable, too, about the fact that I'm not sure why I'm avoiding it. So I tell her the whole story: our trip to Blackpool, my obsession with the Big One, Zoe going on the mouse ride with Scott and then vanishing. And how she never spoke to him again.

'Is that why they split up?' Jess asks, when I've finished. 'Did your mum and Scott split up just because Zoe hated him so much?'

'Sort of,' I say. 'I think it was less direct than that. It was, you know, more the stress of the whole situation. But yeah, it kind of made everything go sour. It made me so angry, losing Dad and then Scott as well, just because Mum and Zoe were so useless all the time.'

'How were they useless?' Jess asks.

But when I try to think about that feeling it doesn't make any sense, so all I can do is shrug. 'I don't know,' I say. 'I just feel like they could have convinced Dad to stay if they'd wanted to. Or Scott, for that matter. But Zoe really hated Scott. Especially after Blackpool.'

'You don't think that—?' Jess starts, before interrupting herself. 'Actually, forget that,' she says.

I don't prompt her to continue, because I'm actually pretty relieved that she decided to stop where she did. I'm fairly certain I know what she was going to say, and I'm only realising, at this precise instant, that the potential for her to say it was the exact reason I've been avoiding telling her about that day.

'Given the circumstances, it must be weird for you being here again, isn't it?' Jess asks.

'A bit,' I say. 'It's where my sister went loopy, so . . .'

'And it's strange that she came back here, isn't it?' Jess says. 'Why do you think she chose here?'

I shrug.

'Maybe it's some kind of healing process,' Jess suggests. 'Maybe she's retracing her steps. Perhaps she's on her way back to you all.'

'Now that I very much doubt,' I say.

We type Zoe's address into Google Maps and then decide to walk back into town. It's another sunny day with blue skies and a breeze. It's considerably warmer than yesterday, too.

'We should have driven,' Jess comments, as we reach the wide promenade. 'We could have finally taken the top down.'

'We can always go for a drive later,' I offer, 'once we've got the Zoe thing out of the way.'

After the fifty-minute walk to Morecambe seafront, it takes another ten to find Poulton Road. The address we've been given is a two-up, two-down house in a side street. It's bang opposite a pub called Smugglers Den.

'The smugglers are missing an apostrophe,' Jess points out.

'Maybe someone smuggled it away,' I joke, turning to face the front door of number fifty-seven and taking a deep breath. 'Here goes,' I say, knocking on the door.

There's no answer, and even when Jess knocks more loudly and shouts through the letterbox there's no sign of movement from the interior. I'm pretty sure the place is empty.

Feeling dejected, we turn to face the pub again. A rough-looking guy with a ratty goatee and tattooed arms is standing in the doorway smoking, staring at us inquiringly.

'Who you after?' he asks, tipping his head slightly backwards as he asks the question. He has a strong local accent.

'Um, Zoe Fuller,' I say, as we cross the road to join him. 'She's my sister. She lives at number fifty-seven. Or at least, she used to.'

'Zoe?' he says. 'Well, now, there's a blast from the past!'

'You know her?' Jess asks.

''Course I do,' he says, dragging deeply on his cigarette and then blowing the smoke off to the left. 'I know all the birds 'round here,' he adds with a salacious wink, and I'm suddenly afraid he's going to tell me how he came to sleep with my sister. He is not a good-looking man, and I'm doing my best to avoid imagining such a scene. 'Moved away ages ago, though, Zoe did,' he adds.

'Right,' I say. 'Any idea where she went?'

'Joined some hippies up in Scotland,' he says.

'Scotland?!' I exclaim.

'Aye. Some commune or sommat,' he says, nodding and blowing smoke out of his nostrils like a dragon. 'Used to bang on about it all the time.' He stubs his cigarette out on the wall of the pub and then drops the butt into a bin. 'Come inside for a bit,' he says, gesturing towards the pub. 'I don't mind a blather but I really need to get back to my mopping.'

We sit on bar stools and watch as he mops the sticky floors of the empty pub. Dim sunlight is filtering through the windowpanes, and there's a strong smell of beer in the air. There's actually something spooky about being in an empty, dingy, unheated pub. Whether it's down to the spookiness or the temperature I'm not sure, but as I sit there I shiver repeatedly.

'So how do you know Zoe?' Jessica asks, and I really wish she hadn't. I wait for the man with the mop to start smirking again before breaking into some sordid story about my sister.

Instead he barely glances up from his mopping as he replies, 'Used to drink here, di'n't she? Used to help behind t'bar from time to time, as well. Nothing official, like, just for free drinks and that.'

'And she moved to Scotland, you say?' I ask. 'To a hippy commune?'

He pauses his mopping and stretches his back. ''S what she said,' he tells me. 'She was dead excited about it, I'll say that much.'

'And this commune,' I say. 'Do you know where it is? Do you know anything else about it?'

'Not really,' he says. 'She was excited, like I say. They grow their own veg and stuff, she said. I remember her talking about that. In some country home, I think it is. Big place, like a mansion or sommat. Like Downton Abbey, she said.'

'And you've absolutely no idea where?' Jess asks. She's simultaneously googling something on her phone.

'On the coast, maybe,' he says. 'Not that far either, I don't think. It wasn't up in the Hebrides or nothin'. I remember that 'cause there's another one right up north, she said. But it was too cold. She didn't fancy that.'

'East Scotland, or west?' Jess asks.

'Sorry,' he says. 'Why you after her, anyway?'

'Oh, their mum's ill,' Jessica says, and I realise that I've forgotten to request that she stop using that particular excuse. 'So Jude really needs to contact her quite urgently.'

'Oh, I'm sorry to hear that,' the man says, propping his mop against the wall and crossing the dark pub to join us at the bar. 'Let me think. 'Cause she was in here quite a bit.'

Jess continues to fiddle with her phone while I watch the man's face expectantly.

'From Buxton,' he says. 'That sound right?'

'That's right,' I tell him. 'We're from Buxton.'

'Nice over there,' he says. 'The Peaks and all that. Good motor-biking roads.'

'You're right,' I say. 'All the bikers love it.'

'So they grow their own veg, but I told you that already, yeah? They've got chickens and I think she said actual cows and stuff. I know this i'n't helpful, like, I'm just . . .' He taps on the side of his head with one finger.

'Any idea how many people there are?' Jess asks, glancing up from her phone. 'In the commune, I mean?'

'Sorry,' he replies. 'No idea.'

'I've got a list here,' Jess says, holding out her phone. 'Could you maybe look at it? See if anything rings a bell?'

The man sighs. 'Sure,' he says. 'But I doubt it. It was a good while ago.'

'How long?' I ask, realising that we haven't asked that yet.

''Bout a year,' he says. 'Maybe more. Maybe eighteen months. They all come down in one of them hippy vans to get her. It had flowers on the side and everything. Right mess, it was.'

Returning his attention to the list, he begins to read. 'Auchinleck, Balnakeil, Bath Street. Corbenic Camphill, Edinburgh. Jees, there's a lot of them, i'n't there?'

'Yeah,' Jess says sadly. 'There are three pages of them.'

'Faslane, Findhorn, Iona. Milltown, Monimail, Newbold . . . Ploughshare . . . Look, I'm sorry but . . .' he says, shaking his head, then, 'Oh! That's it! That's the one.'

I move to his side so that I can see which of the names in the list he is pointing to. 'Portpatrick?' I say.

'That's the one.'

'Really?' Jess says. 'And you're sure?'

'Portpatrick,' he says. 'Definitely. D'you know why I remember, love?'

Both Jess and I shake our heads.

''S me name, innit,' he says.

'Your name's Patrick?'

'That's right. Yes, Portpatrick. That's the one. I remember now.'

We thank Patrick for his help and, promising to return for a drink, we step back outside, blinking, into the sunshine.

'So! Scotland!' Jess says, a mad look in her eyes.

'Jess, we're not going to Scotland,' I laugh.

'Why not?' she asks, apparently without irony. 'It'll be fun. Plus, a hippy commune! Imagine! I may never want to come home again.'

'It's miles and miles away,' I say. 'And she's probably not even there.'

'A hippy commune on the coast?' Jess says. 'Well, I can imagine her there, can't you?'

I laugh again at this and remind Jess that she has never even met Zoe.

'I know that,' Jess says. 'But I'm . . .' She raises her hands and waves them mystically around my head. 'I'm picking up the vibe. From you, and from all these places we've visited.'

'Picking up the vibe, are you?' I ask, sounding cynical.

'Tell me honestly that you can't imagine Zoe in a hippy commune!' Jess says.

'OK, I can,' I admit. 'I can perfectly imagine Zoe knitting her own spaghetti with her sisters in front of a cauldron of vegan soup. But it's still bloody miles away. And I'm worried it'll turn out to be a wild-goose chase.'

'The exciting bit is the chase,' Jess says. 'It doesn't actually matter if you don't bring a goose home. In fact, being vegan, I'd rather the goose escaped to freedom.'

'Great metaphor, Jess. I'm not sure what it means, but I like it.'

'Look. We're on holiday, aren't we?' Jess says. 'Do you have somewhere else you need to be?'

'No,' I admit. 'But what if she's gone even further north? What if she's in that one in the Hebrides?'

'I've got another nine days' leave left,' Jess says. 'We've got the car for another four, and I'm betting we can prolong it if we need to.'

'I wouldn't be so sure of that,' I tell her. 'You know what they're like with these cheap deals.'

'Either way, we've got time. And I'm up for the Hebrides. But she won't be in the Hebrides. I'll bet she's smoking a home-grown joint in Portpatrick as we speak. And according to the map app, it's only about three hours away.'

'Really?' I say. 'That is closer than I thought.'

'So, it's settled,' Jess says. 'The only thing you need to decide is if you want to leave today or tomorrow.'

'Oh, tomorrow,' I tell her definitively. 'It'll give us time to find somewhere to stay in Portpatrick. Plus, we said we'd come back for a drink tonight. And we've already paid for two nights in our luxury retirement home already.'

'Yeah, I am sorry about that, you know,' Jess says, pulling a face. 'You're definitely choosing the next one.'

We're very boring again that evening. As neither of us feel drawn to explore Morecambe's winter nightlife, or even to return to the Smugglers Arms, we eat in the same pub as the previous night and find ourselves back in our granny flat by nine.

'Do you think it's this retirement home that's turning us into old people?' Jess asks.

'Maybe,' I say. 'But I don't think old people do what we're about to do.'

'And what might that be?' Jess asks, all innocence.

'I think you know full well,' I tell her. And then I chase her, squealing, to the bedroom.

Afterwards, we simply fail to really get up again, and by ten Jess is dozing off. 'It's better this way anyway,' she tells me sleepily. 'We can get an early start. It's Scotland tomorrow. My first ever visit to Scotland! Plus, I'm maybe joining a hippy commune.'

'Can I join too?' I ask. 'You wouldn't join without me, would you?'

'Maybe you can come,' Jess says. 'If it's not girls only. I'll discuss it with my comrades and let you know.'

Nine
Mandy

Dr Stevens, the school psychologist, had retired. He'd been replaced by a part-timer called Dr Rufkin. He was a short fat man with bottle-bottom glasses, and I disliked him instantly. He sounded, I thought, a bit like Jeremy Corbyn, who I'd always considered a bit sneery. It always felt like Dr Rufkin was trying to make everyone feel stupid, including me.

Getting Zoe to appointments in the first place was an exhausting, ever-changing battleground of threats and bribes and occasionally even locked doors.

No one strategy ever worked repeatedly, because Zoe was too clever to fall for anything twice. Ultimately, what seemed to work best was making sure Zoe didn't know when the appointments were (so she couldn't vanish entirely) and then throwing a hefty bribe into the mix at the moment the subterfuge was revealed. She was a fifteen-year-old girl, after all. She wanted make-up and clothes and gadgets almost as desperately as she didn't want to be shrinked.

After only a few sessions I came to believe that all the effort to get her there was pointless. Dr Rufkin rarely told me anything about what had taken place in Zoe's session, and I suspected that was because nothing had taken place at all. I could perfectly imagine, as I sat in the waiting room next door, that Dr Rufkin was playing Candy Crush on his phone while Zoe stared at the ceiling in silence. Or vice versa.

One afternoon, after I'd handed the promised twenty-pound bribe over and released Zoe back into the wild, I met up with Celia, a friend from my previous workplace. It was one of those relationships that didn't seem to make much sense now we no longer worked together, but one we intermittently maintained all the same.

Celia, who was aware of Zoe's eating disorder, asked me how things were going with her; and perhaps because I was feeling so frustrated with Dr Rufkin, I told her the full story for the first time ever.

'So she hasn't spoken to Scott since that day?' she asked, her eyes wide. 'Not once?'

I sipped my cappuccino, which because of the length of my story was going cold, and shook my head.

'Not even a yes or a no if he asks her if she wants a drink or something?'

'Nothing. Not one word. It's like she can't hear him.'

'But how do you cope with that? It must be unbearable!'

'It is,' I told her.

'And this shrink at the school, is he making any progress?'

I shook my head again. 'Not really,' I said.

'Has Zoe told him why she's not speaking to Scott, though?'

'I don't know,' I admitted. 'It's like I said; he tells me nothing. He says that their sessions are private. But it might just be that Zoe doesn't say a word.'

'That's just so weird, though,' Celia said. 'How awful for you.'

'I know,' I agreed. 'It's a nightmare.'

'It's a bit like Jeremy's sister, Patricia,' she said thoughtfully, Jeremy being Celia's rather sexy triathlon-champion husband.

134

'Patricia had a huge falling-out with one of their uncles, way back when they were kids. Patricia would never stay in the room when he came to visit – actually, she would never stay in the house. It caused all kinds of arguments, I think. Jeremy only found out once the uncle had died that it was because he was a bit of a Jimmy Savile character. Nothing major. I mean, I don't think he ever actually . . . you know. But he was . . . over-tactile, I suppose you'd say. He was very over-tactile, by all accounts.'

I licked my lips and struggled to swallow.

'I'm not saying that . . . !' Celia said, now noticing my reaction. 'God, me and my mouth! I wasn't suggesting anything, Mandy. Really, I wasn't.'

'No,' I said. I could sense that the blood had drained from my face. My heart was racing and my stomach was churning.

'Anyway, you trust him, yeah? This Scott you're seeing. He'd never do anything like that, would he?'

I stood up so fast that I almost knocked the table over, and muttering, 'Sorry, I, um, have to go,' I pulled my coat on as I stumbled to the door of the coffee shop. I wondered if I was going to throw up.

When I got to the park, I sat on a bench by the pond and cried. I was realising, slowly, painfully, that I had been going to quite extraordinary lengths to avoid that very thought, and I had managed to blank it out quite effectively. But now it was here, bouncing around like an alert on the computer desktop, demanding to be dealt with. I feared that I would never be able to think about anything else again.

Sadly, over the coming weeks, I realised that I was right about that. Whether I was looking at Scott's dreamy features, thinking, *No! Of course he didn't! Of course he wouldn't!* or watching Zoe arching her body away from him as they passed in the narrow corridor, avoiding any possibility of contact, whether I was having sex with him, or (increasingly) making up excuses to avoid having sex, those awful images my mind had manufactured at the instant Celia had said what she'd said were always there, always present, tainting every moment.

I asked Scott a couple more times what had happened on the mouse ride. I asked if Zoe had come on to him, partly because that, too, had crossed my mind, and partly because I wanted to see how he'd react.

Scott just laughed out loud at that. 'She was fifteen. And she can't stand me,' he said. 'Of course she didn't come on to me!'

I tried asking Zoe the question differently, too, adopting the dulcet tones one might use to address an abuse survivor, hoping that this might perhaps produce a response. 'If there's a reason you hate Scott,' I'd tell her softly, 'then you can tell me, you know. If he's ever done anything specific to upset you, then you have to tell me. You can trust me. And if you do, I'll fix it. I promise that I'll do whatever's required to sort things out.'

During one of these conversations I thought I saw a rare flash of recognition in Zoe's eyes. But whether it was recognition of what I was implying, or recognition of something that had actually happened, I really couldn't tell.

I took her to see a specialist abuse therapist in Manchester, tricking her with the offer of a shopping trip and a visit to McDonald's – my vague attempt at humour – and then bribing her with five £20 notes when we got to the practice. Zoe was growing so tall that she needed new clothes. The £100 was really just the clothing budget I'd set aside for her anyway.

There was no clue to Dr McDonald's speciality on the door or in the waiting room – I'd checked that by phone before taking her there. But by the time she came out of the session fifty minutes later, she'd worked it out, I think. There was something different about her during the shopping trip that followed – something cold, something calculating, something watchful, perhaps. She seemed to be eyeing me up intently, gauging my reactions.

I phoned Dr McDonald on the Monday afternoon while Zoe was still at school, and she deigned to talk to me about the session. That, I suppose, is what you get for going private; that's what you get for handing over sixty hard-earned pounds.

'Your daughter's in a lot of pain,' she told me.

'Pain?' I repeated. I was surprised by her opening gambit.

'Yes, psychological pain. She's one very unhappy child.'

'I know that,' I told her. 'We've been trying to help her for years.'

'Do you trust your partner?' she asked then. I could hear pages ruffling, then she continued, 'Scott, isn't it?'

'Yes, Scott, that's right. And yes, I think I trust him.'

'You think you do,' she said. 'That's not really reassuring me. Because if you have any doubts at all, you need to err on the side of protecting your daughter. I'm sure you understand that. Do you know anything about Scott's past relationships? Do you know why they ended?'

'Nothing,' I admitted. And the moment I said it, that struck me as astonishing. 'Did she tell you something?' I asked. 'Has she accused him of something?'

'No,' the doctor said. 'No, not as such.'

'Not as such?' I repeated. 'What does that mean?'

'No, she didn't,' she told me. 'But there's a . . . a black hole, I suppose you could call it, surrounding that day in Blackpool. You told me about it, but Zoe says she doesn't remember it at all.'

'She doesn't remember it?'

'That's what she told me. And my interpretation of that is that either she remembers it, and perhaps not much happened other than her throwing a hissy fit, and so she doesn't want to admit to that; or something happened that was so traumatic, or perhaps so adult, that she can't process it. In which case she's repressed the memory, so it's out of reach. It can be a self-defence mechanism.'

'We're talking abuse, in that case?' I asked. I'd been prepping myself all morning to be able to discuss this objectively, but I was shaking and sweating all the same.

'If that's the case, if she's truly repressed the memory, then we might be talking about abuse, yes. Or at least something that, to her young mind, she interpreted as some kind of abuse.'

'I see,' I said. 'But if she's truly forgotten, surely she has no reason to avoid Scott.'

'Well, we all forget when we first burned our hand in a flame,' the doctor told me. 'But the reflex to jerk the hand away remains for ever.'

'Of course,' I said, visualising, despite my best efforts not to do so, Zoe's body jerking away from Scott's touch. 'I just can't imagine it,' I said. 'Scott's so sweet. I really can't.'

'Sadly, I've heard that many times,' Dr McDonald said. 'Our imaginations often fail us when it comes to imagining such horrors. Especially when it involves those we love.'

'So how do we find out for sure?'

'Therapy,' she said. 'Regular therapy. I'd like to try regression hypnosis, but she's way too refractory at the moment. So I need to build some trust first.'

I'll bet you do, I thought, thinking about the sixty pounds per session she'd be earning while she gained Zoe's trust. 'She's not easy to build trust with,' I said, instead. 'It's almost impossible to even get her to a consultation.'

'Well, you managed it this time,' she said. 'So perhaps you can do so again. But in the meantime, you need to make sure that she's safe.'

'Safe?' I repeated, nausea rising within me.

'Safe,' she repeated. 'No doubts. No excuses. Safe.'

◆　◆　◆

From that moment on, my relationship with Scott was doomed.

I'd suspected it for a while, I think, but I understood it as a fact that Monday afternoon. The whole Zoe issue had lit a fuse beneath us, and I knew now that it was only a matter of time before it exploded.

Within a week of Zoe's session with Dr McDonald I was conspiring, in unspoken agreement with Zoe, to make sure she and Scott never occupied the same space again. I found myself actively helping her avoid him.

I'd stopped having sex with him, too – started even to shrink from his touch. I'd see him heading towards me from the corner of my vision and engage myself in some complex fiddly task, to avoid, or at least limit, the kiss that I knew was coming.

It was ridiculous, I knew that. I had absolutely no proof of anything, nor even any reason to suspect. But I just couldn't stop my mind going to those dark places. And when I asked Scott if he'd be prepared to meet Dr McDonald with Zoe – something Dr McDonald had requested – and he refused point-blank, refused even to discuss it, I knew my last hope had failed.

We began to argue about anything; we began to argue about everything. And Zoe saw it all and rejoiced.

Jude, bless him, actually pulled me to the side on one occasion to ask me what was wrong with me. I'd had a huge, storming argument with Scott. It had been about immigration, of all things, which was ridiculous because we both knew we agreed. But I'd provoked him, knowingly, by taking an opposing point of view, and then pushing him on it until he exploded. And I'd done this for the simple reason that I'd wanted him to leave, because in his presence, the air in the house had become unbreathable.

'I don't know, Jude,' I told my son. 'I don't know what's wrong with me.'

'You're going to drive him away permanently,' he told me, sounding unnervingly adult. 'And then you'll be sad, and I'll have to hate you for ever.'

◆ ◆ ◆

The final straw finally came one Sunday evening. We'd spent a tense weekend together, basically with Scott trying to get close to me and me trying to avoid him doing so. He'd asked me repeatedly what was wrong, and I had obfuscated, insisting that 'nothing' was. I don't know who I thought I was fooling.

About six o'clock, Jude came down from his bedroom and, no doubt driven out of the house by the electricity that was crackling between Scott and me and by the atmospheric pressure generated by the inevitability of the coming storm, he informed us that he was going to his friend Gary's house, and vanished through the back door. Zoe, for her part, had been at her friend Sinead's all weekend.

'So, all alone in the house,' Scott said, raising one eyebrow suggestively, almost as soon as the back door closed.

'Yep,' I replied, business-like. 'D'you want to watch a film?'

'I can think of something else I'd rather do,' Scott said.

'There's a new one on Netflix I want to see,' I told him. 'A thriller. You like thrillers.'

'Mandy,' Scott said.

'I think it's Spanish, but it looked pretty good. You don't mind subtitles, do you?'

'Mandy!' Scott said. 'Stop it.'

'Stop what?'

'Jesus, will you just tell me what's wrong?' he pleaded.

'Nothing's wrong,' I said for the umpteenth time, walking through to the lounge and picking up the remote control. Scott followed me and hung on the doorframe.

'Mandy,' he said. 'You're avoiding me. You're avoiding sex. We haven't done it for weeks. You don't even want to kiss any more.'

I forced a fake laugh. 'Don't exaggerate,' I said.

'Is this because I don't want to see that damned shrink?' Scott asked. 'Is that it?'

'What? No! It's got nothing to do with it.'

'Ah!' Scott said. 'So you admit there's a problem.'

'I didn't say that,' I said. But the tension of the moment, the cumulative stress of the last few weeks, had reached a point where it was unbearable. And avoiding Scott while not telling him why was becoming untenable, I could see that. There was no way we were going to avoid the storm. There was no way we were getting out of this alive.

'But, seeing as we're on the subject, let's talk about that,' I said, some insurgent part of me deciding that now was as good a time as any, as at least the kids were out. 'Why won't you come with us to see Dr McDonald? I mean, if you care so much about this family . . . ?'

Scott shrugged. 'I don't have any issues. I don't need to see a shrink. Zoe has the issues. So Zoe should see him. Simples.'

'It's a her,' I said. 'Dr McDonald is a woman. How come you don't even know that?'

'So Zoe should see her,' Scott said, pedantically. 'And I don't even know that because I'm not that interested.'

'Dr McDonald is interested in you,' I said, with meaning. 'She really wants to talk to you.'

'I don't care. I don't want to talk to her,' Scott said. 'I don't like shrinks.'

'Which is hardly reassuring,' I pointed out.

Scott's features slipped into a deep frown then. He worked his mouth. I could see him slowly, finally, figuring something out. I could see all the emotions – confusion, concern, disgust – as they worked their way across his features, like ever darker clouds swelling.

'Why would I need to reassure you?' he said. 'What the fuck do I need to reassure you about, Mandy?'

'Scott, something happened in Blackpool, you know it did. Something happened on that ride. And Zoe won't, or can't, tell us what it was. And apparently neither will you. And we all, Dr McDonald included, think that's . . . probably relevant,' I said, doing my best to sound reasonable.

'Relevant?' Scott repeated. 'Mandy, nothing happened on the ride. I keep telling you, but you just don't effing believe me!' He was starting to sound angry. 'Nothing happened, Jesus!'

'Well, I'm worried something did, Scott. And so is Dr McDonald.'

'Something like what?' Scott said. 'Why don't you just tell me what you think happened? Go on. Tell me!'

'Because I don't know, Scott. How could I possibly know? I wasn't there.'

'OK, why do you think something happened?' Scott said, visibly struggling to calm down. 'Despite the fact that I keep on and on . . . telling you nothing did, you still do. So why?'

'Look, she hasn't spoken to you since, Scott,' I said. 'Not once. Not one single word. Do you realise how . . . incriminating that looks?' I winced at the word 'incriminating' that had just escaped my lips. I knew instantly that it was a mistake. And then I thought, perhaps not. Perhaps this needs to happen. 'She won't even be alone in a room with you. Not for one second, Scott. And we were all witness to what happened when you touched her the other day. She went completely off the rails. So what am I supposed to think, Scott? Why don't you tell me how I'm supposed to interpret that?'

Scott stared at me, a crazed expression forming on his face. He laughed and gasped at the same time. 'Incriminating?' he repeated, quietly. 'It looks incriminating?' He covered his mouth with one hand. 'God, you think . . .' he whispered, speaking through his fingers. 'Jesus Christ, Mandy! You do, don't you? You actually think that I . . . I mean, Christ, this is me, here, yeah? This is Scott.' His eyes were glistening and he was gently shaking his head.

'I don't think anything, Scott,' I said, my voice wobbling. 'I really don't. It's just . . .'

'Oh, you do,' he said, his lip curling. 'You just won't say it.'

'I really don't,' I said again.

'You . . . wow!' Scott spluttered, now breaking eye contact with me and staring at the corner of the ceiling instead. 'Wow!' He shook his head and exhaled heavily through pursed lips, before continuing, sounding increasingly mean, 'You know, Mandy? It's bad enough that you can even think something like that. But to not have the guts to own it. To not even have the guts to say it to my face. That's . . . bad. That's really fucking evil, Mandy.' And then, his voice wobbling, his face a tormented grimace, he added, 'This . . .' He gestured vaguely at the room, at the space between the two of us, and breathed, 'This is over.'

He pulled the lounge door quietly closed behind him and I sat in the armchair and stared at the blank TV screen, the unused remote still in my hand. Behind the door, I could hear Scott moving around the house collecting his things. A little later, through the corner of the lounge window, I saw him load them into his Toyota.

When he finally reversed down the drive and drove away, I crossed to look out at the empty driveway, at the spot where he'd been parked, and surprised myself. Because instead of feeling devastated, I felt cold, like an assassin – I'd engineered his departure, after all.

I also felt surprisingly relieved. The tension in the house had been quite literally unbearable these past few weeks and I had needed – my sanity and the sanity of my family had required – that by whatever means, it should cease.

The feeling of relief lasted until the next day, when the kids left for school. That's when it hit me that I'd lost Scott for ever. And I was heartbroken this time – truly heartbroken.

Unable to even think about going to work, I sat in that same armchair and let the feeling wash over me. I alternated between feeling disgusted with myself for having let myself suspect Scott of doing anything so horrendous and being disgusted with myself for having trusted him in the first place. Whatever the truth of the matter, there was no get-out-of-jail card for me. I was guilty, either of letting him in or of pushing him out. Tears followed, shocking quantities of tears, and unbeknown to the kids, I took two full days off work just so that I could lie in my bed staring at the ceiling – so that I could cry into a pillow while they were out at school.

It wasn't until Wednesday evening that the kids noticed Scott had taken all his belongings.

'He's not coming back, is he,' Jude asked, more a statement than a question.

I shook my head sadly in reply and ordered my eyes to remain dry.

'I hate you,' Jude said.

As time went by, it became clear that, though he was knocked sideways by it, he didn't actually hate me in the end. Most of the time he put on a convincing show of just how fine he was, despite it all. Just occasionally I'd catch a glimpse of how much the whole mess was affecting him. I'd come into a room and see him staring into the middle distance, an exercise book open in front of him. And when I tried to talk to him about it, he'd say, 'Don't. Just don't.' And then he'd pick up the book and silently go to his room.

Zoe was iridescent in her victory. She danced and sang and even started eating her sausages with us at the dinner table. She put on a bit of weight, too, which only went to reinforce my fears that it was all down to something Scott had done, or worse, had been doing. All the same, I hated her for being so happy about my misery even as I rejoiced in her doing better. It was an extremely complex set of emotions.

The texts started coming about two weeks after he'd left. The early ones were simple messages saying, 'I miss you' or 'You're so wrong about me.' But within a few days they'd evolved to the point where they alternated between – late at night – insults at my 'cesspit imagination' or – in the mornings – love-laden pleas that read like Hallmark cards. I never answered a single message – I just couldn't think what to say.

At the end of the month I changed my number to make them stop because, without overtly naming my fears, there was nothing to be said. And how could I ever tell Scott my fears? How could I ever put words to any of it? I could barely think about it in my own head.

Without him, my life seemed like an empty box. Actually, I felt I'd been destroyed by his departure. I felt as if I was subsisting from day to day, without hope, without pleasure, without life . . . I'd had it all, and I'd somehow lost it. I'd loved Scott far more than I'd ever loved Ian, I saw that now. I'd been ridiculously young when I'd married Ian, and it had been a mistake of youth, nothing more. But Scott? He'd been my soulmate. He'd been The One. But perhaps Rolf Harris's wife had felt that way, too? Maybe Fred West had been Rose's dream guy? Could desire be relied upon to judge these things?

Zoe saw Dr McDonald five more times, and surprisingly, she went to the appointments willingly. Even more surprisingly, it was the doctor who suggested we stop. That she'd willingly give up sixty pounds every two weeks gave me a jolt. I began to think that she was genuine, after all.

Zoe had been playing her from the start, the doctor explained. She was extremely intelligent and understood exactly what was going on. But as nothing Zoe said in therapy was ever true and as she'd proven impossible to hypnotise, there was simply no point in continuing.

'She seems happier since Scott left,' the doctor told me, in our final phone call. 'She looks healthier, too. So I think it's best we just leave it there for now.'

I understood that day that I was never going to find out. I would never get closure on what had happened in Blackpool. I would never know for sure if I'd been wrong about Scott. Well, I'd clearly been wrong about him, but I would never understand if I'd been wrong at the beginning for loving him, or wrong at the end for letting him go.

◆ ◆ ◆

About a month after Scott's departure, Ian reappeared on the scene.

It was about six weeks before Christmas, and at first I feared he wanted to gloat. But as time went by, I saw that he was genuinely concerned for me. I'd let myself go to pot a little, and I'd been assuring only minimal service around the house. It was hard to deny that I needed some support.

Ian seemed healthy and happy, and after all the drama surrounding Scott's final months with me, his calm, good-tempered, familiar presence felt reassuring.

So things between us became civil once again; even friendly, I suppose you could say.

He started to take the kids away to give me a break on weekends, which, though I'd do little but watch soppy films and get drunk, was welcome. People say you shouldn't drink alone, but I honestly think I needed it back then. I needed that time to wallow in my misery, and only alcohol seemed to open the floodgates.

Ian would rent a place, sometimes in Manchester or in the Lake District; one time on the Scarborough coast. There, he'd spend the weekend alone with Jude and Zoe, basically spoiling them rotten. He almost always kept them separate from Linda and her kids, and I never dared to ask why. I was happy that he was taking them and relieved that we were getting on. I didn't want to cause waves.

Sunday nights, when he brought them back, he'd stay for dinner before heading off to his other, duplicate family. On one of these evenings, once the kids had vanished, I told him what had happened with Scott. I'd downed half a bottle of wine before they arrived, so that's probably why my tongue was so loose.

Ian, tactfully, gave no opinion on the matter. He'd only met Scott a few times, and fleetingly at that, so he had no real data on which to base an opinion anyway. But when I'd finished and I'd dried my eyes, he crossed the room and pulled me from my seat to give me a hug. As he left, he promised to find out the truth. I was convinced that was never going to happen, but I was grateful for his concern, all the same. I was thankful that he understood how important it was that we knew.

Zoe was going from strength to strength back then. She was heading for her sixteenth birthday, so it was a huge relief that her school grades had picked up. Her eating problems had eased considerably, too. She'd added potatoes, pasta, green beans and tomatoes (pulped, never whole) to the Quorn and bread on her food list. And I'd invented a surprising number of recipes using just those few ingredients.

◆ ◆ ◆

One cold February evening, Ian brought them home after a weekend away. As I opened the front door to greet them, Zoe pushed past me and ran upstairs, slamming her bedroom door behind her.

147

'Hello,' I said, kissing Jude's head as he entered the house, then turning to Ian. 'You didn't force her to eat broccoli or something, did you?' I asked.

'No,' Ian said, missing, as usual, the fact that I was making a joke. 'Why would I do that? She hates broccoli! No, I told them some news, actually. And Zoe wasn't thrilled about it. And now I need to tell you.'

I invited him into the lounge, and over a glass of white wine he informed me that he and Linda were to be married. She was pregnant as well, which actually surprised me more than the marriage. I had assumed she was too old to have kids. I wondered if yoga had the power to stave off the menopause or if, on the contrary, it had just made her look older than she really was.

'Does Zoe not like Linda?' I asked, confused. I had always heard that they got on OK. 'She's not doing a rerun of the whole Scott thing, is she?'

'I don't think so,' Ian said. 'I mean, they've never been best mates, but nothing major. It's just the shock of it, I think.'

'Yes, I'm sure that's it. I'm sure she'll get over it,' I said.

'I was wondering if perhaps . . .' Ian started, before pausing and sipping his wine.

'Yes?'

'I was wondering, in the car, if maybe we could organise something before the wedding. With you and the kids and Linda and the girls. I thought maybe showing Zoe we can be one big happy family might make her see things in a different light.'

I nodded and shrugged simultaneously. 'Sure,' I said. 'Why not?'

'You'd be up for that?' Ian asked, concernedly. 'It wouldn't be too . . . I don't know. It wouldn't be too hard for you?'

I laughed at this. 'Ian,' I said. 'We've been separated for over four years. We've been divorced for almost two. Why would it be hard for me?'

He looked vaguely disappointed at this, and I realised that my laughter had been harsh. But I'd given up massaging Ian's ego many years before and I wasn't going to start again, now.

'Right,' he said. 'So, how about Zoe's birthday? Maybe we could organise a big party for her sixteenth? All together?'

So that's what we decided to do.

◆ ◆ ◆

Linda seemed OK. She was a little too crystals-and-auras for us ever to be best mates, but I liked her well enough. She seemed jolly and energetic and ready to throw herself into our first joint endeavour.

We held planning meetings in Costa, just the two of us. I'd have a cappuccino and Linda would choose green tea. I wondered how she'd come to stack on the kilos, because though I'd invariably crack for a lump of carrot cake, I never once saw her eat anything. The answer was eventually revealed, though, because Linda was an expert baker. In my experience, you simply can't enjoy baking and be thin.

We agreed to hold the surprise party at our house so that Zoe would walk in on it after school. Though I warned her that Zoe wouldn't touch them, Linda said she'd bake multiple birthday cakes, and her girls would blow up the balloons. I would provide a fake shepherd's pie for Zoe and, because Linda wouldn't give her kids Quorn, which she considered to be a Frankenfood, organic chicken for everyone else. Ian, for his part, had promised to buy Zoe a new mobile phone, a gift she'd apparently been badgering him for since the summer.

With Jude's help I invited three of Zoe's schoolfriends (Britney, Sinead and Vanessa – all sworn to secrecy), plus Jude's best mate, Gary Mason.

We would fill the room with balloons and launch streamers and shout 'Surprise!' And everyone would be happy. That was the plan, at any rate.

◆ ◆ ◆

On the morning of Zoe's birthday, I got up early.

Though I was pretty happy about the party we'd planned, I also wanted a moment of intimacy with my daughter. It had been such a hard year, after all.

I wrapped up a charm bracelet I'd bought her and wrote some heartfelt words in a musical birthday card I knew she'd sneer at. I made her a sausage sandwich for breakfast, and added a flower from the garden to the tray.

When I reached her door, I rested the tray on my knee and pushed the door open before tiptoeing across the rubbish-strewn floor to her bedside.

I glanced around at the mess and decided that today, just this once, I wouldn't moan about it. Instead, I'd tidy while she was at school. I'd make her bedroom look beautiful.

I gasped when I pulled back the covers. Because the only thing in Zoe's bed was her ancient jumbo teddy bear. I laid my cheek to the mattress to test for any residual heat, but it was cold. Wherever Zoe had gone, she'd slipped out some time ago.

I sat on the edge of her bed and ran one hand through my hair. And then I sighed, reached for her sandwich and took a bite.

Ten

Jude

'There's a lodge cabin that looks OK,' Jess says. 'Forty-five quid a night.'

I'm driving up the M6 towards Scotland and, when mobile reception permits, Jess is hunting on her phone for somewhere to stay.

'Sure, a log cabin could be fun, as long as it's heated OK,' I comment.

'A lodge cabin,' Jess corrects me.

'What the hell's a lodge cabin?' I ask.

'I'm not sure,' she says, then, 'Oh, so it's basically a mobile home. I think you're actually supposed to misread lodge for log. It's intentional trickery to get people interested.'

'Then maybe not,' I say.

'Nice view, though.'

'Have you switched on the instant-booking filter?' I ask, and when Jess pulls a face I explain what this is.

'But how do I do that?' she asks, pointing the phone at me.

'Sorry, Jess,' I say. 'I'm driving. It's in the options there somewhere.'

'It's OK, I'll find it,' she says, returning to fiddling with her phone.

A minute or so later, she says, 'Got it. Oh, that's made most of them vanish from the list, though.'

'Because they weren't definitely available for tonight,' I say.

'OK,' Jess says. 'Fair enough.'

By the time we pass Carlisle, she's found and booked what the owners call a gardener's cottage. 'It looks lovely,' Jess tells me. 'It looks amazing.'

At Gretna Green, we see the first traces of snow at the side of the road, and by Dumfries a few flakes are hitting the windscreen.

'D'you want the top down?' I ask.

'Funny boy,' Jess retorts. 'Don't tempt me. Next to driving an open-top car in the sunshine, driving an open-top car in the snow is my second-favourite thing.'

Just after Gatehouse of Fleet, we catch our first sightings of the sea. This puts Jess into shrieky mode. 'The sea! The sea!' she shouts. 'I can see the sea!'

'We only left the sea a couple of hours ago,' I point out.

Jess groans. 'Why do you have to be so . . .' she says, waving one hand vaguely instead of finishing her phrase.

'So what?' I ask.

'I don't know,' Jess says. 'So . . . dour. There you go. That's a good Scottish word.'

'I'm not dour,' I say. 'Am I? Am I dour, do you think?'

But Jess, who has turned to look out of her side window and is now humming a tune, doesn't answer. She's thinking about putting some music on, I can tell. She always hums a bit before that happens. I'm slowly learning to read her on this trip.

I can't help but grin when less than a minute later she plugs her phone into the car stereo and hits play. Cat Empire starts to drift from the speakers, though thankfully not too loud.

I think about the word 'dour', about what a strange word it is. And then, as I drive, I ask myself if it describes me.

On reflection, I don't think that 'dour' is fair to me. I'm more restrained than Jess, it's true. I'm far less likely to shriek, 'Helloooo, bonnie Scotland!' as we drive across the border. But that's got more to do with being nervous about appearing silly, or naff, or terminally uncool than being dour per se.

I scan my body to try to work out how I'm feeling, and I realise that this morning, tense far better describes it.

This trip is, unsurprisingly I suppose, dredging up lots of old memories. I've been thinking about Zoe a lot, obviously, but also about Dad and how I felt when he left, and how depressed Mum was after Scott went, too. I even had a dream about them all last night. Dad, Scott and I had all been in a boat. And we'd dragged Zoe's body from the lake. Only, when we got her back to land and rolled her over, it hadn't been Zoe at all. It had been Jess, who was lifelessly looking up at us, a bit of seaweed coming out of her mouth like an image from a horror film. And then Scott had slipped one hand up her dress and said, 'Now, that's what I'm talkin' about,' and I'd woken in a panic, trying with all my might, but failing, to scream.

'You OK?' Jess asks me, unexpectedly.

So I tell her everything except her part in my dream. No one wants to hear about being dragged lifeless from a river, after all. Not even shrinky-dinky Jess.

'Well, it's bound to bring up lots of memories,' Jess says, once I've finished. 'You're looking for your long-lost sister, after all.'

'I know,' I say. 'But I feel like I shouldn't be feeling stressed about it, you know? I mean, there's no reason to feel stressed, really, is there?'

'Just let yourself feel what you're feeling,' Jess says. 'Don't suffer over your suffering.'

Partly because I'm interested, but mainly because she loves explaining this stuff, I ask her what she means by that.

'Oh, it's a thing a Buddhist friend told me,' she says. 'It's like, if you're upset but you think you shouldn't be. So you feel guilty about being upset. Or upset about feeling guilty, or whatever. Well, that's suffering over your suffering.'

'OK,' I say. 'And the answer is?'

'Just to own it,' Jess says. 'Say, this is making me feel stressed, and that's OK.'

'Right,' I say. 'Got it.'

'Do you think about her all the time?' Jess asks.

'Zoe?'

'No, the Queen.' Jess laughs. 'Of course, Zoe.'

'You mean today, or . . .'

'No, in general. Have you been thinking obsessively about her ever since she vanished?'

'Um, not so much, actually,' I say, feeling vaguely embarrassed about how true this is. 'I suppose I should worry about her more, really, but . . .'

'I think we've established there are no shoulds about these things,' Jess says.

'No,' I say. 'OK. I mean, I did when she first left. But once I went to college I just forgot about her, really.'

'Wow,' Jess says. 'The power of the mind.'

'But then I'd see, say, a pack of Quorn sausages and think about her. That was all she ate for years: Quorn sausage sandwiches. Or on her birthday, I'd wonder if she was OK – stuff like that. But not all the time. Not even that much, if I'm being honest.'

'So why now?' Jess asks.

'Why am I thinking about her?'

'No, why do you want to find her?'

'I don't know,' I tell her honestly. 'Perhaps just because your computer thing made it possible.'

'Maybe possible,' Jess corrects me.

'OK, maybe possible. Why did you look up her address for me? I mean, you said you could lose your job over it.'

'It's true,' Jess says. 'So there was no way I could help you until I trusted you enough. I had to be totally sure that no one was ever going to find out.'

'Right,' I say. 'Of course.'

'Plus, I've come to see how much it's affected you. So I'd like to help with that, if I can.'

'Has it?' I say. 'Has it affected me, do you think?'

'Well, of course it has,' Jess says.

I think about this for a moment, wondering if Jess can maybe see me better than I see myself. 'How, specifically?' I finally dare to ask.

'How has it affected you?' Jess asks.

'Yeah.'

She shrugs. 'I don't know, really,' she says. 'But it's bound to have, isn't it? I bet that half of your relationship issues stem from being abandoned by your father, your stepfather and your sister, don't you?'

'They didn't abandon me,' I tell her.

'No,' she says. 'Sorry. Of course they didn't. But you know what I mean.'

I frown at this but feel reluctant to push the subject any further. The whole thing is making me feel a bit queasy, so I'm relieved when Jess asks, 'Anyway, how far is it now?'

I glance at Google Maps on my phone and tell her it's about an hour.

'Can we stop and get something to eat, then?' Jess asks. 'I'm starving.'

We stop in the strangest store imaginable. It's a huge hangar filled with clothes and lawnmowers and groceries, all mixed up. The coffee shop is at the rear, so we walk along a vast aisle containing some rather nice tartan ties and jackets, some reduced-to-clear Christmas lights and tins of colostrum booster for ewes.

'Oh, I've been meaning to pick up some colostrum booster for ages,' Jess mugs, grabbing a tin and then putting it down. 'Later, maybe.'

There are no vegan options in the café so Jess settles, without complaint, for a cheese sandwich, while I plump for tuna mayo. We're only in the hangar for twenty minutes, but by the time we step back out into the car park it's snowing properly.

'Snow!' Jess says, dancing around like a loon in the midst of our personal snow-globe. 'It's snowing! I love snow!'

'I hope we don't get stuck in it,' I say.

'You see?' Jess says. 'Dour!'

As the first signs for Portpatrick appear, Jess asks me if I want to head for the commune or our rental.

'I'm not sure,' I reply. 'Which one's closest? Is one on the way to the other? Can you look?'

'I think it's going to be the commune,' Jess says. 'Our rental is right on the coast.'

'So shall we go straight there?' I ask. 'See if anyone's home before we get snowed in.'

'See if Zoe's home, more like it,' Jess says. 'And we're not going to get snowed in. The forecast for tomorrow is sunshine.'

'I feel sick,' I tell her. 'I feel, you know, really, seriously pukey.'

'It's normal,' Jess says. 'It's your body getting you ready for a shock. Because deep down it knows that she's going to be there.'

'Don't say that,' I say, a little more sharply than I intended. 'You don't know that. We don't know that at all. And deep down, I can assure you, my body knows nothing at all.'

About twenty minutes from Portpatrick, Jess's phone pings with a rare text from her mother.

'She wants to know why we didn't go to Uncle Will's,' Jess tells me. 'He must have phoned her. I'd better answer her or she'll be worried.'

'You did tell him, though, didn't you?' I ask.

'You know I did,' Jess says, sounding vaguely tetchy. 'I texted him as we were leaving Bristol.'

I frown at the fact that I have absolutely no recollection of her telling me this, but say nothing. She may well have said it while I was thinking about something else – I've been pretty distracted these last few days. Plus, the tetchiness is more, I suspect, to do with the fact that she's thinking about her family.

Jess, who is famed for her endless text messages, taps away at the screen for a while before asking me, 'What's that place we stayed in called? I'm wanting to say Hailsham again, but I know that's not right.'

'Heysham,' I say. 'Hailsham's the one near Eastbourne.'

'That's it,' Jess says, spelling it out as she types. 'H, E, Y, S . . . Even the phone wants to correct it to Hailsham. Is Hailsham famous or something?'

I shrug. 'I doubt it. I only know it because it's one of the places Zoe sent a postcard from. So I looked it up to see where it was.'

'God, the postcards,' Jess says, glancing up from her phone. 'I'd forgotten about those. Do you think she lived there, then? Before Bristol, maybe?'

'No, I'm pretty certain she never sent the postcards from anywhere she lived,' I explain. 'They were always from little villages in the middle of nowhere, I assume so she couldn't be found.'

◆ ◆ ◆

The postcards had started about a month after her disappearance. They'd arrived quite regularly at first, sometimes just a week or two apart. But as time went by they became less and less frequent, until, towards the end, they only ever came on my birthday.

They were sent not to our house but to my friend Gary Mason's place. He lived just around the corner from us, and Gary would bring them into school for me.

Zoe never said much in them, except that she was fine, that I shouldn't worry, and, in the early ones at least, that I shouldn't tell Mum she was writing to me.

The secrecy part of it was challenging, because Mum was worried sick about Zoe. And I mean that quite literally. She wasn't sleeping, and she wasn't eating much either, which was unusual. In the past, Mum had always reacted to stress by pigging out, but this time she looked so pale and thin that one of my schoolfriends assumed she had cancer. So I felt torn between Zoe, who'd made me feel quite special by choosing to secretly send the postcards to me, and Mum, who desperately needed good news.

In the end, it worried me so much that I texted Scott to ask him to call me. It was the first time I'd communicated with him since he'd left, so we chatted for a while, just like old times, and then I explained my dilemma.

He asked me how often Mum made my bed. Though it was a strange question, I assumed he had a plan – Scott always had a plan – and so I told him that she straightened the covers most days and changed the sheets about once every two weeks.

'Hide them under your pillow for a couple of weeks,' he told me. 'And then stick 'em under your mattress. That way she'll find them, but it won't be your fault.'

So that's exactly what I chose to do.

Mum stopped making my bed around then. She even told me, in a fake pique of anger, that she was sick of doing everything and that it was time I made my bed for myself. I was pretty certain that this meant she'd found the postcards, and wanted to continue finding them but without me realising she had. Just to make sure, I arranged them in a specific way and took a photo with my camera so that I could see if they'd moved even the tiniest bit. By the time I got home that night, she'd been at them.

Mum seemed happier, or at least less unhappy, after that, and I got to kind of respect Zoe's wishes. I'd also opened a communications channel with Scott, and I was grateful, now it had happened, to have had such a good excuse to do so. Because chatting to Scott really cheered me up.

About a year after I started college, Gary Mason's family moved to Altrincham, and that was the end of my postcard delivery service.

I went back to his old house just once, a few weeks after my twenty-first birthday. I was visiting Mum and wanted to see if the new owners had received anything for me from Zoe.

A really dodgy skinhead guy opened the door. He had tattoos all up his neck, and more piercings in his nose and ears than I had ever seen on anyone before. As I'd never lived there, I struggled to explain why I thought he might have letters waiting for me, and he didn't seem interested enough to take the time to comprehend what I was saying. He told me there had been 'nowt for no one', and because he was having trouble restraining his equally scary pit bull, I took him at his word; and, feeling a bit like I'd lost my sister all over again, I ran away as fast as I could.

Google Maps fails us. It's the first time on this trip that this has happened.

We're in the middle of a long stretch of uninterrupted country road when it announces, unexpectedly, that we have reached our destination.

I bump the car up on to the snowy footpath and proceed to clamber with difficulty up the steep bank to our right, closely followed by Jess, who with her Dr. Martens has considerably less trouble doing so than I.

When we reach the top we scan the horizon. The countryside is sprinkled thinly with snow. There's a glimpse of sea to our west, and a copse of trees above us to the east. North and south, the road continues, uninterrupted by junctions or side roads, and entirely devoid of hippy communes.

'Maybe it's an invisible hippy commune,' Jess says; an attempt, I think, at cheering me up.

'More like they gave a false address so that no one can find them,' I suggest, my breath rising like steam from a locomotive as I speak. 'Jesus, it's cold in Scotland!'

'You're right,' Jess says. 'It's arctic.'

'There was no phone number for this one either, was there,' I say, a statement of fact, not a question.

Jess shakes her head. 'Pretty, though,' she offers.

'Yeah, well,' I say, 'I didn't drive all the way up here for pretty.'

'Jude,' Jess says, stepping closer to me and stroking my shoulder. 'We'll find it. Don't worry.'

'I'm not sure how,' I tell her despondently. 'The address we got is right here.'

'I vote that we find our gardener's cottage and light a fire and . . .'

'It has a fire?'

'It does! So we can light a fire and cook some food and guzzle down a bottle of wine. And then, once we're too drunk to do anything properly, we can have another look on the internet. Maybe there are two roads with the same name. And maybe you have to be drunk to find the right one.'

'OK,' I say, thinking that, right now, wine and warmth sound perfect. 'Let's do that.'

But as I turn to climb back down the bank, the tenuous grip of my leather-soled shoes on the frozen grass fails and I slip on to my arse, then slither uncontrollably and, judging from Jess's reaction, hilariously, all the way back to the roadside.

'Your bum's covered in mud,' Jess tells me, once her laughter has abated enough for her to join me.

'It's not funny, Jess,' I say. 'These are my only jeans. And I'm soaked.'

'We can wash them,' Jess says. 'Relax, we can hand-wash them when we get to the cottage. It's only mud and grass. I think there might even be a washing machine.'

I'm stretching and twisting to look at my behind. 'Ugh!' I say. 'If I sit in the car, I'll dirty the seats. And then bang goes the deposit.'

'God, you are grumpy since we got to Scotland.'

'Jess, I'm not grumpy,' I say. 'I'm covered in mud!'

'Yep. So you'll have to change,' Jess says. 'Just put on your posh trousers. Where's the problem?'

I run a finger across my muddy back pocket and then raise it to my nose. At least it doesn't smell like dung. 'I guess that's my only option,' I admit.

And so, at the side of the road, in minus three degrees and surrounded by a sudden flurry of snowflakes, I hop from foot to foot as I change.

At the exact moment I'm down to my underpants, an Eddie Stobart truck drives past. The driver honks repeatedly, causing Jess to wave and blow him a kiss before bursting into a fresh bout of laughter. 'I think you've pulled!' she says. 'He was actually quite sexy, too!'

◆ ◆ ◆

It's just after 3 p.m. when we arrive at our rental.

It's a two-bedroom cottage set at the bottom of the walled garden of a country mansion, itself set in the rolling hills above Portpatrick.

We're greeted by a Viking of a Scotsman with a shaggy red beard and freckles. He's so tall he has to duck to get through the perfectly standard-sized door of the cottage. The decor is tasteful, and the place has been thoughtfully furnished with quirky antiques throughout.

Once he has given us a tour of the lounge, kitchen and bedrooms, he leaves by the back door, heading across to the large stately home in the distance.

'It's really nice,' I tell Jess. I pat the top of a funky wingback armchair. 'I love this chair, don't you?'

'Yes, it's nice,' Jess says. 'But it's bloody freezing. We need to get that fire lit. You any good at that? Lighting fires is supposed to be a boy thing, isn't it?'

'I'll light the fire if you wash my jeans,' I say. 'The washing of jeans being, of course, a "girl thing".'

'You're so sexist!' Jess says, glaring at me with mock anger, one hand on her hip.

'Um, I think you started it, actually,' I tell her, grinning. 'But you can light the fire, and I'll wash the jeans if you prefer. If you want get all modern about it.'

'Oh, all right,' Jess laughs. 'I'll wash your jeans, darling. That fire had better be a good one though, cave man.'

Sadly, and despite my very best efforts, the fire is not a good one. Though, technically, it works, it provides about as much heat as a couple of candles.

'I think those peat things are designed to burn gently for hours,' I tell Jess as she hangs my jeans over an electric storage heater. 'Whereas what we need here is a towering inferno.'

We tour the rooms, turning the heaters up to the max, but it's quickly apparent that this isn't going to be enough to warm the thick stone walls of the cottage. My guess is that it hasn't been heated for weeks.

'What we need is proper wood,' I tell Jess.

'Shall I phone him and ask him?' she suggests. 'It's kind of their responsibility, after all.'

I wrinkle my nose. 'We've got to go out for food and wine anyway,' I point out. 'I'm sure we can find something to burn. Let's go see Portpatrick before it gets dark.'

It's a five-minute drive to the village through pretty rolling hills spotted with deep-frozen sheep. I wonder if they're dreading sundown; they must be so cold, the poor things.

Portpatrick turns out to be a cute fishing village nestled in the cleft of the hills. Surprisingly, it hasn't snowed down here.

As I park the car on the almost deserted seafront, a gap in the clouds appears, lighting up a patch of sea on the horizon with visible beams of golden sunlight.

'Wow!' Jess says. 'Selfie! Quick! Before it goes.'

We cross the road and turn our backs to the sea, and by crouching down comically, we manage to take a photo with the fishing boats to my left and the golden patch of sunlit sea above Jess's right ear.

'You look like the heavens have opened to beam you up,' I comment.

As the sun slithers towards the horizon, we walk along the dockside looking at the colourful fishing boats and stand on the seawall and peer out to sea. 'I'm guessing that there's nothing out there till America,' I say.

'Aren't you forgetting Ireland?' Jess asks.

'I think we're too far north for Ireland,' I tell her. But a quick check on my phone proves that I'm wrong. 'So I'm guessing there's nothing out there till Ireland,' I say, sotto voce.

'Do I look like Kate?' Jess asks, raising one hand to her forehead. Seeing that I have no idea what she's talking about, she says, 'Kate Winslet. In *Titanic*? Hello?'

'Oh, you look exactly like Kate,' I tell her. 'In fact, I've rarely seen a black girl who looks more like Kate Winslet than you do.'

There are very few shops in Portpatrick, but we manage to find a bakery for bread and a village store-cum-post office for everything else. Jess puts the ingredients for a minimalist vegan chilli in the basket and I grab two bottles of Chardonnay.

'And the wood?' Jess reminds me, once the cold outside reminds her.

So I duck back into the store to ask for directions to a petrol station, figuring that's where one can generally buy bundles of wood.

The cashier tells me that the nearest one is in Stranraer, fifteen minutes away. I must look disappointed because she asks if that's a problem. 'Running low, are you?' she says.

When I explain that it's not petrol that I'm after but wood, she leads me to the rear of the shop. 'We don't have wood as such,' she says, 'but we have these.' She opens a door revealing an overhang beneath which are stacked packages of the useless peat briquettes, but also compressed-wood heat logs.

'Great,' I tell her, grabbing a pack from the pile. 'If these burn better than those, then it'll be fine.'

By the time we get back to the checkout, Jess has returned from outside. 'It's waay too cold to wait out there,' she says.

'Aye, and snow tonight,' the cashier declares.

'Really?' I say. 'The forecast says sunshine.'

'Sunshine tomorrow, but snow tonight,' she insists. 'You can smell it in the air.'

'I have a question,' Jess says, as the cashier hands me my receipt. 'You don't know where Siochain House is, do you? It's supposed to be in Portpatrick, but we can't find it.'

The woman's demeanour changes instantly. Her face, previously open and welcoming, shuts down. 'Aye,' she says. 'You won't find anyone round here who doesn't know it. And it's pronounced shee-uh-harn, not see-oh-chain. It's Gaelic, dear. It means peace. Which is what I suppose you might call ironic.'

'Could you explain how to get there, maybe?' Jess asks, powering through the woman's clear dislike of the place. 'Or show us on the map thingy on my phone?'

'I could,' she says, emphasising the conditional nature of her reply. 'But I cannae see why two nice folk like yourselves would want to get involved with that lot.'

'We're just trying to track down my sister,' I explain. 'She's gone missing, so . . .'

'His mum . . .' Jessica starts, but I raise a finger and shake my head.

'Sorry,' Jess mutters, looking confused.

'Aye, well, it's up behind the Dunskey Estate,' she says. 'Between the Old Loch and the coast.'

'The Dunskey Estate?' I repeat. 'And if we head for that, will we find Siochain House – did I pronounce that right?'

'Aye,' the woman says. 'Just head for Dunskey and then keep on driving. If the road turns to potholes you'll know you're on the right track. Just follow the trail of burned-out cars and the caravans they've dumped.'

'Burned-out cars and dumped caravans,' Jess comments, once we're back out on the street. 'Otherwise known as how to seduce all the locals.'

'Yeah, it sounds a bit grim, doesn't it?'

'Anyway, what was the thing with your mum? Aren't we using that excuse any more?'

I shake my head. 'Sorry, but it makes me feel uncomfortable,' I explain. 'Like we're tempting fate or something.'

'Oh,' Jess says, nodding. 'Oh, I see. OK. Sorry.'

'It's fine,' I tell her. 'I came up with it, after all. But if we could come up with something different now, then that would be great.'

◆ ◆ ◆

The next morning, our attempts to find Siochain House do not get off to a good start. Though we can see where the Old Loch is on Google Maps, there are precisely zero roads that go out there. So we drive past the Dunskey Estate ('Tearooms, Terrace & Maze – CLOSED') repeatedly, glancing sometimes to our left and other times to our right as we pass by.

We turn down potholed tracks and find ourselves in front of farmhouses, or cattle grids, or dead ends. We see very few people we can ask, but those we do interrogate seem less than willing to help, either telling us that they've never heard of the place, which seems unlikely, or giving us vague or impossible directions.

But it's a beautiful sunny winter morning and, feeling rested after our evening in front of the fire, we attack our quest good-naturedly.

'I feel a bit like I'm in an adventure game, don't you?' Jess says, at one point. 'Trouble is, I always get stuck on the first level.'

Once we've driven up and down often enough to be sure we haven't missed a turning, we start to widen our search, heading as far north as the turning to Killantringan Lighthouse and as far east as the main road to Stranraer, but still we find no burned-out cars or caravans, and not even a tiniest hint of a hippy.

Finally, more bored than upset, I suggest that, for now at least, we admit defeat.

'Can we go to the lighthouse, then?' Jess asks. 'I don't think I've ever seen one for real.'

◆ ◆ ◆

The road out to the headlands is simply stunning, cutting through snow-dusted hills and offering glimpses of white-capped waves beyond the cliffs. Wispy clouds are scooting across a pale blue sky, casting fast-moving shadows on the waters of the bay.

We edge the car through a group of sheep who have straggled from the herd and park in an empty, windswept car park before buttoning up and heading for the lighthouse, which we can see peeping over the top of a hill.

With the sea breeze it's truly too cold for comfort, but there's something magical about the moment, too. It's the light, perhaps, or the sounds of the waves crashing below. Maybe it's the smells of the countryside mixed with the iodine perfume of the sea. Or perhaps it's got more to do with Zoe, with this sensation that she's so close, and yet so far. Whatever it is, I'm starting to feel raw, edgy and unexpectedly emotional.

It takes ten minutes to walk to the highest point, a walled second car park around the base of the lighthouse, and on arrival we make our way to the furthest sea wall, where we lean, looking out at the Irish Sea.

'Isn't this great?' Jess asks, shouting against the noise of the buffeting wind. Her hair is whipping around in the sea breeze and, I notice, starting to frizz quite seriously.

'It is!' I agree. I swipe at a tear on my cheek and Jess somehow detects that the cause might be other than the icy wind.

'Don't worry,' she says concernedly as she takes my fingers in her equally freezing hand. 'We'll find her.'

'It's not that,' I tell her, leaning in close so that she can hear me. 'At least, it's not just that. It's . . . I don't know. It's this,' I say, gesturing at the seascape before us. 'I just feel a bit weird. I feel . . . I don't know.' I shrug and smile at her.

'Alive?' Jess asks.

'Yeah,' I admit. 'Yeah, I suppose that's it. It's just being here, and the wind and the sea and the clouds and the light, you know? It's being here, right now. It's being in this weird place with you.'

Jess laughs.

'What?' I ask.

'I love you too,' she says, grinning broadly and squeezing my hand in hers.

In that moment, I really want to tell her that she's right. I really want to say that yes, that's what I'm thinking: that I love her. That I love this lighthouse, and this wind, and that cloud spinning across the sky, and yes, Jess too. But even now, I still can't say it. I tell myself that it doesn't matter. After all, Jess has just told me that she's understood. Instead I turn and kiss her. It's the best that I can do.

When we get back to the car, she says, 'I want the top down.'

'Um, I think it's just a tad windy for that, Jess,' I say.

'I don't care,' she tells me. 'I paid the supplement and I want the top down.'

'OK. Then at least wait till we get inland a bit. I'm worried the wind will rip it off if we do it here.'

Still feeling raw and unusually present in the moment, I drive us back to the main road and then south towards Portpatrick until I find a suitable siding where I can pull over.

'You're sure about this?' I laugh, as I crank up the car's heater and place my finger over the button.

'I'm sure, Mr Bond,' Jess says. 'Press that button.'

With a click and whirr, the top glides open, lifts and then vanishes magically into the boot.

'Wow,' Jess says. 'How cool is that? That's well worth a fiver a day.'

'Um?' I say. I've been distracted by something I've spotted at the roadside. 'Look,' I tell Jess, pointing.

'What?' she asks, releasing her seatbelt and standing to look over the windscreen. 'Oh, the windmill thing?'

Just a few yards in front of us, planted at the corner of what looks like a farm track – actually, calling it a farm track is perhaps overly generous – is a battered pinwheel in faded rainbow colours, spinning erratically in the breeze.

'Hippies do famously love a rainbow windmill,' I point out.

'So do kids,' Jess says. 'So does every kid on the planet, actually. Plus, the Old Loch's on the other side of the road, isn't it? I thought it was nearer the coast.'

'Maybe she got that wrong,' I say. 'Or maybe she was feeding us duff information.'

'Try it,' Jess says, sliding back into her seat. 'If you think you can do it without getting stuck, then go for it, Mr Bond.'

I bump the car off the road and up on to the track, following it through a wide gap in the hedgerow and along one edge of a snow-dusted farmer's field. I can immediately tell that this isn't right, but seeing a wider stretch further down, I continue in order to turn the car around. However, just as I reach the spot where it opens out, Jessica points and says, 'Look!'

I turn in my seat and follow her gaze to a gap in the hedge. Behind it, in the next field, is a caravan with a flattened roof. My guess is that it failed to withstand the snowfall one year and simply got abandoned.

'Well, it's a caravan,' I say, 'but it's hardly a hippy encampment.'

'Not the caravan,' Jess says. 'Look behind it. Well, behind that bush now.'

I slip the car into reverse and move backwards, and there, barely visible through the gap, behind a distant copse of trees, is an extremely large house.

We climb out of the car and clamber around the caravan to look. I note that my suit trousers have got caught on the brambles and will probably never be the same again, but I say nothing. I'm too excited about the house to care.

'This can't possibly be the main access to that house,' I tell Jess.

'I know,' she says. 'We've fucked up, haven't we? But that might be the place.'

I turn the car around and we bump our way back out on to the main road, then turn left a hundred yards further along into what looks like the drive of a small cottage.

It's only once we're alongside the cottage that it becomes obvious that it must once have been a gatehouse, because behind it the narrow track opens out into a majestic driveway, curving gently around to the house. It's bordered on one side by a pretty lake and on the other by a row of perfectly spaced oak trees.

Eventually, the house comes into view, and I can see that it must indeed have once resembled Downton Abbey. Today the overall impression is more one of lost splendour. Ivy has scaled the walls and half the roof, and what is still visible of the walls is covered in peeling flakes of paint that look like the scales from some dying pink fish.

The house may not be looking its best, but there are no burned-out cars, and other than the one in the field next door, no abandoned caravans either. And yet I'm sure this must be the place.

I pull up on a patch of scrappy gravel in front of the house, next to the only other car present, a surprisingly shiny white Renault.

'D'you think that's a good omen?' I ask Jessica, pointing.

'The car?' she asks me, confused.

'Yes, but what kind of car is it?' I ask, with a wink.

'Ahh,' she laughs. 'A Zoe! I'd say that's a very good sign.'

As we're climbing from the car, a man appears from behind the main building. He's wearing his grey hair in a long straggly ponytail and is dressed in wellington boots, muddy jeans and a number of thick woollen jumpers. As he pushes his wheelbarrow of logs ever closer, I realise that he's considerably older than I had first thought, in his sixties rather than his forties.

When he reaches us, he props up the wheelbarrow and stretches to rub the base of his spine with both hands.

'Ouch,' he says, then, 'Can I help you?'

He has a hint of a smile on his lips, but the overall result is more amused than welcoming. Perhaps he thinks we look out of place here. Glancing at Jess's lime-green trousers and pink coat and the muddy fields around us, I decide that his grin is pretty reasonable.

'I hope you can,' Jess says, stepping forward and offering a hand, which he ignores. 'This is Siochain House, isn't it?'

The man nods. Nothing else about his expression changes, and I decide that he is perhaps not amused after all. I'm thinking that he's almost certainly stoned.

'Thank God,' Jess says. 'We've been driving all over. You're so difficult to find!'

'Which is entirely intentional,' the man says flatly. 'May I inquire what your purpose is?'

'Oh, we're looking for my sister,' I explain. 'Zoe? Zoe Fuller?'

With the same expression of vague amusement, he says, 'Ahh, Zoe. I'm afraid you've missed her.'

'Oh,' I say. 'Do you know when she'll be back?'

'Never is the most likely answer to that one,' he says. 'Though, of course, one can never tell.' At this, he seizes the handles of the wheelbarrow again and starts to continue on his way.

'But we've just missed her, you say?' Jess asks, starting to trot along behind him.

'Oh no, you've missed Zoe by about nine months,' he says, casting the words over his shoulder.

Jess pauses to look back at me and we have an entirely unspoken conversation comprised of raised eyebrows and nods towards the house. As a result, I join her and we follow in the man's wake, past the grand stone staircase to the front door, and around the far corner to a side door.

On arrival, he tips his load of wood on to the bottom step, and then turns to face us once again.

'You're still here,' he comments. Again, his tone of voice is entirely without emotion. He sounds neither surprised nor annoyed by our presence. He's simply stating it as a fact.

'Yep, still here,' I say, wiggling my eyebrows in a vague attempt at charming him.

'We've come all the way from Bristol,' Jess says. 'So . . .'

'From Bristol,' he repeats. 'Yes.'

'Look, can you tell us anything at all?' I ask.

'Oh, many things I can tell you,' the man says, sounding irritatingly like he's channelling Yoda.

'About Zoe,' I say, as flatly as I can manage.

'Ahh, sorry, but Zoe is not my specialist subject,' he says. 'I'm very good on astrology, if that's of use.'

'Is there anyone else here we could talk to?' Jess asks. 'Someone who might know where she went?'

'Nuala will,' he says. 'If she's here. She's far more aware of all the comings and goings than I am.'

'And where might we find Nuala?' Jess asks, tentatively.

'You might find Nuala in the main house,' he says. 'Then again, you might not. She could be out. I really wouldn't know.'

'Do you mind if we look?' I ask.

The man shakes his head gently. 'I don't mind anything at all,' he says.

'How stoned?' I say, once Jess and I have left him behind.

'Quite stoned, I'd say,' Jess says. 'D'you think they grow their own?'

'They might,' I say, emulating the man's flat tone of voice. 'Then again, they might not.'

We walk to the front of the house and climb the curved stone staircase to the main door. As this is wide open, we step inside the porch. One wall is lined with muddy boot-stacked shelves, and the other is taken up by an enormous corkboard on which are pinned posters for long-ago concerts, a couple of bills and tens and tens of scraps of paper with messages written on them.

I scan a few and learn that 'This Monday's house meeting is cancelled' and that 'Electric fires are not to be used in the bedrooms as they overload the wires.'

I cross the chequered tiles and peer through a dirty window-pane in the second door. Beyond it is a high-ceilinged entrance hall, but I can see no sign of life.

We knock a few times on the door and attempt to push an old doorbell button, but it has been painted over long ago.

After a minute or so of knocking, Jess tries the door handle, and when it opens, we step indoors and close it behind us.

'Wow,' Jess whispers. 'It's massive.'

'It's Hill House,' I murmur.

173

'What?' Jess says.

'*The Haunting of Hill House?* You've seen that, haven't you?'

Jess shakes her head. 'No, thankfully,' she says.

'Hello?' I call out. When there's still no answer, we edge further into the cavernous hallway. An image flashes through my mind of a party, in the thirties, perhaps – the house full of men in tuxedos and women in ball gowns; waiters whizzing around serving champagne . . .

I wonder if it's an image I've retained from a TV series or if it's an actual memory the house is somehow beaming into my brain. It wasn't always like this, it seems to be saying. Once upon a time, life was a ball.

A shiver makes me notice the temperature. 'It's colder in here than outside,' I say, my breath hanging in the air as I speak.

'It's like being in a fridge. Someone needs to light that fire,' Jess says, nodding towards a huge stone fireplace on the right-hand wall, around which three ancient sofas have been haphazardly placed.

We cross to the nearest side door and peer into a large lounge with panelled walls. It has French windows looking out over the lake, beautiful worn wooden floorboards and, by way of furniture, a circle of twenty junk-shop armchairs, their stuffing oozing out. The walls have apparently been painted with whatever came to hand, so two are gloss green, one deep red, and the fourth canary yellow. On the ceiling someone has painted, apparently many, many years before, a gigantic yin–yang symbol.

'Hmm,' Jess says doubtfully, as we duck back out of the room then start to cross the hall to the opposite side door. 'Was that a reggae theme?'

'The yin–yang?' I say. 'That's Asian, isn't it?'

'No, silly. The red, green and yellow,' Jess says.

'Ah, right,' I say. 'Maybe.'

'The drawing room?' Jess says as we peer into another room with wall-to-wall bookcases. Again, the outer wall has French windows that reach from the ceiling to the floor, only this time someone has attempted to insulate them with bubble wrap and duct tape. The overall result of beige light filtering through is depressing and their efforts seem to have been in vain anyway, because it's actually colder in here than in the hallway.

'It was once a drawing room,' I reply. With its five single beds and two tables, the room looks far more like an improvised dormitory.

'There's no stuff,' Jess comments, as we step back into the main hall. 'Have you noticed that?'

'Stuff?' I say.

'Yeah, clothes, records, books, plates . . . There's just furniture. Lots and lots of shitty furniture. If people live here, then where is all their stuff?'

We cross the ochre floor tiles of the hallway to the base of the winding staircase. It, too, must have once been pretty grandiose, and it's not difficult to imagine Ava Gardner floating towards us in a ball gown. Sadly, someone with a misplaced sense of taste has randomly painted everything, so the banister poles are all different colours.

'Hello?' I call out again, but there's still no answer, so we duck down a corridor to the right of the staircase. It's about twenty yards long with regularly spaced doors on both sides. As these are all closed and as the only real light is coming from the front door, now some way behind us, it starts to feel quite eerie.

'It's *The Shining*,' I tell Jess. 'Look out for kids on tricycles.'

'Just stop it, will you?' she says, slapping me gently on the shoulder.

We continue to the end of the corridor where a final door is ajar about half an inch, allowing a tiny strip of light to leak out on to the tiled floor.

I push the door and it swings open easily, revealing an industrial-scale kitchen with metal worktops and a twelve-burner gas stove. In the middle of the room, over a wide central island, a rectangular contraption hangs from the ceiling, and hooked on to this are a whole collection of school-dinner-sized pots and pans.

In the middle of the room, with her back to us, a woman is busy cooking.

'Hello?' I call out, because she seems oblivious to our presence.

When she still doesn't respond, Jess and I glance at each other before jointly stepping closer. Her failure to react is a bit creepy, to be honest, and it crosses my mind that she might be a zombie. I guess I've been watching too many horror films on Netflix.

'Hello?' I say loudly, and this time she spins, her knife still in her hand, and on seeing us screams so loudly that both Jess and I jump backwards in fright.

'Shit!' she says, pulling her earbuds out, 'Shit, shit, shit! Shit, you made me jump!'

She's in her mid-fifties, with long, grey hair. She's wearing jeans, dirty Timberland-style boots and a thick, knee-length jumper with almost as many holes as it has stitches.

'I'm sorry,' I say. 'We called out, but . . .'

'Sorry, sorry,' she says breathlessly, gesturing vaguely towards her ears. She blows through her pursed lips slowly. 'It's my fault, really . . . the music.'

'We knocked on the front door for ages, too,' Jess explains. 'But no one answered.'

'Well,' she says, waving the knife around a little nerve-rackingly as she speaks. 'That's like everything else, isn't it?'

'Like everything else?' Jess repeats.

'Never mind,' the woman says. 'It's just, you know, people leaving everything to someone else. It's the cancer of every community.'

'Oh, right,' I say. 'Yes, I'm sure.'

'Sorry, but who are you?' she asks, now pointing the knife right at me. I glance nervously at the blade, and when she realises what she's doing she grimaces and turns and places it on the counter behind her, then wipes her hands on her hips.

'We're, um, looking for my sister,' I explain. 'A guy outside told us to ask for Nuala?'

'Oh. OK, well, you've found her,' she says. 'That's me. But he shouldn't have let you wander around like this. Was it Gunter?'

'I'm not sure,' I tell her. 'It was a guy with a ponytail and a wheelbarrow full of logs . . .'

'Yeah, that'll be Gunter,' she says, her eyes rolling. 'And your sister is?'

'Zoe,' I say. 'Zoe Fuller. Do you know her?'

She nods in sad recognition and then clicks her tongue against the roof of her mouth before replying, 'God, yeah. Of course I do. We all know Zoe.'

She crosses to the cooker, on which there's a frying pan full of onions, and for a moment I think that she's decided to ignore us in the same way Gunter did, that she's simply moving on to her next task. But then she stirs the onions, turns off the heat and returns, walking past us and on into the corridor. 'Come up to mine for a minute,' she says as she passes. 'It's freezing down here. Plus, I have tea.'

We follow her back through the main hall and up the Technicolor staircase.

'It's an amazing house,' Jess says, as we trot along beside her.

'Is it?' Nuala says, then, 'Yes, I suppose it is.'

She leads us along another fridge-cold corridor on the first floor, and once again, almost all the doors are closed. When occasionally

177

a door is ajar, I glance inside to see random collections of furniture, and ever more incoherent colour schemes.

'That's Dillon,' she says, as we pass one open door, and the man in the room waves his fingers at us without even looking up from his book. 'He's a bit antisocial,' she mutters a little further down. 'Don't take it personally.'

At the end of the corridor she unlocks a padlock, pushes the door open and ushers us in. Her bedroom is high ceilinged with another pair of beautiful French windows, this time leading on to a narrow balcony overlooking the lake. Unlike the rest of the house, the decor here is a single colour: a slightly pink-tinged beige.

She has a four-poster bed, a blue velour divan piled with clothes, a desk with a huge iMac computer and a Welsh dresser with cups, plates and a kettle. In the fireplace a two-bar electric fire is running, meaning that this room is slightly less arctic than elsewhere. I think about the warning on the noticeboard and wonder if she's seen it. I wonder if the wires to the sockets are melting at this very moment.

Nuala clears just enough space on the divan for us to sit, and then heads to the dresser to make tea. 'So, how did you find us?' she asks as she fills the kettle from a filter jug and then switches it on.

'It was luck, really,' I tell her. 'We turned down a farm track and then saw the house through the trees.'

'No, I mean more generally speaking,' she says. 'Why did you think Zoe would be here?'

'A guy in Morecambe told us,' I explain. 'He said she'd come here when she moved out, so . . .'

'Morecambe, yes,' Nuala says. 'She was there before. But she's long gone, I'm afraid.'

'So I gather. But the guy outside – Gunter, is it? He seemed to think you might know where she went.'

'Oh, I know exactly where she went,' Nuala says, now dropping teabags into the cups and pouring on boiling water. I've just noticed that the teabags are green tea rather than black. Unfortunately, I'm not a big fan of green tea, but it's too late to say anything now.

'And where is that?' I ask.

'France,' Nuala says. 'Nick found a job out there, so off they jolly well went.'

'Nick?' I repeat.

'If she's your sister, then I'm assuming she told you about Nick?' Nuala says.

I hesitate for a microsecond as to whether it's best to lie and get her confidence, or tell the truth in the hope that she'll explain. The first option wins out, so I nod. 'Of course,' I say.

Jess's brow wrinkles at this, indicating, I think, that this was the wrong decision, so I send her a tiny shrug and a grimace.

'I don't know,' Jess says. 'Who's Nick?'

'Who's Nick . . .' Nuala repeats quietly, her eyes drifting to the window for a moment. She shakes her head slowly. 'Well, Zoe's partner, for one thing. And the last of the youngsters to leave us. It happens to them all in the end.' She crosses the room with our teas and, seeing that we're looking confused, she explains. 'They meet someone on the outside. They fall in love. They bring them back here. It doesn't work out. Everyone argues. And they leave. It's why there are only eight of us left.'

'Eight?' Jess repeats. 'In this huge house?'

Nuala sits on the edge of her bed and sips her tea and nods. 'We're dying, really,' she says. 'No one wants to admit it, but we are. Without fresh blood, we're dying. Like vampires.'

'But it didn't work out?' I ask. 'With Zoe?'

Nuala laughs at this. 'She's a nice enough girl,' she says. 'But suited to communal living she is not.'

'No,' I say. 'No, I can imagine that she might find that challenging. She struggled even with having a family.'

'Who doesn't?' Nuala says. 'Half the people here are escaping dysfunctional families. Zoe never mentioned you, though. She never even hinted that she had any kind of family.'

I sigh at this and sip my tea. There doesn't seem to be much that I can say to that.

'But you definitely know where they went?' Jess says. 'That's brilliant news. Do you have an address or something?'

'I do,' Nuala says.

'Oh, that would be wonderful,' I tell her. 'We've been driving all over the place trying to—'

'I can't just give it to you,' Nuala says. 'That would be . . . No, no, I definitely couldn't do that. I can text them and ask if Zoe minds. Or I can give them your number, I suppose. Yes, that's probably easier. Then it's up to Zoe, isn't it?'

'You know, we've driven all the way from Bristol to find her,' Jess explains. 'So if you could maybe phone and ask, then . . .'

'I can't,' Nuala says, interrupting her. 'I'm on pay as you go. I can't call French numbers. But I can text them for you.'

'We could use mine,' I suggest.

Nuala smiles wryly at my offer. 'Then you'd have wheedled her number out of me,' she says, raising an imaginary gun and shooting me with it. 'So I'd have to kill you.'

'Ha!' I say. 'Maybe not, then. Um, you don't have some sugar for this, do you?' I raise my mug of horrid green tea.

'I've got honey,' she offers, putting her mug down and standing. I'm hoping that the honey's in the kitchen downstairs, because I have a plan. Unfortunately, she just crosses to the dresser, so while her back is turned I mime a person walking from the room by wiggling two fingers at Jess. I point towards the doorway.

Nuala returns with a grubby spoon and a pot of honey, so I smile and sweeten my tea. Jess, I can tell, is still trying to work out what I want.

'Um, could I use your toilet?' she asks, looking at me for clues as to whether she's on the right track. 'We were driving for hours before we got here.'

'Sure,' Nuala tells her. 'It's at the end of the corridor, one floor up. Second door on the right. There's one on this floor but it's out of order. It's been out of order for years, actually, ever since the ceiling fell in.'

Jess catches my eye, silently checking that this is what I wanted. I almost imperceptibly tip my head from side to side.

And then she twigs. 'Oh, could you come with me?' she asks, sounding utterly fake. 'I have the worst sense of direction.'

'Really?' Nuala asks, unconvinced.

'She really does,' I laugh. 'Jess can get lost in her own bedroom. If you let her loose here, we may never find her again.'

Nuala sighs and stands. 'Sure,' she says. 'Whatever. It's just down here . . .'

I listen to their voices fading into the distance, and then I put my tea down and scoot across her bedroom to the iMac.

There's an envelope next to the mouse addressed to Nuala O'Kane. The postal address is the same one we found on the internet, the address that when typed into Google Maps mysteriously led us to the middle of a stretch of main road miles from here.

I pray that Nuala's computer isn't password protected, and I'm in luck because as soon as I touch the mouse the swirling screen saver vanishes and is replaced by Nuala's messy desktop.

I click on the address book icon and type 'Zoe' into the search box. When this fails I type 'Nick' instead. This time, I'm in luck. There are two Nicks in Nuala's address book, one in Manchester and one with what looks like a French address. My heart racing at the thought of being caught, I photograph both of these with my iPhone, then close the window and return to the divan.

181

As soon as I sit down I realise that there's a problem: the multicoloured screen saver has not come back on. If it's anything like mine, it will probably be a few minutes before it does so.

Without any particular idea how to solve this, I return to the computer. I think about switching it off entirely, but that will look suspicious, too. And then, just as I hear their voices drifting down the distant staircase, I have another idea, which, though it isn't much better, is all that I have for now: I open a browser window and Google the route from Portpatrick to Glasgow.

'What the hell are you doing?' Nuala asks, the second she steps through the doorway. She rushes to my side and pulls the mouse from my hand. 'Really!' she says.

'Sorry!' I say, feigning cocky arrogance. 'I didn't think you'd mind. I was only—'

'Mind?' she asks, peering at the screen. 'What are you doing, anyway?'

'Jees, I was only looking at Google Maps,' I tell her. 'We were thinking of maybe going to Glasgow this afternoon, but it's a bit of a long way.'

'Such an entitled generation!' Nuala says. 'Now, if you don't mind, I'd like you to leave. I need to get back to my soup.'

'Sure,' I say. 'Sorry, I didn't mean to upset you.'

'I'm not upset,' Nuala says. 'I'm annoyed. They're entirely different emotions.'

'Um, will you still help us get in touch with Zoe?' Jess asks. 'Please? It's ever so important.'

'You can give me your number,' Nuala says, speaking through a weary sigh. 'I'll text it to them. And then it's up to Zoe what she does.'

I pull out my wallet and hand her one of my business cards. 'Jude Fuller,' she says, reading out loud. 'At least the name matches up.'

'Oh, he's her brother all right,' Jess says.

'Fine,' Nuala says, sliding the card under her keyboard. 'Well, I promise I'll let her know. I can do no more.'

She escorts us back past the reading man and on through the house to the front door. Outside we see two more women of a similar age to Nuala, identically dressed in jeans, boots and multiple layers of jumpers. They look pretty miserable and are alternately carrying and dragging a hefty wooden pallet towards the house, which might explain why. Neither of them acknowledges our presence or even the fact that Nuala is there.

'Can I give you a hand with that?' I offer, but they both reply with thin-lipped shakes of the head.

'A bit cold for open-top cruising, isn't it?' Nuala comments, when we reach the car.

'It is,' I agree. 'But when the lady wants something, the safest thing is to agree.'

'The lady,' Nuala says. 'Huh.' And then she turns and walks back towards the house.

'I can't believe you did that,' Jess says. 'That was so rude.'

'Calling you a lady?'

'No!' she says. 'Using her computer like that! I'm not surprised she kicked us—'

'Jess!' I interrupt. 'I got the address. And the phone number.'

Jess wide-eyes me in astonishment. 'Really?'

'Yep. They were in the address book on her Mac.'

'Really?' Jess says again. 'But that's . . .'

'Brilliant?'

'It's also very naughty.'

'Sure. But admit that it's also quite James Bond-y.'

'OK, perhaps,' she acknowledges reluctantly. 'Just a bit.'

I start the engine and hit the button to close the roof. 'That's the good news,' I tell her. 'The bad news is that it looks like she may really be in France.'

As we bump back down the driveway, and as the house recedes in the rear-view mirror, I ask Jess if she's certain she doesn't want to stay behind. 'You did say you might join the commune,' I remind her facetiously.

'If they're not allowed to moisturise, it's definitely not for me,' Jess says.

'I'm sorry?' I laugh.

'Did you see those women's faces?' Jess asks.

'I thought Nuala looked pretty good,' I say.

'Yeah, OK. She did. But what about the other two?' Jess says. 'I mean, I get the whole no-make-up thing. I even get the baggy jumpers, though personally, if I was spending my days in those temperatures, I'd probably shell out for a decent parka . . . But I'm not having alligator skin for anyone.'

'Wow,' I say, through my grin. 'A woman of principles. Who knew lack of moisturiser would be the downfall of the revolution?'

'I am joking,' Jess says. 'Well, in a way I am. Then again, the lack of moisturiser is kind of symbolic of everything else, isn't it?'

'No heating, no sugar, no moisturiser?' I say, checking left and right and pulling back out on to the main road.

'No joy,' Jess says. 'That's the main thing that seemed to be missing.'

'Yeah,' I say. 'They seemed a bit miserable, didn't they? But I suppose that living in minus five will do that to you.'

'They didn't seem to like each other much either, did they?' Jess says. 'That was the vibe I got, anyway.'

'Not much of a hippy love-in going on there, no.'

'Good on Zoe for moving out,' Jess says. 'Imagine staying there. How long do you think Nuala's been there? Or Gunter, for that matter?'

'Forever,' I say. 'Maybe they're all dead. Actually, that could be it! Maybe they're all ghosts.'

'That would at least explain the dry skin,' Jess says.

◆　◆　◆

I drive back to the centre of Portpatrick and park in the same spot on the seafront. The sky is clouding over again, and with it, the temperature is dropping fast. Even with the car heater on full blast I'm unable to get the Hill House chill from my bones.

We lunch in the first place we find, a seafront pub called the Waterfront.

It has a wood stove in one corner, radiating so much heat we actually can't sit next to it, but it's a cosy surprise after the chill of outdoors and I finally stop shivering.

Though we're the only customers, they inform us that they have everything on their extensive menu. I choose the sea bass in lemon and butter, which is delicious, while Jess plumps for the mushroom bruschetta, which, judging by her expression, is somewhat less successful.

We eat in thoughtful silence, both thinking, I reckon, about the commune, and when we've finished, we order coffees. While we wait for these I show Jess the two addresses I photographed, and she punches the first number into her phone.

'Do you want to call?' she asks. 'Or shall I?'

'I'm worried she'll just hang up on me,' I say. 'And then she'll know I'm on to her, won't she? It might make it harder to track her down. I need to think a bit more before I do that.'

'I could do it and just ask to speak to Zoe, and hang up or something.'

'You could see if she's there and then just pretend you can't hear her,' I suggest. 'Pretend it's a bad line. That might seem less suspicious.'

'OK,' Jessica says. 'I'll do that.'

The first number, corresponding to the address in Manchester, answers immediately. But when Jess asks to speak to Zoe, the Nick on the end of the line denies knowing anyone of that name. As for the French number, it repeatedly connects to a weird semi-continuous tone that neither of us has ever come across before.

'Number disconnected, but in French?' I suggest when Jess holds the handset to my ear.

'Lost in translation, whatever it is,' Jess says, with a shrug. 'Shall we send a text?'

'Saying what, though?' I ask.

'I don't know,' Jess says. 'Ask her to call you back, maybe?'

'I just . . . I don't know,' I say. 'I somehow don't think a phone call is the way. I think she'll just hang up and vanish all over again.'

'But that will happen anyway, won't it?' Jess says. 'Because Nuala is going to text her.'

'Only she doesn't know we have the address. So she's not going to know that we can find her.'

'True,' Jess says. 'So what you're saying is, we need to go and surprise her.'

'Maybe,' I say. 'Maybe we do, one day.'

'Let me look,' Jess says, turning to her phone again. 'Hang on.'

'Look for what?' I ask.

'Well, where Villeneuve-Loubet is, for a start.'

I laugh at this. 'We're not going to France,' I tell her. 'Not now.'

'It's right down south, near the coast,' she announces.

'Even more reason,' I tell her. 'It would take us all week just to get there, Jess. And the cost would be astronomical.'

'There are flights,' she says. 'Actually, the nearest airport is Nice, so there are masses of flights.'

'Jess,' I say. 'Just stop.'

186

'. . . not too expensive either,' she continues, still tapping away at her phone. 'All things considered, that's quite reasonable.'

I reach out and place my fingers over the screen of her phone. 'Please stop.'

She puts the phone down with a sigh, and then flips it over so that it's face-down. 'Am I becoming obsessive?' she asks.

'Just a bit,' I tell her gently. 'We've only got a week left, so let's just get the car back down to Gatwick and go home and relax, shall we? Let's do some fun stuff in London and have a break from chasing Zoe around. I need to think about what to do next. Or if I want to continue at all.'

'OK,' Jess says. 'I mean, she's your sister, so, OK, fine.'

The waitress brings us our coffees, and by the time she leaves the table, Jess is fiddling anew with her Samsung.

'What are you doing now?' I ask, frustratedly. I'm starting to feel like Jessica's phone is a third person taking part in our holiday. She breaks into a grin, and then turns the phone to face me so that I can see what's onscreen. The headline reads 'Nice, France', and below it is a weather forecast comprising a row of little orange sunshine icons. Next to each of these it says, Max 18, Min 7.

'Jess!' I protest. 'No. Just, no!'

'Hey, I'm just saying,' Jess laughs, putting the phone down and sliding it across the table towards me with one finger. She raises her hands in surrender, then adds, 'I mean, personally, I like snow. I have no problem with snow whatsoever. I'm merely pointing out that there are other weather systems out there, if one were to so desire.'

'If one were to so desire?' I repeat, laughing. 'Did you just say "if one were to so desire"?'

'Oh, shut up!' Jess says. 'And stop being so . . . you know! Just stop it.'

Eleven

Mandy

Even as we prepared Zoe's surprise party, we did all the usual things. We phoned around her friends to see if she had stayed with them, and we got them to call others in case someone somewhere had seen her.

The few close friends who'd been invited seemed genuinely surprised at her vanishing act and asked if the party was still happening. Her best friend, Vanessa, reassured us, insisting that Zoe would definitely turn up. 'She thinks she's getting an iPhone 4 for her birthday,' she said. 'She wouldn't miss that for nothing.'

I had no idea how Zoe had found out about the gift, but ultimately I was glad she had. At least she had an extra reason to turn up.

I called her a few times during the day, but her old Blackberry was either switched off or the battery was flat. As neither of these was particularly unusual, I honestly didn't worry too much.

The party that evening was bizarre.

Having Linda helping me set up with her girls running around our feet, and Ian in the house cooking chicken – well, that was all strange enough. But when the moment that Zoe was supposed to arrive came and went and we had to start the party without her, it all started to feel rather surreal.

Zoe's friends abandoned ship pretty early on, and once Jude understood that there was no chance we were going to give him the iPhone in Zoe's absence, he and his mate did the same.

I was left entertaining my ex-husband's new family amid a colourful decor of pointless balloons and excellent home-made birthday cake.

'Are you worried?' Linda asked me, at one point.

Ian answered on my behalf, an old habit of his that had always annoyed me. 'Of course she's not,' he said. 'Zoe's done this thousands of times.'

'I'm not sure about thousands,' I said. 'But yes, she's certainly done it before.'

And it was true. Though I could sense a fairly consequential groundswell of anger rising within me, I still hadn't felt the first twinge of fear.

The following morning, when I got up, I went straight to her bedroom. I sat on her empty bed for a few minutes staring out at the grey morning light, and then went downstairs to pop all the damned balloons.

On Sunday, there was no news, but I didn't worry overly. Even on Monday, as I headed to work, I was still feeling more fury than fear. Sure, there was a vague frisson of concern starting to take seed within me, but it wasn't until that evening, when I called her friends, that I chose to acknowledge the sensation. Zoe had not been to school that day. Still no one had heard anything from her.

On Tuesday morning, before work, I dropped into the police station. Again, because it had happened so often before, they told me not to worry. But by dusk I was scared. The completely sleep-free night that followed left me feeling panicky and febrile.

I managed to take Thursday off work and used it to visit the school, where I interviewed each of her friends. The police had, the kids informed me, asked exactly the same questions the previous day. Through Sinead, I met Zoe's once-upon-a-time boyfriend Gareth. This was something of a shock, as neither Ian, Jude nor myself had ever heard the slightest mention of his existence – I wondered what else we didn't know. But neither Gareth, nor Sinead, nor anyone else had the slightest clue as to where my daughter was hiding, and by the time I got home that evening I was frantic with worry, a horrific state in which time without news seemed to stretch, so that minutes felt like days and days felt like weeks. The worst, though, were the nights. I'd lie in bed listening to the rain and wonder if my darling daughter was sleeping under a bridge, or dying in a ditch, or being raped somewhere. I struggled to avoid thinking about the possibility that just maybe she was already dead.

◆ ◆ ◆

The following Monday morning a policewoman turned up at my workplace. She looked, and spoke, exactly like Olivia Colman.

As our offices were all open plan, I led her to the meeting room. Because all four walls were made of glass, we called it the goldfish bowl, but at least it was relatively soundproof.

I was convinced, as I entered, that she was about to tell me that my daughter was dead, so I lowered the semi-transparent blinds before turning to face her.

'We've found Zoe,' the policewoman told me. 'Your daughter's fine. That's the first thing I have to tell you.'

I doubled up at the news. I thought I was about to be sick. 'Thank God,' I breathed, as the tears streamed down my cheeks. The policewoman crossed the room to my side and gently stroked my back.

'That's the good news,' she said, once I'd recomposed myself. 'But there's some bad news as well, I'm afraid.'

'She's pregnant,' I said, unsure where that thought had popped up from.

'Not that I know of, no,' the officer replied. 'But I'm afraid I have to inform you that she doesn't want to come home.'

I frowned at this. I didn't understand what those words could possibly mean, not in the context of my daughter. 'You mean she wants to go to her father's?' I asked.

The policewoman shook her head. 'No, she's found somewhere else to live, and she seems happy and safe . . .'

'Somewhere else?' I exclaimed. 'Happy?'

'Yes, relatively speaking.'

'But she's fif— she's sixteen,' I said. 'She has to come home. I mean, I don't care if she goes to her father's, but–'

'Actually, the fact that she's sixteen is rather the crux of the matter,' the policewoman explained. 'At sixteen, as long as she's not in danger, she doesn't have to come home at all. She can live wherever she wants.'

'But she's a minor!' I said. 'That's absurd.'

She sighed then, and pulled an expression one might describe as theatrical concern. It involved sticking her lips out, furrowing her brow and tipping her head to one side. 'As a mum,' she said, 'I agree. I really do. But unfortunately, the law says that at sixteen she's reached the age of discretion. She can do just whatever she wants.'

'The age of discretion?' I repeated.

'Yes, that's the legal term.'

'Right, where is she?' I demanded. 'I'll talk to her.'

'I'm afraid that I can't give you that information,' the policewoman said.

'What do you mean, you can't give it to me?' I muttered.

'I'm not able to tell you where she's living unless she authorises me to.'

'But she's my daughter!' I said, my voice rising.

'Yes, I realise that,' the policewoman said. 'And I understand how frustrating this must be for you.'

'Frustrating?' I said. 'Frustrating! Are you out of your mind?'

'She's legally allowed to leave home,' she said again. 'I'm sorry, Mrs Fuller, but that's the law.'

'I think you need to talk to my husband – my ex-husband, her father – about this. He's a lawyer.'

'A colleague of mine is doing that right now,' she said. 'And I think you'll find that he'll confirm what I'm telling you now.'

'Ian will sort all this out,' I said. 'Because this: this is just nonsense.'

I phoned Ian as soon as she'd left, but to my horror he told me that he suspected the policewoman was right. 'I'm going to check with Giles,' he said. 'He's better on family law than I am. But I think that's correct. As long as she's not in danger, there's nothing that we can do.'

'How do we even know she's not in danger?' I asked. 'We don't know anything about her or where she's staying or who she's with or . . .'

'No,' Ian said. 'But the police say she's safe. There's a social worker on the case we can call tomorrow, and once she's spoken to Zoe maybe she'll tell us something. Just try to stay calm.'

'Calm?' I spluttered. 'Calm?!'

Whether we spoke to the social worker or the police, or to specialist legal advisers, all we ever got was more of the same. The law was the law. The age of discretion was a thing. Our daughter was fine, and she didn't want to see us.

She'd stopped going to school, had moved from Buxton and was living with a friend and his father somewhere in the north of England. That was all anyone would tell us.

I was outraged at the situation. I understood for the first time ever what it meant to be spitting mad. 'Wracked with guilt' took on a whole new meaning, too. 'Paralysed with fear', as well.

Most of the time, the combination of these three left me in such a state that I worried I might be on the verge of a mental breakdown. I could quite easily imagine myself ending up in a padded room, rocking gently.

One night, about six weeks after Zoe's vanishing act, Jude came home early. Football practice had been cancelled because of the rain, so he found me in Zoe's room, weeping into her pillow. Even the smell of my daughter was fading.

He dropped his schoolbag in the doorway and sat beside me on her bed and put one arm around my shoulders. 'She's fine, Mum,' he told me. 'Don't worry. She's fine.'

I stopped crying instantly and seized him by the shoulders. 'Do you know something?' I asked. 'You do, don't you? Tell me!'

'You're hurting me, Mum,' Jude said, and it was only then that I realised I'd been shaking him. I forced my hands to release him, raising my trembling fingers to my lips instead. 'Tell me, Jude,' I said again. 'If you know something, you have to tell me. I'm losing my mind here.'

'I don't,' he said, and my tears started to flow all over again. 'I don't know anything, Mum. But the police do. That social worker woman does. And they've all seen her and they all say that she's fine.'

'But that's not enough, Jude,' I said. 'I'm her mother.'

'I know, Mum,' he said. 'I know.'

'I just want to understand,' I told him, my voice wobbling uncontrollably. 'What did we ever do to deserve this? What did we do that was so goddamned awful?'

Jude shrugged. 'Maybe it's not us,' he said. 'Maybe it's her.'

'I don't know what that means,' I told him.

'Look, you know the way Gary's aunt's a bit mad?' Jude said. 'Or, say, that doctor on the telly. Or in *Homeland*, you know the mad one in *Homeland*?'

I wiped my eyes and looked at my son's features. 'I'm sorry, honey,' I said, 'but I'm not following.'

'Maybe Zoe's like them,' he said, nodding earnestly. 'Maybe she's mad, too. And maybe there's no point trying to work out why, because that's just the way she is.'

◆ ◆ ◆

The following weekend, while tidying Jude's room, I found two postcards under his pillow. They gave no real information about where Zoe was living or why she had left, except to say that she was fine, that he shouldn't worry, and that he mustn't show the cards to anyone else. That last request for secrecy felt like having an arrow driven through my heart.

The postmarks on both cards were from Knutsford, and as it was less than an hour's drive away, I jumped in the car immediately.

It was a drizzling April day and wandering aimlessly around the streets looking for my daughter made me feel as hopeless, I think, as I have ever felt.

I showed a photo of her to a few people in shops I imagined she might have visited, but I quickly realised that it was a pointless, soul-destroying task.

On the way home I called into the police station and asked if they could at least confirm that she was in Knutsford. I was desperate back then for even the tiniest nugget of information. I needed to be able to picture where she was and what she was doing. It seemed to me that knowing at least which town she was in would be a help.

The same woman who had come to my office appeared. She led me to a small shabby interview room.

'You know that I can't tell you where she is,' she said, pulling that same fake-concerned expression I remembered from before. 'But I will tell you that she isn't in Knutsford. Now please, go home and look after your son. And when your daughter's ready to get in touch with you again, and believe me, it always happens in the end, then she will.'

Within a few weeks I found a third card, this time hidden under Jude's mattress. In it, Zoe said that she was fine, that she was moving south, and that she hoped Jude was enjoying her iPhone 4. The postcard this time was from Birmingham.

I phoned Ian that evening to tell him the news. We discussed at some length whether I should tell Jude that I'd found them, and decided that it was better not to. We agreed to give him Zoe's birthday gift as well. It was, after all, what she seemed to want.

The cards soon became less frequent. Sometimes a few months would go by and I'd worry that Jude was hiding them elsewhere and have to search every inch of his bedroom. But then a new card would pop up under his mattress from Bristol or Brighton or Canterbury. There seemed to be no pattern to Zoe's movements, and I would imagine her roaming the country with a backpack, like some modern-day gipsy.

Sometimes the postmarks were from villages, and the temptation was too much to resist. I'd jump in the car and drive down to wherever it was. I'd show Zoe's photo to the man in the post office, or the cashier at the village shop, or a busker playing a flute near a cashpoint. But there was never even a hint of recognition, and as Zoe seemed to be constantly on the move, I soon abandoned all hope.

She was somewhere, at least – this I knew. My daughter was alive. They say you can learn to live with anything and, though I would never have thought it possible, I did get used to having a lost daughter.

What with Ian having left and then Scott, now that even my daughter had deserted me as well, I felt hollowed out. In my saddest moments I believed that it was all my fault, that I was the monster who had driven everyone away. In my better moments I simply felt numb, as if a part of me, deep inside – the feeling part – had died. But I was still functioning, still going through the motions, still getting up in the morning and going to sleep at night. And all things considered, that felt like no small victory.

When Jude was eighteen, he, too, left home. He'd been accepted by Manchester University to do a degree in computer science. He offered to find somewhere closer to avoid leaving me on my own, but I insisted that he leave, partly because I felt it was healthier for him to be away from my moping, and partly because I felt I needed the space in which to let myself collapse entirely. The effort of holding it all together had come to feel exhausting.

Once he left, I didn't fall apart after all. Yes, the house was big and empty, and yes, sometimes I was terribly lonely. But I'd trained myself to carry on, and that's what I continued to do.

With Jude away, my supply of fresh postcards dried up, so when he came home that Christmas I broached the subject for the first time. I told him that I knew about the cards, and he told me that he knew that I'd been reading them, that he'd even intended for me to find them.

I explained that I didn't need to know what she'd written – there was never any detail anyway. And I told him that I didn't want to know where they were posted from any more either. I simply asked him to tell me when they arrived, so that I'd know that my daughter was still alive. And this he did, reliably, over the years, invariably around his birthday or at Christmas.

'Zoe's fine, by the way,' he'd say. 'No news, really. Just, you know, the usual.'

'Good,' I'd tell him. 'I'm glad.'

And amazing as it will sound, this was true. I was glad. Knowing that she was alive was enough to turn a day into a good day.

◆ ◆ ◆

Jude had often said that he wanted to return to Buxton after college, and though, deep down, I didn't believe him (I suspected he was simply saying what I wanted to hear), it was a handy excuse not to move.

I also still held on to the tiniest glimmer of hope that Zoe would reappear, so I'd rebuff Ian's requests that I sell up by laying a guilt trip on him about where he expected his children to live, if and when they returned home.

Once Jude had started working in London, the status quo became harder to defend. Jude, Ian would point out, was in a relationship now. Sooner or later, he'd be getting married and wanting to buy a place of his own. I was a single woman living in a three-bedroom house worth almost half a million pounds, and if I would just think about moving somewhere smaller there would be enough money to help Jude put down a deposit.

Half-heartedly, I looked at properties. But not only was I, I think, too depressed to look properly, I'd become somehow stuck where I was. I simply couldn't imagine living anywhere else.

October came, and the day before I was due to take a holiday – a break in which I had nothing whatsoever planned – my boss called me into his office. Business was slowing down, he said, and if the whole Brexit business really happened, he expected things to get even worse. We used to do a fair bit of work for Nissan back then, and they were threatening to leave the UK entirely.

So they'd decided to rationalise the business, he explained. They were closing the Buxton office. There was a job for me in Nottingham if I wanted it, but if not, the only option was redundancy. I drove home in a bit of a daze.

I parked the car outside and looked up at the house I'd lived in for so long, the house where I'd brought up my children – the house I'd planned to spend the next two weeks moping around in. It looked particularly dark and lifeless that day – almost threatening.

I climbed from the car and let myself in. Around me the house was silent.

The strangest feeling came over me. At first it was the tiniest flutter, like a little flame flickering deep within my chest. I frowned at the sensation as I started to wander around the house, going from room to room, suddenly seeing the house objectively, seeing it as a series of cool, uninhabited rooms made of bricks and plaster and wood.

The flame in my bosom grew, and soon it was strong enough that I could identify it. What I was feeling was a sense of relief, for my boss had unwittingly provided an escape route. It felt like a revelation, because up until that point, I'd never even understood that I was trapped.

I went to the kitchen and pulled a ready meal from the freezer and threw it in the microwave. I smiled vaguely, I think, as I watched it spinning behind the glass. And then, as I tipped it on to a plate, I remember the feeling washing over me in a wave, and I gasped. Something had snapped and something else was beginning. I felt unexpectedly submerged in joy.

I was going to Nottingham. I knew it as if I had always known it. I was going to leave Ian and his podgy yoga-teacher wife and her pretty polite girls and their ultra-cute toddler behind. I'd no longer have to pretend to not see the signposts to Bakewell as I drove around town, so I'd finally be able to forget about Scott. I was going to empty Zoe's room so that some other little girl could live in it, and that meant that I'd stop waiting for her to forgive me for god-knows-what and come home, as well. I was leaving the whole sorry weight of it behind me, and not because I was running from it, but because a new chapter had begun elsewhere.

I opened my laptop and, fork in hand, started looking for apartments in Nottingham. I couldn't even wait until I'd eaten to get on with it all.

Twelve

Jude

We're on the M1 heading for London and I am having one of my panic attacks.

We've been driving for seven hours, which is why Jessica has taken the wheel. I'm supposed to be sleeping, but I'm way too stressed to even think about it. In fact, I can barely breathe.

Jessica checks the mirror and changes lanes. She's an excellent driver, as luck would have it. Ironically, this is part of the problem. Because Jessica, bloody Jessica, is just so damned good at everything. It crossed my mind about an hour ago, just after we swapped seats, that she's faultless. And if she's faultless, how will I ever find a reason to break up with her?

This is madness, of course; I can see that. I mean, every guy hopes to meet a girl who's sexy, clever and well balanced, right? So why does this feel like a trap?

She glances over at me now and smiles. 'You're not sleeping?' she asks.

I shake my head.

We pass a sign that says, 'London 50', and I think about cancelling the trip and just going home instead.

Because, yes, I have let Jess convince me to fly to Nice this evening. She's found an apartment to rent and we've booked expensive last-minute flights from Gatwick.

It's just that eight hours is a long drive. And eight hours is a long time to think about the fact that I'm in a relationship with no visible way out, on a holiday that I don't seem to be in control of.

I'm doing my best to work through this on my own, honestly I am. Because I can see just how idiotic I'm being, even as I fail to stop myself. So I'm doing everything I can to spare Jess this latest bout of Jude's silliness.

I've reminded myself that I'm a free man and that I have chosen to come away with Jess. I've reminded myself that we've been getting on brilliantly, and having loads of really good sex.

But, for the moment at least, it's just not working. I'm struggling to breathe, and there's no sensible reason why.

'You've gone quiet,' Jess says. 'Is something wrong?'

'No, I'm just thinking,' I say – a lie.

'Is it Zoe?' Jess asks. 'Is it getting to you? Is this all a really shitty idea?'

'Maybe,' I say. 'I'm not sure.'

'So something is wrong,' Jess says, glancing at me repeatedly despite the traffic. 'We don't have to look for her if you don't want to,' she continues. 'We can just go to the beach or something. I mean, it would seem a bit of a waste after all this whizzing around not to go and find her, but it's got to be up to you in the end. I can't imagine how all of this feels to you.'

'It's not Zoe,' I say, my tone of voice conveying far more irritation than I intended.

'Oh,' Jess says. 'Is it me?'

I sigh and look out of the side window. We're overtaking a livestock lorry. Pig snouts are peeping through the bars. Luckily, Jess hasn't spotted it. She always gets upset about stuff like that.

'So it is me,' Jess says. 'Am I getting on your nerves? Because, like, I know I talk too much sometimes. And we have been together a lot and everything. I wouldn't blame you.'

'You're not getting on my nerves. It's just me being me.'

'Ah,' Jess says. 'You're not panicky again, are you? You're not feeling trapped?'

I shrug. 'Something like that,' I say.

We drive on in silence for almost ten minutes before Jess speaks again.

'Would you rather I didn't come?' she asks. 'Would you rather just drop me off? I mean, we could do that instead of picking up my passport, you know.'

I think about this for a moment and it does make me feel less panicky. Then again, when I picture myself in Nice on my own, the idea strikes me as thoroughly miserable.

'I'm sorry, Jess,' I say. 'I don't know. It's really not your fault. But I don't know.'

'God,' Jess says. 'OK. Wow!'

'And now you're pissed off with me,' I say.

'I just paid two hundred and thirty quid for a flight,' she says. 'So, yeah, I'm a tad pissed off.'

'I'm not saying you shouldn't come. I'm not saying you can't.'

'Oh, well, thanks,' she says.

'I just don't know,' I tell her, my voice breaking a little. 'I'm having a bit of trouble breathing. I think I might be having a panic attack.'

'It's hard,' Jess says. 'To help you, I mean. Because I'm, you know, involved. I need to avoid taking it personally, but that's not easy.'

'I know. I'm sorry.'

Jess sighs deeply and then we drive on in silence for a few more minutes.

'Do you want The Speech?' she finally asks.

'The Speech?'

'Yeah. The Speech. It might help. Then again, it might just annoy you.'

'Try it,' I say. 'I like your speeches.'

'OK, so you're free,' she says. 'You know that, right?'

'Yes, I'm aware that I'm free,' I say flatly.

'We're not married. We're not tied together by any kind of contract. And you don't have to take me to Nice with you, or take me anywhere with you, ever again, in fact.'

'I'm not . . .'

'Don't interrupt The Speech,' Jess says.

'No, sorry.'

'I like being with you. I like your company. You make me laugh. And most of the time I think you're interesting and fun to be with. Actually, and I know you're not comfortable with this word, but actually, I love you. I do. But you know there are people on this planet I love or have loved who I don't see any more, right? So it's not obligatory that we continue to hang out. Loving you doesn't give me any rights, and I know that.'

'OK,' I say, doubtfully.

'So instead of getting into a blind panic, just decide if you want to fly to Nice with me this evening, or if you don't. If you don't, it would be . . . classy, let's say . . . if you reimbursed me for the flight. But we're just two human beings here. Two human beings with free will. And we can decide we want to bump along together for a bit more, for a day or a week or a year, or whatever. Or we can decide that we don't want to do that.

'Unfortunately, in these things, the "no"s kind of have it. So while we'd both need to decide to continue, only one of us needs to decide that it ends. But that's just the way life is.'

'Right,' I say. 'That's a good speech and I—'

'What I'm saying, I suppose,' Jess says, interrupting me, 'is that, well, I already said it, you're free. We can choose different paths at any moment. So we can go to Nice and split up when we get back. Or you can drop me off now and never see me again. Or we can, you know, continue to bump along together. I know which one I want, but if we don't agree, that doesn't count for anything. So it's up to you. Speech over.'

'Thanks,' I say. 'That's . . . helpful.' And it's true. I'm feeling a little less trapped. Because I'm not trapped here at all, am I? No, I'm really not.

'So?' she asks me, ten minutes later. 'I don't mean to pressure you, honey, but some feedback would be good. I kind of need to know if I'm being dropped off or nipping indoors for my passport. We're almost there.'

'Passport,' I say. It's strange, because the word just pops out without me thinking, as if it's come from some deeper place, somewhere that's before, or maybe beyond thought. Like a reflex, perhaps.

'Passport,' Jess repeats. 'You're sure?'

'Totally,' I tell her, managing to smile for the first time in four hours. 'I'm also totally sure that I'm crazy.'

'Yeah,' Jess says. 'Yeah, I worked that bit out for myself.'

The pilot says that Paris can be seen from the right-hand-side windows, but unfortunately I'm on the left, trapped beside a sleeping Jessica and the seven-foot guy crammed into the aisle seat.

Jessica's head is resting on my shoulder. We're both utterly exhausted after what has to have been one of the longest, most tiring days I can remember. But we made it. Somehow, we made it from Scotland to Gatwick, via London.

A surge of warmth washes over me as I think about Jessica. She's amazing. She really is. The way she stays 'up' and enthusiastic about everything . . . The way she remains calm in the face of adversity – the way she copes with my damned moods. I honestly don't know how she does it. I'm one incredibly lucky guy.

It has not gone unnoticed that my emotions are all over the place. And how is that possible? How can I swing from being desperate to escape her presence to this warm feeling of respect and desire? I suppose that there's a word that englobes respect and desire, and that word is probably 'love'. Perhaps it's time that I managed to say it.

But then wouldn't that imply some kind of commitment? And if so, is that the reason it's so hard for me to say it?

I think about Mum saying it to Scott. It used to make me feel embarrassed, the way she said it all the time. And look where that got her. I bet she feels really stupid about it now.

The drinks trolley arrives, whereupon Jess wakes up. We order beers to wash down our rather dry WHSmith's sandwiches and, by the time the wrappers have been cleared away, we're descending towards Nice, the lights of the coast sparkling beyond the windows.

'You OK?' Jess asks, as they dim the cabin lights for landing.

'I am!' I tell her. 'I'm fine!'

'Good,' she says. 'I'm glad.'

'I'm really sorry about before,' I tell her. 'I don't know what's wrong with me.'

'I think I do,' Jess says.

'You do?'

'Well, you lost your dad and your new dad and then your sister, and all in the space of, what? A few years? Maybe that was more traumatic than you like to think.'

◆ ◆ ◆

By the time we find the correct street within the maze that is the old town, it's almost eleven o'clock. We wander up and down trying to find number twenty-two, but the numbers seem to jump from eighteen straight to twenty-six. It's incredibly frustrating.

'I'm just so tired,' Jess moans. 'I'm so tired that, if we don't find it soon, I might cry.'

'I know,' I say. 'It's a nightmare.'

We ask for help in a Portuguese restaurant. The waiter, who thankfully speaks English, is busy stacking tables.

'This is twenty-four,' he tells us. He leads us back out to the middle of the street and points. 'So I think it has got to be this one.'

The ground floor is taken up by an ice-cream vendor and I wonder who on earth buys ice cream on a cold January night.

It's then that I see it, half-hidden behind the chill cabinet: a tiny, half-width door. There's no house number above it, but there is a numerical key pad, so I cross and type in the code we were given. To our relief the little door opens, revealing the steepest staircase I have ever seen.

On the third floor, Jess types the second code we were given, and we're in.

We dump our bags on the orange sofa, and while I open the window and peer out at the street below, Jess heads through to the bedroom. 'Oh, shit!' she says.

I cross the lounge and join her in the doorway. 'Something wrong?' I ask.

'The be-ed's no-ot ma-ade,' she says, her voice wobbling with fake trauma.

'They've left sheets, though,' I say, lifting the pile from the chest of drawers. 'Look.'

'I know,' Jess whines. 'But I'm so-oh tired, Jude, I could die. I might actually be dying right now. I might die before I get the quilt cover on.'

'Would you like me to make the bed, sweetheart?' I ask, grinning. 'Is that it?'

'Oh, would you?' Jess asks, as if the thought had never occurred to her. 'Oh, that would be amazing, Jude.'

'Of course,' I tell her, even though struggling with quilt covers is one of my least favourite things. 'Go and sit down.'

'No, I'm showering,' Jess says. 'But if you could have that bed made by the time I get out, then I promise I'll love you for ever.'

The next morning, I wake up to the chiming of a distant church bell. Jess is still sleeping beside me, so I lie there for a moment slowly isolating all the different sounds. A seagull is squawking somewhere and I can hear a market trader shrieking like a fishwife, but can't hear what she's saying. It actually takes me a few seconds to realise that this is because she's shrieking in French – I'd actually forgotten that we've changed countries here. There's a regular whizzing, grinding noise coming from somewhere, too, plus a baseline hubbub of voices drifting from the street below.

So as not to wake Jessica, I lever myself gently from the bed, then pad through to the lounge. Sunlight is leaking through the slatted wooden shutters, casting patterns across the floor, and when I open the windows and shutters to lean out, an irresistible whiff of coffee hits my nostrils.

I lean on the window ledge and watch French shoppers as they negotiate the narrow street. I spot the coffee shop two doors up, and understand that the whizzing noise is almost certainly their coffee grinder. I see the queue for the butcher's shuffle one forward, and watch a man with a huge bunch of flowers trying to make his way through the queue.

A hand caresses my shoulder, making me jump. I turn to see Jess smiling sleepily at me. '*Bonjour!*' she says. 'This is nice.' She leans beside me and looks out.

'I was just wondering when it stopped being like this back home,' I say. 'You know, the butcher, the florist's, the coffee shop . . . When did everything end up in Tesco's?'

'The butcher, the baker, the candlestick-maker,' Jess says, through a yawn.

'Exactly.'

'There are still places like this,' Jess says. 'Notting Hill's a bit like this on a summer's day. So's Camden. But they tend to be the expensive hipster areas, not your average town centre. God, is that coffee I can smell?'

'There's a shop there,' I say, pointing. 'They grind it. Actually, it smells like they roast it, too.'

Jess leans out further and turns her face skyward. 'Blue sky!' she says. 'Look at that!'

'Do you want me to go and buy coffee?' I ask. 'There's instant in the cupboard, but I think I fancy some proper stuff. Or do you want to go out and get brekky?'

'Would you mind?' Jess asks. 'It's just that I'm not really capable of doing anything until I've had caffeine.'

'Sure,' I say, straightening. 'I'll just nip . . .'

'Stop!' Jess says, turning from the window now to face me and raising one hand. 'I've changed my mind. I want coffee in the sunshine. I want to be waited on by a waiter in a white shirt and a waistcoat. Plus, they'll have croissants, won't they? Proper French croissants.'

◆ ◆ ◆

We drink blow-your-head-off espressos and eat rich, buttery croissants in a café in nearby Place Garibaldi. The waiter is wearing a hoodie, but other than that, Jess declares that it's perfect.

We order a second round of coffees and while we're waiting for them to arrive – and for some reason, they take quite a while – we watch the Sunday-morning crowds going about their business: people leaving Monoprix weighed down with carrier bags, others nibbling the end of a baguette as they return from the bakery.

Though the air temperature in the shade is still in single figures, here, in the sunshine, it's gorgeous.

'People must be happier here, don't you think?' Jess says.

'Than where?'

'Than at home,' she says. 'I mean, just visualise your average Sunday here. Get up. Have coffee and croissants in the sunshine with friends. Wander down to the beach. It's got to be better than Tesco's, Starbucks and the Underground, right? That's got to make people feel happier.'

'It should do,' I say. 'But according to a thing I read last week, the happiest place in the world is Denmark.'

'Denmark?' Jess says, wrinkling her nose. 'But it's cold there.'

I nod. 'Even colder than at home.'

'They've got Danish pastries, I suppose,' Jess says. 'That probably helps.'

'And beer,' I say. 'Carlsberg is Danish, so . . .'

'Beer and pastries,' Jess says. 'Hmm, I still think I'd be happier here.'

◆ ◆ ◆

After breakfast, we meander through the pedestrian streets of the old town. The buildings are all painted in reds and ochres with green or blue shutters. To my eye, the town looks more Italian than

French, and after fiddling on her phone, Jess informs me that the town was Italian, more or less, until 1860.

'What do you mean, more or less?' I ask her.

'It's complicated,' she says. 'Something about Piedmont. You'll have to look it up yourself if you want a proper answer.'

We pass a fish market where I discover that the voice I could hear from our apartment *was* that of a fishwife, and then at the other side of the old town we discover a huge vegetable market as well. On reaching the famous Promenade des Anglais, we cross the road and descend to the beach, where we skim pebbles on the surface of the outrageously turquoise-coloured sea. Afterwards, we stumble across the pebbles for ten minutes before propping ourselves up in the sunshine against a wall.

'It's so warm,' Jess says. 'I can't believe it.'

'I'm actually too hot,' I agree, wriggling out of my jacket.

'So what next, Sherlock?' Jess asks me.

'Sherlock?' I repeat. 'Yesterday I was Bond.'

'Well, if we're looking for Zoe . . .' Jess says, 'Sherlock might be more efficient. Or Holmes. Are we still going to look for her?'

'I suppose so,' I say. 'We need to work out how to get there and everything. She's actually in a different town, isn't she? But we've got four more nights here, so we don't have to do anything today if we don't want to.'

'No,' Jess says. 'No, we can just hang out in the sunshine if you want.'

'I'm a bit knackered,' I admit. 'I could do with a day to just chill.'

'That sounds good to me,' Jess says. 'This was a good idea, wasn't it?'

'It was,' I agree, closing my eyes to the warmth of the sunshine. 'I'm going to be skint for months to pay for it all, but at least I'll be skint with a suntan.'

'I did offer to pay for your flight,' Jess reminds me.

'I'm joking, Jess,' I say, sliding one arm around her shoulder. 'But seriously? Yes, definitely. It was the best idea you've ever had.'

◆　◆　◆

We spend a relaxed day exploring Nice, and I have to say I end up liking the place. It's a pretty, well-kept town, peppered with parks and fountains and cute cafés. The seafront, which is stunning, is omnipresent, and what with the unexpectedly warm sunshine – it feels almost like a British summer day – I quickly come to feel like I'm on a proper holiday.

At lunchtime, with an eye on our spending, we buy sandwiches and cans of drink, which we consume on the beach. The pebbles are pretty uncomfortable, plus, they leave white chalk stains on our clothes; but the sun, hitting us both from the sky and, indirectly, from the surface of the sea, feels gorgeous, and as we sit, and then lie there side by side, I can sense all the January tension in my muscles dissipate.

By four-thirty, we're back in our apartment feeling sleepy.

Leaving Jess zapping through French TV channels, I head to the bathroom. The sight of my reflection in the bathroom mirror provokes a sharp intake of breath, because in the space of a few hours I have dramatically changed colour.

I wash my face in cold water, which actually seems to make the redness deepen, and then step back out into the lounge. I almost ask Jessica if she, too, gets darker in the sunshine, but I think better of it. The answer is almost certainly yes, plus, it's probably something I should know without asking. 'I think I need to buy sunscreen,' I say instead.

Jess, who's stretched out on the sofa watching a game show, says, 'Yeah, I was thinking the same thing,' which kind of answers my unspoken question.

'I'm turning into a lobster,' I say, as I lift her legs and slide in beside her on the sofa.

She glances sideways at me and says, 'God! You are! I didn't notice before. You definitely need some sunblock, otherwise tomorrow you're going to end up in A&E.'

'Not sure about A&E,' I say. 'But, yeah.'

'Not a problem I have,' she says, returning her attention to the TV screen. 'But it's still really bad for my skin.'

'Tomorrow,' I say. 'We can pick some up tomorrow morn—'

'Shhh!' Jess says, raising a finger to silence me.

'Why? You don't speak French, do you?' I ask.

'No,' she says. 'Of course I don't. Which is why I need to concentrate!'

That evening, we walk back to the seafront before heading west towards the port. We stop in a tiny brasserie and drink surprisingly expensive beers, then wander on past the super-yachts and fishing boats and on round to the far side of the port.

One of the restaurants is advertising *Moules frites à volonté*, which Jess excitedly informs me means 'mussels and chips, as much as you can eat'.

I'm surprised by her excitement because, as far as I know, mussels and vegans don't mix. But Jess explains to me, at rather more length than I really need, how various philosophers and biologists have considered the issue and how, because mussels have no brain and because, as far as anyone can tell, they don't have any capacity for pain either, they're considered the highest life form one can ethically eat.

'Wow!' I say when she finally finishes. 'Who knew?'

Whatever the biological reasoning, her eagerness suits me just fine. I love mussels and chips and discover that I like all-you-can-eat mussels in Roquefort sauce even more.

While we wait for our dessert – profiteroles for me and a not-entirely-vegan tarte Tatin for Jess – I research Zoe's supposed address. It quickly becomes apparent that while there is a regular bus service from Nice to Villeneuve-Loubet, the bus goes nowhere near where Zoe lives. The directions given by Google Maps end with the salutary phrase: 'Walk four miles to destination.'

Jess points out that, as with past attempts at finding Zoe, we may well get redirected on further, and as the idea of trying to pursue her via little-understood French public transport seems worse than the effort of renting a car, this is what we decide to do.

So the next morning, after another leisurely breakfast of coffee and croissants in what is already becoming 'our' bar, we ask our waiter, *Monsieur* hoodie, for advice.

He directs us to a nearby agency at the port, but when we get there the cheapest deal on offer is a shocking ninety-five euros per day for a Renault Clio. Jess is eager for us to take it, but I convince her to wait.

We descend to the dockside and, our legs dangling over the edge, I hunt on a comparison site for a cheaper deal. This turns out to be one of my better ideas, because I manage to book an identical Renault Clio for two days for the exact same price that we were going to pay for one. It's not until I've finished the booking process that I realise that I've actually booked it from the same agency we've just visited.

An hour later, feeling rather embarrassed, and also feeling some embarrassment about the fact that I'm embarrassed – what Jess would no doubt call suffering over my suffering – I return to the agency and sheepishly give the same clerk our booking reference. Whether he doesn't remember us, which seems unlikely, or whether he simply pretends not to remember us in order to save everyone embarrassment, I'm grateful for his discretion.

'He'll probably say you scratched it when you bring it back so he can charge you a thousand euros,' Jessica says, once we're seated in the car. 'Serve you right as well, you tight-arse,' she adds with a giggle.

As I turn the key to start the engine, I exhale sharply through pursed lips, an expression of the stress I'm feeling.

'You OK?' Jess asks as she buckles her seatbelt.

'Yep. I've never driven a left-hand drive before, that's all,' I explain. 'I just tried to reach for the handbrake in the seat pocket.'

'I've driven one,' Jess informs me proudly. 'I drove almost a thousand ks in Spain a few summers ago. D'you want to swap seats?'

I sigh with relief. 'Yeah,' I say. 'Yeah, actually, that would be great. If you're sure?'

The route, dictated by Mister Google, takes us through town then along the broad palm-tree-lined Promenade des Anglais and on, out of town on the *autoroute*. Jess takes it all in her stride, from the frantic traffic in the town centre to going the wrong way around roundabouts, to negotiating the *péage* on the motorway. I'm pretty awestruck by how capable and relaxed she is about it all, chatting happily as she drives. 'Now, this is where we should have rented an open-top,' she tells me. 'I wonder how much extra it would have been?'

'I'm guessing a bit more than a fiver,' I say.

Half an hour later, and with less than a minute to go until we reach our final destination, we find ourselves in the middle of a long stretch of A-road cutting through dense woodlands, and for a moment I fear it's going to be a repeat of Scotland – that Google has led us to the middle of nowhere. But then Jess nods at a roadside hoarding and says, 'Le Sourire. It's a bloody campsite, Jude!'

'Shit,' I comment. 'That's not good.'

'Why not?' Jess asks.

'Well, if it's a campsite, she's almost certainly moved on by now.'

'Not necessarily,' Jess says, pointing. 'They have mobile homes. Maybe she lives in one of those.'

I turn to look at the multiple rows of identical mobile homes we're driving past, partly hidden behind a row of trees. 'What do they call them in the States again?' I say. 'The people who live in mobile homes?'

'Trailer trash?' Jessica says.

'Yeah, that's it.'

'God, you're so judgemental!' she laughs.

'I'm not,' I say. 'I was only joking. Plus, you said it, not me.'

'Well, I know where I'd rather be,' Jess says. 'Bristol Filwood or the south of France. Let me see . . .' She indicates, swings into the wide driveway of Camping Le Sourire, then pulls to a halt on the crunchy gravel of the deserted visitors' car park.

The sky is still deepest blue but it's considerably cooler here, away from the coast, and as we step out of the car and walk towards the campsite office, I shiver.

The office is closed and locked up, so we venture further into the campsite. It's pretty quiet, which I suppose is no surprise. We are in January, after all.

We amble past empty, scrubby camping spaces and locked-up mobile homes until we see the first signs of life: two small children playing unaccompanied in a kids' area. We start to head towards them but I spot an elderly man walking his aged poodle in the distance, along the river's edge, so we divert towards him instead.

'*Bonjour*,' Jessica says as we approach. '*Parlez-vous anglais?*'

The man glances at us and, after replying with a simple shake of the head, he returns his attention to his dog.

'*Habla español*, maybe?' Jessica asks, smiling hopefully.

'*Non, français*,' the man replies.

'*Le* owner?' I attempt, in what I'm certain must be abysmal Franglais. '*De camping?*'

The man confirms my fears by pulling a horrific grimace. One would think, from his expression, that I have farted rather than attempted, albeit pitifully, to communicate with him.

'*Où est le proprietario?*' Jessica asks, tentatively. To me, as an aside, she says, 'That's what "owner" is in Spanish, anyway.'

The man shrugs and urges his dog onwards, and I grasp that it's not that he doesn't understand; he just doesn't want to talk to us.

'Come on,' Jess says, pulling at my sleeve. 'Let's see if the kids are more responsive.'

We return to the play area to find that the boy has vanished. Only the little girl remains, sitting on a swing, kicking forlornly at the gravel.

'*Bonjour,*' Jess says, crouching down in front of her.

The girl, who must be about seven, replies in machine-gun-speed French. All I catch is the word *frère*. From her expression, I gather her brother isn't her favourite person right now.

Jess shoots me a sideways grimace. 'God, they speak so fast. I didn't catch a word of that,' she says.

'Perhaps she's speaking a foreign language?' I offer, sarcastically.

'Yeah,' Jess says. 'Thanks for that.'

'*Vous êtes anglais?*' the little girl asks.

'*Oui, anglais,*' Jess says.

'Hello,' she says, in almost perfect English. 'How are you?'

Jess laughs. 'I'm fine, thank you,' she says. 'Can you tell me where your mummy is? Or your daddy?'

The little girl pulls a face and shrugs. Her grasp of our language clearly ends at 'How are you?'

'Mama?' Jessica says. 'Papa?'

The little girl points at one of the mobile homes in the distance. '*À la maison,*' she says.

'*Merci!*' Jessica tells her, straightening. '*Au revoir.*'

But as we begin to walk away, the little girl jumps up and runs to Jessica's side. She takes her hand and walks along beside us until we reach her trailer, where she shouts, '*Maman? Maman!*'

A woman in her thirties with long, lank hair and unfashionable oversized glasses appears in the doorway. '*Oui?*' she says, then, 'Oh!'

The same boy as before now shoots out past his mother's legs, shrieking. He chases his sister, who runs off around the corner, out of sight.

'*Bonjour?*' the woman asks, sounding cautious.

'*Bonjour,*' Jessica says, flashing her broadest smile. '*Parlez-vous anglais?*'

'*Un peu,*' the woman says. 'Not so good. I . . . forget.' She waves over her shoulder to indicate that she hasn't used it for a long time.

'We're looking for the owner,' Jess says. '*Le proprietario?* Of the campsite?'

'*Le proprio?*' the woman says. '*Il n'est pas là.* 'E is not 'ere.'

'Um . . . later perhaps?' Jess says. '*Plus tardes?*'

The woman shakes her head. 'Is winter,' she says. 'Camping is closed.' She pronounces closed 'clo-zed'.

'We're actually looking for Zoe Fuller,' I explain, speaking slowly in the hope she'll understand. 'Do you know her? Does she live here?'

'Or Nick?' Jessica offers in response to the woman's blank expression. 'Zoe's partner, Nick.'

At this her features light up. 'Ahh !' she says. '*Nick et Zoé! Oui, bien sûr.*'

My stomach lurches at this development. My heart rate speeds up noticeably.

She points over at the rows of mobile homes in the distance. '*Numéro vingt-six ou vingt-sept, je crois.* Tweenty-seex or tweenty-sefan.'

'They're here?' I ask. 'Really?'

'*Non, pas maintenant*,' the woman says, speaking slowly.

'Sorry, they're not here?' I say, feeling nauseous.

'*Ils sont au travail*,' she says.

'Oh, they're at work?' Jessica translates.

'Yes, yes,' she says. 'Work. Zoe 'ere at eighteen. Nick maybe eighteen, eighteen and a 'alf.'

'Six, six-thirty,' Jess says. 'Right. And, um, do you know where she works? *Où Zoe travaille?* Is it near here?'

'Not near, no,' the woman says. 'Is a shop making sandwich. In Sophia Antipolis.'

'A sandwich shop, sorry, where?' Jess says. 'Sophie . . .?'

'So-phi-a An-ti-po-lis,' the woman repeats. 'It's town. Maybe ten kilometre from 'ere.'

'And the name of the shop?' Jess asks. 'Do you know that?'

'I'm sorry,' the woman replies. 'I don't understand.'

'*Le nom*,' Jessica says, eliciting another frown.

'Snackway?' I offer. 'McDonalds? Burger King? Um, Prêt à Manger?'

'Ahh, OK,' the woman says. 'Sorry, no. I don't know this. It's not such a big one, I think. Not a . . . *chaîne* . . . Small shop maybe.'

'Right,' I say. 'Got it! Thank you.'

'Best is come back eighteen and a 'alf.'

We thank her for her help then wave goodbye and return to the car.

'So what now, Sherlock?' Jess asks. 'Come back at eighteen and a half, or go looking for Sofia Loren?'

I shrug and pull my phone out. 'Let's see if I can find any sandwich shops,' I say. My voice must have come out a little brittle because Jess puts one hand on my thigh and asks if I'm OK.

I nod and swallow with difficulty. 'I'm just a bit . . . you know . . .' I say.

'Nervous?' Jess asks.

'Um, no,' I say. I find myself unexpectedly struggling against tears. 'It's just, well . . . She's not dead, is she?'

'No,' Jess says, softly. 'No, she really isn't.'

◆ ◆ ◆

Sophia Antipolis is only twenty minutes away and as we have no other real plans for the day, we decide that we might as well visit the three sandwich shops listed by Google. The drive takes us further north, past pretty villages and around the edges of a massive golf course before heading back south once again.

Sophia Antipolis, it transpires, is a massive science park set in rolling hills and woodlands. It's laid out around a seemingly endless series of roundabouts which are so closely packed that half the time the GPS doesn't have time to react between one roundabout and the next; so on a couple of occasions we end up taking the wrong exit and have to double back.

Eventually we arrive in Place Joseph Bermond, a modern reimagining of a village centre, where the first of the shops is listed. It's a weekday lunchtime and we're bang in the middle of a science park, so finding a parking space turns out to be impossible.

After a few laps past the Purple Sandwicherie, Jess pulls into a loading bay. 'Go check it out,' she says. 'If she's there, I'll look for somewhere to park.'

As I walk the fifty yards back to the shop, I try to imagine finding Zoe behind the counter. Having not seen her for seven years, I struggle to imagine her face and even wonder if I'd still recognise her. Above all, I wonder what I might say. Beyond, 'Hi, Zoe,' my mind's a blank.

Le Purple occupies a small shop front with a chill cabinet and seating for twelve on the pavement outside. There are two people working behind the counter; they look like man and wife. I pretend to look at the contents of the chill cabinet before smiling and walking away.

Next door and opposite are large brasseries and, though I peer in just in case, I'm really not getting my hopes up. The woman in the campsite had been pretty specific, after all. Zoe works in a sandwich shop, she had said, not a brasserie.

As I walk back to the car, I see another tiny shop advertising sandwiches, partly hidden behind some trees. This one wasn't listed by Google and, when I reach it, it's the only customer-free commerce in sight. The sandwiches in the window look a few days old, and the owner, a middle-aged woman, glares at me in a most unwelcoming manner as I peer in through the window. Between the wilted sandwiches and her stare, I can understand why the place is empty. I wonder if she's aware that she's about to go bust, and why.

The two remaining addresses are a short drive away in another part of the science park called Garbejaire. It feels a little less swish than the rest of the area; in fact, most of the buildings look like social housing. But again, built on the model of a Mediterranean village and with tree-lined streets and squares, the result is far from unpleasant.

We park up in a side street and, tilting my phone this way and that as we follow directions, quickly manage to find Snack People. Inside, two men are busy assembling sandwiches for a queue of young people that stretches right out the door. Rap music is playing and both the employees are grooving in time with the music as they serve.

We walk the streets for about ten minutes as we try to find Sandwich & Co., but in the end we conclude that it has closed and been turned into either a mobile-phone shop or a poodle parlour, forcing me to admit defeat.

'I guess we'll just have to wait till six-thirty,' I tell Jess as we start to retrace our steps to the car.

'It certainly looks that way,' she says. 'Though I was thinking we should try to be early. We don't want that woman spoiling the surprise by telling her we're in town, do we?'

'No, we don't,' I agree. 'Especially as Zoe would probably vanish if she knew.'

'Do you really think she would?' Jess asks.

I'm just about to answer when Jess stops walking and points down a side road. 'Look,' she says. 'There's a Snackway, too.'

'Are you hungry?' I ask. 'I am.'

'Not for Snackway,' Jess says, dismissively. 'But we should check, shouldn't we? Just in case.'

'Their tuna wrap is pretty nice, actually,' I tell her. 'Plus, I can understand their menu. And they have a vegan option, which, frankly, I don't think you'll find anywhere else around here.'

'They do?'

'They do.'

'OK, Snackway it is,' Jess says. 'Let's just give some of our hard-earned cash to another immense American corporation.'

The side road opens on to another tree-lined square. It's filled with tables and chairs, and the hubbub produced by the large crowd of almost exclusively student-aged diners resonates off the buildings, intensifying the noise level massively.

Inside Snackway, we place our orders with one of three sandwich guys and shuffle towards the cashier. Because I'm watching our guy like a hawk to make sure he's understood that he mustn't put *fromage* in Jessica's sandwich, and because the cashier is wearing the obligatory Snackway baseball cap, I don't see her face immediately.

But when it's our turn and she looks up at Jess, I freeze, my mouth open. Sweat prickles on my brow, and I feel weird and floaty and feverish. Tears start to press at the back of my eyeballs, making them feel like they're bulging with the pressure. A huge lump forms in my throat, making it impossible to swallow.

Jess, oblivious, attempts to pay with her credit card, but there's some problem with it, so she asks me if I can pay instead. I'm semi-paralysed, but I take a gulp of air and somehow manage to tremblingly fumble in my pocket for my wallet and then in my wallet for my debit card.

'Are you OK?' Jess asks, as I hand my card to the girl. 'Are you shaking? You look really pale.'

It's only on hearing us speak English that the cashier finally looks right at me.

'Zoe,' I croak, tears already running down my cheeks. 'Hi!'

Zoe glances from Jessica's face to my own, her expression rapidly shifting through a whole range of emotions before settling into something approximating shock.

She opens her mouth to speak once or twice, but then closes it again. Finally she thinks to study the credit card in her hand and, by the time she returns her gaze to me, I can see that she knows she's not mistaken. 'Jude!' she says, shaking her head gently. 'What the fuck . . . ?'

I nod slowly and attempt to smile, but I'm pretty sure my expression is all mixed up. A tear slithers down the side of my nose.

'You're all grown up,' she says.

I nod again and shrug.

Jess, who apparently has been holding her breath, now lets it out in a sharp exhalation. 'Shit, it's really you?' she asks Zoe, then to me, 'We really found her?'

Zoe looks blankly at Jess and then turns back to me.

'Um-um,' I confirm, unable to string together a meaningful sentence.

'*S'il vous plaît?*' the guy behind me says, leaning forward to catch Zoe's eye. He's clearly in a hurry to pay.

Zoe glances at him only briefly, then raises one hand and says, '*Une minute!*' before addressing me again. 'How . . . why . . . ?' she mumbles. 'I mean, what are you even doing here, Jude?'

'Um . . . kind of . . . looking for you, I imagine,' I say, vaguely.

Zoe nods. 'Right. Sure. Of course,' she says. 'We got a message from Nick's mum, actually . . . But I didn't think you'd turn up here. I mean . . . shit, Jude!'

'*S'il vous plaît!*' the man says again, impatiently.

'*Oui, allez! On y va!*' someone else calls out.

'I'm sorry,' Zoe tells me. 'I really have to . . .' she gestures at those queuing behind me.

'Of course,' I say.

'Maybe we should just take a seat and wait for a lull?' Jessica suggests. 'You seem to have your hands pretty full.'

Zoe nods rapidly. 'Yeah. That'd be good. I'll, um . . . come over as soon as I can.'

She hands me my card back without having debited it, but when I question this she says, 'No, it's done.' I'm unsure if she's confused or giving us a sneaky free meal, but I don't insist.

'Are you OK?' Jessica asks me once we're seated at the only available table, on the far side of the restaurant. 'How are you feeling?'

'No idea,' I tell her, honestly. 'Ask me later, OK?'

'Sure,' Jess says, patting my hand compassionately. 'Of course.'

I glance repeatedly at Zoe as I eat my tuna wrap in silence. I just can't stop myself from looking her way. Partly I'm checking that she hasn't sneaked off, and partly that she's really there, that this is real. It's just so strange seeing her again, seeing her as an adult, seeing her working . . . It's so hard to believe that my sister is truly there, just a few feet away. It makes me feel weird and numb, a bit like I'm in a daydream I can't quite snap out of.

It takes half an hour for the queue to dwindle, half an hour during which I alternate between studying my sister behind the till and staring blankly out at the street. Jess, for her part, catches up with emails on her phone.

When Zoe eventually manages to join us, she dumps her own lunch on the table and says, 'This is mad! I can't believe that you're here, Jude.'

'I know,' I say. 'It's so weird.'

Zoe is looking at Jessica inquisitively, so I introduce them.

Zoe nods at Jess and waves vaguely and says, 'Hi, Jess.' Then, 'And you're Jude's . . . friend, or . . .'

'Girlfriend,' Jess explains. 'Your brother struggles with words like "girlfriend" or "partner", or even "love", in fact, so . . .'

'Sorry,' I say. 'Should I have specified? I didn't mean to be vague.'

'Must be a family trait,' Zoe interrupts. 'I'm not too good with that stuff either.' She takes a bite of her sandwich, which I note is the same as the one Jessica chose. It crosses my mind that a Vegan Deelite is probably the closest thing to a Quorn sandwich Snackway have to offer. Some things, it seems, never change. Zoe, I now notice, has at least put on some weight.

'So how long are you here?' Zoe asks, speaking through crumbs. 'Because I'm not gonna be able to take more than ten minutes right now. Can I see you afterwards? Where are you staying?'

'Do you actually want to see me afterwards?' I ask her.

Zoe raises one eyebrow. 'Well, yeah,' she says. 'I'm hardly going to send you packing, am I, bro? Not after you've come all this way.'

I manage to laugh a little at this, despite my desire to cry. 'Well, good,' I say. 'I'm glad.'

Once we've explained that we have two more nights before we fly home and that we're staying in Nice, we arrange to meet Zoe back at the campsite.

As Zoe returns behind the counter and begins to help clean up after the midday rush, I dump our wrappers in the bin and, after one last glance at my long-lost sister, join Jess outside in the sunshine.

'Well, we found her,' Jessica says. 'That's amazing.'

'Do you think I should tell Mum?' I ask. 'I'm feeling like I should probably phone her. I've been lying to her for years, pretending that I'm still getting postcards. But this time it would be true. I could honestly say that she's fine.'

Jess takes my hand and gives it a squeeze. 'Maybe later,' she says. 'Talk to your sister first. See how she feels about it, maybe?'

I chew my bottom lip and nod. 'I suppose.'

'If you've been telling her Zoe's fine, it's not as if she thinks she's dead or anything, anyway.'

'No, I guess not,' I admit.

'So what now?' Jess asks. 'We've got over three hours to kill.'

I pause and look back at the shop. 'She won't vanish, will she? You don't think she'll just run off again?'

'No!' Jess says, definitively. 'No, she can't, can she? She's at work until six, and then she goes home to where all her stuff is, to where her boyfriend is, apparently. And by the time she gets there, we'll be waiting. So I really can't see any way she could vanish, even if she wanted to.'

I nod and try to take a normal breath, but it's hard. 'That makes sense,' I say. 'It's just . . . well, it's Zoe. You don't know her.'

'That's true,' Jess says. 'But I really think that you'll be fine. And I think she wants to see you. But what now? What do you want to do in the meantime?'

'I've really no idea, Jess,' I tell her honestly. 'I feel really . . . strange. A bit floaty . . . Can you just decide? 'Cause I really don't care what we do.'

'Sure,' Jess says. 'Happy to. So there's a little village we went past, and I was thinking . . .'

Thirteen

Jude

We return to the campsite just after five-thirty. We've spent a pleasant enough afternoon wandering around a nearby village called Valbonne, but I'd struggle to specify anything that we've seen, or even relate any conversation that Jess and I have had. I've been obsessively thinking about Zoe all afternoon, compulsively running potential snippets of conversation through my mind.

Though our day in the sunshine has been nice, it's shockingly cold at the campsite. It's nestled at the bottom of a valley, so the sun has long since vanished behind the hills and an eerie mist is drifting up from the river and swirling around the mobile homes.

I take my jacket off and add a pullover before slipping it back on. Stupidly, I have left my overcoat in the apartment. I hadn't expected to be needing it.

While we wait we walk once around the perimeter, but then, driven by the cold, which is especially intense near the river, we're forced back to the car, where we run the engine just long enough to warm ourselves back up again.

At five past six a little pink scooter comes through the entrance. The rider beeps twice on the puny horn and waves at us before revving up and continuing into the campsite.

'Your sister's a biker,' Jess comments.

'She must be bloody frozen.'

We lock the car and follow in the direction the woman indicated this morning until we spot Zoe's scooter parked up beside one of the cabins. The door opens as we approach and Zoe beckons us in. 'Come inside!' she says. 'It's freezing out there.'

The cabin is basic but warm. Considering that this is where Zoe lives, it's also surprisingly clean. The state of her bedroom had always been something of a standing joke growing up.

When I comment on this, Zoe says, 'Oh, that's not me. That's thanks to Nick. I'm still as messy as ever.'

She makes us mugs of tea and then, somewhat frustratingly, asks Jess how she and I met. Frustrating because I'd much rather be talking about Zoe.

Just as Jess is finishing her hyper-detailed chronology, the door opens and a woman steps in. She must be a very good friend of Zoe's, because without a word of invitation she pulls a fold-out chair from behind the refrigerator and joins us around the tiny dining table.

'Hello!' she says, shaking our hands. 'A family get-together. I wasn't expecting that when I got up this morning. So, what's happening?'

Jess and I glance at each other confusedly and then back at the woman and then at Zoe.

'Oh,' Zoe says. 'Sorry. This is Nick.'

'Oh . . . you're Nick,' I say. 'Sorry, I was . . . never mind.'

'Expecting a guy, perhaps?' Nick asks, sounding amused.

'Not at all,' I say. 'I . . . um, wasn't expecting anything in particular.'

'It's Nicola, actually,' she tells us. 'But everyone calls me Nick, so . . .'

'Sorry, but . . . just to get this clear,' Jessica says. 'You're Zoe's friend, or her partner?'

'Both, I hope,' Nick laughs, shooting Zoe a glare.

'I should have told them,' Zoe tells her. Then, addressing us, she continues, 'Sorry, I should have warned you.'

'Warned?' Nick says. 'Why, is there a problem here?'

'No,' Zoe says. 'Don't be like that. You know what I mean.'

'Is it a problem for you?' Nick asks, looking between me and Jessica.

We both shake our heads in reply. 'Not a problem at all,' I tell her. 'Just a surprise. But then my sister's always full of surprises.'

'She is,' Nick says, reaching out to stroke Zoe's back. 'That's why I love her so much.'

We sit in embarrassed silence for a few seconds before Jess comes to the rescue. 'So, Zoe,' she asks, using her social-worker voice again. 'Did you say something about Nick's mum phoning you?'

Zoe nods. 'She emailed us, actually. The phone's out of credit, so . . .'

'I bought a top-up card today,' Nick tells her, as an aside. 'I just haven't done it yet.'

'Good,' Zoe says. 'Thanks.'

'So the woman we met in the commune, Nuala . . .'

'She's my mum,' Nick confirms.

'Oh,' Jess says. 'I didn't realise. But now you say it, you do look a bit alike.'

'Yeah, people always say that,' Nick says.

'I can't believe you went to Siochain House!' Zoe says. 'What was it like? Who did you see?'

'It was cold,' I say. 'It was really cold. And we saw, um, Gunter, and Nuala, of course. No one else, really. There were two women outside as well, but we didn't really speak to them.'

228

'There was that guy reading a book,' Jess adds. 'Darren?'

'Dillon?' Nick suggests.

'Yeah, that's it.'

'What did you think of the place?'

'It was nice,' Jessica says, presumably being polite.

'Nice?' Zoe repeats, disdainfully. 'Really?'

'Zoe hated it,' Nick explains. 'I'm not that keen these days, if I'm honest. But I grew up there so I have a different relationship with the place.'

'You grew up there?' Jessica says.

'I didn't hate it,' Zoe tells Nick. 'They hated me.'

'They did not,' she replies. 'They may have hated how little housework you did. But they didn't hate you.'

'They did,' Zoe tells me, nodding to reinforce the point. 'But Nick's right. I wasn't into it at all.'

'It's changed a lot,' Nick says. 'When I was a kid it was great fun. There were loads of people living there, maybe thirty or forty adults. And what with the whole free-love thing in the seventies and early eighties, there were quite a few kids there, too.'

This is this first indication I've had of Nick's age. With her short hair and boyish features, she's got one of those faces that makes it impossible to guess. She could be anything between thirty and fifty years old. If Nick was conceived in the late seventies or early eighties, I guess it must be more like forty.

'A few of us didn't know who our dads were, which was challenging, I suppose,' she continues. 'But it was parties for the adults and treehouses and teepees for the kids. I had an amazing childhood there, despite it all being a bit weird from an outside perspective. But of course, that's all pretty much gone now.'

'Nick wanted to move back there,' Zoe explains. 'But it didn't work out. Which is my fault, of course.'

'Not entirely,' Nick says. 'I think my memories were a bit rose-tinted. As a kid, it's all running around and campfires, yeah? But for the adults, I think the whole self-sufficiency thing was pretty hard going. Plus, it's dying, really. It's almost dead, actually. A group of us moved back to try to . . . to try to rejuvenate it, I suppose you'd say. But it didn't really work. The oldies are all set in their ways. No one wanted to change anything to accommodate us. And of course, Zoe didn't fit in at all.'

'So you came here instead,' Jess says.

'Yes, why here?' I ask. 'Why France?'

'Well, I'm a teacher,' Nick says. 'I saw a job advertised at Berlitz in Sophia. And we thought, *Why not?*, didn't we? We both fancied a bit of a change. And some sunshine!'

'You teach in French, then, or . . . ?'

'I teach English,' Nick says. 'To French people, mainly.'

'She's teaching me French, too,' Zoe says. 'She's a brilliant teacher.'

'And you?' Nick asks now, addressing both of us. 'How did you end up here?'

'Well, they came looking for me, didn't they?' Zoe tells her, speaking in that same tone of adolescent disdain I remember from when we were younger.

Nick doesn't flinch. 'Yes, I got that,' she says. 'I mean, how? How did you find us? Mum didn't give you the address, did she?'

'Oh, no. No, she was very careful not to do that,' I say.

'So how?' Nick asks.

'It's, um, a bit embarrassing,' I tell her, gritting my teeth.

'Go on,' Nick urges.

So I explain how I looked in her mother's computer, at which Nick laughs, and then Jess and I spend a few minutes retracing our adventure backwards.

'Wow,' Nick says, once we've finished. 'So, Buxton, Blackpool, Portpatrick . . .'

'Morecambe, too,' Zoe adds.

'Morecambe,' Nick repeats, 'and then here?'

'Via Gatwick and Nice,' I say. 'It's been quite a trip.'

'Sounds it.'

'It's been fun,' Jessica says. 'We've had a great time, haven't we?'

'And all to track down Zoe, here,' Nick says. 'You must have really wanted to find her.'

We all turn to look at Zoe now, which is bad timing. Her eyes are glistening with emotion. 'I'm sorry, Jude,' she says. 'I didn't mean to be so hard to find. It's just . . .'

Nick raises one eyebrow and laughs out loud at this. 'Oh, she did,' she tells us. 'She definitely meant to be this hard to find. But well done. You managed to track her down anyway.'

We chat for about an hour, the conversation flowing relatively easily. We talk about our jobs, first Jessica's and mine, and then Nick's TEFL post at Berlitz. Finally Zoe explains that she'd already worked for Snackway in Blackpool, which enabled her to get the job here, even though her French isn't great. 'Back home, it was one of those shitty zero-hours contracts,' she explains. 'But thankfully they don't allow those in France, so here I actually know what hours I'm going to be working and get paid for them.'

They explain to us how they had driven down in Nick's old camper van, but how the engine had failed one day as Nick drove home from work.

'We were living in a tent, really,' Nick says. 'We were just using the van for transport.'

'But it was full of all our stuff,' Zoe explains, 'so we had to empty it when it broke down. It ended up being scrapped.'

'Poor Victor/Wictoria,' Nick says. 'That's what I called it, by the way. Victor/Wictoria, the VW Van.'

'The owner here offered us this place for the winter and we jumped at the chance,' Zoe says. 'It's really cheap. The only downside is that we have to move out before June. They rent them out to tourists and what-have-you over the summer. So we'll probably look for a proper flat or something by then.'

'If we can save up the deposit,' Nick says.

'Yeah. Neither of us are brilliant with money, are we?' Zoe says, looking at her partner with amused complicity.

Just chatting like this is fine, I suppose. Nick seems nice enough, and Zoe is about as relaxed as I've ever seen her. But I'm also finding the whole thing frustrating. Because with Jessica and Nick present, there's some kind of invisible barrier to getting down to the nitty-gritty. It's as if there's an unspoken agreement to avoid anything intimate, or difficult, or important.

Zoe, for instance, hasn't once asked me about Mum or Dad. And with the ether filled with shallow chit-chat, the space in which I might address the elephant in the room – namely why Zoe ran away in the first place – seems entirely absent. We're stuck in a groove of frenetic banalities and there's no way I can think of to change the record.

By seven-thirty, I'm feeling unexpectedly tired. Something about chatting about one thing while simultaneously imagining what I'd like to be saying is wearing me down. I'm also starting to feel quite hungry, and there's been absolutely no suggestion of food.

'So, tomorrow,' Nick says, after a brief silence. 'Has Zoe spoken to you about tomorrow?'

'Um, no,' I say, wondering when Zoe spoke to Nick about tomorrow. They had clearly hatched a plan before we even arrived.

'OK, well, I'm off in the morning,' Nick says. 'And Zoe's off in the afternoon. So if you fancy it, we could show you around, but it'll have to be separately. We'd have to take it in turns.'

I glance at Zoe, who shrugs and smiles thinly, and from this I somehow work out that this is all Nick's idea, and from this I further deduce that Nick is the one who decides stuff in this relationship. It's amazing how much you can pick up from a glance and a shrug sometimes.

'Sure,' Jess is saying. 'That would be great, wouldn't it?' She glances at me for confirmation.

'Yeah,' I say. 'Yes, that sounds good.'

'That's settled then,' Nick says, standing. 'So, here? Tomorrow? About ten o'clock?'

'Um, great,' I say, making to stand myself.

Jessica is looking between us questioningly. After a moment of confusion she grasps that we're being kicked out. 'Oh!' she says, standing. 'Oh, of course. Yes!'

Seated in the icy car outside a couple of minutes later, she says, 'You know, I kept waiting for them to say something about dinner. I thought they were going to invite us to stay for food, didn't you? But not even a crisp. I feel quite light-headed.'

'Well, food was always complicated for Zoe,' I say. 'Plus, they're broke, apparently. So maybe they didn't have anything in.'

'Oh, I know that,' Jess says. 'But I thought they would suggest a restaurant or something. Then suddenly we were talking about tomorrow.'

'It was a bit unexpected, wasn't it?' I say. 'But in a way it suits me better.'

'It does?'

I nod. 'It was quite . . . intense, I guess you'd say. I'm kind of ready for a break.'

'Oh, right,' Jess says. 'I feel like that, too, but I was thinking that it was just me.'

'No, it was hard work,' I tell her.

233

'Shall we just stop at the first place we come to?' Jess asks. 'I'm starving.'

'They may not have anything vegan,' I point out.

'I don't care,' Jess says. 'I'm dying here.'

We start to head back towards Nice, but when we come to a pizzeria, Jessica pulls into the car park.

'Pizza?' I say. 'Really?' I have never seen Jess eat a pizza yet.

'I'm that hungry . . .' she says. 'Anyway, I'm sure I can ask for it *sans fromage*.'

The restaurant is a basic roadside place. The interior is tiny, but they've added a vast heated tent outside and it's here that we take our seats. Around us the place buzzes with the hubbub of multiple slightly drunk conversations.

'So have you worked out how you're feeling?' Jess asks, once we've ordered and our drinks have arrived.

'I knew you were going to ask that,' I say, smiling weakly.

'And?'

'Hmm,' I say, sipping my beer. 'It's complicated. I mean, I'm happy, of course. Because she's alive and well. And she really does seem well, doesn't she? So yeah, that's good news.'

'I'm sensing there's a "but"?'

'Yeah . . . I don't know. It's also like she's a stranger, really. She's not the Zoe I know, or . . . thought I knew. I mean, I had no idea she was gay, for example. Her living in France seems . . . out of character, I suppose. Plus, I still don't get why she left, you know? And that's kind of the start of the whole story that brings her to where she is now. And none of it makes much sense to me.'

Jess nods thoughtfully and sips her rosé.

'This will sound weird, but I guess I'm struggling to feel like she's my sister,' I say, attempting to work it out in my mind. 'It was all a bit superficial, yeah? So, it feels like I've been chatting to a stranger, almost. And that's always kind of hard work, isn't it?'

'Maybe tomorrow will be different,' Jess says. 'If you see her without Nick being there, maybe you can talk with more intimacy. Actually, perhaps I should stay back in Nice. You might get more of a feel for each other that way.'

I shake my head. 'I don't think so,' I tell her. 'I think I want you there.' I think about how strange those words sound coming from my lips and ask myself if I really mean it. But it's true. For some reason, I can't even imagine doing tomorrow without Jess at my side.

'OK. But if you do need some space . . .'

'If I need you to take a walk around the block, then I'll say, OK?'

Our pizzas arrive at that moment, a Végane for Jess and a Quatre Saisons for me.

'God, they're humungous,' Jess comments, and indeed our two pizzas are so large that they overlap at the middle of the table.

'Good,' I say, salivating as I reach for my cutlery. 'I'm starving.'

Due to the fact that both Jess and I wake up feeling particularly horny the next morning, we're late getting back to the campsite.

We find Nick waiting for us in the car park, sitting on a wall in the sunshine, smoking.

Jess pulls up and parks so that I'm right next to where Nick is sitting. I wind down my window and say, 'Hi.'

'What time do you call this?' Nick asks, tapping the glass of her watch with a fingernail. 'We said ten!' I'm unsure whether she's joking or actually telling me off.

'I'm sorry,' I say, earnestly. 'We left a bit late and then the traffic was bad, too.' This last bit about traffic is entirely untrue.

'It's fine,' Nick says, stubbing her cigarette out and standing. 'I wanted to take you for a walk somewhere pretty, that's all. But I think it's a bit late for that now.'

Jess leans over me and peers up at her. 'Hi, Nick,' she says. 'I'm sorry about that. I would have really liked a walk, too.'

Nick twists her mouth. 'Oh, fuck it,' she says, moving towards the rear of the car and opening the door to climb in. 'Let's do it anyway.'

Once Nick's aboard, she directs us to drive inland.

'So where d'you eat, last night?' she asks, leaning forward so that her head appears between our shoulders. 'Anywhere nice?'

'A pizzeria just back the other way,' I say, twisting in my seat to address her.

'L'Authentique?' she asks.

'Yes!' I say. 'How'd you know?'

Nick taps the side of her head. 'Psychic,' she says, and though this has to be a joke, again she sounds totally serious as she says it. 'Good pizzas there, huh?'

'Yeah, really good,' Jessica says. 'They even had a vegan one for me.'

'I would have suggested we all go there together,' Nick says, 'but Zoe's weird about eating with other people. I guess you already know that, Jude.'

I tip my head from side to side. 'More or less,' I say. 'Food was never a simple thing as far as Zoe was concerned.'

'She ate with us in Snackway,' Jess points out.

'Yes, she's OK as long as it's something she's happy to eat. And she's fine with their veggie baguette thing. But she can't stand restaurants where she has to choose something different. People always end up trying to get her to try new things because they just don't get it, and that drives her crazy.'

Nick directs us to a small village fifteen minutes away. It's called Pont du Loup, which she explains means Wolf Bridge, the Loup – 'Wolf' – being the name of the river.

The village itself isn't that special, comprising just a few shops on either side of a fairly busy main road. But it's set at the bottom of a gorge, and the grey cliffs rising either side are dramatic and beautiful. A series of stone pillars rises out of the valley, the remains of the famous bridge, now defunct.

Leaving the Renault in a small car park, we follow Nick along a footpath down to the river and then on up into the gorge, where the path tapers to a simple hiking track.

The river is the same crazy turquoise colour as the sea in Nice and when I comment on this, Nick explains that the sea is this colour precisely because these rivers release their waters into the bay. 'It's flecks of silica from these rocks,' she tells us. 'The rain washes tiny particles into the river, and they reflect the light, making the water look turquoise.'

'It's beautiful,' Jessica says. 'It's almost fluorescent.'

As the path follows the river up into the hills it rises in places, leading us into woodlands, and then drops back down to meet the rapids again. It soon becomes so narrow that we have to walk in single file, Jessica out in front, then Nick, then me.

'So, Nick,' I ask, as we walk, almost shouting so that she can hear me. 'How come Zoe moved around so much?'

'Did she?' she says. 'I know she was in Bristol with some guy before Morecambe, but . . .'

'Yeah, she used to send me postcards from all over the place,' I tell her. 'Knutsford and Canterbury . . . Brighton . . .'

'Hailsham,' Jess adds.

'Yeah, Hailsham, too. Loads of little villages.'

'Oh, she knew this van driver,' Nick says. 'I think she used to get him to send them.'

'Oh, right,' I say. 'Any idea why?'

'So you wouldn't know where she was living, I imagine.'

'Yeah, but why didn't she want me to know?'

'Ah, you'd have to ask Zoe about that,' Nick says.

'Right,' I reply, pulling a face at her back. 'I just thought you might know, that's all.'

'Are these hills part of the Alps?' Jess asks, clearly trying to calm things down a little. I guess I am being a little over-eager in my information-gathering attempts.

'Yep,' Nick says.

'Amazing.'

'And have you noticed all the layers?' Nick asks. 'Look.' She points to a rise of rock to our left, where layers of sediment, presumably once horizontal, have been pushed up until they're almost vertical. The rain has then worn away the softer layers, leaving strata of rock sticking up. They look a bit like the fossilised ribs of some vast dinosaur.

'It's pretty,' Jess says. 'Do you walk here a lot?'

'Not often,' Nick says. 'There are so many great walks around here. Zoe hates walking, of course. But I often go for a hike on Saturday morning, while she's working.'

'So, was Zoe dating guys before you met her?' I ask.

I regret my clumsy question even before Nick replies. She looks back at me and shoots me a lazy smile. 'You can quiz Zoe all afternoon,' she says. 'For now, let's just enjoy the nature, shall we?'

I sigh silently and drop back a little, feeling half-embarrassed at my lack of tact, but also a bit peeved. Because, yes, the walk is pleasant and, yes, the surroundings are stunning. But that really isn't why I'm here. The reason I've travelled hundreds of miles over the last ten days is to find out more about my sister, and I only have a few hours in which to do so.

The path opens out a little, so Nick and Jess end up walking side by side while I'm forced to trail behind them. They chat easily about the weather and driving in France, and about whether Nick and Zoe think they'll move back home one day. Slowly but surely, Jess manages to guide the conversation towards the things she knows I'm dying to find out more about. She's clearly much better at this than I am.

'So can I ask you a personal question?' she asks Nick, about half an hour into the walk. 'It's just something I've always wondered about being gay.'

'God, you're not going to ask what we do in bed, are you?' Nick asks.

'No!' Jess laughs. 'Don't be daft!'

'People do,' Nick says. 'You'd be surprised.'

'Oh, I can imagine,' Jess tells her. 'But no. No, the thing I always wonder is how you meet people, if you're gay. I mean, there's the internet and everything, isn't there. But if you're at work or whatever, well, it's delicate, isn't it? Because you can never really tell.'

'Yeah, I know what you mean,' Nick says. 'Sometimes it's complicated.'

'So, say, for you and Zoe. How could you tell? Because I'd never guess that either of you were gay. Or is gaydar a real thing?'

'I don't think so, really,' Nick says. 'But the pub I met Zoe in was a gay one. So that was a bit of a giveaway.'

'Ah, right,' Jess says. 'Thank God for gay pubs, then. Are there lots of them, even in little towns like Morecambe?'

Nick laughs. 'Not one!' she says. 'No, we met in Blackpool. And there's only one shitty pub there.'

'Blackpool scared me a bit,' Jess confides. 'We got hassled on the seafront. Some racist idiot started making monkey noises.'

'I'm not surprised,' Nick says. 'It's rough. Personally, I'd never live in Blackpool. Even Zoe couldn't stomach it for long, and let's face it, not much fazes Zoe.'

'I think it's funny that she ended up in catering,' Jess says. 'I mean, what with all her food issues. It seems a strange choice.'

'Just the luck of the draw, I think,' Nick tells her. 'A guy she met fixed her up with the Snackway stint. She'd already worked in a chippy, too, I believe.'

'Yes, in Bristol,' Jess says. 'We went there. Horrible, horrible chips. In the roughest part of Bristol. Zoe certainly chose some strange places to live. Before here, I mean. Because it's gorgeous here, isn't it? I'd love to live somewhere like this.'

We're reaching the narrowest part of the gorge now, and the noise of the river cascading against the rocks is deafening; so I'm unable, for about five minutes, to hear their conversation. Frustratingly, by the time the valley opens out again, Jess is telling Nick about our lives instead.

It's just after one when we get back to the car, so we offer to buy Nick lunch in a café somewhere. She declines, telling us that she's 'out of time'. She also informs us that Zoe is bringing sandwiches home for us all, so instead we return to the campsite, where Nick climbs into a beaten-up Renault van and, telling us that Zoe will be home 'pretty soon', she waves and starts the engine.

As she pulls out on to the main road, leaving a cloud of diesel fumes lingering in the air, I realise that I'm not sure if we're even going to see her again. Perhaps we should have said our goodbyes in a more definitive way.

But Jess tells me that we're eating with her this evening. 'She said she'd be back around six.'

We sit on the wall in the sunshine, and while we wait for Zoe to return, Jess fills me in on the other bits of conversation I missed out on: namely that Zoe's moves to Bristol and Blackpool and Morecambe had all been related to different men she'd been dating.

'So she's flexi, then, is she?' I ask, frowning in confusion. I've only just got my head around the fact that she's gay.

'I don't know,' Jess says. 'But I'm guessing that she must be.'

◆ ◆ ◆

Zoe arrives just after two, a plastic Snackway carrier bag hanging from the handlebars of her little scooter. When we reach the cabin, she is in the process of moving three chairs to the middle of the access road that runs through the middle of the campsite. The cabins are so closely packed, I realise, that the winter sun can't penetrate between them.

'It's a bit public,' Zoe says, as she unfolds a small camp table, 'but at least it's in the sun. Plus, there's hardly anyone here at the moment anyway.'

She tips the contents of the Snackway bag on to the table, and it's an exact repeat of what Jess and I ordered yesterday: a tuna wrap and a vegan baguette with a Coke and an orange juice. I'm quite touched that she has remembered. She was always so self-centred back in the day that this simple attention to our tastes is quite surprising. I suppose even the Zoes of this world get to grow up.

'You're not eating?' Jess asks.

'I ate at work,' Zoe says. 'I was hungry.'

'You're quite early,' I point out. 'Weren't they busy?'

'Oh, queuing out the door, like every day,' Zoe says. 'But Jacques, my boss, he's quite cool. I told him it was exceptional circumstances. *Circonstances exceptionnelles.*'

'And they're nice?' Jess asks. 'You like working there?'

'Snackway?' Zoe says, laughing. 'No, they're slave-drivers. And everyone's on minimum wage. But it's, you know, a job. At least until we've got a flat sorted out, and until Nick gets more hours at Berlitz . . . well, we need the money. Actually, there's a risk that Berlitz will lay her off completely, so that's a worry, too.'

'I like Nick,' Jessica tells her. 'She's really easy to get on with, isn't she?'

Zoe shrugs. 'More famed for being direct than "easy", but, yeah, she's OK. She's fine.'

'Is she your first girlfriend?' Jess asks. 'Or . . .'

Zoe blushes visibly at this, causing Jess to apologise before she's even had a chance to answer.

'No, it's fine,' Zoe says in the end. 'I just . . . Um, yes. The answer is yes.'

I open my mouth to ask Zoe when she first realised she was gay, but then hesitate between trying to demonstrate that I'm cool with it and avoiding making her uncomfortable.

'I dated guys before, so . . .' Zoe says, partly answering my unspoken question. 'I'm not a militant lesbian or anything. Not like Nick.'

'You're not?' Jess says. 'Oh, right.'

'It's just the person, yeah? You fall in love with a person, not a gender. And I fell for Nick.'

'Sure,' Jess says, smiling reassuringly. 'Of course.'

'Anyway, it didn't really work too well with guys,' Zoe adds. 'This seems to suit me better, for now.'

'Was it a guy when you left?' I ask her. 'I mean, did you meet someone? Was that where you went?'

It's the subtlest way of edging the conversation in the direction I want it to go that I've been able to come up with. But my angst has leaked into my voice so that it hasn't ended up sounding casual at all.

Zoe shoots me an inquisitive glance. She looks scared, momentarily, like a tiny cornered rodent, but I shoot her my best smile and she relaxes a little. 'It was the delivery guy,' she says. 'You know about that, right?'

'The delivery guy?'

Zoe nods. 'The QuickParcel guy. The one who brought all the stuff Mum used to order online.'

'Really?' I say.

'Don't you remember him? Blond guy. Really cute. Massively gelled-up hair. I'm sure I told you I liked him . . . Anyway, I used to go round the corner and smoke joints with him in his van.'

'You did?'

Zoe rolls her eyes and glances at Jessica. 'Boys,' she says. 'They notice nothing.'

'Um, Mum didn't spot that one either,' I point out.

'No, well, I made sure of that,' Zoe says.

'And that's where you went when you left home?'

Zoe nods. 'Well, to his dad's place in Macclesfield. But he creeped me out – his dad, that is. I think he wanted a bit of . . . you know . . . the action. So we went to Dwayne's mum's place instead. That was all the way down in Bristol.'

'Ah, so that's how you ended up going to Bristol,' Jess says. 'We did wonder.'

'It was rubbish,' Zoe tells us. 'His mum lives in the middle of this housing estate. There's nothing to do there at all. I was bored stiff. And it didn't work out with Dwayne either. He was pretty pissed off with me about his dad, as if that was my fault . . . He hated his new job as well. He ended up working for some local courier company and they were pretty horrible to him, so he was angry about that, too. So in the end, I left.'

'We went there,' I tell Zoe. 'We met Dwayne's mum. She said she liked you.'

'Yeah, she was OK,' Zoe says.

'And then we went to a horrible place in Princess Anne Road or something.'

'Queen Ann Road? You went there?' Zoe says. 'Oh, God . . .'

'Pre-tt-y horrible,' I tell her.

Zoe nods. 'I know,' she says. 'But I was going through a bad patch. I got into smack, actually, if you must know. But I didn't stay there long, and I'm off it all now, thanks to Nick. So . . .'

We sit in silence for a moment as we continue to eat our sandwiches. Zoe looks lost in her memories, while I'm trying to slot this new data into my previously sketchy understanding of events. But though this explains where she went, it of course doesn't explain why she left. And it certainly doesn't explain her absolute avoidance of any contact with any of us ever since. I try to find a clever way to ask the question indirectly, and eventually decide to pursue the Morecambe connection.

'So, why Blackpool, Zoe?' I ask. 'Why Morecambe?'

'They were just, you know, things that happened,' Zoe says.

'Things that happened?'

'Yeah, you know . . . This guy I met in Bristol was driving to Blackpool,' she tells me. 'I wanted to get away, so I got a lift. He was kinda cute, so . . . I mean, I thought I liked him at first. But then he tried to jump me at the motorway services and that was the end of that. But anyway . . .'

'And Morecambe?'

'Oh, some bloke offered me a cleaning job up there,' Zoe says. 'I needed the money and it came with accommodation. They never paid me what they owed me in the end. But it was OK. It was a friendly house. I was sharing with this gay guy called Paul. He actually took me out in Blackpool, which is where I met Nick. And the rest, as they say, is history.'

'And that's the only reason you went to Morecambe?' I ask.

Zoe shrugs. 'Well, yeah,' she says. 'I needed the job.'

I sigh at the dead end we have reached, and glance at Jess, who I know can see what I'm trying to do. She raises one eyebrow at me almost imperceptibly.

'Mum's fine, by the way,' I say, attempting a different tack. I'm tempted to add a sarcastic, 'Not that you've asked,' to my phrase, but I just about manage to restrain myself.

'I know,' Zoe says, shocking me once again. 'She's moving to Nottingham, right? Selling the house and everything.'

My mouth, still full of tuna wrap, falls open at this. I cover it quickly with my hand. 'How can you possibly know that?' I ask, once I've swallowed.

'Sinead told me,' Zoe says. 'She gives me occasional updates on you all.'

'Sinead?'

'Yeah, my friend from school. Don't you remember her? Redhead, curls . . . You fancied her when you were about eight.'

'Did I?' I ask, frowning. I honestly have no recollection of Sinead.

'Anyway, her mum ended up working with our mum. So she finds out stuff and tells me.'

'And Sinead's mum is . . .?'

'Cynthia,' Zoe says. 'Cynthia Hubert. I'm not sure if you know her. We never saw her much, back then. But Mum got to know her when she was at Publicis. And then they sort of kept in touch.'

I bite my bottom lip and exhale sharply. Because for all these years, I've been telling myself that my sister didn't give a damn about any of us. And that belief, I'm only now realising, really hurt me. 'And me?' I ask her. 'Did she tell you stuff about me as well?'

Zoe laughs. 'Of course,' she says. 'You're living in London. You did a degree in electronics and got some top-notch result in your exams.'

'Computer science,' I correct her.

'Same thing,' Zoe says, dismissively. 'I know about Dad marrying that yoga bimbo, too. And having a kid and calling the poor fucker Terra.'

'Linda's hardly a bimbo,' I say. 'And that poor fucker Terra is our half-brother.'

'If you say so,' Zoe says. 'She used to drive me crazy with all her crystals and meditation and shit, though.'

I catch Jessica's eye again and I can see that she's willing me on. She wants me to be brave and ask the question: *Why, Zoe?* But I can't seem to find a way to get there. Or perhaps I'm too scared of what her answer will be.

'Shall I go for a walk?' Jess asks. 'Maybe I should give you two some space?'

I wonder if it would be easier if she did, or whether that would actually make things even harder. She's so good at getting people to talk, after all. She's so much better at all this than I am.

But before I can decide, let alone answer, Zoe has replied for me. 'No! You're fine,' she says, definitively. 'She should stay, shouldn't she?'

I guess from the panic in her voice that Zoe's afraid to be alone with me; she's afraid of where the conversation might go. She's perhaps afraid of how angry I might get as well.

It dawns on me that this is what I'm afraid of, too. I understand only now why the question is so hard. I'm afraid of my own anger. Of course I am.

'Yes, stay, Jess,' I tell her. 'You should definitely stay.'

'It's just, I don't really see why,' Jess says. 'I'm sure you two have private things you need to talk about, don't you?'

'I'd far rather talk about you than me,' Zoe says, and I think, *Yeah, I bet you would.* 'You're a social worker, you said, right?' she prompts.

So Jess ends up telling Zoe all about her job, a tale which includes a lengthy description of the famous Baby P case of 2007. I feel frustrated by the length of the detour, but also strangely relieved that we've managed to avoid talking about our family for a little longer.

Eventually, having explained that though she obviously wasn't working in Haringey in 2007, the ricochets of the Baby P case have changed just about everything in child protection, Jess winds up her strange monologue.

'Shall we go for a walk or something?' Zoe says, and from the fact that she asks it in the split second following the end of Jessica's story, I can tell that she's been thinking about her next move even while Jess was still talking. She's been deciding how to continue to fill that oh-so-dangerous void without getting personal. 'Because if we are, we should probably make a move before the weather turns.'

'The weather?' Jess says.

'Yeah, it's going to rain, apparently.'

'The weather forecast said sunshine all week,' Jess says. 'In Nice, at any rate.'

'Oh, Nice has, like, its own special climate. Sometimes we have storms here and in Nice it's boiling.'

'Oh,' Jess says. 'Right.'

Even though clouds do seem to be building further inland, the temperature on the coast is a full eight degrees warmer than on the campsite. The sun is shining and it's positively balmy, making it hard to imagine that it might rain.

Directed by Zoe, we have driven to a long strip of pebble beach, sandwiched between the road and railway tracks on one side and the turquoise waters of the Med on the other. Because of the train tracks

247

it's one of the few areas on the coast that hasn't been built up, and this gives it an entirely different feel to the rest of the Côte d'Azur.

'This is the barbecue beach,' Zoe tells us as we lock the car up and head to the water's edge. 'In summer this is wall-to-wall people cooking food and picnicking. It's really good fun. People play music and dance and all sorts.'

'That does sound cool,' I say.

'Nick's not so keen,' Zoe says. 'She says it's the ugliest beach in the area. But I kind of like it because it's a bit shabby.'

'I like it, too,' Jess says, picking up a smooth pebble and chucking it across the beach to the sea. 'It's cinematographic, somehow. I think it's the light. It's like a scene from an American road movie or something.'

'Like a scene from our road trip movie,' I say.

'Yeah,' Jess says, shooting me a smile. 'Yeah, I guess it is.'

We walk the length of the beach, past fishermen and dog-walkers, pausing to take photos of the snow-capped Alps in the distance and to skim stones across the waves.

Behind us, back towards Zoe's place, dark clouds are swelling; but for now at least, we're still blessed with blue sky and sunshine here on the coast. Eventually we reach the outskirts of Marina Baie des Anges, a development of high-rise ultra-modern apartments that ripples along the coast like some massive wave-shaped sculpture. At the edge of the development is an incongruous café comprising a small wooden hut and few red plastic tables scattered among the pebbles. Here, we buy cans of Coke and turn our chairs to face out to sea, side by side. It's kind of strange having the turquoise sea and sky above and in front of us, even as the sky behind our backs shifts to deepest grey. I keep glancing over my shoulder just to look.

'I'm glad you found me,' Zoe says, unexpectedly. 'I mean . . . I know it's my fault and everything . . . the fact that we've seen so little of each other . . .'

My eyebrow twitches irrepressibly at this massive understatement, and Zoe notices and corrects herself. 'OK, that we haven't seen each other at all, then,' she says. 'But I'm glad you found me. Hanging out like this. Well, it's nice.'

I nod and swallow with difficulty. My emotions are so confused that I'm struggling to work out what I'm feeling.

'And your mum?' Jessica asks. 'Do you think you'd be ready to see her as well?'

I'm a bit stunned by Jessica's intervention. I hadn't been expecting that at all, and now I hold my breath as I wait to see how Zoe will reply. But she just shakes her head vaguely and then sips at her can of Coke.

Why, Zoe? The question is there once again, waiting on the tip of my tongue like a slowly melting acid drop. But I still can't say it. Saying it out loud is somehow beyond my physical capabilities.

Jessica, apparently, has no such issues. 'Why is that?' she asks, provoking another sharp intake of breath on my part.

'I don't . . . really . . .' Zoe mumbles, glancing off along the beach – anything to avoid eye contact.

'You don't really what?' Jess asks softly, reaching out to touch her arm. 'What is it?'

I put my drink down and start to chew a fingernail. I, too, look away along the beach, but in the other direction. The tension of the moment is becoming unbearable.

'I don't really want to go there,' Zoe says, now turning back to face Jessica and beginning to sound a little annoyed. 'If it's all the same to you?'

'Well, I don't think it's all the same to Jude,' Jessica says. 'Do you realise just how hard this has all been for him, all this not knowing?'

Though I can see what she's doing and why, and though I understand that her motivations are all good ones, the fact of her asking the question in this way is unbearable to me, and for so many reasons.

249

I begin to list and decode those reasons: that Jessica is trying to get my sister to tell me something I'm too scared to ask her myself; that her doing so implies a sort of shared ownership of the problem, the sort of suffocating coupledom where one partner feels authorised to speak for the other; that she's talking to my sister about something that is my problem with my sister, that has nothing whatsoever to do with Jessica, and that she's daring to tell Zoe how hard this has all been for me when she really has no idea how hard it's been, when neither of them do, because it's been so fucking hard that for most of my life I've had to pretend that it's all fine and that it's had absolutely no effect on me whatsoever. And even now that I'm starting to accept that's maybe not the case, I still can't find a way to think rationally about it or even begin to quantify what effect losing two dads and a sister within the space of a few years – as Jess so rightly pointed out – might have had on me.

'The thing is, Zoe—' Jessica says.

But suddenly, it's all just too much for me. 'Stop, Jess,' I tell her.

'But you two really need—'

'Just stop!' I say sharply, my anger leaking out.

'But you need to talk about this,' Jess insists. 'You have to.'

Only I don't. What I need is for Jessica to stop. What I need is to get away from both of them. What I need is to be able to breathe. I stand and walk – almost run, actually – off along the beach, leaving them sitting in the café behind me.

'Jude,' Jess calls out, pleadingly. 'Jude!'

But I don't pause, and I don't look back.

Once I start walking, I find I can't stop. I'm feeling angry and upset, incomprehensibly scared and confused, and the more distance I put between myself and Zoe, the better it feels. And so I continue to walk.

Halfway along the enormous beach, I pluck up the courage to look back. Neither Jessica nor Zoe appear to have moved from the café, and I'm relieved to see that they haven't been following me. My breathing is starting to ease.

I sit down at the water's edge and see some tiny fish nibbling at some algae. I watch a cormorant dipping and diving until it finally comes up with a fish in its beak, and then glance up to see that the line of cloud has advanced so far that it now ends directly above my head.

I think about Jessica tramping all over my private garden in her yellow Dr. Martens boots and feel angry at her lack of discretion, at her failure to understand the impossibility of asking that question, or more precisely, her failure to realise that if it had been askable, I would have asked it myself.

I think about her reasons for having done so and force myself to understand that she had merely been trying to help.

Only at the end of this process do I think about the fact that she's right – of course she is. Zoe and I do need to have this conversation. That conversation is the reason I am here today; it's the reason we've tracked her down. I need to take my courage in both hands and let her tell me what happened all those years ago, because time is running out.

Yes, I've been pretending, for years, that I'm fine. I've been telling myself that none of this really affected me. I'm a bloke, after all. I'm solid. It's all cool. Only it isn't, is it? Because look at the state of my relationships . . . And look at the state of me now.

I sigh deeply and shiver. The winter sun, still visible in its ever-shrinking strip of blue sky, is already dipping towards the horizon, and the temperature is dropping quickly. I glance back up the beach and see that Jess and Zoe are heading my way.

Seeing that I'm looking at them, Jessica now points towards where our car is parked and beckons to me. I stand, take one difficult gulp of air as if in preparation for a dive, and then head across the beach to join them.

The drive back to the campsite, towards the menacing gloom of the storm clouds, takes place in complete silence. It's not an empty silence, or even an angry silence. Neither Jessica nor Zoe seem upset with me, which is a relief, but they both seem pretty strange. Actually, they both look as if they've been crying, which is weird. It's what people in novels call a pregnant silence, I suppose – a silence desperate to be filled; a silence biding its time before delivering its secrets.

The first drops of rain start to plop on to the windscreen at the exact moment we pull into the campsite. Jessica takes the keys from the ignition but then, placing one hand gently on my thigh, instructs me to stay put. 'Zoe has something to tell you,' she informs me, her voice unusually brittle. 'I'll go for a wander.'

I glance back at Zoe in the rear of the car and see her reach forward with her own keys. 'Take them,' she tells Jessica. 'You can wait in the caravan. I think it's going to chuck it down.'

Jess nods and takes the keys from her grasp. 'Thanks,' she says, then to me, 'Be calm. Try to understand. And don't forget to breathe.' As she pushes open the door of the car and stands, she adds, '. . . Love you.'

'You coming up front?' I ask Zoe. My voice is gravelly with fear.

Zoe shakes her head. 'I'm fine here,' she says.

I shift in my seat so that I can face her. I think about the fact that she feels safer with the headrests separating us and wonder what she's going to tell me. 'Whatever,' I say.

Zoe turns away to look out of the side window. I follow her gaze and watch Jess until she disappears from sight behind the campsite office. A sudden flurry of raindrops hits the car, wetting the windscreen and hammering on the roof before abruptly stopping again.

'So?' I prompt. 'What do you want to tell me, Zo?'

When she turns back to face me her eyes are watering. 'I . . .' she says.

'Yes?'

'I . . . think it was easier talking to Jess,' she says.

'Because she's a woman?' I ask.

Zoe shakes her head.

''Cause she's not involved?'

Zoe nods.

'So you told her, then? You told her everything?'

Another nod, then, 'Pretty much. Maybe you could just get Jess to tell you? That might be easier.'

I snort. 'No, I don't think so, Zoe,' I say. 'I think this is something we need to do, don't you?'

Zoe shakes her head. 'It's just . . .' she says. 'I'm just . . .' She sighs and brushes a tear from her cheek.

'You're what?' I ask her gently. 'Tell me, Zo.'

'It's so hard,' she says. 'That's the thing, Jude. I'm so ashamed.'

'Is it Scott?' I ask. 'Did he do something?'

But Zoe is shaking her head.

'He didn't?' I say, frowning. I'm thinking both, *Of course he didn't do anything*, and, *But he must have done something*. I realise that I've been living with these two incompatible thoughts stuffed away in my subconscious for years.

Another shake of the head.

'Then tell me,' I say. 'Just tell me what happened, Zoe.'

'I'm not sure if I can,' she says, her voice wobbling.

'You can,' I say. 'You have to.'

Zoe chews her bottom lip and nods. 'So, it's all about that stuff, back then. Why I left and everything.' She shakes her head and says again, 'I'm just so ashamed, Jude.'

253

'You don't need to be,' I tell her, softly. 'You've got nothing to be ashamed of, have you, Zo? But I think you need to tell me what happened, don't you?'

'It wasn't Scott,' she says. 'It was Dad. The reason I left was 'cause of Dad.'

'Dad?' I say, breathing the word more than saying it.

'I wanted him back, that's all.'

I frown. 'What? What do you mean you wanted him back?'

Zoe's features are crumpling and tears are running down her cheeks. In a strange symmetry, the drumming of the rain on the roof suddenly intensifies again. 'You won't understand,' she says. 'Even if I tell you.'

'Try me,' I say.

Zoe covers her eyes with one hand and starts to judder in the effort to hold back her sobs. 'I thought . . . I thought they'd get back together,' she says.

'Who would? Mum and Scott?'

'No, Mum and Dad.'

'What?'

'I thought Dad still loved . . . us. I thought he and Mum still loved each other. I thought he'd come home if I could just get rid of Scott.'

I flinch. I cover my mouth with one hand. 'You mean . . .' I gasp. 'You mean, you did it on purpose? You broke Mum and Scott up on purpose? Or have I got that wrong?'

Zoe peeps over the tops of her fingers at me and nods, makes a groaning sound and breaks into a fresh batch of tears.

'But we thought . . . I mean, you let us think . . .'

'I know . . .' Zoe whimpers. 'I'm sorry . . .'

'But Zoe, Mum loved him,' I say, my own tears rising, despite my best efforts to keep them down. 'I loved him. We were . . . we were happy, Zoe.'

'I know,' she says again, her voice squeaky and strange.

'You made Mum think he'd . . . done something to you, Zoe. You do get that, right?'

Zoe breaks into a series of breathy, juddering gasps. Without looking up from her hands, which she's wringing in her lap, she nods. 'It wasn't my idea, though . . .' she whispers. 'I never said he'd done nothing. It was just what everyone thought. It was that shrink Mum took me to see, asking me all those disgusting questions. I hadn't even thought of it till then.'

'But you could have said,' I say, struggling not to cry again. 'You could have just told us. Why didn't you just say? They split up because of you, Zoe! Mum was miserable for years. I was miserable. Scott was heartbroken. It was fucking horrible for everyone. It destroyed her. It fucked up our whole family.'

'I know,' Zoe whispers, peering up at me, red-eyed. 'I'm sorry.'

'But why? I still don't get it,' I say, my tears morphing to anger.

'I told you,' she says. 'I thought . . .'

'Oh, don't give me that,' I say, my anger starting to leak out. 'You knew full well Dad wouldn't get back with Mum! You knew he was marrying Linda. We all did.'

'But I didn't,' Zoe sobs. 'Really, I didn't. I thought he loved me. I thought he loved Mum. I thought he'd come back so we could be a proper family again.'

'But Dad told us about the marriage!' I say, struggling to keep myself from shouting. 'So that's bullshit, Zoe.'

'I know,' Zoe says. 'That's—' But the rain abruptly hammers on the rooftop, drowning her words.

'What?' I shout, now that the rain has given me an excuse. 'That's what?' Shouting feels better, in fact. Shouting seems to help.

'I said, that's when I realised,' Zoe says, speaking more loudly in order to be heard over the crazy drumming of the rain. 'That's when I saw what I'd done. That's why I had to leave.'

'But Scott did nothing?' I say, outraged. 'Are you really fucking telling me that there was no reason you hated him like that? That he did nothing at all? Well, except be nice to us. Because he was really fucking nice to us, Zoe.'

Zoe drops her face to her hands and starts to weep uncontrollably now, but I'm way too angry to feel sorry for her. 'You . . .' I murmur. But none of the words that I can think of are strong enough. 'You fucking . . .' I splutter, trying again. 'Jesus, Zoe . . . I . . . I'm fucking speechless.'

And it's true. I'm so utterly, massively furious that I'm unable to speak. It's never happened to me before, and in fact, I can't even think of a word strong enough to describe my anger. It feels like a sort of burning white hole melting in the middle of my brain, like an overheated film spool or something. The edge of my vision is red-tinged, too, and I feel as if I might actually explode with it all if I don't hit something. Or someone. Is there a limit to how angry one can feel, I wonder? Do you just die of a sudden heart attack or a burst blood vessel if anger exceeds a certain threshold? Because right here, right now, death, actual death, wouldn't really surprise me at all.

'I'm sorry . . .' Zoe splutters, reaching hesitantly for the door handle. 'I don't know what else to say. I should go. I'm sorry.'

She glances at me one last time, but I turn away, scared of my own anger – terrified, in fact, that if I look at her for a minute longer I will find myself leaping through the gap between the seats to punch her in the face. These are emotions I have never had before, and I have absolutely no idea how to deal with them.

'Just tell me one more time, before you go,' I suddenly shout, lurching between the seats to grab her by her sweatshirt as she moves towards the door. 'Tell me that Scott didn't do anything. Tell me that he never did one single fucking thing to piss you off.'

Zoe turns to me and shakes her head. 'I'm sorry,' she squeaks.

She tries to prise my fingers from her shoulder, but I'm hanging on tight. 'TELL ME!' I shout.

'He didn't,' she weeps. 'He didn't do anything at all.'

I release my grip and wipe the steamed-up windscreen with my sleeve so that I can look out at the rain. It's quite shockingly dark outside. I silently shake my head as I hear the sound of the car door. Once it's closed, I turn back and watch her blurred form through the window as she leaves, her hands over her head to shield herself from the torrential rain, and I think, with relief, that I will never have to see her again. And once she's gone, once she has vanished behind the campsite office, I bang my fists on the dashboard of the Renault, and when that doesn't seem to help as much as I'd hoped it would, I do it again and I let out a deep, soulful, animal wail.

Over half an hour has passed by the time Jessica returns, half an hour during which my emotions have been all over the place, swinging from utter speechless fury to sudden bouts of tears, and then back again to anger. At the precise moment that a very wet Jessica slides back into the driving seat beside me, I'm stuck in silent fury all over again. It's one of those moments in life when you realise just how little separates us from the killers, from the murderers, from the psychopaths. Because right now, in this instant, I swear I could kill with my bare hands.

'Are you OK?' Jessica asks quietly, as she dries her face on her sleeve and then slides the key back into the ignition.

And how to even begin to answer that? I turn to look away from her, out of the side window. The rain has dwindled to drizzle now, and it's got a little lighter. 'No,' I say, simply.

'I'm not surprised,' she says quietly. She reaches for my shoulder, but I shrink from her touch. 'Do you want to talk about it or . . .'

'Not talk about it,' I say, and in my efforts to avoid shouting at her, the words have come out so quietly that I fear she hasn't heard me at all.

'OK,' she says, eventually, her voice a little wobbly. 'OK, I understand. Shall I just drive, then?'

I close my eyes and nod rapidly. 'Yes, please,' I say, once again in a whisper.

'You don't want to wait for Nick to—'

'No,' I interrupt. 'No, I want to get out of here, please.'

'OK,' Jess says. She pulls a handkerchief from her pocket and rather ineffectually wipes the windscreen and side window, then starts the engine and pulls on her seatbelt. She reverses out of the parking space, flips on the windscreen wipers and engages first gear, but then pauses. We sit there in silence, the engine ticking over quietly, the wipers slapping back and forth across the rain-splattered windscreen.

'Just one thing,' she says. 'Your anger. It's not with me, is it?'

I shoot her a glance and manage, just about, to shake my head. But that shake of the head is a lie, really. Because yes, I'm feeling angry with Jessica as well. I'm feeling furious with her for getting Zoe to tell me what happened, for having forced that conversation between us. Because, wasn't it better not knowing?

I'm aware, though, that this is what people call 'shooting the messenger'. Even through the illogical red filter of my anger, I can still see that this isn't actually Jessica's fault. And so I have lied by shaking my head.

'Good,' Jess says. 'Let's get you home, then, shall we? Or back to Nice, at any rate.'

'Thanks,' I say. 'That would be good.'

'And then I'm guessing it's Buxton, here we come?' Jess says.

I frown at her confusedly. I don't answer.

But as we drive back to Nice in silence, I realise that she's right: that the one and only thing to do now is to go and talk to Mum. Jess amazes me sometimes, she really does.

Fourteen

Mandy

I'm standing looking out through the living-room window at the darkened street beyond. Most of the snow has now melted, thank God, leaving only slushy leftovers on the pavements. More snow would have been bad news, not only for Jude but for my imminent house move as well.

I've been standing here street-watching for almost an hour. Oh, I've tried to concentrate on the television burbling away in the background, but on the eve of moving house, and while awaiting the arrival of my son, it's impossible. So I've abandoned myself to my desire to simply stare out at the street.

I sip my glass of white wine and think about the fact of Jude and Jessica's unexpected visit. It's not the best day for it – not by a long shot. The removal guys are arriving at ten tomorrow morning, and I'd just about finished packing when Jude called. But I've now abandoned myself to this idea as well. I'm quite thrilled, if the truth be told, that they're coming. And I'm excited about whatever it is they're going to announce.

I've been running all the possibilities through my mind as I pack up the final pots and pans and unpack sheets and pillows for their arrival. Though it doesn't quite make sense to me – it doesn't seem to match the urgency of the visit, nor the stress that oozed from Jude's voice over the phone – I've come to the conclusion that they're going to get married. I'm now certain that this is what they're coming here today to announce. Jude's always had a few issues about committing to relationships, and I've decided that this must be the reason for his angsty-sounding phone call.

Images of a marriage now play across the cinema screen in my head, superimposing themselves on the view of the cold, slushy street beyond the window, glistening in the orange light from the streetlamps.

I imagine Jessica in a wedding dress and feel certain that she'll look like a model. She's a pretty girl with a great figure anyway, but it's her sense of style that really sets her apart. Her clothing combinations are to die for. Jude, of course, will wear a suit – he rarely wears anything else. Perhaps he'll even want top hat and tails, I figure. Any excuse to dress up; that's my son.

I glance at the mantelpiece behind me, which is silly because not only is it completely empty (its usual contents having been long since scooped into a box) but the photo I was thinking of, my wedding photo with Ian, hasn't resided there for years.

Headlights outside catch my eye, so I turn to look, but it's just a battered old Renault 5. As Jude has to use hire cars when he visits, I deduce that this can't possibly be them. I let out a sigh of disappointment and imagine, terrifyingly, that they've had an accident somewhere. Picturing your kids trapped in folded metal is the mother's curse. It happens pretty much every time you know your child is driving.

The Renault is now pulling up outside; in fact, it's parking right outside my house. And when the driver switches off the headlights, I can see through the windscreen, and it is indeed Jude and Jess who are sitting there, talking.

By the time I reach the front door, they're on the doorstep.

Jude's wearing an expensive-looking blue checked suit and Jess a striped jersey dress with olive-green leggings and a lime-green mac. They look, as ever, quite amazing. It's funny, really, because before Jess came along, I always worried that Jude looked a bit like an accountant. He hasn't changed how he dresses at all, but together with Jess, it somehow works. They look like a couple of eighties pop stars.

'I didn't think it was you,' I say as Jude steps forward and hugs me with unusual intensity. 'What's with the old banger?'

'I borrowed it from Steve, my flatmate,' Jude explains as he separates from my embrace. 'I couldn't find a decent rental for tonight, so he lent me his.'

'It runs really well, actually,' Jess says. 'And the sound system's amazing. It's like a night club.'

'Yeah, Steve's a musician,' Jude says. 'I think the sound system cost more than the car.'

I kiss Jess on both cheeks and lead them into the house.

'Shit, Mum,' Jude says, running one hand along the wall of boxes in the hall as he enters. 'Someone's been busy.'

'It's tomorrow, Jude,' I say. 'Of course I've been busy.'

'I still think we should have been here to help,' Jude says.

'Me, too,' Jess agrees.

'It's fine,' I tell them. 'It's just boxes and bags. The removal guys are doing all the hard lifting tomorrow. And now you're here to help as well.'

'Well, we got the food, anyway,' Jess says, raising a carrier bag in one hand.

I can smell the contents from here.

'And yes, we went to Ip's,' Jude says, 'before you ask.'

The kids take their coats off and hang them over the backs of the chairs, and then we all move through to the kitchen, where I've already laid the table.

'Do you want to eat right away?' I ask.

'Yeah, while it's hot,' Jude says. 'Plus, I'm pretty hungry, aren't you?'

Jessica nods. 'Me, too,' she says. 'It smells so good. My mouth was watering in the car.'

While I pour them glasses of wine, Jude and Jess divvy out the contents of the aluminium trays. Then we raise our glasses in a toast.

'To you,' I say, thinking that it will lead us on to whatever this is all about.

'No,' Jude says. 'To your move! To Nottingham!'

And suddenly I'm less certain as to why they are here.

'So, to what do I owe this pleasure?' I ask, another attempt at moving things along.

Jude licks his lips and glances at Jess, who shoots him a reassuring smile.

'Maybe after dinner,' Jude says, turning back to face me. 'I've got a bit of an announcement to make, but it might be better to eat first.'

'Oh, God,' I say. 'I'm not going to need champagne, am I? Because I definitely don't have any in. But there's still time to nip up the road to—'

'No, Mum,' Jude says, solemnly. 'No, you definitely don't need champagne.'

I tut. 'I hate it when you get all mysterious on me.' I turn to Jess and tell her, 'He used to do this as a kid, you know . . . say he had something to tell you but then make you wait until later on. A terrible desire to intrigue, my son.'

Jessica just nods, while Jude, for his part, says, 'Yeah, I'm famed for it. All the same, let's just eat first, OK?'

'So, um, are you all ready for your move?' Jess asks. She's clearly decided that it's time to change the subject.

'Pretty much,' I tell her, still trying to figure out what's going on with the two of them. 'Except for all the stuff I had to unpack for you two.'

'Oh, I'm sorry,' Jessica says.

'Actually, it's fine,' I tell her. 'It was nothing: just a couple of sheets and what-have-you.'

'We brought sleeping bags,' Jude says. 'They're in the boot.'

'I'm not having you in sleeping bags,' I say. 'This is still your home, after all.'

'For one night only,' Jude says.

'Don't be like that, sweetheart,' I say. 'You know I'll have a spare room for you in the new place, too.'

'I meant it's one night only, sleeping in sleeping bags,' Jude explains.

'Well, it isn't that either. It's one night only in a nice comfortable bed.'

'Jude says the new place is pretty awesome,' Jess says.

And so we talk for ten minutes about my new flat, which, with its views of the River Trent, is actually pretty awesome.

'Anyway,' I say, once I feel that we've covered that subject, 'what about you two? Tell me about your holiday.'

'Oh, it's been crazy,' Jess tells me. 'We've been all over the place, haven't we?' She glances at Jude then, and I see him send her a hint of a glare.

'We have,' he confirms.

'Where did you go?' I ask. 'Your text said you were in Nice. Was it nice in Nice?'

'Yeah,' Jude says, either missing or ignoring my admittedly lacklustre joke. 'It was fine.'

'It was really hot in the sun,' Jessica tells me, sounding desperately like she's trying to throw something positive into the mix. 'Jude even got a bit sunburned.' She turns to look at Jude and adds, 'Though it's pretty much faded now, thank God.'

'I looked like a lobster,' Jude tells me.

'Not a problem I have to deal with,' Jessica says. 'We had a weird sudden downpour as well. It clouded over, bucketed it down, and then half an hour later it stopped.'

'And where else?' I ask. 'You were going to Cornwall to start with, weren't you?'

'Yeah, but we never made it there, did we?' Jude says.

'No,' Jessica agrees. 'No, we didn't. Bristol was the closest we got.'

Seeing that both Jude and Jessica have finished eating, I fork a final mouthful of mushroom chop suey into my mouth and push my plate to one side. I could probably eat more, but the truth is that I'm too eager to hear whatever's coming next.

'So, come on,' I tell Jude. 'Spill the beans.'

Jude sends another complex glance in Jessica's direction and she replies with a sort of you-might-as-well-get-it-over-with shrug. 'I should go,' she says, beginning to stand. 'I should go and leave you two to it.'

'Jess,' Jude protests. 'We talked about this in the car. I want—'

'Yes, we did,' Jessica says, interrupting him. 'But I changed my mind. This really needs to be just you two. Trust me.'

'But—'

'I'll be just next door,' Jessica says. 'If you need me, I'll come back. OK?'

She then sloshes some wine into her almost empty glass and apologising, perhaps for having served herself or perhaps for leaving, she exits the kitchen, pulling the door firmly closed behind her. I glance at the closed door and feel nervous: we never really close any doors in this house. When I hear her close the lounge door as well, I start to feel quite scared.

'What's this about, Jude?' I ask.

He finishes filling our wineglasses and then chews his bottom lip for a moment before replying. 'OK, so . . . it's . . . Well, it's Zoe, Mum,' he says breathily. 'It's about Zoe.'

'God, she's dead, isn't she?' I say. 'Is she dead?'

But Jude is already shaking his head, cancelling out that particular terror before it even gets started. 'No, she isn't, Mum,' he says. 'She's actually living in France.'

I gasp and raise one hand to my mouth. 'Then you've seen her?' I whisper. 'Is that it? Jesus!'

My son nods. 'Yeah,' he says quietly. 'Yeah, Jess and I tracked her down.'

My vision is blurring as tears of relief well up. My heart's in my throat, making it almost impossible to speak. 'But that's wonderful news, Jude,' I croak. 'Isn't it?' Something about his delivery tells me that there's more. Something about his demeanour doesn't fit with the sense of relief that I'm feeling.

'I suppose so, yeah,' he says, confirming my fears. He sips his wine and glances regretfully towards the lounge.

I have so many questions I want to ask him. I want to know how Zoe is; I want to know exactly where she is, what she's doing . . . There's so much I don't know that I don't even know where to start.

'She's . . . I mean . . .' I splutter. 'She is OK, isn't she?' Because something tells me that she isn't. Perhaps she's ill, I think. Perhaps she has cancer, or HIV, or hepatitis or . . . Perhaps she's having a baby and there's something wrong with it. Maybe she's on a feeding tube in a hospital in France.

'Yeah, she's fine,' Jude says, blinking slowly and nodding. He clears his throat, and I brace myself for whatever's coming next. 'She's living on a campsite,' he says. 'Well, in a mobile home, actually. A caravan park, I suppose you could call it.'

So she's broke, I think. That's it. She needs money. She wants to come home. But that's OK. That's the least of my worries.

'She's working in Snackway,' Jude adds, unexpectedly.

'What, the sandwich place? Or . . .'

'Yeah, a sandwich shop. In a science park.'

'They have that in France, do they?' I say. 'Snackway?'

'Apparently so,' Jude says.

'OK,' I say, starting to frown. My mind's running out of scenarios here, so I need him to get on and tell me.

'She's learning French,' Jude says. 'Her, um, girlfriend is teaching her French.'

'Her girlfriend,' I repeat.

Jude nods and bites his lip. He looks down at his dirty plate and starts fiddling with his fork.

'She's with a girl?' I say. 'Is that it?'

Jude nods again.

'Oh!' I say. I hadn't seen that one coming. 'OK, but that's all right, isn't it? I mean, as long as she's happy . . .' Having a lesbian daughter may not be every parent's ideal, I suppose, but I'm surprised to see Jude this upset about it. Because frankly, that she's not ill, or in hospital, or dead, means that all I'm feeling here is a huge sense of relief.

'Yeah, it's fine,' Jude says. 'Nick, her girlfriend, seems nice enough.'

I put my glass of wine down and run my palm across my eyes. I brush a tear from the corner of one eye with my middle finger. 'You don't seem thrilled about something, Jude,' I say. 'Did it not go well? Wasn't she happy to see you? Because something's wrong, isn't it? And I wish you'd just tell me what it is. Because I'm struggling to make sense of all this, sweetheart.'

Jude stares at his hands and continues to fiddle with his fork, pushing a lone grain of rice around the plate. The noise, though hardly deafening, is setting my nerves on edge and I have to fight the desire to rip it from his fingers.

'Sorry, this is hard,' he says, glancing briefly up at me.

'What is, Jude?' I ask. 'I really don't get it.'

266

'It made me so angry when she told me,' he says. 'That's why I'm a bit scared, I guess.'

'You're scared?'

'Of how you'll react.'

I reach for my glass and take a hefty gulp of wine, then put it down and reach for my son's wrist. 'I won't,' I tell him. 'Whatever it is, I promise I won't get angry. You know not to be scared of me.'

'Sure,' Jude says. 'It's just . . .'

'It's just what?' I ask. 'What's this all about?'

'It's why she left,' Jude says. 'She told me why she left.'

Despite my best intentions, I pull my hand back from his wrist and use it to cover my mouth instead. 'Oh, God,' I say. 'Is it bad?'

'Well, it's pretty fucking upsetting,' Jude says. 'Sorry, but it is.'

'Was it Scott?' I ask. 'God, it's Scott, isn't it?'

But Jude is shaking his head.

'It's OK if it is,' I tell him. 'I mean, it's obviously not OK. But it's OK to tell me. I need to know anyway.'

Jude shakes his head again. 'It's not Scott,' he says. 'Scott never did anything.'

I gasp at this, a gasp of relief and shock combined. 'So what, then?' I ask, my brain struggling to think beyond the mantra of *Scott didn't do anything, Scott didn't do anything*, lovely, beautiful, sexy Scott, the love of my life, didn't do anything. Of course he didn't. How could he have done?

'It's, well . . . it was nothing, really, Mum. That's the thing. That's what's so hard about the whole thing.'

'Nothing,' I repeat.

Jude shrugs. 'She feels really ashamed about it, if that helps. I'm not sure that it does, really, but she kept saying it anyway. She kept saying how ashamed she felt.'

'Ashamed about what, though?' I say. 'I don't get it.'

'She wanted you to split up with Scott. She thought that you'd get back with Dad.'

I exhale slowly and close my eyes. I massage the bridge of my nose. 'I don't understand what you're saying.'

'Well, no,' Jude says. 'It's a bit mad, that's why. It doesn't really make any sense.'

'Then start again at the beginning,' I say. 'Tell me exactly what she said.'

'She spoke to Jess first, and she told her that she was in love with Dad,' Jude says, blushing as he speaks.

'She was in love with him?' I repeat. 'Or she loved him?'

'She was in love with him,' Jude says. 'Jess says it's the Electra complex or something.'

'The what complex?'

'Electra. It's the female version of the Oedipus thing or something. But you'd have to ask Jess about that. You know how shrinky she is.'

'OK . . .' I say, doubtfully.

'But that's what Zoe told her. That she was in love with Dad. She said she worshipped him, actually.'

'Well, she was always a bit closer to your father, but that's not unusual for a girl.'

'And when he left, and she had to stay, she says it made her go into meltdown. She thought that you'd get back together, that's the thing. And when Scott came along, she decided she needed to get rid of him.'

'Get rid of him?'

'That's what she believed. She told Jess that she used to have daydreams about killing him. Poisoning him and stuff like that . . . Because she was convinced that, with Scott gone, you and Dad would get back together.'

'So what are you saying?' I ask. 'That everything she did was on purpose? That these were conscious decisions that she made?'

'Yeah, kind of.'

'But . . .' I close my eyes again as I try to run a condensed version of events through my mind. Wasn't it true that Zoe was always happier when Ian and I were getting along? Had she really been imagining that we were making up? And Scott, my lovely Scott: was he really nothing but an innocent bystander? And if that's the case, how stupid was I to let him go?

'And he kind of was keeping you two apart, in a way,' Jude says.

'What do you mean?' I ask, struggling now to stay calm. 'I was never going to get back with your father. That was never on the cards, and you know it.'

'I know that,' Jude says. 'You know that. But Zoe, well, she believed that it could still happen. And Scott did stop you seeing Dad. You know how jealous he used to get. So none of us got to see Dad much and, in a way, it was because of Scott.'

'Jesus, Jude,' I say, now standing and crossing to the bay window. I look out at the darkened garden, then focus on my son's reflection in the window instead. 'But Scott . . . I mean, she let me think . . . she pretty much let me think that he'd done something terrible.'

'She did,' Jude says. 'I told her that. I mean, she knew what you were worrying about, obviously. For what it's worth, she said the idea came from that shrink you took her to see.'

I spin on one heel now to face him. 'What do you mean, it came from the shrink?'

'Apparently, she asked Zoe questions about Scott. To find out if he'd been touching her up or whatever. Zoe said she hadn't even thought of it until then.'

'And?'

269

'And . . . I don't know, Mum,' Jude says. 'I'm just trying to work out this shit myself.'

I understand, from his defensive reply, that I'm sounding increasingly angry. I consciously attempt to soften my tone. 'It's not you, Jude,' I tell him. 'You know I'm not angry with you.'

'I know,' Jude says.

'So the shrink gave her the idea that . . . that what exactly?'

'That if she carried on blanking Scott, we'd all assume something terrible had happened. And then you'd dump him. She said she felt disgusted that anyone could even imagine something like that, but I suppose she saw it as useful, too. I mean, it's true that she never actually said it out loud. She never accused him or anything.'

'But she didn't have to,' I say. 'God, she didn't have to, did she? She just let us think it, and we did. But that's so . . .'

'Shitty?' Jude offers.

'It's outrageous, is what it is.'

'Yeah, it is. I was so angry when she told me. I was . . . speechless. I was literally speechless, Mum. I couldn't say a word.'

'So it was all so that Scott would go away?'

'Pretty much,' Jude says. 'Yeah.'

'And that was all so that your dad and I would make up?'

Jude nods.

'Christ!' I say.

'I'm still trying to piece it all together,' Jude says. 'I mean, she had half a conversation with Jess and the other half with me. I was so angry I didn't ask the right questions, really, so it's a good job she spoke to Jess as well. But it's a real cluster-fuck, isn't it?'

'Yeah,' I say. 'I'm not keen on the term, but yes, I suppose that does describe it pretty well.'

'Once Scott left, we did see more of Dad, too. So that made Zoe think she'd pulled it off, I suppose.'

'Until he announced he was marrying Linda.'

Jude nods sadly. 'Just before her birthday . . . She told Jess that it blew a fuse, like, in her brain. She says that when he told her, she just lost it.'

'Right,' I say. 'Well, I suppose it makes a kind of sense. I mean, it's an insane kind of sense, but . . . That still doesn't explain why she ran away from home, though.'

'I think it was the shame,' Jude says. 'Once she knew he was marrying Linda, she saw what she'd done. She realised she'd split you and Scott up for no reason. She understood how stupid it all was. That's when she got that you were never getting back with Dad. So she hated Dad then, and she hated Linda for taking him away. She hated everyone and felt too ashamed about Scott to look you in the eye, let alone join in a big double-family birthday dinner.'

My legs are feeling weak, so I pull out the chair at the head of the table and sit, cupping my jaw with my hands. I stare into the middle distance for a moment, remembering Zoe's fleeting regard. A few tears slide silently down my cheeks. I run the whole thing through my mind once again as I desperately try to piece it all together. Scott, I think again. My God, poor Scott.

'She ran off with some delivery guy,' Jude says. 'Did you know that? She couldn't stand the idea of her birthday bash, what with Dad and Linda and you and everyone being there. So she went off with some delivery guy who'd been chatting her up.'

'Not that blond guy from QuickParcel?' I ask. 'The one with the spiky hair who was always flirting with her?'

'Yeah, I think so,' Jude says. 'That's what she said. She stayed with him in Macclesfield for a bit. But then she ended up moving all over the place. She was in Bristol for a bit with him. He was working as a van driver. He posted the postcards from all those weird places.'

'So she wasn't even there? All those places I went to try and find her, and she wasn't even there?'

Jude shakes his head.

'And do we know why she never came back? I mean, if nothing had really happened, why stay away?'

'Like I said,' Jude tells me, 'it's just the shame of it all, I think. She told Jess she was so ashamed she wanted to kill herself, and I kind of believe her. She got into drugs, apparently.'

'Drugs?'

Jude nods. 'To try to forget, I think. She lived in some real shit-holes, too.'

'But the drugs,' I ask, surprised at the lurch my heart is still able to make at the thought of my daughter being in danger.

'She says she's clean,' Jude says. 'She was just getting into heroin when she met Nick, but Nick helped her get off it all.'

'Heroin?!' I exclaim, my heart in my mouth again.

'Relax, Mum,' Jude says. 'She only dabbled, apparently. And she only ever smoked it. She never got as far as injecting, thank God. And she's totally clean now, thanks to Nick.'

'But heroin!' I say. 'Jesus, Jude!'

'I know,' Jude says.

'And this Nick . . . So that's Nicola, is it?'

'Yeah. But she calls herself Nick. She's quite . . . you know . . . blokey. But nice. She was really nice, actually.'

I nod slowly. I try to reach for my wineglass – I need a drink. As it's too far away, I stand and return to my original seat opposite Jude. 'It's just so crazy,' I tell him, noticing that my hand is shaking as I raise my glass to my lips. 'I can, you know, piece it all together, what you're saying . . . But it doesn't really make sense, because it's mad. I mean, it is all just a bit insane, isn't it?'

'Yeah,' Jude says, with a shrug. 'Yeah, it's pretty fucked up.'

'And Jess?' I say. 'She knows all this too?'

'It was Jess who got her to talk the most, really,' Jude says. 'I was so pissed off I couldn't really think straight.'

'And what does Jess make of it all?'

'Well, like I said, she's got this whole theory about Electra and what-have-you. It's something to do with Dad being absent at a really important time for Zoe. Jess thinks that mucked up her development or something, so she ended up sort of fixated on him and heartbroken when he left. But you'd have to talk to Jess about that. Freud and Jung and whatever, that's more, you know, her thing than mine. Do you want me to go and get her?'

I shake my head. 'No,' I say. 'Not yet.'

'Are you OK?' Jude asks. 'Because I pretty much blew a gasket when she told me.'

I'm tapping the table with one fingernail. I'm wiggling my foot beneath the chair. 'I think I'm OK,' I say.

'The whole Electra thing—' Jude starts.

But I interrupt him. 'Would you mind if we took a break?' I ask. 'I think I need a moment on my own.'

Something is rising within me. For the moment I'm not sure if it's sorrow or rage, but whatever it is, it feels massive and uncontrollable and I need to be alone with it. I need to not be in this tiny overheated room with my son.

'I might go out for a walk,' I say. 'Would that be OK?'

'A walk?' Jude repeats. 'But it's freezing out, Mum.'

But I'm already standing, I'm already in the hallway, grabbing my purse from the windowsill and my puffa coat from the hook. 'Don't worry,' I call back to Jude. 'I'll be back in a bit.'

The second I close the front door behind me, it swings open again. Jude calls after me. 'Your phone,' he says. 'Don't forget your phone.'

I spin on one heel and return to take it from his outstretched hand. Telling him, in the most reassuring manner I can manage,

'Don't worry, I'm just going for a walk around the block,' I turn back towards the street and stride rapidly away.

I walk to the top of our road and then turn instinctively towards Solomon's Temple. I walk past Zoe's old school and then, realising that, in muddy darkness, Solomon's Temple is impossible, I take a right and head back towards town.

My mind, for the moment, contains nothing but a blur of images – it's as if someone has thrown my thoughts into a spin dryer. There's so much to think about, that's the thing. There's so much to think about and so much to avoid thinking about that I don't know where to start or where to make myself stop.

Eventually, I reach the edges of the town centre and, as I walk past the Old Clubhouse, I glance in through the window and see the flickering log fire and the cosy glow of the bar. *Whisky*, I think, which is a strange thought for me to have, as I've never been a whisky drinker in my life. But I suppose it's what people do in films, isn't it, when faced with impossible situations? Perhaps they all drink whisky because it helps?

I take a seat at the bar and when the barman, who looks too young to be working anywhere let alone in a bar, appears, I ask him for a double whisky.

'Whisky,' he repeats, then, 'Any particular whisky?'

Something about the word sounded wrong coming from my mouth. Whisky, perhaps, isn't me, I think. 'Actually, make that a large house white,' I say. 'I've changed my mind.'

Once he's served me and I've paid, I move to a corner seat. The bar is pretty much empty. Just one young couple are present on the sofa, by the log fire, and a businessman in a suit has just entered and is standing at the bar. None of them even glances my way, and I'm glad to be able to imagine that I'm invisible.

I take a hefty sip of wine and wonder if it was a mistake, not ordering whisky. The wine seems somehow too ordinary for such exceptional circumstances. My phone buzzes in my pocket, so I pull it out and check the screen. On it is a text message from Jude. 'Are you OK?' it says, simply.

I reply that I'm fine and that I just needed a breath of fresh air. 'I'll be back soon,' I tell him, and I wonder if that's true.

The text sent, I take another swig of wine. It's surprisingly good for a house white. I suspect that it's Pinot Gris. Ian always had a thing for Pinot Gris.

I push the phone around with one finger. Ian, I think. I should call him. We could talk about what happened with our daughter.

But what did happen? Jude said that nothing had really happened, but of course from Zoe's point of view everything had happened. Her beloved father had left not only me, but her as well. He'd even told her he didn't want her to live with him. He'd replaced me, Zoe, Jude – all of us – with a new fully formed family.

Suddenly, I'm catching my first glimpse of the turmoil that must have been present in my adolescent daughter's mind. Had I been too selfish, too wrapped up in my own misery, to imagine what my daughter was feeling? Perhaps I had.

I click on the contacts list and swipe my way down to the letter 'I'. I look at Ian's number for a moment, but then continue swiping my way down to S. Scott's number is absent. Of course it is. I google 'Scott Theroux, tree surgeon' just to see if I can, just to see if I actually have that option.

'Call this number now,' his webpage says.

I tap my fingers on the table top for a full minute before thinking, *What the hell*, and click on the inviting green button.

Scott answers immediately and just the sound of him saying, 'Hello?' is enough to make my heart ache.

'It's me,' I say, quietly.

'Sorry, who is this?' Scott asks. I can hear the television set playing in the background. Canned laughter. Applause.

'It's me. It's Mandy,' I say.

There's another much longer pause, during which I listen once again to the sound of the TV. It's a Jimmy Carr thing that he's watching, I can tell. I'd recognise Carr's fake laughter anywhere.

'Are you OK?' is what Scott finally says. Scott, as always, is Scott. And the first words he says after a full eight years of being avoided are words of concern for my well-being.

'No . . .' I say, starting to cry. 'No, Scott, I'm not OK at all.'

'OK . . .' he says. 'Are you at home?'

'No,' I say, barely able to speak through my sobs. 'I'm in a pub, in town.'

'Tell me which one and I'll come,' he says. 'I can be there in about half an hour.'

◆ ◆ ◆

It takes Scott just over twenty minutes to arrive – twenty minutes, during which I repeatedly pick up the phone, fully intending to tell him not to bother. It seems absurdly unfair to be asking Scott for help after everything that has happened, plus, the conversation we need to have seems impossible – I just can't imagine which words I might use. But try as I might, I can't think of anyone else on planet Earth I want to talk to right now, so each time I put the phone back down on the table and push it away from me with one fingernail.

He bursts through the door at twenty past nine, scans the room and strides urgently across the bar to join me. He's aged considerably in the eight years since I last saw him. He's filled out, gained a few smile lines around his eyes and even started to go grey at the temples. But age suits him, it really does. If anything, he looks even more handsome, even more rugged, than before.

He crouches beside me and says, 'Thank God! I was sure you'd be gone by the time I got here.'

'Nope,' I say, my throat tight. 'Still here.' I nod towards the bar. 'Go get yourself a drink.' I need a few seconds to adjust to the sight of him, to get used to the fact that he's really here.

Scott nods and stands. 'Yeah,' he says. 'Good idea. Refill?'

I shake my head. 'I'm already squiffy,' I tell him. I raise my half-empty glass. 'This is my second.' Thinking about what I drank at home, I add, 'Actually, my third. At least.'

I watch him at the bar, alternating between his usual easy manner with the barman and worried glances sent my way. When he returns, pint in hand, he sits opposite me.

'So what's happening?' he asks. 'I could hardly believe it when you called. Talk about out of the blue.'

I open my mouth to speak but I don't know where to begin. I close my eyes and shake my head and try to hold back a fresh bout of tears, but I can feel them slipping down my cheeks already.

Scott takes my hand and the sensation – the warmth of his skin, perhaps a full degree warmer than my own, the roughness of his gardener's hands – feels so familiar, feels magical, really. My tears start to flow freely.

'What's happened?' Scott asks, squeezing my hand in his. 'Tell me. Is it Jude? Is Jude OK?'

I nod and shake my head confusedly, attempting to answer both questions at once. 'He's fine,' I say. 'Jude's fine. It's me, Scott. I'm such a terrible person. I'm so sorry.'

'You're not,' he says, almost amused. 'You're one of the nicest people I know.'

'But I'm not,' I say, struggling to speak in a normal voice. 'I'm horrible. The things I let myself think . . .'

'What's happened?' he asks again. 'Tell me what's happened. Because otherwise . . .'

I release his hand and push it away from me. Physical contact with him is making me emotional and, if I'm to navigate these waters in any meaningful way, I need to hold it together – I need to avoid falling to pieces.

I pull a fresh tissue from my pocket and use it to blow my nose. I look at the ceiling for a moment and force myself to take a deep breath. 'Sorry,' I say. 'I'm sorry for all . . . this . . .' I gesture towards my eyes. 'It's been a tough day, that's all.'

'Yeah, I can see that,' Scott says, frowning with concern. 'But Jude's OK, is he?'

I nod. 'He's fine.'

'And Ian?' Scott asks.

'He's fine, too,' I tell him. 'Well, as far as I know.'

'So, what?' Scott asks. 'You're not ill or anything, are you?'

'It's Zoe,' I tell him. I blow through pursed lips, trying to find the strength to say what needs to be said. 'Jude tracked her down. She's in France. And she told him everything.'

Scott visibly stiffens. He shuffles uncomfortably in his seat. 'She told him what, exactly?'

'She told him that nothing happened. She admitted to doing it all on purpose.'

'OK,' Scott says, dubiously. 'She admitted doing what on purpose?'

'To splitting us up,' I tell him, speaking through tears. 'To letting me think that . . .' I look back up at the ceiling as if this will somehow keep the tears inside me. 'I'm such a terrible person, Scott,' I say, my voice wobbling all over the place, 'for even imagining anything like that.'

Scott puts his beer down. He chews at a fingernail and sighs. When I look him in the eye, I see that his own eyes are glistening. 'It's not your fault, Mandy,' he says. 'It's really not your fault.'

'Only it is.'

'Why, though?' Scott asks, slowly shaking his head. 'I mean, why did she do that? Why did she hate me so much? Did she explain that?'

And so I tell him what I know. I tell him how Zoe wanted her father back and how she thought that Scott was the only obstacle to that happening.

'So it wasn't me at all?' Scott asks, once I've finished. His voice is thin and breathy. 'It wasn't anything I did or said?'

'No,' I tell him. 'It wasn't anything to do with you at all.'

'I tried so hard with her, too,' Scott says.

'I know you did,' I say. 'I remember.'

'And the little bitch is OK, is she?' he asks, a hint of laughter in his voice. I must wince at this, because he apologises immediately, saying, 'I'm sorry. I know she's your daughter and everything. But . . . Jesus!'

'It's OK,' I tell him. 'You're right to be angry. I'm really bloody angry myself.'

Scott nods and sips his beer. He sighs repeatedly and then massages his brow and says, 'Fuck!'

'Can you forgive her, do you think?' he asks, eventually. 'Because I suppose you have to find a way to do that, right? I mean, she's still your daughter and everything.'

'Yes, she's my daughter,' I say, vaguely, thoughtfully. 'And I suppose, one day, I'll have to. It's what mothers do, isn't it?'

'I guess.'

'But I don't know how, yet. Perhaps if I can work out why, you know? Maybe if I can understand better what went wrong, that might help. But it cost me so much . . .' Fresh tears are rising again, and just the thought of them leaves me feeling exhausted. But there doesn't seem to be anything I can do to stem the flow. 'It cost me you, Scott,' I say.

'Yeah,' Scott says sadly, resting his head in his hands. 'It cost me you as well.'

'And you?' I ask, my voice trembling.

'Me?'

'Do you think you can ever forgive me?'

'For what?' Scott asks with a hint of a shrug.

'For thinking . . .' I say. 'For imagining . . . God, I still can't even say it.'

'It's OK,' Scott says, softly. 'You don't have to. I know exactly what everyone thought.'

'You know I didn't,' I tell him, only realising as I say it that it's true. 'I used to try to imagine . . . something like that. But I never could. I never believed it.'

'Then why?' Scott asks.

'I couldn't quite rule it out either,' I say. 'Not one hundred per cent. There was this tiny, minuscule smidgen of doubt that just ruined everything. I promise you that's true, though. I never believed it was possible that you'd . . . that you could have . . .'

'Our Zoe put on a pretty convincing show,' Scott says.

'Yes,' I say. 'She did. But all the same.'

Scott screws his face up now as he tries to master his emotions. 'It . . .' He clears his throat. 'It . . . hurt, you know . . .' he says quietly. He nods gently, visibly remembering. 'It really hurt me that people, that you . . . could even think something like that.'

'I know,' I say. 'I'm so, so sorry, Scott.'

Scott shakes his head violently as if to shake off the tears. He runs his hand across his face like a flannel. 'It's the times we live in,' he says. 'That's part of it.'

'I'm sorry?'

'Oh, you know,' he says, sniffing. 'What with the priests and the TV hosts, what with Savile and Rolf Harris and Jackson . . . It's like everyone's been at it. For years everyone kept a lid on it all and no one wanted to see anything. And now no one can work out if they're being too suspicious or too trusting. So everyone's terrified of making the wrong call.'

'Yes,' I say. 'Yes, I suppose that's true. It was the shrink who first gave Zoe the idea, you know? The one I took her to in Manchester. She was an abuse counsellor.'

'I don't remember that,' Scott says.

I think about this and remember that, of course, I had never told Scott that Dr McDonald was an abuse counsellor. So the original thought crime, if there had been one, was mine. I'd taken Zoe there because of my own doubts.

'It is my fault,' I say. 'I'm . . . I know it's not enough, but I don't know what else to say to you, Scott, except that I'm sorry.'

'Try to go easy on yourself,' Scott says. 'It happens more than you think. You'd be surprised.' I frown at this remark, so he continues, 'Jen, that's my girlfriend, she had a similar thing with her youngest.'

My heart lurches at this mention of a girlfriend and as he continues to speak, I take note of my shocked state and wonder what it implies. Had I really imagined Scott single? Had I really imagined that, even now, even after everything that had happened, we'd make up? *Zoe's not the only one who needs to see a shrink*, I think.

'. . . at the school,' Scott is saying when I tune back into the conversation. 'I mean, he's only six, for Christ's sake. And kids of that age, well, they all say shit like that, you know?'

'What did he say again?' I ask.

'That if he didn't give him his sweets back, he'd pull his willy off.'

I nod. 'You're right,' I say. 'Kids do say rubbish like that.'

'But the school made it into this whole thing,' Scott tells me. 'They thought that someone in Jen's entourage might be abusing him or something, yeah? She had to be interviewed by the school

281

shrink, and then the kid had to see a specialist and . . . Anyway, it was a nightmare, apparently.'

'You didn't have to get involved, did you?' I ask. 'You didn't have to go through all that again, surely?'

'Oh, no,' Scott says, with a tight laugh. 'No, this was all before we met, thank God. I don't think it did much for Jen's previous relationship, though. But it's like I say. Nowadays it's complicated. Because no one wants to suspect for no reason, but everyone's scared of being blind to it, too. So we're all just trying to find a balance. But that really isn't easy.'

Scott asks me some questions about Zoe next, so I tell him what I can. He wants to know why Zoe stopped talking to him in Blackpool, and I admit that I still don't know. He wants to know how Jude found her, too, but when I open my mouth to answer, I realise that I don't know that yet either.

I'm just thinking about the fact that I need to get back to Jude when my phone begins to buzz with an incoming call from him.

'Mum!' he says, when I answer. 'Where are you? You're scaring us.'

Us, I think. I'm pretty sure it's the first time that I've ever heard Jude use 'us' in that way. *And so it begins*, I think. 'It's OK,' I tell him. 'I'm with Scott.'

'Scott . . .' Jude repeats, the surprise audible in his voice.

'Yes, Scott,' I say. 'I'll be home in twenty minutes.'

'I can drop you off if you want,' Scott says.

'OK, so, Scott's going to drive me home,' I tell Jude, 'so it's going to be more like ten minutes.'

'OK,' Jude says. 'I'll wait up.'

We stand to leave and Scott, chivalrous as ever, helps me on with my coat.

Outside in the cold, walking to his car, I feel like I should ask him about Jen, but my heart isn't strong enough for me to fake that conversation right now.

'New car,' I say instead, hating myself for the banality of the remark.

'Yeah,' Scott says, as he opens the passenger door for me. 'Yeah, the old one died just about when . . . Ages ago.' He coughs, then walks around to the other side and climbs in.

He drives me to the beginning of my street before thinking to ask me if I still live there.

'I do,' I say, laughing weakly. 'Until tomorrow.'

'Tomorrow?'

I nod. 'Yeah. I'm moving to Nottingham tomorrow,' I say.

'Oh, OK,' Scott says. 'You mean literally tomorrow, then?'

'I mean literally, 10 a.m. tomorrow morning,' I say.

'Oh,' Scott says. 'OK.'

I wonder about that hint of disappointment in his voice.

'New fella's in Nottingham, is he?' he asks, sounding fake-casual as he pulls up outside my door.

I turn in my seat to face him and reach out to stroke his bearded cheek with the back of my hand. 'There is no fella, Scott,' I tell him. 'There hasn't been a fella since you.'

'Oh?' Scott says again. 'OK.' And the optimistic shift in his intonation makes them sound like two different words this time around. 'Do you, um, want me to come in?'

'No, thanks,' I say. 'You'd better get back to . . . Jen . . . was it?'

'Yeah,' Scott says through a long exhalation. 'Yeah, I suppose I'd better.'

I open the door and climb down. 'Thanks, Scott,' I tell him. 'You saved my life tonight.'

He nods gently. 'Any time,' he says.

I close the door and he hesitates for a few seconds, staring at me through the side window, before he revs up the engine and lurches away.

I manage to walk as far as the front door before the tears return. I pull my keys from my pocket but, instead of opening the door, I turn instead and lean against it. I close my eyes and let the sadness roll down my cheeks.

After a minute or so, I let myself in to find Jude in the lounge, fiddling with his phone while watching TV with the sound turned low.

'Mum!' he says, jumping up and crossing the room to meet me.

'I'm fine,' I tell him, patting his arm. 'I'm sorry if I scared you, but I'm fine.'

'Is he with you?' Jude asks, nodding towards the hallway.

'Scott?' I ask. 'Oh, no, dear. No, he had to get home to . . . He had to get home.'

'Right,' Jude says.

'To his girlfriend,' I say, squinting a little as protection against more tears. 'He, um, has a girlfriend.'

'Yeah,' Jude says. He sucks his bottom lip for a moment then says, 'Jen, is it?'

'Yes,' I say, frowning. 'But how did you know that?'

'We, um, always kind of kept in touch,' he says.

'Oh!' I say. This day clearly hasn't finished surprising me.

'I always really liked him so we . . . kept in touch. Nothing major. Just, you know, a phone call from time to time.'

'Fair enough,' I say, then, 'Is she nice?'

'Who? Jen?'

I nod.

'I don't know,' Jude replies. 'They haven't been seeing each other long, so . . .'

'OK,' I say. 'And Jess?'

'Yeah, she's nice,' Jude says, deadpan.

'I meant . . .'

'I know,' Jude interrupts. 'Yeah, she turned in. She was knackered from the drive and everything. We both are, really.'

'Yes, you must be exhausted,' I tell him.

'Actually, we had a bit of a tiff. Nothing major, but . . .'

'Oh, gosh,' I say. 'Do you want to talk about it, or . . . ?' I'm feeling emotionally overwrought and I could frankly do without Jude's relationship angst tonight, but I brace myself all the same.

'She just gets annoyed with me sometimes because I'm not as expressive as her.'

'Expressive?' I say.

'Yeah, you know . . .' Jude says. 'Lovey-dovey and all that.'

'Well, perhaps you need to work on that,' I tell him. 'If it's important for the person you want to be with, then maybe it's worth the effort.'

'Yeah,' Jude says. 'I suppose . . . Can I ask you a question?'

'Of course,' I say, praying that it's not something that's going to make me cry again.

'You know how lovey-dovey you always were with Scott . . .'

'Lovey-dovey?'

'Yeah . . . you used to tell him that you loved him like a hundred times a day.'

'I don't think it was a hundred times a day,' I say.

'No,' Jude says. 'But you know what I mean.'

'Sort of,' I say. I clear my throat. 'So, what's the question?'

'Did you feel stupid about it once it all went wrong? When he abandoned you, despite it all, did you feel like . . . I don't know . . . like you'd been silly to get so soppy over him?'

'No,' I say, honestly surprised by the question. 'Why?'

'Never?'

'No,' I say again. 'Why would I?'

Jude sighs. 'I just wondered,' he says.

'And he didn't abandon me, Jude,' I say. 'We agreed to separate. Because things had become impossible. But that didn't take away anything from the time we had spent together. I still treasure the good times we had. The same goes for your father. All relationships end, either in separation or death. All of them. But that doesn't make them any less worthwhile. You don't not do things because one day they'll have to end.'

'No,' Jude says. 'No, I suppose not. Anyway, I'm knackered, so . . .'

'Jude, I'm glad I told him I loved him. I'm glad I let him know how I felt. It's important. Words . . . are important. Honesty is important. And you should never regret being honest.'

'Sure,' he says. 'OK, thanks. I'm gonna crash.'

'I'm going to bed now, too. We've got an early start tomorrow, after all.'

'Oh, God,' Jude says. 'Yeah, the move. Did you say ten?'

I nod. 'Ten o'clock, sharp. But we need to get the final bits and pieces boxed up first so I'll be up pretty early, I imagine.'

'Right,' Jude says, lingering in the doorway. 'Night-night, then.'

'Night, Jude. I love you.'

'Yeah,' he says. 'Yeah, you too.'

Once the house is silent, I climb into my bed and look at the piles of boxes around me. The main curtains having been removed and bagged up already, the room is vaguely lit by the orange glow of a distant streetlamp.

I pick up my phone from the bedside cabinet and fiddle with it thoughtfully.

I open up the call list and verify that I now have Scott's mobile number. I add an entry with his name to the contact list, then delete it and then add it all over again.

I type, and delete, a text message to him, three times in a row. 'I love you,' it reads. 'It was only ever you.' But in the end I chastise myself for even thinking of sending it. I have, I reckon, caused enough havoc in poor Scott's life. And now he's seeing someone else, of course. For all that honesty is a good thing, surely this would be one of those rare occasions when I'd end up regretting it. I switch the phone off and fall quickly into a deep sleep of angst-filled dreams.

I wake up at six the next morning, a full hour before the alarm clock goes off. The first pre-dawn light is already leaking into the room.

I reach for my phone and switch it on. I check my emails and then my text messages.

I gasp. Because there, onscreen, is my message.

'It was only ever you,' it reads. 'You're The One.'

Oh God, I sent it, I think, my mouth falling open in horror. 'No, no, no!' I groan. 'I didn't send it. I'm sure I didn't.' But the evidence is there, on the screen. The proof is right there in front of me.

My phone vibrates and a second message adds itself to the conversation. 'Are you awake yet?' it says.

I rub my sleepy eyes and stare at the screen uncomprehendingly. And it's only then that I understand that I was right. I didn't send Scott a message at all. The text onscreen is on the left-hand side. It's not from me at all.

My phone screen is starting to blur now, so I wipe my eyes on the duvet, and then as I focus on it once again, a third message pops up beneath the other two, and only now as I read all three from top to bottom do I begin to believe what's happening here.

'It was only ever you. You're The One.'

'Are you awake?'

'Call me when you are. We need to talk before you go to Notts.'

I inhale sharply and cover my mouth with my hand as a fourth message arrives.

'Please. I'm still in love with you. Scott.'

Subject: Sorry

From: Zoe Fuller (Zoe.Fuller147@bigfib.com)
To: Amanda Fuller (fullermandy@bestukbroad-band.com)
On: 12 June 2020 at 22:47
Subject: Sorry

Dear Mum,

I'm really sorry I haven't been in touch. I thought about writing to you all the time, honest I did, but I just didn't know what to say. It wasn't till I spoke to Jude last winter, and Nick, my girlfriend, since then, that things have started to come clear in my head. Because she's better with words than me, Nick's helping me write this letter, too, so here goes.

I'm so ashamed of everything I've done, Mum. And I want to start this letter by telling you that I honestly do get how bad everything I've done is. And I want you to know that I don't expect you to ever forgive me, so please don't think that's why I'm writing to you now. I'm not asking for anything.

I'm sure you've spoken to Jude by now, but Nick thinks it's important for me to tell you myself exactly what I did and (as far as I can explain it) why.

I split you and Scott up on purpose, Mum. I was an absolute bitch, I know I was. Bitch probably isn't a bad enough word, but I know how you hate the other one, so I won't use it.

I wound him up, I wound you up, and then when I realised you were all getting worried that he was maybe a bit of a paedo, I did everything I could to make sure that seemed like a real possibility.

God, it's hard writing this, Mum. I keep wanting to cry, and I can hardly breathe so I'm writing it one chunk at a time. Nick has to keep giving me hugs to calm me down.

It's truly unforgivable, and like I said, I don't ever expect you to forgive me.

But I do think I went a bit crazy, Mum. In fact, I bloody know I did. So maybe that's a sort of excuse?

It just killed me when Dad left us. I don't know why I felt the way I did, but it didn't feel to me like he'd left you at all. It felt like he'd left me. I was so hurt that he didn't want me, Mum. The day Dad left, the bottom fell out of my world, really.

I loved you both (I really did), but everything I did, I did for Dad. We always knew that you loved us, there was never any doubt about that, not even at the end. But with Dad it was a bit more on and off, you always felt like you had to earn it, somehow. And I only ever felt good about myself when I was in his good books.

Do you remember how I used to clean his car for him? I was thinking about that this morning, and it's so not me to do something like that, but I used to feel really good about myself whenever I did anything for Dad, or whenever he told me I was doing well at school or looked pretty or whatever. But from when I was about ten it seemed like he was losing interest, really. I wonder sometimes whether he was already seeing Linda and starting to think about her and her kids more than us, whether that's why it felt the way it did? It felt like he wanted to be somewhere else all the time. Do you know what I mean?

Anyway, I think that's why I started playing up and being funny with my food and everything. I think I was trying to get his attention back. I was trying to get him to show he still cared.

When he left, I was so upset I started cutting myself with a knife. You never knew about that because I did it on my groin, just below the waistline, and I made sure that no one ever saw. I can't really explain to you why I did that, except that when I was doing it I used to think about how Dad didn't love me any more, and how useless I was, and how I wanted to die, so Nick says it must have been to do with feeling unloved by Dad. I've still got horrible scars down there to remind me. I'll never be able to forget all the things I've done.

When he left, I thought he'd come back. Actually, it was more than just a thought. I believed it the way some people believe in God, if that makes any sense. It just didn't seem to me that there could be any other way, really. But then Scott came along and I got really scared, because with him taking Dad's place at home, and in your heart, Dad couldn't come home any more, could he?

I started praying for Scott to just sod off and leave you. When he didn't, I read up about how to cut his brake pipes to make him have a car accident. I even tried to find some deadly flowers out in the woods so I could poison him (I couldn't find any – I don't think it was the right time of year or something) and for what it's worth, I don't think I would really have dared even if I had found them.

Do you remember when we went to Blackpool, Mum? It was a weird day, because Scott was so nice to me that I actually started to like him. I'd been putting all my efforts into hating him, and I think we will both agree that I was pretty good at that. But I was beginning to think that he was OK that day. It was like I was running out of steam trying to hate him or something. I could feel myself caving in.

But then I saw you with Dad and it changed everything. I was up on some rubbish mouse ride with Scott, and I saw you down below, talking, and I thought you'd arranged to meet up in secret, that you'd stuck me and Scott on a ride so you could hang out with Dad. When the ride went around a second time I saw you kissing, too, and I just knew that you were going to get back together so I sort of forgot about how nice Scott was being and doubled down on trying to piss him off so much that he'd leave. It seemed like all it needed was one last push and he'd go and everything would be like before, when we were happy.

After Blackpool, you sent me to that shrink McDonald in Manchester (she was really horrible, by the way. I hated her almost as much as I hated Scott). And she gave me a grilling about what she called my 'physical relationship' with Scott, and I suddenly realised that everyone was worried he'd been touching me up. I was so disgusted the first time she hinted at that, Mum. I felt sick, like proper sick, when you have food poisoning. I couldn't even eat my sausage sandwiches. I got really, really skinny then, do you remember? But you started being a bit nicer to me. You even told me you'd sort it out if Scott had 'done something' to me, so I thought that if I just carried on, he'd have to leave. And of course, it worked, because he did leave, and I was really, madly happy because I just knew that Dad would come home.

Only, he didn't come home, did he? He decided he'd marry Loony Linda. I'm not sure if he ever told you this, but I threw up when he told me they were getting married. He put it down to something I'd eaten, but it wasn't anything I'd eaten. It was just the shock of it, I think. The shock of realising that he was never coming back. The shock of realising she was pregnant, that they'd been making babies and whatever made me feel really queasy, too. Plus, the shame of it all. I wanted to die, really, because that's when I realised what I'd done to you and Scott. And that's when I realised it was all stupid and childish and pointless.

I felt sick all the time after that. In fact, the only time I felt a bit better was when I was smoking joints with Dwayne, this guy I was seeing on the sly. He was a delivery driver for QuickParcel, and I used to skive off school and drive around with him in his van all day. I'm not sure if you ever found out about that. Perhaps Jude told you?

Anyway, when you and Dad and Linda got chummy and started planning my big birthday surprise (which wasn't a surprise cos Sinead told me), I asked if I could move in with him, and he said sure, why not? He was really easy-going at the beginning.

I felt so bad about everything, Mum, so ashamed. I felt like I was drowning in shame or something. But I couldn't just tell you to go and get Scott back, could I? Not without admitting to what I'd done. And I was way too scared to do that, Mum. I thought you'd kill me if you knew. Actually, I thought you'd disown me, which was worse.

So I asked Dwayne if I could stay with him for a bit.

You mustn't blame him for any of this. He was really nice to me, Mum, honest he was. And until the police turned up at his house that first time, he thought I was eighteen because that's what I'd told him.

I had a pretty bad time after that, Mum. Things were really, really awful, actually.

Everywhere I stayed things turned to sh*t, really. Dwayne's creepy dad tried it on with me, so we had to leave there. We went to his mum's place in Bristol, which meant that he had to change jobs, and the new one didn't work out. I couldn't find a proper job, just a few hours here and there in a chippy. So I got really bored and started hanging out with some real losers. I did some really stupid things in Bristol, Mum, but I don't think I want to tell you about them now, or perhaps ever. And then, when I left, things got even worse. I was scared and lonely and hungry sometimes, too. I had to sleep with some guys I didn't really want to and I slept under the pier in Blackpool a couple of times too. There were loads of junkies there and it was really scary and I wanted to come home so much, but I was too ashamed. So I just sat there under the pier and cried. I just want you to know that when I met Nick in Blackpool, it was the best thing that ever happened to me. Because she saved me, Mum. She really did. She gave me somewhere to stay and bought me clothes and fed me (never easy, as you know!) and helped me get back on my feet, and all for nothing in return.

We're still together, and still in France. My email address is above in case you want to write back, but don't worry if you don't. I'm not expecting much. I'd totally understand if you want to disown me or whatever and forget about me for ever more. God, it makes me breathless to even think about the fact that maybe I'll never see any of you again.

Nick lost her teaching job recently, and so we're thinking of moving back home, but we can't really decide where to go. Nick grew up in a hippy commune in Scotland (she doesn't like me calling it that, but that's what it is) and we could go there, but I don't want to really. Not for long, at any rate. Nick's mum lives there and she's nice, but I don't think I'm cut out for communal living. That's what Nick says, anyway.

I kind of thought about moving back to Buxton, but I know you're not there any more, or maybe to London to be near Jude, but that's probably too expensive and he seems to hate my guts anyway. Don't worry, we're not thinking about Nottingham cos I'm sure you don't want to be bumping into me in Tesco's on a Saturday morning.

But if we do move, I'll write to you again so you've got my new address. Just in case you want to send a proper letter or something one day.

I'm so so so sorry, Mum. Jude said I've fucked up our whole family (I know, swear word, but that's what he said), and I know he's totally right about that. I don't expect you two will ever forgive me for taking Scott away from you. I know how much you both liked him. The really sad thing is that, deep down, I think I did too.

Anyway, please tell Jude I'm sorry. Tell Scott, too, if you ever bump into him.

I hope you're OK and you've managed to put your life back together in Nottingham.

Lots of love from your very bad, very sorry, very sad daughter, Zoe.

Re: Sorry

From: Amanda Fuller (fullermandy@bestuk-broadband.com)

To: Zoe Fuller (Zoe.Fuller147@bigfib.com)

On: 13 June 2020 at 05:25

Re: Sorry

Hello Zoe,

I'm so happy you wrote to me! I burst into tears the second I saw your email.

I wanted to write to you last year after Jude got back, but he convinced me that it was best to wait for you to make the first move. But I kept writing letters and binning them all the same. I've written at least ten.

Firstly, please stop feeling bad about what happened. This family has had enough suffering, and now it's time for it to stop.

I've been thinking about this all night, and really, Zoe, the one thing that I want is for us to draw a line under this so that we can enjoy being a family from here on in.

I know you don't have any children of your own, so you won't understand this, perhaps, but I never stopped loving you, Zoe. I never wanted to disown you. All I ever wanted was to make things right for you, even when you were being awful. Because I'm not going to deny that you were, truly, awful!

But you're my daughter, Zoe. I know it will make you queasy, but you came out of me. My body made you. I carried you inside me for nine months. And that bond, well, I honestly don't think there's anything stronger on planet Earth. I suppose it's not likely that you'll be a mum one day, but I hope you will. It's a very special feeling and one that never goes away, no matter what happens.

I'm also very sorry, Zoe. I'm really, really sorry for what happened to you. I know how traumatic Dad leaving was for you and I know exactly what you mean about him not being that interested in us towards the end. Because yes, your instinct is right. He was already seeing Linda for some time before he left.

I'm sorry, too, if I wasn't everything I needed to be for you. I tried really hard, but I'm human and fallible, too, Zoe. I was pretty young, still, and hurting from having been dumped. And then I was madly in love with Scott, and if I'm perfectly honest, I didn't really know how to deal with your pain either. But know that even if I was a bit 'rubbish', as you would say, I was doing my best. And hear me again when I tell you that I never stopped loving you.

Now that you've written, please don't ever stay away again. Please, please, please keep in touch, even if it's just by email. I've missed you so much. I've got so much I want to say to you. God, I'm crying now, as I type this.

I'm just so, so happy you're back!

Come and visit me, please, or tell me if I can come and visit you in France, maybe.

And if you want to move back, please get in touch so we can talk about it.

I'm back with Scott (ever since the day Jude got home from seeing you, actually) and we have two places between us, one in Nottingham and one in Bakewell, so I'm sure we can put you up for a while if you need it. I'm dying to meet Nick, too. From what Jude and Jess say, she sounds really nice.

Scott, who is as lovely as ever, and who is sleeping upstairs, told me to give you his love if I write to you. He also said to tell you that if you 'ever start all that shit again' he'll 'whack you one'.

And don't worry about Jude either. He'll be fine, I promise you. He's your brother.

He and Jess are getting married on the 3rd of July, and you should definitely come. Don't ask him, or tell him you're coming. Just come. I promise I'll make sure it's all OK. My heart's been broken since you left, Zoe, so please come home. Please come home and let us be a family again.

Your loving Mumsy.

Epilogue

Zac hugs his mother's leg as she pours ground coffee into the cafetière.

'Zac,' she says. 'Please don't hang on me like that. Not first thing in the morning.'

'I'm sleepy,' he says.

'Then go back to bed.'

'I'm not that kind of sleepy,' he says. 'I'm waking-up sleepy.'

'Then please go and wake up somewhere else, babe,' she tells him gently, smoothing his hair. 'Just give me half an hour and I'll do something with you, OK?'

'Like what?' Zac asks.

'I don't know. Whatever you want.'

'Like Pixtures.'

'Yes, OK. If you want, we can play Pixtures. But you have to give me time to wake up first, Zac. OK? You know I don't function properly before coffee.'

'Can I go and see Grandma?'

'Grandma won't be up yet,' she tells him as she presses on the plunger of the coffee pot.

'Grandma gets up really early,' Zac says. 'I bet you she's been up for ages and ages.'

She rolls her eyes and sighs silently, then crouches down so that she's at the same height as her son. 'OK, I'll tell you what you can do, OK? You can creep very quietly up to the house and look in the kitchen window. And if Grandma's up, if you can see her in the kitchen, then you can knock very gently on the window, OK? But quietly, so you don't wake the whole house up. Because even if Grandma is awake, everyone else will be asleep, OK? Not everyone wants to get up at crazy o'clock.'

Zac nods, his eyes wide with excitement at the idea of this morning mission.

'But you have to be quiet, and if Grandma's not in the kitchen you come straight back here, OK?'

'OK!' Zac says, already running towards the door.

'Zac!' she calls out. 'Shoes!'

'Oh yeah,' he says, changing direction to the cupboard under the stairs, which he opens to retrieve a pair of small white trainers. 'Do I have to do socks?' he asks, sitting on a kitchen chair and pulling back the Velcro fasteners.

'No,' she says. 'No, you don't have to do socks. We'll do socks later after you've showered.'

He pulls the trainers on to his bare feet and stands again.

'And remember,' she says. 'Don't—'

'Don't make a noise. I know.'

'And if Gran's not in the kitchen, then—'

'Don't wake her up. I know!'

'That's right,' she says. 'Good boy.'

He slides open the French window and steps out into the early-morning air. The sun hasn't been up for long and the garden is still damp and fragrant with dew, but even this early, it's not cold. The last few days have been hot, like when they went to Spain last summer. He likes it when it's hot because they let him use the blow-up pool.

His arms stretched like wings, he runs through the garden, weaving back and forth between the neat rows of vegetables. He pauses as he passes the raspberry bush and picks a berry and puts it in his mouth, but it's not ripe and it tastes so acidic that it almost hurts, so he spits it out and says, 'Yuck,' and runs on.

When he reaches the house, he stands on tiptoe and sees Grandma sitting at the kitchen table, so he raps on the window and she startles and turns to look at him and smiles.

'Morning, Gran,' he says, before she's even finished opening the door.

'Morning, early bird,' she says, sweeping him into her arms and then snuffling his neck like a monster. 'Lordy, you smell good in the mornings,' she says. 'You smell like honey and flowers and caramel. How do you manage that?'

'Mum said you'd be asleep,' he says. 'But I knew you'd be up already.'

'Shh!' she says, gently. 'You have to whisper. Everyone's still asleep.'

She returns to the kitchen table and sits with him on her lap.

'What are you doing?' he asks.

'I'm just looking at these old photos,' she says. 'I should get your mum to put them in the mat thing, really.'

'She's probably already got them,' he says. 'Mum's got everyone's pictures in her PhotoMat.'

'Not these,' she says. 'These are old ones. Look.'

She leafs through the photos and then pulls one out to show him. It's a faded, dog-eared picture of a man in a suit and a woman holding a bunch of flowers.

'Is that Mum?' he asks.

'No, that's me!' she tells him. 'That's on my wedding day. That's the day I married Grandad Ian, a long, long time ago.'

'You were pretty,' he says, pointing at the bouquet of flowers.

'You're supposed to say that I still am,' she tells him, tickling him until he giggles.

301

'And who's that?' he asks, pointing at another photo.

'That's your mum when she was about thirteen,' she says. 'And that, next to her, is Uncle Jude.'

'She's skinny like String Lady in the cartoon,' he says. 'And that doesn't look like Uncle Jude at all.'

'Well, no. He was only twelve when I took that photo.'

'He was lucky to have a sister,' Zac says. 'I wish I had a sister.'

'Well, I think you're right,' she tells him. 'He was lucky. But back then, I'm not sure he would have agreed with you. They didn't always get on so well, you know.'

He pulls the box of photos towards him and starts to look through them, but quickly loses interest because he doesn't recognise any of the faces. 'Are there any of Mama?' he asks.

'No, those ones are in the PhotoMat,' she says. 'But I can't seem to find it.'

'I think it's in the garden house,' he says. 'Mum borrowed it to show Mama the pictures. Shall I go get it?'

'They're not asleep, are they?'

He shakes his head. 'No, they're awake,' he says. 'Well, Mum is, anyway.'

He pushes out of her lap and runs to the back door. 'I'll be back in a minute,' he says.

She watches him go and then returns her attention to the box of photos. And here is a photo of Jude on his birthday. And here is another of Zoe, about a year before she vanished. She strokes the photo gently. *Kids*, she thinks, *they bring so much heartache. But so much happiness, too.*

She sifts through the photos, catching glimpses of her own mother and father, another of Jude, Zoe as a baby, and then she finds Scott's business card. She remembers finding it in the old house, just before she moved out of Buxton. She hadn't had a single photo of Scott, because somewhere along the way she'd lost all her digital pictures. *Sadness*, she thinks. It would be so much easier to bear if we could only convince ourselves how temporary it is.

The back door bursts open again and Zac runs in, brandishing the aluminium tube of the PhotoMat like a sword.

'Careful with that, it's expensive!' she says.

'It's in a tube,' Zac says. 'It's metal. You can't break it, Gran!'

She smiles wryly at his mocking tone of voice and wonders if he's going to be as much trouble as Zoe. She hopes not, for Zoe's sake.

'So, come on,' she says, patting her knee until he climbs back up.

She takes the tube from his hands and unscrews the end. She pulls the rolled PhotoMat from the tube and lays it across the table like a place mat.

'I'm not sure how to switch it on,' she lies. 'Do you know?'

Zac looks up at her and nods proudly, then presses one corner of the mat far harder than necessary. The PhotoMat lights up and a series of icons fills the screen.

Zac starts stabbing at the screen immediately, so she grabs his hand and restrains him. 'Wait,' she says. 'I want to look at them in order.'

She jabs at a few icons across the top of the screen until a column of numbers appears on the left-hand side, running from 1990 to 2039. *Have I really lived through all that?* she wonders. Just the concept of having reached 2039 makes her feel tired.

'Mum says she wants to put all your old ones in as well. She says she's gonna ask Mama to do it for her.'

'That's a very good idea,' she says. 'But she's been telling me that for years, and I'm still waiting. Actually, some of these are ones she's scanned. Look.' She clicks on one of the photos from 1994 and the image of her wedding to Ian comes up. 'So who's that?' she quizzes Zac, pointing.

'That's you with the pretty flowers,' Zac says. 'And that's Grandad Ian.'

'Very good,' she says, jiggling him on her knee. 'So you do listen to what I have to say.'

'Are there any pictures of me?' Zac asks.

'I'm sure there are,' she tells him, clicking on the years one after another and glancing at the thumbnail pictures that appear. 'But I want to look at these others first. Don't worry, we'll get to you in a bit.'

She clicks on 2021. 'So this is your mum's wedding to Mama. This is when they got married in Nottingham.'

'Mama looks like a man,' Zac says, causing her to laugh out loud, which, in turn, provokes a fit of coughing. 'You're right,' she says, once she's regained her composure. 'She used to have her hair short back then. And she insisted on wearing trousers and a shirt for her wedding. See how pretty your mum looked, though? I bought her that dress. She wanted a wedding dress but thought it was excessive. So Granny had to surprise her with it.'

'What's excessive?' Zac asks.

'Excessive is like too much,' she explains. 'She thought it was too much to wear a white dress, that it was over the top.' She scrolls back to 2020. 'And this is Uncle Jude's wedding to Jess.'

'Her dress is bright orange,' Zac says.

'Oh, I know!' she laughs. 'I did everything I could to talk her out of that, but she thought she knew everything about clothes. She's usually so good with fashion, too . . .' She shakes her head as she remembers. 'But there was no telling her. And she's regretted it ever since. She won't even look at the photos, these days.'

'Uncle Jude looks silly, too,' Zac says.

'Yes, that white suit was a mistake as well,' she tells him. 'He spilt wine all down his trousers at the reception. He had a big red stain in his lap. Anyway, once all the drama was over, it was a lovely day. I haven't danced so much . . . ever, actually. My legs ached for days afterwards.'

She swipes at her eyes so that she can see clearly again. All these memories are making her feel emotional. She clicks on through the images.

'Who's that?' Zac asks, pointing at a photo of two women in strange puff-sleeved linen dresses.

'Ah, those are two of your aunties being bridesmaids at someone's wedding. I don't know whose wedding it was, but I think that's your aunty Janis on the left,' she says, pointing. 'And that one must be Harmony. And that boy in the background is Terra.'

'Uncle Terra?'

'Yes.'

'He looks a bit like me,' Zac says.

'You're right,' she tells him. 'He does. Terra was a terror, like you. Did you see what I did there?'

Zac looks up at her and frowns.

'Anyway, I think he was about the same age then as you are now.'

'So what's all this, then?' asks a voice from the doorway, and they both turn to look. 'The early-bird club, is it?'

'Grandad!' Zac exclaims, and she can see him wince at the appellation. He's tried to get the kid to stop calling him Grandad, but he just can't seem to make anything else stick.

'We're looking at old pictures,' Zac says. 'Uncle Terra looks just like me.'

'He really does. Come and look, dear,' she says.

So, yawning, he crosses the room to join them. 'Gosh, he does look like you,' he says, crouching down and leaning in to push his head between the two of them. He pecks them on the cheek one after the other. 'Any of me in there?' he asks.

'Nothing before 2019,' she says. 'You know how I lost all the photos from before. It's such a shame. I hate digital.'

'Well, that's not such a bad thing,' he says. 'Some things are best forgotten.'

'You!' she says, laughing and elbowing him in the stomach. 'But you're probably right about that.'

He reaches forward and presses 2021 and then 2022. 'There we go,' he says. 'Look how hunky Grandad was back in the day.'

Onscreen is a photo of him topless, his muscular torso shiny with sweat. He's leaning on a garden fork.

'You're still gorgeous,' she says, reaching up to run one hand down the grey, bristly hair of his beard as she continues to look at the screen. 'But it's true, you looked bloody amazing back then.'

'Grandma!' Zac says.

'It's OK,' she tells Zac, wiggling her knee up and down. 'Old people are allowed to swear. Just don't tell your mothers.'

She clicks on another photo taken at Jude and Jess's wedding. 'Ooh, look at you, all suited and booted,' she says, her eyes vaguely watery again. 'I was already past my prime, but you . . . you were at peak gorgeousness . . . Grrr!'

'You just said I'm still gorgeous,' he laughs. 'Or was that a lie?'

She turns in her seat and appraises him playfully, twisting her mouth and nodding thoughtfully. 'Nah, you're still looking pretty good,' she says. 'My toy boy.'

He snorts. 'Yeah,' he says. 'That'll be right. The toy boy's fifty-six in three weeks.' He straightens and heads towards the back door. 'I'm just going to water those lettuces,' he says. 'Otherwise they'll be cooked by the time we get back from the wedding. I swear, if it doesn't rain soon . . .'

'What's a toy boy?' Zac asks, once he's gone.

'It's when an older woman gets together with a younger man,' she explains. 'But it's all a bit sexist, so you can forget that I told you that straight away.'

'Mum says Terra's too young to get married,' Zac says.

She smiles. 'Well, Mum may be right about that,' she says. 'But don't ever say that to anyone else. Someone told me that on my wedding day, and they were right – I was too young. But that didn't stop me being upset because someone had said it. So, especially don't say it today, OK?'

'OK,' Zac says. 'My lips are zipped.'

'Good. You're a good boy, really, aren't you?'

'Does everyone have to get married?' Zac asks as she continues to click through the photos. 'Will I have to get married?'

'Not at all,' she tells him. 'Grandad and I aren't married.'

'Why not?' Zac asks.

'Well, I was married to Grandad Ian, once upon a time. And then we got divorced so that he could marry Grandma Linda and so that I could be with Scott. And I just felt like I'd been there and done that. Does that make any sense?'

'Uh-uh,' Zac says, frowning and shaking his head as he starts to stab randomly at the screen again. A selfie of her and Scott appears. In it, she's standing beside Scott in the garden of this very house. Scott has a hosepipe in one hand.

She can remember the day clearly. It had been after Zoe and Nick had decided to come back from France, and she and Scott had just had a conversation about where to put them up once they arrived. Scott had said, quite casually, as if it was nothing, 'Why not lend them your place?'

'Sure, but where would I live?' she'd asked.

'Well, here, of course,' he'd said.

'Oh, OK,' she'd replied. She was hating her job in Nottingham anyway. Plus, time spent apart from Scott felt like physical pain, while time spent with him felt like joy. So it had seemed the most natural thing in the world. Neither of them had hesitated. The decision had been made in that instant and she'd taken a selfie in order to remember it. She'd wanted to remember how ordinary yet monumental the moment had felt.

'Sometimes people love each other so much that all they want to do is get married,' she tells Zac. 'And other times people love each other so much, they're so sure that they're with the right person and that they're going to be together for the rest of their lives that there doesn't seem to be much point getting married at all.'

'That doesn't make any sense either,' Zac says.

'No,' she agrees. 'No, you're right. It probably doesn't.'

She glances at the clock on the refrigerator. 'Now, do you want to do something for me?' she asks. 'Do you want to go and wake Jude and Jessica up so they've got time to get ready for Terra's wedding?'

'Mum says people don't get up at crazy o'clock,' Zac tells her. 'Only you.'

'Well, it's actually gone eight o'clock and the only people I know who think that's crazy o'clock are your mothers. Plus, Jude needs to iron a shirt and Jess, her hair. So can you do that for me, do you think?'

Zac nods and jumps down from her lap.

'Do it gently,' she tells him as he leaves the room. 'Don't jump on them or anything, OK?'

'OK, Gran,' he says, climbing the stairs one by one.

'And knock on the door first!' she calls out after him. She grimaces vaguely to herself. 'Maybe not your best idea, Grandma,' she mutters. *Grandma*, she thinks. Jesus, when did that happen?

She clicks again on the photo of Scott looking gorgeous in a suit and then remembers other moments from Jude and Jessica's wedding in London, where the photo had been taken.

It had seemed, initially, as if convincing Zoe to come back for a surprise appearance at the wedding hadn't been her best idea either.

Jude, who'd dropped in unexpectedly the evening before the wedding, had turned quite green once he'd discovered Zoe sitting in the hotel lobby. He'd caused quite the scene, screaming and shouting as he furiously told her that she'd ruined the first fifteen years of his life and that she wasn't going to ruin his wedding as well.

Mandy had spent hours calming Zoe and persuading her not to leave. However, just as she had managed to do so, Ian and Linda had appeared, ready to check in, and Zoe had fallen apart all over again. But Ian had surprised Mandy, because for once he'd lived up to the requirements of the moment.

He'd asked Linda to retire to their hotel room and sat with Mandy to help calm Zoe down. He'd admitted for the first time ever that everything that had happened was at least partly his fault. 'I'm so, so sorry, Zoe. I was a selfish bastard,' he'd told her. And then, as Zoe had collapsed into his arms for the first time in years, he'd peered over their sobbing daughter's shoulder at Mandy, looked her straight in the eye, and croaked, with a gentle nod and a long, slow blink, 'I'm sorry for what I did to all of you. I really am.'

Mandy had replied with a simple but heartfelt, 'Thank you.'

Finally, once Zoe's tears had ceased, Ian and Scott had taken a taxi over to Jude's flat, where they'd spent half the night talking him down.

Things the next day had remained nerve-rackingly edgy – it had felt as if a row could erupt at any moment – but they had somehow all got through the service without a major incident.

At the reception party, a pretty drunk Jessica, sick to death of the tension, had demanded that her husband make up with his sister. Zoe and Jude's dance together had begun frigidly, under duress, but had quickly morphed into a tearful hug that made all the onlookers well up, too. Pretty soon, Ian had invited Mandy to dance and Scott had asked Linda, and so mixed-up couple by mixed-up couple, the dance floor had become filled with teary parents and wet-eyed brothers and sisters, and half-brothers and half-sisters, until they had all, as if drawn magnetically together, ended up in a big, emotional family crush in the middle of the dance floor. Though no one had thought to take a photo, it remains, to this day, one of the most beautiful moments of her life.

She glances back down at the PhotoMat, at Scott, suited, in his mid-thirties, and then clicks again on the photo of him gardening bare-chested. She growls quietly once again and then, laughing at herself for staring at a photo when she has the real thing outside, she rolls up the PhotoMat and slides it back into the tube.

She crosses to the kitchen door and peers out.

In the garden, Scott is watering the vegetable patch, playfully arcing the jet of water so that the droplets sparkle and glitter in the sunlight. Her eyes mist up again. Weddings, damned weddings . . . they always make her feel emotional.

Still, today is a good day, she thinks. She's got her whole family around her and they're off to Manchester to meet the other half of the Fuller clan. She's had bad days and good days over the years. Actually, she's had some bloody terrible days, way back when; of course she has. But what followed has reduced them to the status of footnotes, thank God. The twenty years she's spent with Scott have made the eight years they spent apart feel like nothing more than a blip.

And yes, today is going to be a good day. She can sense it in the morning air, just waiting to be picked and peeled and enjoyed, like ripe fruit hanging from a tree.

She opens the door and calls out, 'Scott? D'you want some coffee?' And when he looks up and smiles at her, when he nods enthusiastically and winks, her eyes mist all over again.

ACKNOWLEDGMENTS

Thanks to Lolo, Charlie and Titou for the mad brainstorming session during which the ideas for this novel hatched. Thanks to Rosemary for being my writer's touchstone. Thanks to Apple for making reliable work tools and, above all, thanks to everyone at Lake Union for all their hard work on this novel.

ABOUT THE AUTHOR

Photo © 2017 Rosey Aston-Snow

Nick Alexander was born in 1964 in the UK. He has travelled widely and has lived and worked in the UK, the USA and France, where he resides today. Nick is the author of fifteen novels, including *The Other Son,* named by Amazon as one of the best fiction titles of 2015; *The Photographer's Wife*, published in 2014 – a number-one hit in both the UK and France, and *The Half-Life of Hannah*, the fourth-bestselling independently published Kindle title of all time. Nick's novels have been translated into French, German, Italian, Spanish, Norwegian, Turkish and Croatian. Nick lives in the south of France with his partner, three friendly cats and a few trout.